Copyright © Lee Kerr 2010

www.leekerr.net

The right of Lee Kerr to be identified as the author of this work has been asserted by him in accordance with the Copyright, Designs and Patents Act 1988.

ISBN 978-1-326-35633-0

This novel is entirely a work of fiction. All characters in this publication are fictitious and any resemblance to real persons, living or dead, is purely coincidental.

All rights reserved. No part of this publication may be reproduced, stored in a retrieval system, or transmitted, in any form or by any means, electronic, mechanical, photocopying, recording or otherwise, without prior written consent from the author.

WELCOME TO THE APOCALYPSE

Lee Kerr

"It is perfectly true, as philosophers say, that life must be understood backwards. But they forget the other proposition, that it must be lived forwards."

Søren Kierkegaard

Danish philosopher, theologian and poet.

May 1813 – Nov 1855

STORIES

1. To shop, to drop

2. Your money means nothing

3. Beg, buy, but never borrow

4. All that is so obviously hidden

5. What is truth if not real?

6. Do not disturb

7. In all but the darkness

8. The enduring inevitability of corporations and cockroaches

9. That secret slice of life

10. Welcome to the apocalypse

Saturday 13th August – London

To shop, to drop

'Why are we here again?' she asks, as they walk towards Big Blue.

'I don't wanna go and Jade don't wanna go, neither. There's nowt we need,' Cortnee says, her arms flapping by her side.

'And nowt we can afford, anyways,' Jade says.

Mum quickly clips Cortnee around the ear, although it's less of a slap and more of a tickle, on account of the child being considerably taller, and by Mum's own admission, her big, fat chicken wings are not able to lift up much these days.

'Your Ashley needs a new mattress. He's pissed enough in the last one.'

His two sisters point at him, making it clear where their laughter is directed. Ashley says nothing. He walks forward, his head bowed down and his shoulders hunched forward as he tries to block out his horrible siblings' howls, which echo around the empty car park.

'Meatballs,' Dad says.

Mum looks at him, her fists clenched, her head shaking. She knew it was coming and yet she can still feel the anger stirring deep within her. She takes a deep breath, which must never be mistaken as a sign of forgiveness, or even any level of understanding, but rather a chance to ever-so-slightly calm her frayed nerves. 'Yeah, we'll get you some bloody meatballs.'

'We have to get 'em here because yours are so shit!' Ashley shouts and starts running, ever so slowly, knowing she will give chase but entirely confident she won't ever catch him.

And sure enough, Mum breaks into a small run and pursues him for a second a two, just until her back starts to hurt or her knees start to ache, or her boobs begin chafing against that cheap, ill-fitting bra. The reason barely matters in the shadow of her obvious lack of willingness to continue. She puts her hands on her knees, her back bent over, not sure where the pain is coming from, as she looks around at the two girls who are still laughing. She looks at Dad who, in her opinion, ain't doing nothing worth doing. 'Mine not good enough for you, eh?' she asks.

He doesn't say anything, just shrugs his shoulders and walks through the entrance. The girls run in and Mum takes up the rear, counting up how much is in her purse, knowing they will just about be able to afford the meatballs, but it will be just one refillable juice to share between the kids and one coffee for the adults. Anything else they want will have to be swiped, and the only thing that will go through the tills will be Ashley's new mattress.

If Ashley pisses on this one too she has said he will go back to nappies, because it's getting stupid now, she thinks. After all, whoever has heard of a fifteen year old lad having to wear nappies? But then again, who ain't thinking it's gross that he's still pissing in his bed when he's so close to being a proper man.

Hypnotherapy could cure it, the consultant had said. Hypnowhat? My ass, she had thought. We can't be affording that, and besides ain't nothing a wipe down mattress protector can't fix, at a fraction of the price of some posh doctor, she reckoned.

And so, as Mum closes her purse and pushes her husband onto the escalator, telling him it ain't nothing to be worrying him, it is only Ashley who stops to think. He stands at the entrance and looks around the car park, all the time thinking that he has never seen this place so empty. Sure, it's early in the morning but there should still be people in the outdoor car park. He knows the multi-storey don't be filling up unless the rain comes or there is a queue for the surface one. But there are always the keen people who want to do all them home improvements at the weekend. Ashley thinks that one fine day he might come here as one of them, and not as part of this family outing. They always come here early, before there is too many staff on shift, meaning that their swearing and swiping is likely to be spotted.

As he moves up the escalator he can't help but think that this place is not like it normally is, and there aren't many other customers or staff members inside, either. He runs to catch up with his family, his mum is still shouting at his sisters.

'Mum,' he says, hoping she'll listen to him, just this once. 'The telly was saying we should stay indoors today. Don't you think we should maybe listen to what they is saying?'

She stops and looks up at him, and for a second he thinks he might have actually got her attention. She holds his gaze as he watches her eyes for any hint of understanding. She stares back at him, as if she is actually thinking about this as a genuine problem. But she says nothing and eventually pushes out her backside, releasing a loud, prolonged fart – one of those very satisfying sorts that gets both ass cheeks flapping together. 'That's what I think of that bollocks virus shit they're talking about.'

The girls start laughing, and then, once they get wind of the deathly rat smell, start running. Ashley looks at his dad but he don't have nothing to say other than the usual: 'meatballs.'

Mum smacks dad hard around the face but he doesn't move, so she smacks him again. 'You'll get your fucking meatballs when we've got this little pisser's mattress sorted and not a minute before.'

His dad still doesn't move, not even to tense his arms. Ashley still remembers the days when his dad would come home and hear about whatever shit him or his sisters had caused their overworked mother that day. He would calmly listen to her for barely a minute, nodding all the time, before he would throw whatever child was most guilty over his knee. Ashley was often the easy target, being the only boy, so whenever he took his punishment he would watch his old man's muscles flex and his tattoos grow, like they were swelling with such purpose, wanting his kids to be better than he had ever been. Ashley wanted muscles like that, but he always wanted to do something better with them.

'Can't we go straight to the good stuff?' Cortnee says.

'Yeah, the stuff that's ripe for the picking,' Jade says, licking her lips. 'Look, there's like hardly any staff on duty.'

Mum makes a swing for one of them, either of them, but misses both. 'Yeah and there's no fucking customers about neither, so we bloody wait until this place fills up. You know I can't afford to get caught again.' She pushes forward, forcing the family to follow. They didn't dare to be separated in public. 'I wanna look around, anyway. If we get that pay out from your dad's accident then we're gonna do the whole house up.'

'And what about them council vouchers?' Jade says.

'You can piss right off if you think we is using them in 'ere. If we ever get them I'm getting the bathroom done but it ain't gonna be this posh.'

'Why are we looking around in this bit then?' Ashley asks, rubbing his eyes, trying to wake himself up, knowing the answer but not wanting to hear it come from his mother. 'This stuff won't be here next year, anyway.'

'Bollocks,' Mum says. 'It's all the same shit, so we're looking around the whole place and I don't wanna hear any more moans. I've been standing up all week in the chippie, so today I'm gonna chill and you bastard kids are gonna behave! Are you getting me?'

And so each of them nod in turn, as the family start their journey, snaking their away around living rooms and then towards bedrooms. The girls sit on every sofa and lie on every bed, making sure that they rip anything they really like, always hopeful they'll see it in the reduced section next week. As they do so, their mum reminds them that if they get caught they should say the security guard touched them. As Ashley blocks out this usual chatter he looks around, seeing that he can count the number of staff in here on one hand, all of them wearing worried expressions, and this time he doesn't think it's his family visit that's got them all flustered.

*****

The police car speeds through the streets quicker than any of the four officers have ever known before. Despite having a combined sixty years of experience, none of them can ever recall a time when they made it around the A406 so quickly, and especially without a few near misses along the way. But today is different, as if half-term has been combined with a day where England are playing in the World Cup – that's the only combination of things that could ever clear the usual, grinding congestion from this inner London road.

Luke starts to wonder whether maybe all Saturdays in the summer months are like this. He sits quietly, keeping a tight hold of the handrail, as the car swerves around the corners, far quicker than he's used to. Although the officers in the car have vast combined experience, his own makes up less than ten percent of this total; he's still in his first year as an armed police officer, but he already knows he's enjoying it far more than his previous beat around Wembley and Ealing High streets.

This job still fills him with excitement. No, that's not the right word. It's more like adrenaline mixed with slight fear; a sense that the unknown is waiting for him each time they speed off. Sure, you still have to do the regular stuff – the traffic violations and the petty theft – but then you get to carry two weapons; solid steel instruments, at your side, ready to obey your every command. He's still to do it, still waiting to shoot someone. Maybe he'll never get the chance, and although he won't admit it to his sergeant or any of his colleagues, he feels that to never unleash this power on another person would, in some way, be a real shame.

Of course he means to let it loose on a bad person; someone entirely deserving of the cold touch of steel with skin, all from his steady aim. He wonders if today might be the day; there's certainly a different buzz on this shift, a feeling that something is looming, something that none of them can quite get a handle on.

Every officer in his station has been called into work, so he knows that something big is happening. The briefing seemed deliberately vague, telling them their task today would most likely be urban pacification. When they left the station he noticed that half of the officers were being kitted out in riot gear, and everyone knows that when that happens, the press will be all over it in hours.

'Okay, remember to keep a low profile,' his Sergeant shouts from the front passenger seat.

Before Dave has even finished talking, Luke gives a quick nod. He listens intently, filtering out all the radio chatter and the blasts from the siren, so he can hear every word from his boss, an experienced police officer who has been in the force for years. He's one of the best, Luke assures himself. Nothing seems to panic him and you know that if he feels the need to start shooting then you just aim at whoever he's pointing at and let rip.

'We set ourselves up in strategic points and let the beat officers take all the attention. We expect the streets to be clear this morning but eventually the curiosity will get the better of most people, especially when they see all this activity on the news, so just be ready.'

'And what exactly are we getting ready for?' Mike asks, from beside Luke.

Dave looks ahead, no doubt checking that they are on a straight road, and when he sees that the next few seconds are clear he turns himself around fully, letting him see the whites of their eyes. 'I don't know what we're getting ready for. You know what I know, and that's as good as today gets.'

'So this could be a training exercise, for all we know?' Mike asks, looking at Luke and then back to Dave. Mike asks more questions and gives more opinions than most of the guys

Luke has worked with so far, which he thinks might be because of his age, as well as that thing you often hear that he has 'been there, done that and never got the promotion.'

Dave looks back at Mike, but he doesn't really nod or shake his head; he just stares at him. 'That's what you want it to be, and that's what I want it to be, but the reality might just be something different, so you just remember that.'

Mike nods and then shrugs his shoulders. 'Sure, boss.'

The car suddenly takes a left turn, leaving the longest convoy of police cars Luke has ever seen. He watches as a couple of cars turn with them whilst the rest speed ahead, all of them looking like they're bumper to bumper. Luke can't even see the first car anymore but it has been replaced by identical blue and white cars, which are followed by many ambulances, moving a little slower, but just as determined to get to somewhere.

'This is no training exercise,' Mike says, speaking only to Luke, his voice barely above a whisper. 'There's no way we've got the money for this to be some sort of training day. We didn't even get this paranoid during the Olympics or the jubilee, or the NATO Summit.'

Luke stares at Mike but he doesn't know what to say, what else he can add.

Mike simply grins back. 'Not even the royal wedding got this much attention.'

Luke looks forward, thinking only about his training, reminding himself that there is no difference between an exercise and a real life need to fire a weapon. 'We will do whatever we need to do,' he says.

Mike laughs. 'I can tell you're still a newbie. You actually think we're doing something noble that also happens to pay the bills.'

The car comes to a halt and Dave leans around again. 'Right, you two get out here and set up a control point. Give it one sweep of the area and then base yourselves with whatever uniformed arrive shortly. Keep channel one open at all times and report anything suspicious.'

Luke gets out of the car as Dave puts down his window. 'We'll be two blocks away and if it gets nasty out there just remember that you control the situation.'

Luke nods, taking hold of the steel object draped around his shoulders. As the car speeds off he checks the safety catch for the hundredth time today. He also checks he still has his side arm, as if it could actually just disappear. After a few seconds he remembers to check for Mike, and finds him standing behind him, laughing and shaking his head.

'It's nice of you to remember me,' Mike says, before marching forward towards the biggest building in the immediate area.

Luke quickly follows him, wishing that he was with Dave, wishing he was with anyone but Mike. He breaks into a short run, just so he can get close enough to visually inspect Mike's weapons, and he sees that his rifle already has the safety off.

Mike catches Luke looking at him but he doesn't rectify his blatant breach of procedure. 'Today is no training exercise, and today is not going to end well.'

*****

'I like this one,' Mum says, sitting on a sofa and looking at each of the kids as they stand around, tapping on their phones and playing with their hair. 'What do you lot think?'

No one answers. Not Dad, not the girls and especially not Ashley. He just wants to get his mattress and get back home, hopefully grabbing some tinned food and bottled water on the way. That's what the news people have been telling everyone to do. Whatever is happening, it is the only thing on his phone. All the different apps have been telling him the same thing: get indoors and stay there.

Mum huffs at the lack of response and it's Dad who gets the slap. 'Well your ass seems to be liking it, don't it?' she says to him.

The kids all laugh, pointing at their dad's fat ass spread out across the crack somewhere between the two large cushions. He looks up, catching the eyes of each of them in turn, but he has nothing to say.

Mum fills the silence with another long fart until her bowels have been emptied of all available air. The pungent scent gets muffled by the immense stretch of fabric underneath, but eventually reaches its victims nonetheless. She gives a satisfied grin, like she's marking her territory. 'Beans for breakfast do the trick nicely.'

All the family laugh again, even Dad this time. This faint hum slips out of the side of his mouth for just a moment, just long enough for him to be recognisable from that previous life.

'Let's see them greedy bastards sell this now,' Mum says, holding out her hand.

Ashley does his duty and pulls her up, hoisting her out of yet another piece of furniture that they won't be buying until Dad gets himself back into a job, which looks like it will be sometime close to never.

'Don't like it anyway,' she says. 'That colour looks like dog-shit-brown to me.' She crinkles her nose as she starts down the long path towards bedrooms, with dining and casual chairs still to get through. The family follow, the two daughters heaving their dad out of his comfy chair. He would have told them he had enjoyed that, if he could just have found the right words.

'Oi! Why's it so quiet in 'ere?' Mum shouts at two staff hanging around the display rugs.

The first one shrugs her shoulders, and then carries on with her tidying and shuffling about. Mum stares at the other one, determined that she will not be looked down on by these little slappers, all dressed up as wannabe till tarts.

'It's the virus, innit,' the other one says, still playing with the stock, not wanting to look up at the woman.

'See! I told you about that!' Ashley shouts out.

He gets a quick smack, a bashing on the back of his head that warns him not to push his luck. 'That's total bollocks. There's always some flapping about MRSA or bird-shit flu in this shithole of a country, plus all that other crap going round from all them foreigners.'

'This one's for real though, they reckon,' the staff member says. 'Our supervisor is probably gonna close the store soon, especially since there are only a few customers in here.'

'Oh, Mum, we ain't been to the marketplace yet!' Jade shouts.

'And my mattress,' Ashley says, tugging at her arm.

'Meatballs,' Dad says.

Mum pushes Ashley off and holds out her hands, silencing all. 'What a load of shit. I can't believe any of you is gonna believe this. You remember when we came back from Majorca? When them cabin crew reckoned we got some bug from the hotel and they wouldn't let us get on the plane?'

The kids nod, all of them suddenly reliving that particular nightmare.

Mum looks at each of them and then turns to the staff member. 'Well, that ain't happening to me again, so is that restaurant still open or what?'

She nods. 'It is for now.'

Ashley hears this; he knows how long a trip to the restaurant will take, and he taps his mum's arm again. 'Please, Mum, what about my mattress?' he says, desperate to get it. After all, if they are going to be holed up indoors for weeks then he doesn't want to be sleeping on a piss-soaked bed any longer, especially as he thought this sort of thing was now consigned to that past life he doesn't ever want to remember.

She pushes him away. 'It's not all about you, Ashley!'

He looks down at the floor, knowing it's never about him, but knowing better than to argue with her in public.

Mum makes a loud tut, telling everyone how pissed she is. 'He ain't ever gonna shut up. It's like having a three year old all over again. So, let's all go and get young Ashley's piss protector and mattress and then we can finally get some nosh.'

Most of the family cheer, and then Ashley's sisters remember that they need to laugh at him for still wetting the bed. They point their fingers at him, all the time calling him 'pissy pants' and never once wondering if this constant taunting was in any way contributing to him wetting himself in the middle of the night.

Ashley hasn't always wet the bed; he is a teenager, after all. He did it a few times when he was younger – like, much younger. Then it started again, sometime between him starting school and his balls dropping, and once he had got a few slaps from his mum, he realised that his life would be much easier if he simply didn't wee himself in the middle of the night. He approached this as intelligently as he could, by reading online about the causes of bedwetting. The best and simplest – and, of course, cheapest – piece of advice was not to drink anything from eight in the evening onwards – three full hours before he went to sleep. He used to go to bed dying of thirst, his still-digesting dinner demanding some liquid to help the process, and he used to wake up with a thick layer of fur across his tongue and his lips cracking from his self-imposed torment. But, however dry his mouth was, so was the rest of the bed, and so to Ashley it was worth all that suffering.

Two weeks ago it all started again. He woke up with a big wet patch all around him and his boxers drenched. He had stopped his routine of not drinking before bed some years ago, since his mind had clearly become able to control his bodily fluids while he wasn't awake, so he was pretty annoyed with himself that this particular problem had come back. He hadn't dared ask his mates, and of course his sisters would have had no interest in helping, other than to tell his so-called mates, just to make sure everyone knew how weird Ashley was. He did ask his Dad, hoping a man-to-man chat would sort things out, but of course, he got nothing back of any substance, just some rambling and a few shrugs of his shoulders.

When he had found the courage to approach his old man, he hadn't realised that his mum had been listening from the kitchen. Hearing that he wasn't getting anything helpful from his dad, she chose to fill that void with her own opinions, frying pan in hand, which Ashley could definitely vouch for how much that hurts when it catches the side of your head.

In that painful moment, as Ashley's Mum continued to chastise her son for something that was arguably out of his conscious control, she obviously thought that bellowing at him with all manner of her own issues, whilst brandishing her favourite sausage pan just above his head, would somehow solve the problem. And while she screamed that 'I really don't fucking need this,' and 'I ain't washing your pissy sheets no more,' Ashley thought that if she had just asked him why he was wetting the bed again then he would have happily told her.

To Ashley, there was an obvious reason why this problem had returned, and that reason was the stress they were under. He often spent the final few moments of any evening looking at this family unit that had fallen into chaos. It had never been particularly strong at the best of times – certainly had never been a team – but when his dad was normal, things at least happened.

Every night before heading to bed, he would take a final look at his old man, and he would always find him staring blankly at the flickering TV screen. He would then look over at his mum, who was always asleep on the sofa, her oversized, snotty nose scooping up all the air and her fat, greedy gob pushing it back out again. He knew she was slowly poisoning the place he once called home but any love for her had left a long time ago, and once his dad had sort of left then there was no actual reason for him to stay.

The family make it to the bed section before Ashley can sort any more of these thoughts out in his head, which he is strangely okay with. He knows that if you can't fix something then you put up or get out. He just needs more time and, quite obviously, a lot more money. The scary shit that was going on right now wasn't helping but there was little he could do about that either.

'We'll head to the knick-knacks downstairs,' Cortnee says, 'if Dad gives us the car keys.' She winks at her sister, as if Mum might just buy this and let them go down there without her. She has done it before, sometimes finding it better if she lets the kids do the nicking on their own. That way if they get caught she can come over and give them a good telling-off, and hopefully convince the Manager to let them go, assuring him that she would give them some proper punishment once they got home. The telling off was never faked: she was always pissed when they got caught while swiping the things she wanted.

'Yeah, we ain't that hungry,' Jade says, standing shoulder-to-shoulder alongside her sister.

She gets a slap back, not being quick enough to move this time. 'No, you bloody well won't. We all stick together today.'

'That's probably a good idea,' Ashley says. 'The virus warning is all over north London now,' he says, looking at his phone.

Mum takes a deep breath, her eyes shut. 'Will you shut up with that virus bollocks?'

He nods back at her, almost knowing this is the only response he will get. His phone credits are nearly gone, so it won't be long before he loses this source of information. It doesn't seem to be doing any good, but he would at least like to know what's coming next.

*****

Luke watches Mike as he talks to the uniformed officers. He has finally decided to lock his weapon, which, strangely, has calmed the situation. At least that's how it seems to Luke who is standing next to him, not really listening to the conversation, holding his weapon in both hands as it hangs across his chest. He spends his time staring at the patrol officer and then takes in the wider area. He times how long it takes him to complete a 360 degree survey, his overactive mind absorbing the view of the car park and shops in just over ten seconds.

Luke has already forgotten the names of these new guys, who have been drafted in from South London. He wonders how happy they are at being called up this way, and if they are going to be any help if they have to give chase through the surrounding housing estates. Not that he has any idea of what they might be chasing, but he is fairly sure that today is going to involve some running.

Perhaps it might be running away, Luke thinks. Mike certainly doesn't look ready to run anywhere; his feet are locked in formation and his index finger regularly brushes against the trigger, like he's almost teasing it before the main event.

'I've heard it's spreading quickly, like wildfire,' Mike says, his thoughts mainly directed at the other two, because he knows that Luke doesn't want to hear any more of his views on this subject. 'It's important to ensure you know as much as possible in these situations.'

The other officers nod. One of them has his phone out and is checking for live updates to add to the discussion. The radio chatter is pretty basic, and the regular briefings don't appear to be giving any more information beyond what's already on the news.

'What you got?' Mike says, looking at the officer with his phone out.

He looks up. 'Not much, to be honest. Just the same stuff we've heard already. The BBC think it's a virus that's spreading quickly, starting from Heathrow Airport and making its way further into London.'

'So the host has gone dark?' Mike says, like he's a detective now. He's talking like he's part of the solution, part of the team who are fixing the bigger problem. Luke wants to tell him that he's not, that they are only part of a huge ground team, dealing with a very tiny part of whatever is actually happening. They are small part of the massive numbers who are here to fix what they've been told to fix, and he wishes he was with someone who understood that.

'We should do another patrol,' Luke says.

Mike puts a hand out in front of at him, indicating to Luke that he should calm down. 'Yes, in a minute. Let's make sure we know all the facts first.'

'What, from a few newsfeeds on a mobile phone?'

The other two laugh, their heads nodding, hopefully agreeing with him. 'He's right, you know,' one of them says. 'The BBC say it's a virus but Sky News are saying it's a possible terrorist attack, and that we're not being told so we don't go and shoot the wrong people.'

Luke watches as Mike strokes his weapon, clearly reflecting on this possibility. He looks like he's keeping it just on the right side of calm, like a dog about to start sprinting. Luke spots that the other two have noticed the same thing and he isn't sure if they wish they had what he and Mike are carrying, or if they're just glad they won't be at the front, having to make the most difficult decisions.

Luke looks around, surveying the area, looking for anything different whilst mentally preparing for what will hopefully be an extended patrol. McDonald's seems a little busier, despite the fact that they've already ran out of buns; the local residents clearly topping up their supplies from wherever they can get them. The main store still looks quiet – far too quiet for a Saturday morning. The doors are still open, which he takes as a good sign. There is now also less twitching of curtains and more people on the streets.

He looks across the vast, empty space, towards the car park entrance, and he sees another group of officers, and that they have a constant stream of people coming up to them, asking what he thinks must be all manner of questions. He notices that they don't linger for long, clearly not getting much in the way of answers from his colleagues.

The clouds are hanging low and he hopes more than anything that it doesn't rain. He looks around for Dave and his car, but they are nowhere to be seen; he hasn't seen them for at least half an hour now. He looks around for possible shelter but the trees are far from big enough and he doubts he'll be allowed to patrol the multi-story car park for the rest of his shift, however long it might be.

'There's a briefing coming through,' Mike says, tapping his earpiece.

One of the others puts his radio on speaker and they all gather around. He's still flicking through his phone, probably ready to compare the quality of what they are hearing to what's freely available to everyone. They listen carefully and quietly, as if there is no one else around them who really matters.

'So we have a possible containment issue in this area?' Luke says.

'Oh, great, so we all get infected,' Mike says, shaking his head. 'I was due to start my holiday this week and I bloody wish I had. I could be on a beach right now.'

No one says anything; there isn't much to say. They all start to look around, trying to spot the real issue in the masses of potential problems.

'Remember to look out for any strange behaviour,' Luke says, trying to keep it real, trying to keep everyone focused. 'They expect anyone infected to be aggressive or disorientated.'

'And don't let them touch you, for Christ's sake,' Mike says.

One of them nods but Luke spots that the other one is looking at his phone, playing around with the settings. He finally looks up at everyone, his face white and his eyes blank. 'There's no signal anymore and no 4G either.'

Everyone shakes their heads but Luke tries to keep calm. How many times has that happened before? If it happened in the middle of your day off, when you're shopping or chilling out, you wouldn't think of it as anything more than a mild annoyance. But he also knows that this could be something very serious; the networks do get shut down in the event of a threat, and this could signal big trouble ahead. He feels worried and annoyed at the same time – being expected to show bravery, yet being treated just like Joe Public.

'Go to McDonalds,' Mike commands the other two. 'See if you can get on the Wi-Fi.'

Luke doesn't say anything to them, as he turns back to Mike. 'Dave confirms it's a network blackout and we need to be ready.'

Mike simply nods, and the moment the other two are out of earshot he checks the view ahead through his holographic sight, nodding to himself again as he looks around.

Luke looks up at the sky again, seeing the cloud formations that seem to be joining together and tightening up, doing their best to block out any remaining blue sky. He almost feels the tension in the air and he can't help but agree that this isn't a training exercise.

*****

'Meatballs,' Dad says, as a plate of meatballs is put in front of him. This is followed by a plate of chips, and a glass of Coke. He looks up at her, his face slightly creased.

She knows what he's thinking and soon pulls a cake out of her coat pocket, wrapped in a napkin, the chocolate smeared across it. She puts it down and licks the runaway chocolate off her hand.

He looks down at it and then looks up at her.

She gives him a smack, staining his cheek with sticky proof of her uncontrollable frustration. 'They ain't got no other cake that I can fit in me pocket, so that's what you're getting. And we're sharing pop so you're getting up to refill the bloody thing.'

The kids set down their food and start to pull out their own extras from their pockets. Ashley notices one of the staff looking at him but they don't seem in the slightest bit bothered. He knows that this has to be because of what is happening today. They've probably been recorded on the camera but he's not sure anything will ever come of it. 'Why can't I have my mattress?' he asks, in between mouthfuls of chips.

'Oh, fucking hell, Ashley,' his mum says, spitting juice all over him and the table. 'I told you already they ain't got the cheap one in stock and I ain't forking out a hundred quid.'

'So I have to sleep in my own piss?'

His sisters start laughing and shouting 'Pissy pants, pissy pants, who's got pissy pants?' Cortnee gets onto a chair to do a dance; they don't look like they're going to stop any time soon as she wiggles about and her sister calls out some beats to help the rhythm. Ashley starts to feel the anger swell within him; anger at being part of such a shocking family, and fear that he has another whole year to go before he can escape.

At this moment, as Ashley is considering how he will ever cope with this until he reaches sixteen, his sister, who is still dancing above him, a drink in her hand, has a bright idea: she decides to pour it all over his trousers. Her aim is impeccable, and most of the liquid lands square on his crotch, soaking its way into his light blue jeans before he can think of moving.

By the time he pushes his chair back and gets out of the way, the damage has been done. He looks at those around him, his family – the people who are supposed to look out for him. His sisters are still screaming 'pissy pants', one from above him and one from across the table. His mum soon joins in, a finger pointed at his crotch, as she laughs at him. He feels the absence of any love, so much so that it causes him to choke. He looks at his dad, the one person who would always have stood up for him in the past; the man who might give him a slap when he deserved it, but who would just have easily rubbed his hair and told him that the re-gearing of his bike chain or the shelf he put up in the kitchen was spot-on. But now there is nothing, as the thing that only looks like his old man shovels food into his gob, completely oblivious to what is going on.

That really is the last straw for Ashley; his dad has gone and he has reached his limit. He looks at his mum, who is still laughing her head off, and then he looks across the table at his sister, who is grabbing Mum's arm, desperate to keep on the right side of her. Time seems to move slower now, as he looks up at his other sister, still laughing from up high, always looking down at him.

He leans down and grabs two of the chair legs, properly bending over, making sure he gets all the weight into his legs, and with one final glance up at his sister he knows she can see what's coming. She tries to move as she lifts a leg to leap onto the table, but she's too slow. Ashley pulls the chair with both hands. He puts every ounce of energy, of passion, and hatred into pulling that chair up and away, and does so with such force that it swings behind him and then flies across the restaurant.

He looks to see where it lands, impressed with how far it went, and when he turns back he sees his sister landing on the table, squashing the food and sending a scattering of chips and juice across the floor. She's screaming now and Ashley feels eternally disappointed that her head didn't hit something, so that his mind could be given a bit of a rest.

His mum and sister are yelling too, as they furiously scrub the meatball juice off their clothes before it dries. No one helps Cortnee as she scrambles around on the table, desperately trying to pick herself up as her hands slip on the plastic covering, now coated with all manner of sauces and crushed food.

Ashley starts to laugh, first at his sister and then at his dad, as he sees him picking around his daughter's body at the surviving food.

'Don't just fucking sit there!' Mum shouts at him as she looks on in horror.

But that's exactly what Dad does, keeping low and calmly rescuing what food he can. He's not just tucking into the food on his own plate anymore, but whatever he can salvage. He helpfully picks a meatball out of Cortnee's mangled hair, everything going into his mouth before it gets squashed by her frantic movements.

Mum looks over at Ashley, her face creased with anger. 'You're going to get the belt across your fucking back when we get home. You're sisters are gonna hold you down and I'm going to lash you raw, you filthy, piss-stinking little faggot.'

Ashley says nothing, as the family fall silent, everyone allowing his mum's sharp tongue to do its worst.

She takes a chance to look around, to savour her victory, and then he looks at Ashley. 'Now, help get your sister down off that fucking table.'

Ashley nods, looking down at his sister. She is lying still now, clearly expecting him to help her. She thinks about the punishment she's going to dish out, far in excess of whatever their mum does. The lashing will probably start just before *The X Factor*, and he'll be left in his room to nurse his wounds, with no supper and certainly no TV. And once the show is over then her and Jade will get on with the night of torment. She thinks she will start with shaving his eyebrows and then try some more extreme ideas. She thinks about leaving him tied down and using him as a toilet all night; his own piss combined with whatever she and her sister can expunge from their bowels onto his stinking face.

She looks up at Ashley and he looks back; he knows what's in store for him. You don't have to be a genius to work out that if he goes back to the house tonight he will face horrors far worse than whatever is lurking outside the store. It is at that moment that Ashley truly knows he is on his own, and when you acknowledge that you've only got yourself left in the world, your perception of the rules seem to change.

'I'll help you down, dear sister,' he says, taking hold of both her legs.

Cortnee hears the tone in his voice and realises that she is too exposed. Ashley has always been bigger than his age, and these last couple of years have seen his muscles grow and his puppy fat disappear. Even through all those baggy jumpers he always wears she could see the change. What she will never know is that Ashley has been doing five hundred push-ups every day, ever since the day he first realised it was taking both of his sisters to pin him down. And now with just one to deal with, it was no difficulty at all to swing her off that table and onto the floor. He couldn't have timed it better: her head hit the leg of the table behind, making her scream out in pain. It's not quite hard enough to knock her unconscious but it is enough to set blood streaming down her face, which pleases Ashley greatly.

It is also enough to send his other sister flying around the table towards him. Jade charges at him like she's about to deal death to her brother, but he stands there calmly, and only when she gets within striking distance does he raise his arm and smack her straight in the face. Blood gushes out of her nose as she falls backwards. She stumbles towards her dad but he simply moves away; it's been years since he's cradled this bitch in his arms.

Upon seeing blood flowing out of her sister's nose, Cortnee quite rightly decides that this isn't going to end well for Ashley. Since he has crossed a line that the family will never tolerate, he is now what she would describe as openly fair game. And by this she means it is now entirely acceptable to bury a fork into his leg, which she attempts to do by picking up the one lying next to her. She doesn't hesitate, taking a firm hold of his leg in one hand, and lifting the other, the fork clutched tight.

It's almost as if everything the members of this family have ever done to each other has led to this moment; her mind providing her the graphic instructions as to how to best hurt her younger brother. On one level she thinks this might be a bad idea, especially as if he ends up in A&E, as then she won't get the evening of punishment that is clearly due. But, on balance, she is fairly confident she can convince her mum that he can be patched up at home, and his back will still be ripe for a good belting.

Of course, that isn't what Ashley has in mind: his years of being tormented by his two sister's means that he knows if one of them is hurt, the other is always waiting to strike. They are, by their very nature, a two-headed monster. They have different bodies, but barely manage one brain between them. Ashley laughs at his sister as she lifts the fork up. He leaves her holding his left leg as the other one kicks her between the eyes. The force of the heel of his boot sends her head colliding with the floor, the shock taking a moment before the screams of enduring pain follow, like no words could ever replace what has just happened.

As both of his sisters lie down, nursing their broken noses, he feels strangely satisfied. He looks at his mum and he knows he'll never be going home because he'll never be allowed to live if he does. He keeps an eye on her, wondering what she is truly capable of, as she looks around for the best tool available to hurt her unwanted and ever-neglected son. He needs only to pat his pocket, to feel his dad's car keys still in there, which he had swiped half an hour ago while his mum was yelling at him because the cheapest and thinnest mattress was out of stock.

He gets ready to run, knowing that all he needs to do is beat them to the car. He just about knows how to drive, and is fairly sure the roads will be clear. As long as he can win the race back to the house then everything he needs is in the one bag in his wardrobe – always packed, always ready. If he thinks he has time he will give the house a trash too, mainly his sister's bedrooms. He'll at least have time to show them what a pissy mattress really smells like. And so he steps away from his family, from his mum, and from his bitch sisters. He looks at his dad, who has finally stopped eating to look up at what is happening.

Dad has nothing to say as he watches the boy step away, moving backwards through the maze of tables and chairs. He briefly wonders why the other two kids are on the floor, but he knows it will be because of some drama that will eventually turn out to be his fault.

'Goodbye, Dad,' Ashley says, as he turns and runs.

His dad smiles at him, and from the depths of somewhere in his vacant mind he wishes the boy luck. He thinks that in that previous life he should probably have been nicer to the lad, but those finer points all left him the day he fell down the hole on that building site. A sharp smack across his head brings him back to the moment, as he looks up to see his missus shouting at him. He can't really hear what she's saying but he has a feeling that in his old life he put up with too many of these slaps, and the odd punch, and he wishes he had given a few back when he was well enough to do it.

She smacks him across the face, as hard as she can, her rage towards the boy now funnelled entirely at his dad. 'Where are your bloody car keys, has he got 'em?' she yells, knowing that little shit is more clever than he looks.

Dad just looks back at her, as she keeps shouting at him. 'Meatballs,' is all he says, knowing how much this winds her up. Somewhere deep inside himself he's laughing.

Her face scrunches up, the rage swelling through her. She believes it's a feeling of anger at him and what he has become. But if she was ever brave enough to look into her own mind, she would know it is anger at what she has allowed herself to become; deep down knowing she could have been a good parent if she had just kept that demon at bay.

But that monster is loose now and it's growing within her. She smacks him again, sure that her hand is hurting far more than his face ever will. She looks at the table, still hunting for what she can use. The only things she can see are those few remaining meatballs, and so she scoops them up and then smears them all over her face. They sting a little but since they're nearly cold she thinks it's probably her pride rather than her skin that is hurting. 'There… are you fucking happy now?' She grabs his face with one hand, digging her nails into his skin as she continues to rub the meat and juice all over her face. 'Will this make you give me any more attention now?'

He looks up at her, seeing the thing he used to call his wife. He never wanted to marry her; he just wanted a few shags. Back then he liked her best mate way more, but she never put out and never showed any interest. A few shags can become quite expensive when you're on the dole, and the fact is that condoms become a luxury you can't afford. He stares at the beast in front of him and remembers that night when they had finished off the vodka and she had promised she would step off just as she finished him. But she never did, and as he lay there knowing the climax was coming, begging her to jump off now, she just ground him down a little bit more, keeping all her weight on him. It was quite a lot of weight, as he recalls, and she's been doing that ever since.

'Well, do you want to fuck me now, do you?' she shouts at him, that same face from 20 years ago now coming back to haunt him.

He looks at her one more time and then looks down at the table. 'Full up,' he says.

She screams and then hits him several more times, lashing at his head and shoulders, all her anger stemming from their poor choices and her eternal desperation to be loved.

The girls come together to watch, never having quite seen their mum lose it as much as she is now. She eventually wears out and looks over at them, her mind ticking away. After a moment she scrunches her face up again. 'Ashley,' she grunts. 'Where is that little fucker?'

No one answers as she continues her demanding glares, and then she starts to run, tearing up a path through the tables towards the escalator, throwing aside anything that gets in her way and screaming out her son's name like she will hunt him to hell and back.

The sisters and Dad watch her disappear out of the restaurant, and so do the poor staff who have had to witness all of this. 'She's crazed, something has taken over her,' one of them says into the phone. 'The whole family just lost it.'

On any other day the operator would have just ignored this description as a little over-the-top, caused entirely by the adrenaline of the moment. The first time she took a call about a shoplifter becoming violent she felt some degree of shock, but after ten years on the job it was just another routine call. But on this day she didn't feel like that; everything is different now and no experience from the past can change that. She follows the strict instructions she has been given to send out a quarantine order on the immediate building, to inform the surrounding officers, and raise the alert level for the entire area.

After all, this isn't the first time she did this today, and it is starting to become something of a new routine.

*****

Mike and Luke nod at each other as they hear the quarantine order come through.

Luke's heart is pumping wildly now, as the realisation hits him that this has just become real for them. He thinks about how many officers must be standing ready, as he is, just looking and waiting until that call comes through. And now that whatever is happening is hitting his world, he knows that fate has turned up to see just what he does.

'Mike, Luke, stand ready, please,' Dave says through their earpieces. 'We're on route to you, sixty seconds out.'

'Acknowledged,' Mike says, looking over at Luke, staring at him with burning intensity, as if he is now the target. He has a panicked look, as though he's all alone in this. 'Get your fucking safeties off and stand ready!'

Luke jolts backwards then obeys, a battle raging in his mind between remembering his training and following Mike's lead. He thinks about keeping it real, staying in the moment and always thinking about what is happening around you. Everything is moving too fast to take it all in, and the only thing he can truly rely on is his partner. Mike moves forward and so does Luke. He looks briefly behind him to see the two officers from earlier.

'Armed police!' Mike shouts, pulling Luke's attention back to what's in front of him.

He tries to take everything in, but what he can sees battles against the flurry of information in his earpiece, as he tries to figure out what is most important right now.

'Subjects are showing signs of infection,' a voice says. 'All units please be aware that the quarantine must be maintained.'

'Armed police! Stop where you are!' Mike shouts again, towards the front of the store.

'I got your back,' Luke says to Mike, suddenly glad of his experience, and that he is confident enough to do what he needs to do.

'We give this kid one more chance,' is all Mike says in return, never looking away from his eye-piece.

'Stop now or we will fire!' Luke shouts, announcing himself.

'Officers behind you,' someone calls out. Luke quickly turns to look.

The interval between him calling out that he is armed and turning around seems to last forever, and when he turns back he sees some kid kneeling down a few yards ahead of them, begging not to be shot. He looks scared but harmless, rational and in control; showing none of the symptoms of the virus that they had been told about.

But then someone else runs out of the building, her eyes wild and her skin covered in what looks like rashes and boils. Her arms are swinging everywhere as she makes her way straight towards the boy, her frenzied screams echoing across the big, open space. Luke is clear that this lad has now become a potential victim and obviously needs protection.

Mike is shouting the standard warnings, as Luke trails his crosshair on her. He hears the sirens in the distance, he hears the repeated warnings over the radio to maintain quarantine and he knows that Dave is coming. But he also knows that his boss will be too late. By all means protect innocent civilians, Dave had said, but don't you dare break that thin wall of invisible protection for anything or anyone.

She doesn't listen to any of the warnings like a rational human being would. In both Luke and Mike's minds she is clearly possessed, which makes her fair game in this new, chaotic world. Shooting is a last resort, any officer will tell you that, but set against the backdrop of only what they know, the stakes soon rise and those quick decisions matter more than ever.

It's the boy who helps make up their mind, as he turns around to see just how close she is getting. He's in between her and the police, making a shot to the leg all but impossible. But when he shouts 'she's crazy!' and 'she's got it in her blood!' there really isn't much else that can be said.

The deafening sounds of bullets travelling from the barrels of two guns, and the screams of one crazy woman are quickly met with silence in just seconds. Her frantic cries are replaced by instructions from the officers to stay down. The boy turns around, ever so slowly, not wanting to provoke the same reaction from them. He looks over to the thing lying on the floor, the pool of blood trickling out of its head, and he knows that he wasn't lying when he said he has always known she was crazy, way before today ever arrived.

He doesn't really have any other thoughts about her, or what has happened, even when he sees the blank eyes of his dead mother looking at him. But at that moment something makes him look up to a window in the store, where he sees the silhouette of a man looking down, and he realises he does have one more thought.

'Best shopping trip ever,' he whispers, watching the shadow as it slowly disappears.

Sunday 14th August – London

Your money means nothing

He looks at me with that stupid grin and I know what's coming next. I know he will silence me with a kiss on the lips and then tell me how great everything is going to be. And sure enough, just before the lift stops he leans towards me. I let him plant his soppy, wet lips onto mine. I've given up telling him that we're not 16 anymore.

The lift doors open and I see another couple standing in front of us, waiting to get in. They don't look as embarrassed as I would have expected and Stan probably hoped; in fact they look like a potential copy of us, just a lot younger and healthier. Age is the last thing on my mind and since I have nothing to say on the matter I prepare to exchange places.

It's Stan who has to make a scene, has to make something out of nothing. 'Oh, I'm so sorry you had to witness that. It's like our honeymoon all over again!'

He's still babbling away as I get out of the lift and the other couple get in. They still say nothing, but their facial expressions say it all. One of them presses the button repeatedly, and I grab our suitcase, pulling it along the corridor, knowing that eventually Stan will follow.

'Well, they didn't seem very happy to be here,' he says. 'One of the best hotels in London and they still can't even break into a smile.' He takes the suitcase from me and starts making his way down the corridor, but after only a few short paces he turns around. 'I bet they are so used to places like this that it simply bores them. Can you ever imagine us being like that? There was once a time we could only dream.'

'Yes, Stan,' I say, pushing him forward. 'We could only dream.'

I follow behind him as we walk along the corridor. He looks at every door, checking each room number to make sure that it isn't ours, that we don't miss it – that we don't miss a thing. I watch him constantly cross-check each door with our room card, his anxiety so obvious, so out of place for somewhere like this. I suddenly notice that his jeans are too ill-fitting, his shirt is too tight around his increasingly unpleasant girth, and his blazer is obviously oversized. It's the only remotely posh thing he owns these days, and in even a few short hours he has managed to coat the top of it with a thick line of dandruff.

When we reach our room he holds up the key card like he's presenting it to God. 'We've made it, Gloria! We're finally here! I never thought it would happen but now it has. I am literally opening the door to our new world!'

I nod and sigh. 'Well, Stan, you can get that door open whenever you like.'

He lunges towards me and kisses me again, first just a simple peck on the lips, but then his mouth gapes open. My lips don't move, forcing him to suck my face like he's some desperate fish fighting the side of its tank, desperate to be noticed. I'd always hoped that after thirty-something years of marriage I would still want to suck the face off my man, but the reality is that the appeal disappeared somewhere in the '80s.

I push him away, more forcefully than I had planned.

He backs off and nods, looking at me and then looking to the floor. 'This time it will be different, Gloria. I really promise you that.'

'We're in our sixties. How could it not be different?'

'You know what I mean,' he says, and then finally pushes the door.

As it opens, I breathe a sigh of relief. I half-expected the key card not to work, thinking that my credit card's feeble limit had already been reached, that our inability to survive in a place like this has already become clear to those at reception and that they had cut us off from ever being able to experience what awaits behind that door. For the last 48 hours I have been convinced that all of this is a dream, but as I follow Stan into the room, I finally start to allow myself to think that this is real, that this is something I deserve.

I pull our suitcase into the room and look around in astonishment. It's huge, easily the size of a small suite. Stan is in the middle, his arms held out wide as he shows off what he has found for us. He quickly turns, pointing out all the things I can see for myself, before he stalks his way towards me.

'Didn't I say it would be great?' he says, stroking a finger down my arm. 'Didn't I say that I would give you only the best from now on?'

I silently nod as I look around and count the pieces of furniture. There are so many: different chairs for different purposes, and more tables and dressers than I could ever spread our few possessions around. And then I see it – the imposing four-poster bed. It takes up one whole corner, a declaration of importance.

He's suddenly behind me, taking my breasts into his grubby hands, his gravelly voice ringing in my ears. 'Didn't I promise you the bed would be perfect?'

'Perfect for you,' I say and then push him away. I walk towards the bathroom, not wanting to picture that bed for one more second. 'I'm going for a shower. It's been a long journey.'

'I could join you?' he says, his face full of sickening hopefulness.

I quickly shake my head and only then do I think to force a smile. My desperation to get away from him combines with my need to get through the next few hours, and I come up with a solution that has him touching me as little as possible, without arousing too much suspicion. 'I need some lady time,' I finally say.

'Well you come back quickly, babe,' he says and winks. He watches me leave, picking up the phone. 'I'll get us some champagne. It must be at least ten years since we've ordered room service.'

'More like twenty,' I mutter, slowly closing the door to the bathroom. I lock it, quietly, yet symbolically putting a physical barrier between us. I turn around and take a look at my opulent surroundings. The room is white marble from floor to ceiling; the many bath sheets are all crisp and white and folded to perfection. I look at the oversized shower, then at the bath in the other corner and I smile, allowing myself this small victory as I look through the vast selection of toiletries I have not been able to afford for such a long time.

I think about starting with a shower and then moving onto a long bath, but however exciting that sounds I know that I will do it alone, with him always and forever in the next room. As sad as that feels, it is far preferable to having to spend it with his hard cock poking at my back as his slippery tongue lashes at my neck. That lost its appeal somewhere in the '70s.

I can hear Stan shouting things to me but I let the shower drown him out. I let it splash water all over my body and I don't make any attempt to answer him. When I've finished scrubbing my body, washing off the effects of the long journey, as well as any trace of him, I smother the sponge with a new product. I take my time to rinse and repeat, lathering my body and washing off every trace of the past. I inspect each new bottle, breathing in the scent of my future, rubbing them all over my body like I'm marking my new territory and I dare anyone to try to take it away from me this time.

When I finally walk back into the bedroom I expect him to jump in front of me, immediately throwing his overbearing desires to make everything good in my face with a complimentary glass of bubbles. Having relaxed I feel ready to do battle again, to show enthusiasm where none exists, but I'm met with only silence and I don't see him at first, until I look over to the bed and see him lying on the pure, white sheets, his body spread-eagled and his cock hard.

'Please!' he says, somehow knowing that I'm back in the room; his cock pointing to the ceiling, the black mask and restraints lying casually next to him.

I sigh but don't say anything, as the life I desperately want to leave behind invades this place I hoped would become neutral ground. My head shakes, feeling a familiar sense of anger, as that odour of leather and sweat, which reminds me of only an unhappy past, starts to smother the pure and floral scents of my new future.

'Oh, please do it now. Oh God, Gloria, please do it now.'

'You've sniffed poppers, haven't you, Stan?'

'Oh, God, yes, just before you came out. Come take hold of it now. Oh, please, now!'

I turn and move to the window, sitting down in the oversized armchair that's angled perfectly so that I can see everything happening in the big, exciting world outside. 'Not right now. I'm not in the mood.'

He's still pleading, his cock jerking as he teases it himself and I quietly stare out to the unknown. I try to get as far away from him as possible, my gaze casting its way down the street. It's quieter than I expected for Central London, yet the streets still have a frantic feel to them. People don't seem to be walking with the confidence I remember when I was here in the early '80s, the last time that Stan and I stayed in a swanky London hotel.

I turn to him, forgetting his devious plan for our afternoon. 'Don't you think the streets are a little too quiet, and the people around here seem a little frazzled?'

He stands up, muttering to himself, putting his pants back on as his little man tries to poke through the hole in his baggy briefs. 'And what would you know about what London is like?'

'I know it should be different to this. It didn't feel right when we got the cab from the station, it didn't feel right when we checked in, and it doesn't feel right now.'

He comes over and kisses me, wrapping his arms around me like I should somehow feel safe just because he's here. He smiles, making sure our eyes connect. 'It only feels different because we're different now. We are never going to have to worry about money ever again.' He holds out his arms in celebration. 'We're rich!'

'Not until we meet with them tomorrow and the money is in our accounts.'

'Honey, do you have to keep saying *our* accounts?'

I nod, entirely sure that there will forever be two accounts. 'The money will be split, and I'm not having this conversation again.'

He nods back, knowing better than to start this again. 'From tomorrow everything will be fine. *Our* money will be in *our* accounts, and *our* marriage will be back on track.'

'You had better hope so because we only have this place for one night.'

He steps away, his hands planted on his hips. 'Do you think I would have wasted our last remaining savings if everything wasn't guaranteed?'

'It was the last of *my* savings that we used, and the last few hundred on *my* credit card.'

He smiles and nods. 'And it's *my* lottery ticket.'

I keep quiet, knowing that the power I hold comes from the past, and the power he now has comes from the future. I must remember what is still to come, and until I have half of that money in my account I need to keep my place.

He lurches forward and kneels down in front of me, taking my hands in his. 'You're my wife, so what is mine is yours. We've shared the good times and the not-so-good times together, so my win is a reward for both of us. Now we can start a new life.'

I simply nod, knowing the game we are playing. He squandered our savings and threw our life away but he's still my ticket to a happier world, and so I kiss him. I kiss him so hard that his cock rises to the occasion. I grab it and I tease it, just how he likes it. I don't jerk at it like some violent monster, trying to quickly placate it. No, this moment requires me to play the game. Two, maybe three, dirty sprays from that ugly, veiny, red thing, and only one more fake orgasm from me and then my escape plan will start in earnest.

He suddenly pulls away from me. 'The champagne still hasn't arrived.' He walks to the phone, his eyes still on me. 'We need to start celebrating, don't you think?'

I nod and continue looking out of the window as Stan taps away on the phone. I watch the few people scrambling around beneath me. 'I haven't seen a black cab or any other car pull up outside since we got here.'

Stan doesn't hear me as he taps a finger on the oak table. 'No one has picked up yet. Can you believe this? It's supposed to be one of the poshest hotels in London and no one has bloody answered.'

'Give them a minute. Perhaps they're just busy.'

'They might be busy, but it's still their job to answer the phone and make our stay a comfortable one.' He heads to the bathroom, finds his white bathrobe and puts it on. 'I'm going to go down there and give them a piece of my mind.'

'Why are you doing that?' I ask, knowing that Stan getting involved in anything is never a good idea.

'Gloria, we deserve some bubbles, and I'm going to get us some, okay?'

I pick up the phone and redial the number, hoping that someone will answer and solve this minor issue, wanting to stop Stan going down there and giving them grief. Much to my relief, someone answers. 'Could I possibly get some champagne to room 412 please?'

'I'm not room service,' the voice says, slow and ever-so-slightly sarcastic.

'Oh, I'm sorry,' I say. 'Could you please put me through to them?'

'Room 412, you say? I'll be up in a few minutes.'

The line goes dead but I take this as a success. I don't bother to mention how abrupt his tone was to Stan: the risk of him demanding to see the manager is just too great.

'Well done to my darling wife,' he says, and drops his gown on the floor, the poke in his pants back for another round.

I turn on the TV and start flicking through the channels. 'After some bubbles, perhaps,' I say, giving him a quick glance, and seeing that pathetic, sad face staring back at me.

I watch the news as he watches me. Despite the immediate future looking bright and hopeful, I can't help but feel that this is the lowest point in my life. I feel depressed, my husband is sat next to me and the grey world outside seems bleaker than I have ever known it. Only Stan and Gloria could turn a stay in the best hotel in London into something so shit; everyone else's dream just the climax to my lifelong nightmare.

'Someone was shot outside Ikea yesterday,' Stan says, focusing on the TV, quickly revealing that I'm not concentrating at this important moment.

'What?' I say and turn up the volume.

'Well, coming out of that place it was bound to happen.'

I tut at yet another view of his that has changed. 'It's nice – we have been there lots of times and you never complained before.'

Stan shakes his head, frowning at me like I'm stupid. 'We haven't been there in years and we will never set foot inside there again. It will be only the best for us from now on.'

I don't answer and instead I realise that Stan is right. I've been to Ikea a lot lately but not with him. I think about how many times Antonio and I have been there in the last few months and I suddenly see the how easily I could have been caught. It was all I could afford to help him sort out his little place and it desperately needed some colour, some organisation, and most of all a woman's touch. The few hundred pounds I spent on kitting out mine and Antonio's little love nest is the only secret I've ever kept from Stan, and it still pales into insignificance to the thousands he squandered. Despite the big dent it made in my small, secret savings account, it was worth it all to see Antonio's bright young face when we finished decorating. That day was the most pleasurable one of my dreary existence, as I watched my Spanish lover do all the work, admiring his ripped, smooth torso, covered in splashes of white paint. When he finished the last wall he smiled at his work, then silently ripped my skirt off and took me in every position we could think of.

I remember every bit of him was primal. He had teased me for hours as he stretched and worked, before silently letting his pants fall around his ankles and my lips settle around his monster cock. The smells and juices that ooze from Stan would normally make me feel sick, and since at least the '80-s, I have refused to go down on him unless he has showered thoroughly, but with Antonio those scents were like an intoxicating drug to me. That night he fucked me into heaven, and every night since then, I have wanted only him.

'Are you okay, darling?' Stan says, tapping my arm.

'Yes, I'm fine,' I say, as I stand up and head to the bathroom.

Stan doesn't say anything as he watches me leave. I know his gaze is fixed on the door as I slowly close it again; his beady little eyes watching the lock turn, no doubt.

I turn on the shower and sit on the toilet as I leave Antonio another voicemail. There's still no answer but this time I tell him everything I've wanted to tell him for so long. I tell him about the lottery win and that I intend to spend all of my side of the winnings on our new life together. I whisper, ever-so-quietly, as I confess my plans for us both to escape the chains that keep us from being together forever; his student debts and my indebted husband – both of which will be a thing of the past in just a couple of days.

I put the phone down and imagine Antonio and I sitting on a first class flight, the ching of our champagne flutes as the plane takes off. Stan will likely be at home, trying to figure out where I am and when I will be coming back. I won't leave him a note; I won't tell him anything. He will forever wonder where I have gone and he'll never be able to trace me. I will transfer the money to Antonio and we will live together in a Spanish villa by the beach. Antonio will swim every day as I lie on a sunbed. I imagine watching him walking out of the sea, water dripping down his muscled body, both of us smiling at what lies ahead of us.

We'll be happy and Stan will be nothing. While he wastes his share of the winnings I will build a new life with the kind of lover who should have been mine from the start, my real man – half Stan's age and double the man he will ever be.

I suddenly hear a tap on the door. 'Gloria, are you okay?'

I sit forward. I know he is not about to burst into the room and discover my darkest secret, but I clear my phone's call list anyway. 'Yes, I'll be out soon.'

'You won't believe it, they're saying zombies have started appearing and they have shot one in West London. The world has gone crazy, I tell you.'

'Okay,' I say, as if that's a half-good answer to what he has just told me. 'I'll be out to look in a minute.'

He says nothing back and for a moment I think he's gone, until I see a shadow moving, creeping across the small gap at the base of the door. I wait, wondering if he's listening – both of us quietly sizing up the other's movements. 'I'll get ready,' he finally says, and the shadow disappears.

My heart sinks as I let out a gasp. I imagine what will be waiting for me on that bed, his darkest desires overshadowing any genuine concern for the world outside. I load up my pictures of Antonio on my phone, using the secret app he showed me – his clever way of letting him always be with me – all of them taken by me and hidden by Antonio. I flick through them, taking every part of him in, from his cute young face; a few days' stubble on it, to his thick cock, bigger than I even thought was possible. The first few times he stripped off I always wondered why he wanted to be with me, a woman twice his age. I would look at my body, my desperate attempts to make myself appear younger, and then I would look at his smooth, tanned skin and I never understood what the attraction was. But as we spent more time together, our experiences growing, I realised that what I offered him other women of his age never could. I brought depth and experience to his flat life, and as our love-making sessions got longer and more intense I forgot about the age issue, just as he stopped letting my lifelong wisdom and so many more stories than him be anything but a clear turn on. I think now of all those times together and how it couldn't just be about money, couldn't just be sex, and so could only be love, separated by decades but has now finally come true.

I hear the main door open and feel thankful that the alcohol has finally arrived. I decide that I'll down two glasses and do all I can to keep the memory alive of my darling young man. It should just about be enough to get me through the next half an hour or so.

I move to the door and wait for the attendant to leave. The leather gimp mask and assorted tools are no doubt laid out on the bed, and although I have a good idea of what they will have seen, I can at least choose not to let myself become a face in this desperate tale. The room service attendant will no doubt tell everyone about it but I will just be thought of as the secret mistress; a dirty little title without any real identity.

I suddenly hear a thud and I wonder what has happened now. I lean my ear against the door, wondering if they have already left. 'Stan?' I shout.

'I'm not Stan,' this voice says, sounding like it is coming from just the other side of the bathroom door.

I push myself away, back towards the toilet. I wait, and I say nothing more, realising that this dark voice matches the one I heard on the phone.

The handle slowly moves, making its way down until it's stopped by the lock.

I gasp, finding a boundary he is willing to push. 'Stan? Is that you? Stop playing around.'

The handle returns to its safe place. 'I told you, I'm not Stan.'

I feel scared, and involuntarily let out a whimper. I dial 999 and think about what I can say, ready to whisper, knowing that the precious lock won't help me for long. No one answers my call, no one seems to care. An automated message tells me that all lines are busy and that, wherever possible, I should seek local help and medical assistance. I try Antonio again but it won't connect to him, either.

I look around the bathroom and then at the base of the door, watching for a shadow that isn't there. I take a brave step forward and put my ear back to the wood, listening for Stan or for anything that will give me a clue as to what's outside. I picture the path to the main door in my head and I think about whether I can make it out of here. Thinking of the bright new world that I am going to create with Antonio spurs me forward; I won't let circumstances or the actions of others hold me back any more. I take a deep breath, tuck my hairspray can under my dressing gown, and then unlock the door.

When I step into the room I see Stan on the bed, tied up with the gimp mask on. I think that maybe it was him all along, and that the person who delivered the champagne is long gone. I consider heading to the bed to take part in whatever new fantasy my husband has created. My overworked mind has obviously been creating nightmares. But then I think about that voice, so out of place for the world created by this hotel and this brand, and so I immediately check my path to the door.

I soon realise that it was not just my imagination, seeing that the coffee table, sofa and chest of drawers are all lined up against my only way out, creating a barricade. I let out another whimper, feeling there is someone behind me.

'Do you like what I've done to your place?'

I turn around to see a man standing in front of me. He's middle-aged, bald, and his blood-red eyes tell me more than I ever want to know. I step away but he moves closer. I look at him, trying to take in as much as possible, hoping that within the hour I will be reciting this in a witness statement to the police, who will have traced my call and come to my aid. He's wearing a suit jacket but I notice that underneath is a pair of jeans and a ripped t-shirt. The jacket is covered in red splashes, which I keep telling myself cannot be blood.

My heart beats faster with every little detail I take in. The name badge that says 'Robert' and the title underneath that states 'Manager'. I step back further and think about how much damage a blast of hairspray could do to his eyes, and whether that would give me enough time to pull all the furniture out of my way. Only in the last few seconds of my simple plan do I give Stan any thought. I make one quick glance his way and silently tell him that he's on his own; it was always going to happen, although I never would have dreamt up this situation in my worst nightmares.

'I think these places are far too orderly,' the man says, throwing a chair across the room. 'I think a little chaos is exactly what we need in times like these.'

I hold my hands out. 'Please,' I say, my eyes filling up and my whole body shaking.

'Just come here,' he says, his own arms spread out like he's offering some sort of silent assurance that he won't hurt me.

I don't believe him and so I take my chance, the only one I may get, and pull out the hairspray. I quickly aim at his eyes and press the top of canister. It's a new can, bought especially for my new life, and I let it all go now. It jets out a mist towards him and I hold down, firing as much of it as I can. It seems to work: he staggers backwards and starts rubbing his eyes. It's enough for me to grab my chance as I turn and start pulling at things. I claw at whatever I can get my hands on, frantically pulling at the solid, luxury furnishings, whilst screaming as loud as possible that someone needs to help me.

I start to see that I won't be able to clear a path before he recovers and I realise that I have made a mistake: I should have hit him with something. I quickly turn, looking around for the heaviest thing I can pick up. It proves too late as I find him in front of me. I step backwards but he grabs me and smacks my head.

'You clever little bitch,' he says, before smashing our heads together. A daze falls over me as I realise that I'm on the floor and he is dragging me. I feel him lifting my body as I land on a sofa, the one nearest to the bed, and then I feel his breath on me. He is licking his way up my chin and across my face. 'I like the creative ones. The better the fight, the less pain I will cause you in the end, you have my promise on that.'

We are both disturbed by Stan as he suddenly moves and I hear the muffled screams coming through that thick mask. His naked body struggles, so obviously fighting against the restraints.

The man looks over at him. 'Oh, he's finally awake. I assume I was about to interrupt something between you.'

'No,' I say, my desperate head shaking. 'I was going to stay in the bathroom whilst we have guests. Two other men are coming over and they'll be here soon. It's what he likes.'

He turns towards me and punches me in the face, before jumping up and grabbing at his head and rubbing his eyes, like he's trying to make sense of this as much as I am. 'What a lie! You and I both know that no one is coming. Have you not seen the shit-storm out there?'

I shake my head as I try to make sense of where the pain is coming from, whilst tears flow freely down my cheeks. 'Please let us go and I promise I'll give you money.'

His thick hand is suddenly around my throat as he pushes hard against my skin. 'Oh, I bet you can. All you fuckers have now is your money. You live your lives of debauchery and promiscuity while the rest of society goes to hell, and then you think it is your money that will save you.' He pushes harder, forcing the back of my head deeper into the soft fabric of the sofa. 'Why should people like you survive all that's coming?'

'No, we're just like you,' I say, as he releases my grip a little. 'We won the lottery. We're collecting our winnings tomorrow. We can split it with you, I promise.'

He grabs my arm, and a knife appears from nowhere. 'You're nothing like me,' he says and slices my pale flesh like it's raw chicken on a board.

I scream out before the pain even registers in my mind. It's not long before he has me pinned close to the sofa, his hand around my throat again. 'When you get that money I already see what you two will become. You'll join them – the ranks of the so-called elite. You new-money people are even more clueless than the wealthy fuckers out there now, earning all those bonuses just for screwing over the little guy.'

I try to shake my head, hoping that this will allow me to take in some air. I look at his name badge again and I wonder why the manager of a hotel is doing this.

He catches me looking and laughs. 'I'm not Robert. The last time I saw him he was slumped in his chair with blood flowing out of his neck and down to his shiny boots and his immaculate beige carpet. A fitting end for a tool of capitalism, don't you think? He will no longer do his masters' bidding – keeping you people in a state of luxury that you don't deserve, whilst the rest of us fight in the arena of the real world.' He pulls a sock out of his pocket and stuffs it into my mouth as my answer; my pleading and begging seem of no interest to him. He pushes it down deeper until my mouth is filled with the tinge of iron.

'Sorry about the blood, but I didn't think Robert would need these anymore.' He leaps up and looks down at me, his face calm, and the knife still in his hand. 'Now, you stay there and observe. If you play nicely I will end you quickly, just as soon as we finish making love.'

It's too much to imagine, too much pain to endure after a lifetime of regrets, and so I scream out, my hands pulling at his sock until welcome air fills my lungs.

I see the rage swell in his eyes as he quickly leans back down and punches me. He hits me again and again until I stop moving. I sit quietly this time, letting him stuff the sock back in my mouth without resisting, as he uses the other one to bind my hands together. I don't dare fight back and I don't even think about the end that will come. I think only of Antonio and how, at any cost, I must get out of here and find my way back to him.

The man soon leaves me and makes his way to the bed. I watch my husband as he registers the weight of someone else next to him, and then starts wriggling and struggling. He runs the cold blade up Stan's thigh and around his wrinkly testicles, making the sounds coming through the mask even more desperate. I know this is a scream like no other; nothing like any of the noises I have ever heard him make. I have helped my husband become primal many times, his wildest kinks simply a mindless chore for me, but I have never before heard a noise like this.

Our intruder lets out a laugh, and I realise that he has been observing me as I watch my husband. 'I think you both enjoy this.'

I shake my head, desperately trying to tell him that I am not enjoying this, and that I have never enjoyed these moments. I think back to the hundreds of times I have been forced to tie him up, as tight as I possibly can, making escape near impossible. I remember the countless whines and moans he would make as I worked his cock to a climax, always making sure none of it hit me. Then I would quietly release a restraint, always just one, leaving the rest to him as I retire to a long, lonely bath. I thought that life was nearly over for me, but now it's on show for someone else to see, someone who believes I actually got happiness from it. I think of those decades of silent bitterness, always hoping for escape, always held back by having no money.

'I shouldn't be cruel, your husband clearly has some needs,' he says, putting the knife down next to one of Stan's legs.

My heart starts to slow down, just a little. He seems to relax; his movements with the blade become just that little less sinister. He starts to run his finger down Stan's chest, first teasing his nipples and then ending on his belly button. He plays with Stan's floppy cock and strokes his hairy, grey pubes as if it's just the two of them, together in this new nightmare. I soon realise that he's doing a better job than I have done in the last couple of decades. I huff, almost involuntarily, when I see his cock jerk. Only Stan, my pathetic husband, could eventually get some kicks out of this.

'I think he likes it,' the man says, grinning over at me.

I don't say anything but sure enough, Stan's cock grows and I see him reach his lowest point in all our long years together.

The man seems absorbed in this moment, giving my husband all the attention he has lacked from me since the day he first brought home the harnesses that would chain me as much as they would him. I silently watch, forced to endure all of Stan's moans and noises. He's not really here anymore and I know that it no longer matters who has hold of him. His dark world is a simple one; a few sensations and the power of his imagination are all he needs to get off now.

'Is that it?' the intruder asks, his hand enveloping the entire girth of my man.

I say nothing, thinking only about Antonio, thinking about how even in Stan's youth he was nothing compared to the man I have now, the one I desperately need to find and keep.

'Is it?' he shouts, pulling Stan's cock as he makes his demands of me.

I make my muffled 'yes' through the fabric that still restrains me, as I look at what is presented before me and realise how much more I could have had.

'Would you like it now?' he says, grinning over at me.

I shake my head, not wanting to imagine him forcing me to grind up and down on Stan's body as he gets his kicks. I know how that will go, how quickly it will be over, and how the man will inevitably decide that I need far more than my husband can give me.

'Oh, I think you do,' he says, pulling Stan's cock up as much as it will go, forcing his body to lift up with it, his bum rising just a little up off the bedsheets.

I shake my head again but I don't think he's listening. He's not interested in what I want.

'I'll give it to you,' the man says, his eyes wild. He grabs the blade with his other hand and with one quick slice he cuts Stan's cock clean off. He throws it over to me, the thing I have held so many times now detached from the real world, and sitting on my lap.

I hear fresh cries from Stan travel through all his boundaries; the longest and darkest scream that comes from this new, harsh reality. There is nothing he can do; blood spurts out of the gaping wound. The man screams too, and as a haze comes over me I realise that what I can see on his face is pure delight, as he watches the blood that is quickly draining out of my husband cover his clothes.

I see the devil in front of me stand up, his triumphant yells echoing throughout this apparent paradise. I look down at the lump of skin on my trembling lap; the remaining blood now soaking into my white gown.

It's the last act, enough to take me away, and as the tingling in my hands signals the collapse of my mind I think only of Antonio. I think of him on that beach, my protector and lover; he would never have got us into this mess.

*****

I wake up to muffled moaning and it takes me a moment to realise where I am, then the memories come slowly flooding back into my mind. I think of the man, of Antonio and of the future I had so hoped would come true. And only then, tracing the source of the constant whimpers, do I think of Stan. I look over at the bed and see that he is still tied up; the once clean and white sheets are now covered in the fresh stains of my drained husband.

'Don't worry, he'll be dead soon,' the man says. He's at the other end of the sofa, perched on the corner and looking at me. His face is still covered in the blood of his last victim, my partner of so many years, and the knife is still in his hand.

He moves towards me and I cower, my most basic instincts the only thing still with me. I pull away until I fall onto the floor, and then I simply kick out towards him and drag my body across the carpet. I know that even considering all the despair I have experienced – my husband ruining my life, my constant fears about Antonio leaving me – nothing will compare to the horror of what is approaching now.

He's telling me to be quiet, to calm down, but all I can do is scream through the bloodied and dirty sock that belonged to a man who has already fallen victim to this monster. He suddenly picks me up, pulling me towards him.

'Sssshhhh, I told you it will be quick.'

I shake my head, not sure what I'm denying. He ignores my muffled pleas and sets me back down on the sofa, pulling the sock out of my mouth and then cutting the fabric tying my wrists. I feel a simple and immediate sense of relief as my body sucks in as much air as I can take, like I'm quenching a thirst I have never experienced before.

He moves back to his perch on the edge of the sofa, and then he pushes the knife into the cushion, like he's thrusting a sword into the ground. He looks at it and then looks over at me. 'I promise I won't use this on you. Your husband has taken the blade so that you won't have to. I'm sure you appreciate his sacrifice, don't you?'

I look over at the remains of my dying husband. One simple cut has made an unimaginable mess that can never be fixed, but I don't feel sympathy for him. I'm not sure that I feel anything; my own situation now seems far more real than whatever he is experiencing. I watch, seeing that his faltering heart still beats, although it's clearly a struggle and the end must be near. I curse Stan – only he could survive such an experience, still lingering on when the rest of us would have taken the hint by now.

'He's only alive because he's lying down. But it won't be long now and I don't imagine that he will feel much of anything anymore. Does that give you comfort?'

I shake my head. 'I get no comfort from knowing you are a vile murderer!'

He simply laughs, immune to anything I tell him. 'If you were to survive my visit then you would meet many more of me in the new world, I can promise you that.'

'What are you talking about? And why are you doing this?'

'It's not that simple to explain what is coming but it will change everything. You see, I have seen things and I know that you have to be fit to survive the storms that are approaching. Do you think you're fit enough, Gloria?'

'How do you know my name?'

He smiles. 'You filthy rich have created such a cushioned life that you take for granted so many of the basic things. The computer flashed up your name when you called, and so I decided to pay you a visit. You could say that fate brought me here because if you hadn't called for champagne then the chances are I wouldn't have visited this room for some time. You might have moved on by then, or you might have been asleep by the time I arrived. I might simply have cut both of your throats in the night.'

I whimper again, my whole body shaking.

'But instead, I was brought here. Our destiny is to meet for longer than the quick slice of my blade, of that I am sure.'

I shake my head, showing both my surprise at his honesty and my denial of the plans he has for me. I think about my options and spot a glimmer of hope: there may still be a chance of talking my way out of this. Perhaps the money could be my ticket out of here. If I can only get out of this room, I can get away and into the arms of my Antonio.

He is still staring at me, still looking me up and down like he is sizing up his prize. 'You can tell a lot in these situations and I'm a good judge of character. For instance, I can tell that you don't love him, and yet you are "Mr and Mrs" on the computer.' He walks over to the bed, to Stan, looking down at him. 'Explain this to me, please. I'm very interested.'

I shake my head, my worn-out mind not able to grasp the complexity of this moment. Nothing makes sense in this new, cruel reality and I have no answer that would help him understand.

His face turns red in response to my continuing silence, and it's not long before he pushes down on Stan's chest. He thumps it hard with both hands, forcing another scream out of my husband and causing blood to jet out of the gaping wound.

I start to scream and cry, the horror of what he has just done coming back to me; the fear that beats though my own veins so entirely real.

'Tell me!' he shrieks, getting ready for another thump on Stan's chest. 'You have until your husband takes his final breath to help me to understand the very interesting, yet ultimately complex inter-personal relationship you two have, so I suggest you start talking!'

I hold out a hand, begging him to stop, silently asking for more time.

He takes a deep breath, as if calming himself down, and then nods as he sits back down next to Stan. He rests his body on the blood-soaked sheets as if he doesn't see a difference in what they are and what they shouldn't be; doesn't see what he has caused.

'We won the lottery and we're here to claim our winnings. We have never stayed in a place like this before. We have fought to make enough money to live on and now just want to start a new life.'

He nods again, matter-of-factly, as he takes it all in. He seems to absorb every word that I say. 'How much did you win?'

I take a deep breath, trying to figure out what motivates him – other than killing people – then say '20 million,' staring at him and hoping it will be enough. I consider offering him half the share, all of it even, but I'm not sure he is in the same place as me anymore. 'We just wanted to have some happiness for ourselves and then help other people, like charities and those in need, those just like us.'

He laughs, then gets up from the bed and comes towards me, like a predator stalking its prey. When he reaches my face he takes a long sniff, sucking in all the air around me. 'You really want me to believe that, don't you?'

I close my eyes, unable to bear having his angry eyes or hellish face so close to mine. I try to imagine him believing me, try to imagine him simply leaving the room, giving me a few minutes to do what must be done to Stan, then allowing me to walk out of the building and into the arms of the nearest policeman, or anyone in authority.

I feel a hand on my throat and I gasp as his fingers push against my skin and his grip tightens. 'Why should I believe that? Tell me one thing that will make me believe you.'

I open my eyes and stare at him, at the man who has become my judge and probable executioner. 'Because I am a good person, I'm in my sixties and I would never able to spend that much money in my lifetime. If you don't believe me then let me sign it all over to you, to do with it what you please.'

He smiles and then slowly licks his way up my face, starting from my neck and not stopping until he reaches my forehead. 'You are a nice person, Gloria. I can tell you are one of the good people, but I still can't believe you. If you truly cared about worldwide poverty and the state of our planet more than your own well-being then you wouldn't be staying in this hotel. You wouldn't be preaching to me dressed in an expensive bathrobe, drenched in the scents of high society, and you wouldn't both be pursuing such perversions of the mind. If you were pure then you would not be in this place of judgement.'

I can't answer him, cannot deny what is so obviously true. We are both distracted by coughing coming from the bed and I look over to see Stan's body convulsing as his head moves from side to side.

The man is quickly beside him, putting his face next to the mask that hides my husband from me. I pray that he doesn't take it off; I don't want to see him, not like this. He licks the mask and then spits across the room.

'There isn't much time, Gloria. He will be dead soon, and once he passes then it will be your turn. I still don't understand enough about you two, about how you have come to be in this moment.' He turns to look at me. 'There is more to you, I can sense it.'

'You are murdering my husband!' I scream. 'What more can you possibly want to know?'

He walks back towards me. 'No, that is where you are wrong. You are slowly torturing your own husband. You haven't once tried to go over to him, to offer comfort or to even ask me if I can ease his suffering.' He sits on my lap, gently placing his body on top of mine. 'You could have asked to borrow the blade at any time, and with one simple slice you could have ended his life and allowed the judgement to start on yours.' He stands up and walks over to the blade, picking it out of the sofa. 'Do you love him, Gloria?' he asks and stares at me.

I pause for a moment, remembering some of the many times I asked myself that question, all those many years ago. I have known the answer for so long yet done nothing about it. I finally shake my head and then let it bow down in shame.

'I knew that,' he says, and then looks down at Stan's pale body. 'I think we all knew that.'

'I could end his suffering now if you would let me,' I say.

He looks at the knife and then back to me. 'I think that would be the right thing to do.'

I stand up, cautious, not sure if my captor will ever actually allow me to do such a thing, or even if I am capable of slicing my husband, or this evil man, should the chance present itself. I don't really know what I'm doing; none of this seems real yet I know it is happening.

He moves closer and fearlessly holds out the knife, despite it being obvious what I am thinking of doing. He calmly nods, looking at me, almost smiling. 'Let us finish him and then decide what we will do with you.'

I nod back, playing along in a game I know I'm never going to win. I take hold of the knife and see that he is standing at arm's length from me, making a swing unlikely to succeed. I look at the bed and at the body of my husband. He doesn't even look like my Stan anymore – he's just the shell of the man I chose to stick with. I move closer and our intruder takes up position at the other side of him.

I don't know what to do and so I lean myself onto the mattress, trying to avoid anything stained with the horrors of this last hour. Stan's body isn't moving anymore and I'm not sure if it is over already. I think of the pillow, the easiest option for both of us. But then I have these cruel, selfish thoughts. I need to use the knife; I need to have the weapon in my hand and find the opportunity when I can strike. I start to see Stan as a practice run, wondering how I should do it. Perhaps this is my payback for all his years of inadequacy, or perhaps this is the kindest way to end the torture he has been going through. I look at the intruder to see that he is staring at me, his face wild with excitement. It's so obvious that he gets his kicks from the pain of others.

'Let's get his mask off him,' he says, excited, like my husband is a present waiting to be unwrapped.

'Perhaps we should leave it on?' I say, not wanting to see those dying eyes. Right now, he can't see me and I cannot see him, and that is the way this should end.

This man gets hold of my hair before I see him coming. He pulls hard, forcing my head to land on Stan's chest. I feel the touch of his curly hairs, the smell of blood and sweat, his body now as lukewarm as our forty years of marriage have been. He eventually lets go of my hair and allows me to sit back up. 'You will look into his eyes at the end, just as I will look into yours. It's the fairest thing we can do.'

I slowly nod, now clear that I should throw myself into this moment, as I prepare myself for seeing Stan's fearful and confused face.

The mask comes off quickly, and I realise that the intruder didn't secure the rear fasteners. It was too loose – something Stan would never approve of. He always had to have an entire vacuum around him when held captive, his body and senses sealed in a world he couldn't escape from. I almost feel like apologising to Stan for the half-arsed job this monster did of securing him, but instead I take one final look at his gaping wound and get ready to tell him not to look down; to tell him that it isn't as bad as it must feel.

As the leather mask comes away from his head I see that there is a trail of blood dripping down his chin, and then I see his eyes, which are grey and unmoving. I look down at him but I don't actually feel upset; I don't even feel pity. I feel angry. Angry that he has left before me – this was my escape, my chance to walk away and leave him scared and alone, never to know what had happened. And now, as I look at the two men before me, I realise I have not even found that dignity to be the first to get out of this lifetime trap.

The man who has just officially become my husband's killer starts moving around, his hands digging into Stan's mouth. 'Look, Gloria, he actually bit a part of his tongue off. It must have been the pain or the shock. I wonder if he intended to do that.'

I look across the bed and see what a horrible thing man can turn into. Money, greed or power could never change him from what he has now become. I look down at Stan, at his mutilated body. 'He only ever wanted to bring me to London to collect our winnings and then start a better life. That's all he hoped for and you've taken that away from him.'

He pays me no attention and continues to examine the body, checking for a pulse and then putting his ear to Stan's chest. 'He has already passed away, Gloria. That's such a shame. I was looking forward to seeing you push the blade into his flesh and the remaining blood spill out from within him.'

My body shakes as I look down at the weapon in my hand and I realise how tight a grip I have on it. I let go, just a little, seeing the immediate indent it has made on my skin. I look back at him and then make my grip firm again.

He looks at me and then back to Stan, his mind obviously preoccupied with whatever he is planning to do next. He doesn't seem bothered that I am still holding the knife, but I'm distinctly aware that it is my only chance to get out of here and that he will soon turn all of his attention onto me.

'Are you sure he's dead?' I ask, knowing how obvious the answer is to that question.

'I think so,' he says. I don't know if he is playing along or is genuinely not sure. He checks for a pulse once more. I find his thoroughness scary, thinking about how it might soon be my turn to face this nightmare.

He bends his head down and pins his ear to Stan's chest, then waits for a second to see if anything happens. I know that this is my moment and as he starts to talk about how you can tell if a person is really dead, I visualise the best place on his body to drive this knife into. I settle on his neck, hoping that it will sever an artery or perhaps enter his head and slice through his corrupted brain. I move quickly, turning the knife in my hand until it's at the right angle to do as much damage as possible, and then I lunge towards him.

Everything seems to move slowly. He moves his body back, forcing me to thrust forward. I lunge quickly, stretching over Stan's cold corpse. The knife stays on course until the last moment, puncturing the skin and penetrating his shoulder, but I know this alone is unlikely to kill him. I imagine that he must have been almost hoping that this would happen – my assault upon him ending any truce that might have existed between us and now justifying any attack he will now make upon me.

He screams out in pain as I feel the blade hit a bone, my determination driving it onwards. He falls back onto the floor and I think about leaping over the bed and continuing my assault.

But then I remember his strength, and the possibility that this wounded bear still has a good deal of fight left in him, and so I decide to drop the knife and make my way towards the door.

As he shouts and screams, I try to get the coffee table out of the way. I pull at the top of the sofa, but my blood-soaked hands are not able to get a firm grip on it, then I manage to get hold of the bottom and start dragging it away from the door, knowing that more obstacles still stand between me and my freedom.

I look over to see he is getting up from the floor, his hands pulling at Stan's legs in order to help himself up.

'Clever, Gloria, very clever. Your punishment will now be even greater – your pain now prolonged.'

His words are enough to give my body strength I didn't know I had. The sofa moves a little, enough for me to get to the small dresser. I pull at it and with one shove it lands on the floor. I can see the door and my freedom but then I see the lock and the handle that has been broken off.

I turn around to see him standing up, the knife now in his hand, blood running down his shoulder. He looks at the door, to where the handle should be, and he laughs. 'Your judgement and death in this place was always inevitable.'

As he starts to make his way towards me I give in and run to the bathroom. He staggers in the same direction, but just in time, I push the door closed and manage to lock it, just as he gets hold of the handle.

I stagger backwards, sitting down on the toilet seat, all the time watching the handle move up and down. His screaming is drowned out by his banging on the door and I don't know how long it will hold. I look around for a better weapon than the last one, but in this moment of darkness I see nothing but Antonio's sweet face.

I pull out my phone and dial his number, knowing that it will never work. I wait as the network decides what it will do; I seem to remain in that limbo between a ringing tone and a voicemail that seems to last for an eternity. When it starts ringing I feel a rush of hope, even when I think about the impossible odds. All I know that he has gone to his family in the south of Spain. When he got the message a week ago, he left immediately; he didn't know what had happened, but his family had said it was urgent. Now I need him here, far more than they ever will.

'Hello?' the voice says. It is obviously Antonio, but he sounds different somehow. I can barely hear his voice over the background noise of shouting and cars beeping.

'Antonio! Oh, God, Antonio! Where are you? I desperately need you.'

'Gloria?' he says, sounding doubtful. 'This is a difficult time for me, for all of us. I cannot talk now and I must go.'

'Please don't... please don't do that,' I shout, trying to force my desperation down the phone line and into the mind of my only real lover. 'I really need you. Listen, I'm still in London. I have so much to tell you, but someone is attacking me.'

He doesn't say anything in return. The noise in his background is deafening and sounds like many sirens are all around him.

'Did you hear me, Antonio? Someone is attacking me and I need you!'

'People are being attacked everywhere. You see what is happening? You must see it?'

I don't answer, seeing the handle stop moving and the door start shaking as my personal devil bashes against it.

I don't know what else I can do, what else I can say and so I start to cry. 'Antonio, I'm so scared. Please help me.'

'I cannot help you because I must get home to my family before it's too late. You must realise that this is goodbye, Gloria.'

'No, please!' I scream, competing with the sounds of crashing fists against thin wood, as I look up to see his angry face appear through the hole he has just created. 'I love you Antonio, I love you so much.'

But he doesn't say anything back. I hear the line go dead, and the next thing I see is the hand of my attacker reaching through the hole and unlocking the door.

I look around one more time for a weapon, realising I have wasted my precious time on a youth who would never have stayed with me, never have protected me in my darkest hour. I was only ever a limited something for him; some company for one small part of his long life. I realise that now; at this end I finally accept that I have never found what I really wanted. I have never experienced true and mutual love, and for that I can only judge myself.

The man I only know as Robert bursts through the broken door and I don't even try to stop him. He takes hold of me, spitting blood and sweat all over my face, shouting all manner of graphic threats about what will happen now that he has me.

'The money,' I say, my one last attempt. 'I'll give it all to you.'

'Your money means nothing,' he says, as he drives that bloody and well-used dagger into my lonely heart.

Tuesday 16th August – Arabian Peninsula

Beg, buy but never borrow

I look into the mirror and something looks back at me. It's an absent stare; a look without a cause. I'm not sure what it says, not really clear about what I actually am. Even laid bare I don't know what I'm supposed to be other than skin and a scattering of hairs. I tap my stomach – it's firm and toned; what was once slim and scant is now properly sculpted. My stubble is trimmed as close to my skin as possible, utterly refusing to be bent into any kind of beard. Those black eyes stare back at me, dark and empty, giving nothing away – not sure what I have to give.

An Arabian prince is what she called me. I'll always remember the first time I stripped for her on webcam, how her eyes were wide as I teased every part of my body. It was all for her, however she wanted it. I was pleased with my work – my hours of gym and endless running had given both of us what we wanted.

'Do it gently,' she would say, as if she was with me, caressing my body with those small, feathery fingers. She moaned as I moaned; our distance climaxes were as real to me as if she had my manhood in both her hands, which she assured me would be needed. I always did as she told me, angling the camera and working my body as she demanded, her entire mind seeming to be mesmerised by me. And in return, she was the only woman I had ever obeyed, let alone talked to on any sort of equal level. I wondered if all Western girls would feel the same about me – whether my body and name would be as exotic to them as I hoped, and whether I would allow others of her kind to command me, as she had done.

After these thoughts I would always chastise myself, assuring my fractured mind that I would be faithful to the one who had found me first – forever ignoring the many more who would offer themselves freely to me. Her loyalty would be rewarded, if I could just be with her. She never knew that what she believed me to be is actually what I am. I never got to tell her the truth about me – the truth that the robes I took off were as real as my birth right to the empire around me. I wanted to tell her. I desperately wanted her to know that we could have been more than virtual lovers. We were so close yet so far.

I only ever got to show, never to reveal. I came close to sharing my plans with her. The further they came to becoming a reality the more I wanted to confide in her my deepest hopes: that soon we would be able to embrace as one. I would be in America within the year. If she could wait that long I would make it worth her while, giving her all the treasures that my land could ever offer. It was a question I was dying to ask but I never got the chance.

When they found me exposed, close and entirely in the moment, my father's first threat was to have me executed. He screamed at me; I felt as though I'd been unfaithful to a cause without even knowing it. He said that I should be sent back to the moment when I was at my lowest; my most depraved, and that is how I would be buried.

But the beauty of being the only one left in a family where bloodlines matter most, so obviously brings a blanket of safety that cannot easily be thrown away. She screamed for me when they shot the lock and stormed into my room, carrying me away as I commanded, perhaps begged, them to stop. When they finished hosing me down with cold water my father finally let me put a robe on and then he sat next to me, his face level with mine. He said she was still on the screen when he finally entered my room, her pale face staring back at him. He told her who he was, and who I was, and helpfully informed her that the things we had done together were sins in the eyes of anyone who mattered. He forgave me but said he could not do the same with an infidel such as her. He had kept her online as his men found her real life location. She had threatened to call the New York Police Department, but this meant very little when our spies got to her.

As he told me this story, he grabbed my manhood, balls and all, and lifted me up, staring into my eyes as he promised that she had paid dearly for my mistake, and that this was the last time we would ever talk about the USA. He said that if I was doing such things then I would never study there, exposed to all that corrupting filth. I could not be trusted, and so my computers and passports would all be removed from my possession, just in case I had any more foul ideas.

In many ways it was as if he had blinded me; he took away my ability to communicate with the outside world, with the friends I had found in that place with few boundaries – no physical boundaries, at least. The virtual me wasn't held back by my looks, my future or my place of birth. I could be someone different and I often changed exactly who that person was, trying out new versions of myself, finding the one that best showed who I wanted to be.

I told none of this to my father, although I'm sure his men found out all of my secrets on the laptops they seized. I made no effort to hide any of it, having hidden enough of myself all over the planet. I wondered if all those distant friends I made would ever remember me, or if to them I would go forever offline - followed but forgotten – nothing more than a memory of the past that only ever hung around the edges of their waking lives. My father didn't understand anything about this new world and became convinced that I needed a simple life, to enable myself to remember who I was and what I would become. And now with each layer I put on my body I hide further away; busy being the person I am supposed to be, never the person I want to be.

When I'm finished I look in the mirror that's leaning against the wall. The breeze from the balcony and the fans on the ceiling are doing little to help me. The heat from all these garments is stifling and they work together to form a blanket that slowly suffocates me, giving me no freedom to be who I really am. My real self remains hidden somewhere deep inside and I somehow tolerated this for so many years, knowing that there was always a possible way out. I had been looking forward to a year in the United States of America with every ounce of my being. I planned to quietly disappear while my brother continued to charge forwards, only a short step behind my father, preparing to lead to the family while I happily shrank into oblivion. It would have been my chance to be different, to find myself – to be me. After that I had many ideas of what my future would look like, mostly centring around my eventual and eternal escape.

The knock on the door comes on cue, barely a second after I have fixed my turban and taken a deep breath. I don't answer at first, but there is no second knock; the handle turns, and I am imposed upon.

'Shouldn't you knock again, Abdul?' I say, turning to look at him.

He looks back at me, dressed in his simple suit – so entirely boring next to everything I am forced to wear, like I'm the only one to go on stage – the only one who requires a costume in these uncertain times.

'A prince deserves the respect of a second knock, don't you think?' I say, desperately trying just to elicit a response, let alone assert anything that resembles authority. I know that in this place I have none.

Abdul doesn't answer, instead choosing to fuss around me, pulling my robes tighter and searching around for the appropriate shoes. 'A prince has to earn that right, Jalal,' he says, focusing on hunting for my footwear instead of looking at me. 'I'm sure you'll agree that you certainly have not earned that right.'

I don't answer, instead sitting down and watching my own personal dictator rummage through my things, both of us knowing there is nothing left that should be hidden. I watch and wait for him to throw the shoes in my direction, which he does, silently demanding that I comply. The man who is supposed to be my advisor, my confidant and my voice of wisdom simply walks across me and stands back at the doorway, tapping things into his phone and telling me that I need to hurry up.

'The Americans will soon be here,' he says, as we walk along the marbled corridor. I follow him, always one step behind, his little legs doing a great job of setting our hurried pace, as if he is floating through the palace on a cloud of nervous energy.

'Why do they want to meet me?' I ask, stopping still. I wait, somehow finding the courage to anchor myself in one spot, hoping for an answer that will make moving worthwhile.

He stops and turns around but doesn't walk the few steps back towards me. Instead he tuts and sighs, as if this only re-enforces his feelings of frustration at decades of being stuck with me. The man who has been telling me what to do since I was a small boy does the same again, demanding that I come to him.

'I'm not a fucking dog!' I shout.

It's enough to bring Abdul tearing towards me. We both look around to see the guards who were lingering behind pillars and on balconies suddenly come into view. He smacks me on the arm. 'Why must you constantly embarrass me? You must learn to behave like a prince and not a petulant child.' He rubs his eyes, his head shaking, as he takes time to properly massage the exhaustion out of his weary head. 'You do realise that your brother would never have behaved like this.'

His eyes reach into mine, and I somehow find courage from my growing rage. 'My brother is no longer here. You must accept that and start treating me like a prince. I will be in charge one day, Abdul. You had best remember that.'

He takes a deep breath, bringing himself closer to me, his mouth near my ear. 'You think you will ever be in charge of anything? Your father grows older but because of you he must still produce another son. This is a great burden you have placed upon him, and yet you show no remorse.'

My mouth falls open quicker than I can collect my thoughts to defend an impossible position. I know that these insults to my honour will continue forever, no matter how much logic is on my side. I wasn't there that day, deep in the desert, when the cars were ambushed. I wasn't involved in the route planning or the security precautions, wasn't one of those brave few who tried to save half of the royal family. It didn't take long for me to realise that had been my biggest mistake and it meant I was forever on borrowed time, the days and hours counting down until my absence from everything state and family-related would be my ultimate undoing.

When that long day finally ended my father found me on the southern terrace, just as the sun was setting. I was watching the wisps of sand flying across the distant hills, imagining it was my mother, her spirit still looking out for me, her echoes of understanding travelling across the land. She was the only one who had really known me; although she couldn't always accept that I was somehow different, but she at least realised it was true. On that particular night she was not looking out for me, not able to hold him back this time. As he beat me until the sun finally disappeared I knew that somehow it was my fault, and it always would be, because it hadn't been me in the convoy that day, and my brother hadn't been safe within the palace walls. It should have been me. He told me, without saying a single word. The loss of his wife was bad enough but the loss of an heir with the energy to carry on the name and to lead our people was impossible to comprehend.

'I have caused this?' I say to Abdul, already knowing the answer, already regretting giving him such an easy way in.

'Yes, you!' he shouts, as he digs a finger into my chest. 'You and your western thoughts. Somehow the capitalist devil got into your head and I've tried everything to get him out.'

I shake my head, unable to find the right words to match my dismay. When my father first said the Americans were coming I got so excited. I would get to meet them and we would talk about my future, all of us having a say in deciding what university I would attend and where I would live. Even when my father made it clear that their visit was about oil, trade and money, and that my year away was only an afterthought, I still got excited. Just knowing that this was a chance for a better life was enough to make me smile every day, even if three body guards and the never-happy Abdul would have to come along with me. I never once wondered how many barrels it would take to buy my freedom; only the thoughts of different shores mattered.

'I'm not going to America now. I'm never going to leave this place and we both know that, so why would the Americans ever want to meet with me?'

He prods my chest again. 'You never listen to anything I tell you. The Americans *will* be meeting with you, which means that all the trade discussions will be in your hands.'

'But where is my father?' I ask, not believing that I will be alone, unable to comprehend the thought that I could be trusted with anything more than visits to our most remote settlements.

'He had to leave immediately and so he will not be joining us. Something is happening in the south and the military has been put on the highest alert. He has personally gone to investigate.'

'And I am only being told this now?'

Abdul starts tapping something into his phone and when he eventually looks up he smiles. 'You only needed to know this now, and that is why you have just been told.'

'So, I have been left in charge?'

He takes a deep breath and mutters a prayer as he looks up to the ceiling and then at me. 'You must understand that we had no other choice.'

He starts to walk away but I stand still, refusing to leave this place without the respect I deserve. 'Perhaps I will not see them. Perhaps I will be the petulant child that I appear to be so good at. I could sit here and leave you, the mere advisor to the lowly prince, to see them and to negotiate on behalf of the palace and my father.'

He turns on his heels so he can look at me, refusing to move back. 'Perhaps you do that and then we both know that you will never get to the USA. You long to travel to that arrogant land, yet I pray every night that you will somehow find a way out from under the vast shadow of your late brother, and finally prove your worth to your father. Act as a petulant child and you will simply confirm everything he knows to be true about you. But achieve victory in this meeting and you will earn some much-needed respect, which will be good for both of us.'

I think for a moment. I think about the United States and I think about myself; the two always joined as one in my desperate mind. It doesn't take long before I nod and walk forward, coming to my master like the dog I am, knowing my place and what my biggest needs are. As we walk along the corridor I wonder how the relationship of two countries could be left in my care. I am about to be locked in a room with a monster, desperate and hungry for what we have, and yet it still excites me. I have what it wants – I'm literally sitting on barrels of it and a passage out of here is all I really care about.

Abdul grabs my arm, squeezing it tight, as if he can guess the thoughts that are running through my corrupted mind. 'Our relationship with the Americans is nearly over and we are ready to burn it. It is clear that they are falling from grace and they are nothing more than a frantic and plagued people. Once their military machine runs out of power it will die like a horse that has ran out of water, so you must not give them anything of value. In fact, you must do the opposite and give them nothing.'

I shake my head, openly willing to refuse this order, feeling closer to the future I want than I have been in a long time. 'What is the point of them being here if we are not to negotiate?'

He shakes his head at my continuing lack of understanding of our political and economic place in the world. I think I understand it better than he ever will; the divide between our generations and our different desires is never as obvious as when we discuss the land of the free. 'You will do nothing but listen and remain firm,' he says. 'You must say very little and remain aloof and disinterested whilst Hamza and I do all the talking.'

I throw my hands by my side, behaving exactly as I have always been forced to, playing a role, one that has by now become very easy for me. 'Hamza will be in the meeting, too?'

'Why would a general not be in attendance at such an important meeting? He has deliberately remained behind to meet the Americans, and then he will fly to the south when they leave.' He shakes his head at me once more. 'You will never know how much it pains me that you cannot be trusted to conduct these negotiations on your own. General Hamza should be with the scouting party and yet he has to be here, with you. If anything should happen to your father then this will be entirely your fault.'

I say nothing and rub my face, playing with the stubble that should be a beard by now. I wonder why I have never allowed it to grow into what it is supposed to be. His stare tells me more than I want to know. He looks at me as though I am an outsider who somehow got inside this palace but also into my mother's womb. I imagine in the USA that many people will be running through all those corridors of power that I used to see on my television before it was taken away, all of them focused on today's important visit. I remember all those many rooms, with their big, over-the-top titles on every door. I truly believe it would be a nightmare to make any major decision, but it symbolises all these people working together to create something bigger than any individual could ever be. And here, it is just one person, in one room, who makes all the decisions that matter. When that person disappears and I am relied on, I don't know what I will do, or how I will ever make a success out of today.

Adbul pulls me out of my thoughts and onto the balcony, and I immediately see three helicopters approaching. They look big, even from this distance, and extremely powerful yet utterly exciting. They hold formation like they were made to fly together, until they get close enough that all I can hear is the deafening sound of their blades. One of them suddenly moves forward and I assume it is the one with the cargo – the passengers of importance.

I glance to my left for just a moment, just long enough to see Abdul shouting into his radio, his angry screams competing with the unstoppable sounds of our new visitors. I look around to see our soldiers getting themselves ready, perhaps for a fight; if nothing else, wanting at least to look strong against the small, yet deadly force that has arrived. I look around and see chaos, but I still don't see the sinister aspects of what is approaching. All I see is opportunity.

The lead helicopter finally lands, still flanked by the other two, as though they are playground bullies who always stick together, knowing that strength comes from numbers.

'American arrogance knows no boundaries!' Abdul shouts, louder than I have ever heard him before, as if he hoped they would hear it from inside their big metal toys. As if they could; as if they would care if they did.

'They were supposed to land at the back, not on the new lawn!'

I don't answer him and look down to see servants and soldiers shouting and waving their arms, pointing to the back of the palace.

'These bastards landed on the moon first and now they think it gives them the right to land wherever they like and do whatever pleases them.'

'And clearly it does,' I say, with a smile.

Abdul suddenly grabs me and pushes me back into the room, pinning me against a wall. We're inside enough for the Americans not to see but still close enough that I can feel the sun beating down on one side of my face. I don't look at him, even as he shouts at me; instead, I look outside, hoping the Americans don't ever see me like this – as the weak and imperfect person that I am. They will think of me as sheltered and unimportant, and however true that may be, I don't want them to know me as everyone else does.

'These people only want our oil,' Abdul says, his thin fingers digging into my neck. 'And our oil is all we have. Do you understand me?'

I shake my head, my body forcing against the hold he has on me. 'It is not all we have.'

'Oh, but it is. Do you think that tourism will save us? And do you think at the end of Western civilisation that anyone will still come? I promise you they will not. This will only ever be about our desert and what hides beneath those dunes. Today we will see how much they are willing to pay and then they will leave with nothing, because it is most definitely not for sale.'

'He is right, young Jalal,' this voice says from the doorway. I quickly realise it belongs to Hamza. He stands there in his full military outfit, a rifle thrown over his back as though he feels it is his duty to fight off the advancing hordes single-handedly. 'We might seem like nothing more than a small pile of rocks and barren sand but we will not be beaten by these vile beasts.'

'Hamza is right and you will do well to let him do the talking today.'

Hamza advances towards us both, his eyes on our violent embrace. 'And you, Abdul, would do well to release your prince. However much a worm he is, he is not ours for squashing. We must all be focused on the real enemy that awaits us downstairs.'

Abdul seems to think carefully for a moment and then releases me and nods, patting down my arms and slowly stepping back. 'You must forgive my enthusiasm, we both know I only wish for you to finally listen to my experience and wisdom, so that I may make you the prince we all hope you can be.'

Hamza grabs both of us and pulls us closer, as the smell of sweat resulting from this morning's mobilisation floods my senses and makes me want to choke. 'The purpose of today is to see them beg and then later this evening you will tell your father the tale of how they were on their knees. You will bathe in the glory of our nation's reserves and offer them only enough for their return journey to whatever archaic battleship they have moored wherever they are still welcome. They will land back on their ship with nothing but a realisation that their world is coming to an end and that a new power will be born and a new world formed. Whatever plague they have created for themselves will be their undoing and we will only benefit in this new world.'

Abdul bumps his head into mine. 'Follow our lead and do as we tell you and tonight we will comfort your father with stories of how they left us, never to return, and how we paved the first steps into the future of our people and our mighty country.'

I look at him but I cannot speak; I cannot even offer a fake nod. I don't like the old world but the new world I envisaged didn't involve my best hope of escape leaving without me. They will never return again, never again give me such an obvious opportunity. Abdul and Hamza smile at each other, and all I can think of is how I am about to lose something before I even gain it.

*****

I walk into the reception room and feel an immediate chill. I'm not sure if it's me and the burden I am now bearing, or if it's simply the constant buzz of the air conditioning that has slowly absorbed its way into the marble, making every step a cold reminder that I did not expect to find myself in this position today, or any other day.

Hamza suddenly grabs me and prevents me from moving another step further. 'You will stand here,' he says, his thick hand anchoring me in position, his eyes fixed on mine. 'Do not move any closer towards them and at all times make them come to you.'

Abdul stands next to me. 'And do not speak unless it is to reinforce what we are saying. You must remain proud and reserved, leaving us to do the talking.'

'You mean I am not to speak because I cannot be trusted?'

Hamza laughs, before taking a couple of steps away from me, placing himself where I assume he would have been with my father, my brother and all those before me.

Abdul is still staring at me, his beady black eyes looking me up and down for what must be the hundredth time today. 'You believe whatever you think is best and we will think whatever we believe is right.'

I look back at him, casting a probing gaze over him until he notices what I am doing. 'You're still sulking over the helicopters on the lawn, aren't you?'

'How dare you?' he says, his hands ready to make their mark, our battle never over.

'Enough!' Hamza shouts, silencing us both as he looks towards the entrance.

We both look forward, just in time to see the Americans coming down the hall. They move quickly and with absolute purpose; the people of importance flanked by marines dressed in full combat gear. I look down at my robes and up at the visitors in suits and battle armour, and I realise how little and irrelevant I really am.

The marines push the group forward, their eyes observing everything, like they are assessing every possible threat. They look so noble, so proud of who they are and where they come from. I cannot help but admire them and everything that they symbolise. They suddenly separate, making way for the formation behind them to continue the journey into my room, leaving the soldiers outside. It is the generals, diplomats and ministers who will have the adult discussion with me.

I watch them enter: two suits and a soldier; two women and a man.

I'm confused; the vision in front of me is entirely different to what I would ever have expected and difficult to understand. I can't see the obvious leader or understand who is in charge. I stare at this small group as they settle themselves into their new surroundings, their differences to each other both obvious and unexpected. Instinctively, I look at the only man, but he seems small and insignificant; his skinny frame barely filling out his pin-stripe suit. The bigger of the two women is the one in the general's uniform – a woman in warriors' clothing, with a build appropriate for her position. She stares down at me as I look up, admiring her ability to be who she wants to be – her nation allowing her the freedom to fulfil her own destiny.

I turn to see that the third visitor is staring at me through eyes as dark as mine. I gasp as my mind takes me straight back to my last American love, to the sense of perfection and meaning I felt back then, even through the eyes of a simple webcam. I look at her again, and it's as if she's become one with my previous love, the first and only woman to be of significance to me. This thing of beauty stands before me now, dressed in a tight-fitting black suit, which exposes a pale, perfect body, like the one I remember.

My eyes rest upon her, and I wonder if they will ever be able to leave what I have now found, as she stares back at me, clearly confused by my long hesitation. I take a deep breath, seeing more than what a thousand cameras could ever give me; my loyalties to that forgotten, long dead girl in New York now mean nothing to me.

The man in the suit steps forward, his hand extended. 'Young prince, I'm Ambassador Richard Nevins. I don't believe we have had the chance to be introduced.'

I look at him as he stares back at me. His beady, grey eyes look at me through small, wiry glasses. We both wait for me to say something, as everyone else stands patiently. I don't find that I'm scared of not having anything to say, or of saying entirely the wrong thing, but rather of feeling different. I start to think like I am actually someone of importance, that fate has finally made me into something special, even if it is only for a short time and not what was intended by my elders. I'm no longer on the edge, uninvited; I'm now the centre of all that matters.

'No, we have not met before, but I welcome you to my palace anyway.'

'The imperial palace,' Abdul says, as he leans forward and takes the Ambassador's hand from me. 'The king cannot be here right now, for which we offer our sincerest apologies.'

I hold up a hand to the man who has cursed me from the shadows since the day I was born. 'I am dealing with all matters of state whilst my father is away, so no apology is required.'

'Well, it's great to finally meet you,' Nevins says, looking between us. 'Perhaps I should introduce the rest of our delegation?'

'Perhaps you should,' I say.

'May I introduce General Martha Edwards, and this is Jessica Adams from the United States Treasury Department.'

General Martha holds out a hand, forcing it towards me, but Jessica Adams just stares at me. I stare back at her, repeating that name, seeing how it feels as I say it in my head in different ways.

She smiles but doesn't move. It's like her body is a statue that has been brought into the room to haunt me for what I have missed all my life and may never see again. I watch her face, wondering how someone so beautiful could work in such a boring place. I imagine all those old men staring at her as she walks around the office, much like the programmes I used to watch on television.

I feel the grip tightening around my hand and realise that General Martha has taken hold of it. I look up at her and feel a slight squeeze that demands to be recognised. Whatever words she has just spoken were wasted but the connecting of our eyes seems to placate her as she lets go.

Before I can say anything, I feel a tap on my shoulder, a reminder that the act must begin. I invite everyone to the seating area, realising how little effort I have put into being the host and how little interest I have in these formalities. I sit in the larger chair, the one always reserved for my father, and I realise just how frustrating I have been for Abdul and any other of the aides as they have tried to mould and shape me into the man I was meant to become.

'We were sorry to hear about the loss of your mother and brother,' Ambassador Nevins says, as positions are taken and tea is poured. He watches me, waiting for a reaction, clearly hoping for an acknowledgement. He will never understand what she meant to me and when I give nothing back he shuffles in his seat, looking around the open room. 'We are also wondering where your father is, if I may be so bold to question his absence?'

'He is not here and I am, and this is all you need to know.'

The big general sighs and shakes her head, and Hamza sits forward, perhaps wanting to confront his opposite number on my behalf. Abdul looks into the shadows around the room but says nothing. He most likely shares their frustrations and it's clear that none of us want to be here, in this situation, with me as the man tasked to pull this together.

The ambassador leans forward, taking his time to look at each person. 'With all due respect, young prince, I think I speak for all of us when I say that we worry you might not be enough. Not when we consider the gravity of what we must discuss.'

'I will be enough or I will be nothing and that is down to you to decide,' I say, and then sit back, somehow happy with my choice of words – it was like a riddle, the kind that would normally come from Abdul's sharp tongue, except that this one actually made sense.

She finally takes her chance to speak: the only one I see, the only one I will ever listen to. 'We're here to discuss the purchase of oil and we need you to take this seriously.'

'The world is changing,' Ambassador Nevins says.

'I know this, I have heard.'

He looks at his general, then my general and then back to me. 'Well, I'm not sure you all realise just how much it is changing. We have new intelligence about what is happening and we *could* put ourselves in a position where we can share this with you.'

'You have probably heard about everything that has happened in Eastern Europe?' General Martha says. 'The whole continent could be a graveyard by the weekend.'

'We have heard many stories,' Abdul says, looking at his hands and absently picking dirt from his nails. 'None of them have proven to be more than what I think you call 'old-fashioned wives' tales.''

General Martha nods, seeming to admit she has heard a few of these stories for herself. 'The tales of zombies and killer viruses are, as best as we can tell, isolated instances of false information based on variable sources. However, let me be clear, there is a very real threat that affects all of Europe that could soon spread across the planet if not contained.'

'Europe is not our concern,' I say, sitting back, trying to make my body represent my views, even though my mind is scattered. I curse myself as these words leave my innocent mouth, because how can I say that Europe is not our concern when I truly have no idea how much oil we pump to them every day? It could be thousands of barrels or it could be none, but my naivety seems to know no bounds and I know the Americans will spot this.

'Of course Europe is all of our concern,' Abdul says. 'Our prince knows the worth of every country but we will not be intimidated into giving you our natural resources based purely on unsubstantiated stories, just so you can fuel your endless military operations. We know that it is only our oil that you want.'

General Martha leans forward, her head shaking as she looks at Abdul. 'Let me tell you specifically what your precious oil would be fuelling. It will be going into aircraft carriers, fighter jets and tanks. If we are going to get control of this situation then we need these things and you will need us. You should just remember that.'

This is enough of a bold statement to make everyone starts talking, all wanting to have their say – and everyone aims it at me, as if I'm the one to blame for everything. They don't get a chance to present their individual thoughts as Jessica coughs loudly, which makes everyone else stop to look at her, although I'm sure my keen eyes get there first.

'If we accept that Europe is in big trouble then it looks to me like you will need a new customer and we're clearly in the market for buying,' she says, looking at everyone before winking at me. 'I suggest you come to a solution, boys. And you do it quickly.'

The ambassador looks at me and nods, his eyes almost pleading. 'Time is running out and we need a solution today. We are getting ready to intervene across Europe. It is not our homeland, but we know that if the world is to remain secure then our involvement will be required. Having access to your oil will greatly accelerate our efforts, and ultimately, it will protect your country as well.'

I stare back at him, unsure what he expects me to do. I wonder if he thinks I have any power or the ability to make any important decision. I'm simply a victim of circumstance; I have nothing to sell and nothing to bargain with and what I want in return I cannot ask for. I think about trading a few million barrels – if we even have that many – in return for safe passage to the United States. I know that this isn't just a one-off trip anymore; it's about my future, a new life in a different world, which I have to buy by the barrel.

'Well, can you help us?' the ambassador says, staring at me.

I look around to see that everyone else is doing the same; all staring and pinning their expectations on me. Half of the group want to see the others begging for the world's most precious resource, and the other half want to buy something I cannot sell. I'm stuck firmly in the middle: my needs are not known by those around me, and will never be discussed.

'We can sell you what you need, but I warn you that it will be costly,' I say.

Abdul and Hamza gasp, both of them openly shocked by how I have departed from the script. I wonder if they will go along with me, on the assumption that I intend to make the Americans beg for our liquid gold, or if they will drag me out of the room and then shoot the guests so that no one ever finds out about my insolence. I imagine my treachery being seen by all. I imagine them burying the bodies and repainting the helicopters, and my father returning home to hear how I have let him down, yet again. I have been doing that since I was born, but we all know that this time would be the last time, and that this story would inevitably make me the fourth grave, lined up next to our American visitors.

I hold up a hand, hoping to keep my story going for just a little longer, wondering if I will survive the day. To my surprise they both stay silent, both waiting to see what I will do. Everyone looks at me, no doubt asking themselves if I have the guts to follow through on what I have started.

In the silence I have now created it is the woman of my dreams that are yet to come who speaks first, as I am still wondering how I survived so long in a world without her. 'We will take everything you have and based on the scale of the purchase we can offer you 40 dollars per barrel.'

I'm still doing the maths in my head as Hamza laughs and Abdul shakes his head. 'You must take us for fools,' Abdul says. 'The scale of the worldwide crisis has pushed the price up, not down.'

She shakes her head and taps things into her tablet, working out sums that don't exist in anyone but the Americans' minds. 'You misunderstand the fundamental issue here: the value of world currencies will also diminish. As the weeks go by and global commerce stops, the value of whatever gold you have will decrease drastically. Tourism will stop and no one will buy anything from you, making this your last chance to sell what you have.'

The ambassador leans forward, looking at Abdul and then Hamza, then finally at me, making me wonder if I'm actually important or I'm just an afterthought. 'We are on the edge of what is to come and if we boil your economic survivability to its simplest form, your current revenue stream will cease and only what you have buried out there can ever help you,' he says, looking out of the open window. 'The vast majority of people are aware that something is happening but they are still in the denial stage. Those who haven't seen anything or who aren't directly affected by what has happened will continue to lead their lives as normal, but when the oil runs out and the supply of food is restricted they will realise something is very wrong and they will demand a resolution.'

Abdul laughs and I know his mind is working through how to phrase the inevitable rejection. 'You would like to borrow our oil so that you keep up with the demands of your people, and what is more you offer payment with barely a few coins that will be worth even less in a few weeks' time?'

The entire American contingent nods in unison, giving the impression that they have already foreseen this and planned for every possible eventuality. General Martha is the one who sits forward, looking at me. 'The offer made to you by us today is simply a nominal fee. What you really get is protection from what is out there and what is yet to come. Lend us the oil and we will sign a pact to come to your aid whenever it is needed. You know that we must work together to survive.'

Hamza laughs. 'We would be better keeping our oil where it is and spending it on our own military. Why should we see it disappear across the ocean when we have our own issues to deal with?'

Abdul suddenly stands up, and General Hamza quickly follows his lead. 'Our general is right: we need the oil for our own uses. Whatever the new world looks like, we will need it to trade with whoever is left, which may or may not be you. At this moment in time none of us have the answers, so I believe this concludes our negotiations.'

'You are making a big mistake,' General Martha says. She is still sitting, but this doesn't make her seem any less dominant. 'You will need allies and if you won't provide what we need then perhaps we will have to go to one of your neighbours.'

'Do you think we are a stupid people?' Abdul says, pointing a finger at the general. 'We are fully aware of what is happening out there and nothing has happened to us. You are scared because you know you are next. The western world is finally meeting its maker and you think that fuelling your military machine will save you, but it will not.'

'We must secure our place in this new world,' Jessica says, looking only at me.

I try to answer but I am too confused. I hear what she is saying but I think that everyone here takes different meanings from her words. I desperately try to think of how I can find safety in this frantic new world that she is describing. I look over at the ambassador and Abdul; I see that they are arguing but I can't hear any of the words.

Absently, I sense Hamza pulling at my arm. He is still shouting and is trying to get me to stand up. I cannot move and only stare at Jessica, taking in all of her beauty. She is so entirely unique. I look at what I want, what I have always wanted and I find it staring back at me. It's too much to ignore, too big to turn away.

'Take me with you,' I blurt out, loud enough for everyone to hear, although only one person notices.

She frowns and leans back, clearly confused.

I lean forward, desperate for her to listen, for her to see that I need a reason to continue 'You can have the oil for the price you are offering, as long as you promise to protect my people and take me with you. I need full residency, forever. You know that I will never be able to return here.'

She stares at me for a moment, her mind clearly evaluating my proposal. It sounds simple to me, and the only possible answer is yes, but nonetheless she seems to carefully consider every aspect of what I have suggested.

'We have a deal,' she says, quietly, smiling only at me.

I breathe properly for what seems like the first time in days, feeling the rush of escape. My new life is finally on the horizon, and I start to think through what I need to take with me and how little time I will have to gather my things. I decide I will take nothing, wanting to make a quick departure, and as I think this, I look around and see that everyone else is still distracted. Hamza is shouting into his radio whilst Abdul is still arguing with the ambassador. I really start to believe that I can pull this off: a prince walking freely out of the palace with those American marines positioned either side of me.

'We have a deal,' she says again, this time louder, as if she is announcing to the world that I have finally done something of significance with my life. She quickly turns to the general, and starts whispering into her ear whilst pointing to me. The general looks at me and nods back, clearly confirming that my passage is guaranteed – that I have got what I have always dreamed of, in return for all my people's oil and their pointless prince. I already know which one they will miss the most.

'What do you mean: "we have a deal?"' Abdul shouts, his angry face appearing before me like a viper waiting to strike. His eyes look into mine and they express only one emotion – betrayal.

'Your father is returning!' Hamza shouts. 'He will deal with this mess!'

'There is no deal!' Abdul shouts. 'You will all leave now.'

'Guards!' Hamza shouts.

Neither of them takes their eyes off me, their anger directed only my way, which I realise is their biggest mistake. They have never realised my needs, never appreciated that I am different and that my desire to be unique would always eventually lead us to this point. The day my brother died we all knew that my father had now lost both his sons but although everyone mourned, no one asked about me. They never saw me for what I am, let alone accepted that things would have to be different. As I see our palace guards flood into the room I also see that our American visitors have not sat quietly: they have whispered and planned, and their minds now seem to work as one tight unit.

'Get out!' Hamza shouts. 'You will leave with nothing!'

'We have a deal,' the ambassador says. 'We have conducted negotiations with your prince, the most senior person in your palace, and we have agreed terms.'

'Come with us, Prince Jalal,' General Martha says, an arm outstretched.

I don't move, still frozen by shock at what she has called me. A click of her fingers tells me not to think twice and so I nod and move towards my new master, feeling more of a sense of belonging from that one simple gesture than I have from the past decades of existence in an unwelcoming world.

'There is no deal!' Hamza shouts again, spitting anger and hatred over all of us.

'You are not in a position to decline an offer that has been made,' Nevin says, still so calm and assured. 'You have agreed a sale and we have formally accepted.'

'I will do more than decline your offer,' Hamza shouts, as he pulls the gun from his holster and fires several shots into Nevins. Hamza's creased face and rotten teeth seem to fire the bullets themselves, and he screams in anger as the deafening sound of the gun echoes throughout the room. This one action pushes us all into an entirely new place. Blood splatters everywhere as his body falls backwards over the chair and crashes onto the floor.

I fall downwards, pushed by the American hulk who then pulls out her own pistol. She fires bullets into Hamza like they have been mortal enemies since the dawn of time, and I hear metal tear through his thin combat shirt and into his flesh.

'Kill them! Kill them all!' Abdul shouts, as he falls to the floor in front of me.

I look around; my eyes are the only senses that still work. My ears are ringing and my nose is filling with smoke. I see our many palace guards pulling rifles and firing as they run towards the marines. What I see in return is pure preparation, as the marines throw grenades and tear gas, followed by red dots trailing ahead of their steady aim, giving them all the opportunity they need to select their target and fire. So few are ranged against so many, but there is no anger, no shouting – simply precision.

I keep my head down, feeling as if I'm in a war zone of my own creation. Abdul looks at me and shakes his head; to him, all of this is my fault. He reaches for Hamza and feels his comrade's throat to see that he is truly dead. I look around, trying to catch sight of the ambassador, as Abdul grabs a gun and shoots the American general, taking clear revenge for the death of his oldest friend. I cannot look, cannot dare to see my new protectors fall one by one. Somewhere inside I can hear myself begging for my new life not to end here.

When he has finished firing he turns to me, summoning all those decades of contempt. 'Your father will blame you for this and we will both face certain death. In these last few hours you just remember that it is you who has ruined everything.'

I want to answer him, to tell him that I am not going to be blamed for today or any other day, but as I start to shout he doesn't say anything, just staring at me. He looks ready to speak, ready to scream at me, but instead he just smiles, a trickle of blood flowing out of his mouth. I look around and then back at him; I'm so conditioned by his constant chastisements that I still expect some kind of response from him. I hear the thud of his gun hit the floor, and see both of his hands fall to his stomach as his shirt turns red.

He goes limp, and instinctively I grab him, cradling him in my arms. He tries to speak, desperately clawing at my face with a blood-stained hand, but he doesn't have the energy to sustain the movement, and it just brushes against me. I tell him to calm down, that I will get help; that I still somehow care about him. I turn to see what has happened and where the bullet came from, and I immediately see that General is still standing, still very much alive.

'Mission lost. The Palace is going into lockdown. Confirm this is a no deal. Blow the lot,' she shouts into her radio as she looks at me, her face expressing nothing – no hatred, no disappointment – nothing I can use. One of her men is wrapping a bandage around her arm as another starts to escort Jessica away. She looks down at me for a moment, her face not moving, as I see that she is willing to only offer me what I think is a look of genuine pity.

'Please take me with you,' I shout, still holding Abdul in my arms, hoping that that she will hear my plea over the noise of firing guns and shouting men, and that she will honour our hasty deal.

She shakes her head but says nothing as the group moves away, stepping slowly towards the door. She doesn't know of my dreams, of America and now her. She cannot know of my desperation but she must be able to see it.

Abdul suddenly grabs me, blood still trickling from his mouth. I look down at him; his body is still entwined with mine. He tries to mouth something, his weak hand only able to lightly smack my face. I shake my head, telling him that I have no time for him now; he's my past and I'm fast losing my future. He jolts forward, his body wrestling with mine like a baby trying to escape the embrace of a parent. He coughs and his blood stains my clothes.

'Don't say anything,' I say, knowing there is nothing that can undo what has been done.

He shakes his head, pulling himself up just a little, his breathing erratic and fading. 'You have always disappointed me.'

I drop his body to the floor, screaming at him, screaming at everything I have been made to become. I watch his body jolt and shake a little more, his mouth still moving, still trying to tell me what a terrible person I really am. I watch for a moment, until that mouth stops telling me things I don't want to hear and those disapproving eyes no longer move.

I look up to see that my future is almost gone. 'No, wait!' I shout, but get nothing back. Instead of an answer a deafening sound comes from afar and the palace shakes like an earthquake has hit us without any warning.

I get up and a few more guards run into the room, but quickly fall to the might of the marines who are walking backwards, pointing their rifles at anything that moves. These silent, red dots immediately remind me of my limited worth, my lost opportunity and the time I have borrowed. I run toward them, and their attention turns to me, their guns ready to do to me what my father will inevitably do later. I think about my options: do I prefer being killed efficiently like this or several prolonged beatings before the eventual mercy of a firing squad.

'Stay where you are,' two Marines shout together.

'The deal!' I shout. 'We have a deal!'

'The deal is off. Stay where you are or we will fire.'

I stay still and look down at the two red marks still positioned on my body, each competing with the other to find the centre of my chest. I'm struck by the fact that the only ones now interested in me are the soldiers, the experts in war, who were not even in the room when I bought my short-lived freedom.

Once they disappear around the corner I look out the window and see the helicopters blades roaring into life as they prepare to leave me. I don't know what to do; I am still as trapped as I always have been, and my world has changed so drastically, yet I still face a future that is no different from what it was before. I wait for a moment, hoping that Jessica will come back, running into my arms and pulling me with her to the safety of her distant home far across the ocean.

She doesn't appear and nothing happens, and just as my chapter in this story seems to be ending, I suddenly hear Abdul's voice. I turn to see him standing back up and shouting at me.

'You have done this! You have caused all of this!' he screams, in between gulps of blood that spill out of his mouth and splatter onto the floor. 'You have betrayed your mother's faith in you and failed your father, and now you have destroyed your country!'

I cannot hear anymore and I run at him, screaming with hatred that has grown over many years, from of all that I have been told and all that has been denied. By the time I reach him he is lying flat and unmoving, but it doesn't stop me from hitting him. I smack him across his cheek, catching his nose for good measure, thinking only of those decades of torment, sending blood and bone splattering across the marble floor. I hit him again and again, not stopping to think what I'm doing. I lift his body up and smash my head into his; my clear payment for his absolute abandonment of the boy he was supposed to protect.

When I finally stop I can no longer recognise the face of my eternal tormentor, and I know that he won't ever move again. I take one final look at him, at the twisted corpse that will take a new place in my nightmares, and once I can no longer face him I turn and run. I run past the bodies of people I know, and through smoke-filled corridors filled with screaming men and expanding pools of blood.

Once I get outside I finally understand what I have caused. In the distance there is nothing but fire and fumes, funnelling their way deep into the clouds. Our world burns with flames so big I am sure you can see them from space. I was told to make them beg for the oil, told never to sell and not to lend, but now these oil fields are ablaze for as far as my eyes can see; worthless in the eyes of everyone who matters.

I look around for someone to help, for some way out of this, but all I can see is my father's convoy heading towards the palace, a trail of dust following them as they speed along the long road. It's enough for me to realise that I have only one choice – one final chance – and so I run towards the helicopters, towards my only possible source of freedom. As I fight my way through the grounds I think only of the world I have wanted to be in for so long, now so close and yet still so far. I look up to see more palace guards above me on the roof, aiming a rocket launcher at the helicopter.

'Don't shoot!' I shout, but they either don't hear or don't want to listen to little me.

Before they can fire anything a splatter of bullets from one of the other helicopters sprays across the roof, and I realise that its friends never left it. The two airborne gunships are still flying around like bees protecting a nest, killing anything that moves.

I keep running, praying that if I'm hit now that the bullets kill me. My eyes are focused only on my only escape out of here, which is about to take off. I think how likely my death is now and how unlikely it has become that I will find a way out, and it's enough to make me pick up a rifle, hoping my father will somehow believe I am still loyal, so obviously one of the brave few who fought off our attackers.

As I reach my ticket to freedom I see the door is still open and I wonder if they are waiting for me. I soon realise the reason for their delay is the general, as I see her shirt ripped open and some sort of drip being hooked into her veins. I keep shouting and look around the helicopter. I finally see Jessica's slender frame hiding in the corner, a white ghost who will now forever appear in my dreams and my nightmares. I stop shouting and stare, hoping that someone will notice my silence.

She sees me as she talks on her phone. She keeps talking but looks at me with this gaze that my frantic mind interprets as flirting; she seems to be enticing me to come closer. The marines have their guns pointed my way again but it doesn't stop me. I drop my weapon and grab hold of the door.

'Please, take me with you. We have a deal,' I plead.

She puts the phone down and leans forward, pushing the marines out of the way, her face near to mine and her sweet breath close enough to taste. 'But you have nothing to offer us.'

I think for a second, desperately trying to find an answer that will help, willing to offer her anything. All around us the skyline burns, a red blaze that seems to come up from the sand like it has travelled from the depths of hell pull everyone under and make them pay for my mistakes. 'You know that if I stay I will die. I made a deal and you blew up our oil.'

Those eyes look at me but don't show a fraction of the passion I want to see. 'It was never your deal to make,' she says and smiles. 'You played a game and you lost, and we cannot afford any passengers where we are going.'

I shake my head, refusing to listen to her, although I already know that what she is saying is true. 'Please, I want to go to America.'

'You shouldn't beg,' she says, and then leans back.

It's a cue for the marines to push me away; my grip weakens and only my desperate pleas remain. I fall to the floor, my back hitting the dusty ground that I have had to call home for all my life.

The helicopter finally takes off, still flanked by its smaller, deadlier friends. The sound is deafening. A dust cloud surrounds me and I lie back to see the belly of the beast as the helicopter leaves, its blades spinning faster until I'm forced to close my eyes.

I wait for the storm to pass before I open my eyes again and stand up, now without any cause or options. I see that my only chance to escape the darkness of this place is departing towards the distant, golden sun, leaving me behind with only my fading and ultimately borrowed time.

Wednesday 17th August - Thailand

All that is so obviously hidden

It's our summer break, so what are we supposed to do? Hang around midtown and loiter like we actually matter to anyone? We could have gone to the beach to watch the boys surf all day and long into the evening, until the sun fades and we would light fires and drink beer. Our youth is supposed to be for these wasted moments; that gap between nothing and something meaningful.

It was my father who suggested a month of charity work, the flight and accommodation paid for by him. I have to admit that it did sound a little more appealing than lighting a beach fire and piling firewood on top of yesterday's wood, all the time wondering if tonight Angelica would get screwed by Brad or Cody, or maybe by both of them. I always thought that it would be a delightful change if for once Brad could pound Cody into the dunes whilst everyone else watches. That would hold my attention far more than the set-menu jock-and-cheerleader routine I'm so regularly forced to endure.

If you knew me it would come as no surprise that none of those ideas met with my approval. I had no intention of standing with the other mannequins on the boulevard, handbags as red as lipstick, their bitch-rays on full blast to anyone not in designer everything. I was not going to lay with the other dolls on the beach, either – the ones who at least try to relax, even if it is in the name of a messy fuck somewhere deep in that big, adult sandpit. And as for a month of sweating in Africa, my feet blistering and my hands torn from battling with rock and wood? Well, I told dear Daddy if some village wanted the luxury of fresh water then its lucky inhabitant's best get digging their own well.

I did, however, take him up on his offer of a flight and accommodation, and I even managed to convince a few others to con the same out of their parents. And so five college friends have come to Thailand for a summer break that I hoped would turn out to be legendary, for more reasons than I care to share.

At some point during the flight here I realised it was unlikely we would all be friends forever, not when you consider the intertwined secrets of our past, created for nothing but my amusement and known only to one person. Looking around the plane that evening, the rest of them asleep, I realised the nightmare I had created and brought onto this trip was far worse than whatever random stuff that was making the news lately. And in relation to that weird shit going down, we all decided to get the flight anyway, and as soon as we landed I knew that we all needed to make the best of whatever happens next.

We are a small group – a collection of young, twenty-somethings who will move on to become doctors, lawyers and other incredibly helpful people. We set out to study hard and play harder, especially when it's on some other mug's doorstep. We will dance naked on the beach, we will drink vodka and we will smash our glasses onto the floor. Our indiscretions will be tolerated; one of many down-payments made for all the future value we might one day contribute. But we're nothing unique, nothing but young kids carving out a world for ourselves, feeling as if we're the only things the universe should be paying attention to.

You might think we are five testosterone-riddled young men who are staying in cramped, yet utterly fantastic beach huts – the kind of places where you hear the waves all day and night, where we spend all of our time topless and barefoot, our modern loin cloths and chilled bottles of Bud the only thing that separates us from our cavemen ancestors.

You'd be very wrong. We're just two weird couples and Austin, and we're stuck in a beach resort, entombed in concrete and trapped by eternally happy service people who put our pathetic needs ahead of anything else. Even if they found twelve puppies drowning in a pool, my need for another mojito would come before any sense of rescuing them. The question you should be asking is why aren't we dancing around those raging fires, our sweaty bodies exposed to the burning flames, as we perform our own strange moonlight rituals? It's all because of the princess two doors down – the poor little thing who can't possibly be away from everything clean, crisp and sanitary. It's because of her that we're stuck in this white-walled, ordinary, lifeless place.

As angry as I am I will never hold it against her – never could and never will. She has been through too much and I know how much this break means to her; it means a lot to all of us in some way or another.

Speaking of a princess, my own little precious thing has just come out of the bathroom. I sit on my bed and stare at him as I contemplate the inevitability of my recent choices. Eric has a towel wrapped around his waist and is standing still in the middle of the room, just a few paces away from me. He starts prodding at his chest, desperately trying to find something that isn't there.

'It's looking a little more defined, don't you think?' he says, his hands pulling at the skin that's sucked to his tight body, his eyes not daring to meet with mine. 'I definitely think so.'

I don't say anything as I slowly move off the bed and snake my ways towards him, passed the suitcase I still haven't unpacked, moving around the used clothing that awaits rescue by someone who isn't me.

As I reach him he finally looks up, desperate for an answer, begging for validation. My approval means everything to him; like it's a stamp from God – a passport to acceptance. I circle around him and stare, so obviously taunting him, so openly playing with his fragile needs that I'm often shocked he still hangs around me. I say nothing, knowing that there is still more to do, acutely aware that I must nurture what I have created.

'Well?' he says, stepping away from me, just slightly, but enough to demand that I take in the whole of him, not just the microscopic bits I'm so obviously overanalysing.

'I'm not sure,' I say, and then kneel down. I take prolonged yet genuine time to properly look at his flat stomach, all thanks to his Asian genetics, which seems able to remain unaffected by any of his American vices.

'So, you're saying that an entire semester in the gym has done nothing?' he says, his skinny arms hanging by his sides like lonely, limp posts, desperately wanting a flag to carry and a burden to bear.

I look up at him. 'Your stomach looks no different. It's as flat as the Nevada dessert.'

He lets out a long huff, like my opinion is the only reality he will accept, as if my words can override what a thousand mirrors might otherwise tell him differently.

'Tense your body,' I say.

He immediately obeys, starting with his stomach. I have to admit that something appears; some vein resemblance of abdominal muscles. I touch them and he shudders, giggling like a girl whilst still managing to hold his pose. I trace my fingers along them, finding small yet obvious grooves between each muscle. It gives me hope – hope that he can yet be moulded; hope that what is still hidden can come out and be noticed. These small muscles that are forming are symbolic of Eric – a reflection of his future self. He is still trying to shed the skin of his current being. And where muscles grow, confidence will follow. I jab him in the stomach. 'I think I've found your ribcage but that's about it.'

I don't give him time to sulk, now demanding that he shows me what his arms have gained. He obeys and tenses them, putting all of his energy into forcing two small tennis balls to form under his skin. I tense with him, showing how it should be done.

He suddenly laughs, losing his pose. 'Your boobs look firmer when you do that!'

I jab him again, reminding him who is in charge. He quickly returns to his original position, both arms curled up and stretched, his eyes checking that this posture is the best for showing off what he has created.

I grab one of his arms and put my hand around it. I can no longer wrap all the way around – a sure and irrefutable sign that progress is being made. 'There is definitely something there,' I say, and then take a step back. 'You see, I made you, so it's important that I see progress is being made to make my investment worthwhile.'

He nods back, showing a cowardly acceptance of my demands. He's happy to be moulded, happy to be in the hands of someone else. He's my puppet of progress.

I quickly pull his towel away, managing to get it off his waist and away from him before he can grab it back.

'Anna!' he shouts, covering his tackle with his hands, his face in shock. He looks over his shoulder and I can see he is thinking about fleeing to the bathroom, but he probably knows that it will do him no good. For however long he could hide in there I would be waiting out here and if he pushed me too far I'd start throwing his clothes over the balcony.

I calmly place his towel on the bed. 'Eric, remember that I made you. When we first met you were some geeky boy, far more Chinese than American, but now I've cleaned you up. We've said goodbye to the bowl haircut, and you've finally come around to my way of thinking that a bit of stubble works well on you, whatever your mother thinks.'

He shakes his head and opens his mouth. I stop his challenge; I openly refuse to accept any defence of his faraway and entirely archaic mother. 'And I've got your body on track and your mind focused.' I open up my arms and hold out my hands. 'There's a lot we should celebrate.'

He frowns, keeping his hands where he thinks they should be. 'I'm not hugging you,' he says, half-shouting, half-laughing at the idea.

I laugh back. 'Why can't I see it? We both know two hands is overkill.'

'How do you know?' he says, his mouth gaped open. 'You can't know that.'

'Because, Eric, genetics leave nothing hidden.'

He shakes his head. 'You didn't make down here and you can't change whatever its size or shape is. It's the one thing you'll never be able to change.'

I narrow my eyes as I consider if I want to test that theory, wondering how far I could push him. I imagine myself sitting in some hospital waiting room, absently flicking through a magazine, while he's lying on an operating table, about to get it lengthened. I laugh to myself when I imagine a less sinister version of this future being played out in my mind – one where I find myself inserting his floppy cock into a vacuum pump, his whiny voice begging me to stop, and my voice, calm and chilling, telling him that it will work and that it must be done.

I finally sit on the bed. 'I bet Austin is hung.'

Eric laughs, his face filled with a smile. 'I bet he is.'

I jump up, grabbing at his hands, which are encasing his small jewel, hoping to catch him off guard. 'Eric, show me. I need to make sure you have trimmed.'

'I'm not trimming!' he shouts.

I let go of his wrists and encircle him with my arms, knowing that my way in is through his mind. I stop when I'm behind him, and then push a hand against him, forcing him to arch his back, just a little.

'A tidy ass crack is very important these days.'

'It's as smooth as a baby's bottom,' he announces, validating what I can already see.

I walk back in front of him and place my hands on his forearms whilst I look into his jet-black eyes. 'This moment is symbolic, Eric.'

He's still shaking his head, his mind denying that the ultimate reveal should ever happen, but his hands eventually start to separate from his body.

'Close your eyes,' I say, as I slowly guide them away from his cock and rest them by his sides. I look him up and down, taking all of him in. I see the beauty of his simple body and for the first time in our few months together I see him for what he truly is. He will never be my lover, or my boyfriend – he will simply be Eric. And there are a billion more Eric's out there, all with their tight, slightly off-white skin. They're like clones, coming off the production line with their shiny, black hair and petite little figures, all accessorised with a slightly oversized bush around purely functional genitalia.

But this Eric is different now; I've taken this model and customised him the Anna way. Eric is my past as much as my future; he's like the Barbie doll my once parents gave me – the doll I painstakingly accessorised with all manner of combat gear, a machine gun for a handbag, and a tank for a house. Eric's scrunched up face reminds me of their horrified expressions all those years ago, how their faces screwed up when I showed them Barbie's head glued onto the body of GI Joe. It was my best work at the time and I personally liked what it stood for – the ultimate symbol of a women thriving in a world dominated by men.

'Keep those eyes closed,' I say and then step away from him. I start to strip off, calmly letting each item of clothing drop onto the floor around us.

'Anna,' he says and gulps. 'What are you doing?'

'Stay still,' I say, as I keep peeling away the layers of our friendship. I know that touching his flesh with mine will make us stronger, meaning that our relationship no longer has any physical boundaries.

His eyes are still closed as we stand opposite each other. I copy his movements: his nervous smiles, flashing white teeth, the way his hands scratch his body before returning to his sides and swinging nervously around. I want to touch him, to tease my way down his chest and see his reaction as I run a finger past his cock and onto his balls.

'Open your eyes,' I say, softly, more erotically than I had planned.

He obeys, but upon seeing me naked he immediately brings his hands up to his mouth, openly horrified. He looks around the empty room, as though hoping to find an audience to validate his shock.

'Why are you laughing?' I ask, but get nothing back. His gaze darts around the room, desperately searching for a safe place to look.

'Eric!' I shout. 'Why are you laughing?'

'We're both naked,' he says, his hands back around his tackle. 'It's totally weird!'

'Take a hold of your cock with one hand.'

He shakes his head, denying the possibility of what could happen.

'Do it!'

He jumps back and freezes. He looks like he's thinking through what is happening, and the obvious consequences that would come from refusing my request. He eventually does what he is told, taking a hold of his manhood, grabbing all of it, like it's his new pet gerbil.

I run a finger down my breasts while I stare at him. He looks back at me in pure confusion; his innocence is being taken away from him, inch by inch. All the time I focus my eyes and my mind on his tackle, but no matter how deep I go nothing moves, nothing stirs. I know that he's trying, trying for me. He wants it to grow, more for me than ever for himself.

I move closer to him, as close as we can get without touching. I interrupt him, his eyes now closed and his imagination somewhere else, as his body gently sways. I kiss him on the cheek and he opens his eyes, his disappointed look so obvious.

'Eric, we will be friends forever.'

'We will?' he asks, his arms now folded across his stomach, clearly seeing no point in hiding anything. 'Even after this, after what we have just done?'

I throw him his towel and start putting all those layers back over my body. 'Especially after this. We both know what you like and it's important that you embrace it. Promise me that you will embrace it.'

'I promise,' he says, too casually, the towel still hanging at his side.

'And promise that you will obey me.'

He laughs and nods. 'I have trusted you this far, haven't I?'

I nod. 'We're late, and you need to trim and get dressed.'

He looks down. 'Really?'

'Embrace and obey, remember?'

*****

When we get to the bar Austin is already there, sitting on a stool, a beer in front of him and his headphones still plugged in. He doesn't look up, doesn't do anything, and I immediately think he is loyal and brave in equal measure – happy to wait for his friends to eventually arrive, not wanting to go and sulk at a corner table where no one can see him.

He's the poor guy who has a room to himself. That's what everyone has said to him from when we first planned this holiday, when we were on the plane and ever since we arrived in this overcomplicated place. I personally think he is the luckiest person here: he has enough space to do what he wants and can keep the people he loosely calls friends at arm's length. I've twice asked to swap with him, much to Eric's horror and a confused look from Austin.

I embrace him as soon as we're close enough, forcing a kiss onto each cheek, then giving him an overly long hug. Even though we only left each other's company only a couple of hours ago I insist upon this intimacy because I like the feel of his skin. He is most definitely the right shade of dark; his skin is soft and smooth, and his body perpetually tanned and toned. The moment I first met Austin I knew I had to add him to my collection. You can't meet someone who looks like he just came from a sunbed in heaven and not keep him around for as long as possible. He's everything that I imagine a real angel would be. Why would you make them pasty white and hairy when you can have perfection wrapped in forever-bronzed skin? I look at him and he looks back at me, and I know that if I become God he will be right by my side, or perhaps slightly ahead and to my left, giving me a regular glance at those generous abs.

He's everything Eric isn't and it fascinates me each time I see them next to each other. This holiday is a perfect chance for me to observe their physiques, to consider why I feel that they were created for very different reasons. Time on the beach and by the pool has allowed for ample examination of tensed arms and muscles that double in size with a simple flick of his wrist, and a hopeful answer as to why their snakes are such different sizes.

I look at them both now and see a fascinating mix of colours and vibes. I wonder what their children would look like, however impossible it would be to create such a thing, and as they awkwardly embrace each other I wonder what it would be like to see them fucking. I watch them quietly fumble and half-hug, picturing them entwined as one, their sweating bodies rubbing against each other as they pant and moan.

'Drink?' Eric asks, waking me from my thoughts.

'Of course,' I say, smiling at them both.

'What strange ideas just crawled out of your mind?' Austin asks, still perched in the same position as when we arrived. He is sitting still, kitted out in a trendy tee and a cool cap, the night still young and offering plenty of time to change, should the mood take him. I'm impressed that although his body has not left his seat, he has managed to bend and contort around us with very little effort, every part of him inviting and welcoming.

'Don't you worry about what I was thinking,' I say, as I position myself between the two of them. I look at each of them and immediately decide that I have overdressed Eric. His skinny jeans and tight shirt are obviously doing their job, but maybe the little bow tie was a step too far, despite how adorable it looks.

He leans over the bar, desperate to get the barman's attention, as Austin calmly spins on his stool. After what seems like an eternity of Eric being ignored, Austin tries to get served and immediately succeeds, and as our drinks are made we sit next to him, and for me it all becomes a little too standard. We're back in the brochure – a photo of close friends at an amazing bar. I look around to see if I can spot a photographer to snap us all smiling together; it would be a moment caught and recorded for all of history, but all out of context and with the real emotions entirely missed by a simple lens.

'So, Austin,' I say, turning my stool to face him, needing to quickly create entertainment for myself. 'Eric and I were just talking about genetics.'

'Genetics?' he asks, packing his headphones away into his small bag.

'Yes, we were just saying that you are probably quite hung.'

He smiles and lets out a short laugh, showing Eric how he should have reacted.

I look at Eric, but his gaze is elsewhere. This isn't a conversation he wants; it's not a competition he can win. I grip his knee. 'But you wouldn't be Eric if it was any different.'

'What are you talking about?' Austin asks.

'Nothing,' I say. 'But does genetics always mean stereotyping? Doesn't it leave something to be hidden, to be different to what we expect?'

Austin suddenly smiles. 'Girl, you need a drink,' he says; on cue, they arrive in front of us. 'Sip it down and I'll get the next one.'

I obey, but I don't sip. I let it all flow into my throat, feeling like I've opened a passageway straight to the numbness I desperately need. As the alcohol reaches my stomach I keep my eyes on Austin alone, knowing that he's the kind of person who would stand a chance of keeping me. His face will always keep that calm façade; I know he won't judge me as my views become more extreme with each drink I consume. I know that later in the evening, when I start to falter, his ample body will shield and hold me, and then his smooth voice will soothe me to sleep. I look at those arms again and I know I want to be wrapped up in them.

'Where are the other two?' he asks.

'They're probably still fucking,' Eric says.

'Well you two finished that pretty quickly,' Austin says, a grin spread across his face, not looking as jealous as I want him to.

I choose not to answer him, partly wondering what Eric will say but mostly wanting Austin to have to work at it for a bit longer. I think of the other two and laugh at Kyle rampantly fucking while she just lies there. I'd bet all the money in Thailand he doesn't hit one of her spots – that would take more effort than he will ever be capable of.

'Do you think Kyle is hung?' Austin asks, this cheeky grin forming across his face.

I rub his arm, taking every chance I can get to touch him before it's just too inappropriate. 'Oh, you like my little game, don't you?'

He nods and laughs. 'I'm an outsider to your little clique, but your games help me to forget that.'

I shake head violently, my mind furious that he can think such things. 'You are a little less familiar but no more of an outsider than anyone else. And believe me, this isn't the clique you think it is.'

Austin nods back and grins, seemingly happy about what he hears.

'But to answer your question, I think the order goes Eric, then you, and then Kyle.'

Austin laughs, his head playfully shaking. 'You think some mouthy jock wins because he's got a bit of muscle on him?' He flexes his own muscles and invites me to wrap my hands around the thickest part of his arm.

I do as I'm told, my heart racing as I connect with him, as if it's just the two of us. 'I might have to see it to believe it,' I say, my defences temporarily down and allowing myself that small window of lust that I have learnt to keep in check. These feelings, if not kept on a tight lead, can open up into a chasm of emotions, which I find impossible to sort in my head.

I see him look behind me, towards Eric, for the third time this evening. This acts as my signal to let go, to stop enjoying the situation and to close that window forever. 'Damn, you've gone quiet, boy,' he says to him.

'It's not my favourite conversation,' Eric says, his gaze somewhere just beyond us, like we've lost him, and he's trapped in a place where he doesn't want to be.

Austin gives him a slow wink, dressed with a grin – the sort that, if I allowed it, would melt me into a desperate puddle of neediness. 'What you got or ain't got don't matter when you've got a face like that.'

Eric suddenly smiles; it seems as though his whole world has just changed. I look at him at just the right moment and catch sight of it – the instant when his life and everything he thought he knew suddenly changes. I see a look that should be captured for all eternity. Frown lines that he has always hidden suddenly appear, born from a smile grander and more pronounced than I would ever have thought him capable of. I slowly turn, seeing that their gazes have met and created something special. I see Austin's arm stretched across me to touch Eric's shoulder, and I feel the new connection between them. In this world that is changing around me I see what was hidden now comes into plain sight and it is truly beautiful. I now feel like an intruder on something that should last forever – forget their first kiss or their first orgasm; don't bother to accelerate forty years to find them still deeply in love. I say take this moment and hold it forever as the true meaning of hope and a real symbol of love without any boundaries. Everything that follows will never be as good, never as deep.

'What the fuck are we interrupting?' Kyle shouts from across the room.

I curse under my breath as we untangle from our intricate web and return to our drinks as he makes his way towards us. He's still shouting crap, his arms are waving everywhere; Jessica is clinging onto him, her slight body being tossed around as he attempts to throw some playful insult our way.

'So, come on, what were we interrupting?' he asks, pretending to stick two fingers down his throat. 'It looked so beautiful.'

'You weren't interrupting anything, except a whole bar full of people,' I say, as the only person I believe to be truly qualified and able to put him back in his place.

He quickly reaches down the back of my jeans. 'What's got you so uptight?' he asks, and then laughs at himself, probably knowing that no one else on this holiday ever will.

'I see you've been on the beers already?' I say.

Kyle keeps laughing girlishly, despite his athlete's body. He was born to perform and excel, but it's all wasted on such an undeveloped mind; he never seems to realise what he could be if he just said nothing. 'We're all on holiday, so don't be such a bitch… you bitch!'

I turn around on my stool, ready to remind him that he's not on tour with his football buddies, and that this really isn't an appropriate place to act like a dick. Before I can say anything, Eric passes the drinks from the bar to Austin and he hands them out with a calm grin on his face that says it's going to be okay.

'What you doing?' Kyle asks, as he slaps Eric on the back, looking him up and down. 'You finally got a job here? You fit in pretty well, my man!'

Eric sighs, as I imagine he wonders for the hundredth time why he's on holiday with this caveman. 'No, Kyle, I don't have a job here.'

'I think he looks perfect,' I say, ready to defend my boy until my dying breath.

Kyle looks at me and then grips Eric's shoulder, before running a hand through his greased hair. 'She's been styling you, hasn't she? Don't let her do that too often otherwise she'll be fucking with your head before you know it.'

I stand up, deciding that I've truly had enough. I look Kyle up and down, wondering why I ever bothered. He still has that old, over-gelled spiky hairstyle, showing just how much I tried and failed to change him. He refused to listen, couldn't see how good he would have looked with a comb-down and some big glasses. I look at his arms and his tight t-shirt; I can easily remember everything that sits beneath – every mole and every hair – and I'm entirely clear that he doesn't deserve what he has, and that he most definitely doesn't know how to use it.

'Problem?' he says, looking down at me, a hand still on Eric's shoulder.

'I've been in Eric's mind for quite some time, and I'm pretty pleased with how it's going,' I say, and prod Kyle's chest. 'At least he can learn and adapt, unlike you.'

'And what the fuck gives you the right to screw with people's minds? You know that no one has asked you to do this, don't you?'

I shake my head, wondering how I can best hurt him. I want to silence him in the most painful way possible, to make him shut up for the whole evening. I want him to crawl away and lick his wounds, wondering why he ever chose to argue with me tonight, why he ever came on holiday and why he ever dated me in the first place. I prepare my answer, knowing that I will be revealing more than I should, but before I can say anything, a declaration from Austin fills the air and silences everyone.

'I think Eric looks awesome,' he says, looking straight at my man with those dark, strong eyes.

I smile, knowing it is happening – seeing something which has made sense in my head since before we got on the plane finally become reality. There are some things you just know, future events that you can connect together like dots on a page. These new connections are being made now and it feels so very special.

And now that Austin has openly declared his interest in Eric, and Kyle is showing how much he hates Austin for siding with me, I turn all my attention to Jessica. She looks fragile and silly, curled up in a chair whilst staring up at one of the television screens. It's obvious that she hasn't heard anything that has been said, let alone picked up on the subtle cues being given off by our small group. I focus on her as she watches some drama unfolding on a television above our heads, giving everything she has to a different reality. She scrunches up her slender frame, wrapping her long legs around her body as she absently plays with those shiny, golden locks of hair. I was always jealous of how easy she made it all look, always finding ways to stay controlled, styled and flawless, no matter her situation.

'Where is that?' I ask, looking at the same picture, seeing buildings burn and people run.

'It's a film,' Austin says. 'It's been on for a while.'

Jessica suddenly turns, and I see her absence from the conversation is not as total as I first thought. 'It's not a film. It's happening right now.'

Kyle buries his head in his hands and then rubs his eyes. 'Oh, Jesus, don't get her started on this. It's all she's been watching since we left the pool.'

She ignores him and looks straight at me. 'The fires have been going on for hours,' she says. 'Arabia is burning.'

'Aladdin burns!' Kyle shouts out, banging his hands on the bar. 'But who gives a fuck?'

I'm about to launch into another tirade at him, but the lights suddenly go out. The darkness is followed by nothing but silence, and for a moment, everyone waits, expecting that the lights will come back on and people will resume their conversations; life will continue, just as it always has and always will. A pause is just a pause; when it ends, our world as we know it will prove once again that it is the stable and solid rock that we are used to.

I sit quietly, secretly hoping that it doesn't, contemplating what will happen if our precious reality doesn't return with the much needed light to allow us to function as a normal, modern society.

I seem to be getting my wish: it remains dark. I hear people fumbling over their chairs and voices seeming to become clearer, as our eyes are now of limited use. At first people are calm, slowly moving around. The service people find candles and open all the blinds, letting the moonlight do what it can. I sit and watch different people shuffling and scurrying around in the shadows, seeing no point in moving myself. They declare that they are going to their rooms, making mention of obvious compensation, placing sole responsibility for everything on the poor staff, who can say nothing other than 'so sorry.'

The lights start to flicker, like they're at least trying to come back to us. This brings with it another period of silence, as people wait to see what will happen. They stare up at the ceiling, or at the bar staff, their demanding glances fading in and out of visibility with the failing light from the bulbs.

The lights give up again, plunging us back into near darkness. The void of silence returns and our eyes start to adjust to the candlelight again. I close my eyes and quietly wait, preparing myself for all those sighs and tuts; all those angry people making it clear that their dream holiday has been stolen from them.

I take a deep breath, but the moans of the many don't ever come. Instead they're replaced by a sound of screaming which drowns out everything else. This new sound is coming from a distance, from outside this room, but it still floods my senses, like a wave of fear that is spreading through the hotel. I try to figure it out, listening closely, trying to hear and trying to understand. I hear cries from countless mouths travelling across the complex – it's in the distance, but getting closer. The news has been very weird lately and this new sound is enough to make everyone run in the opposite direction.

I grab Eric and push us forward as chairs and tables screech across the floor and those who were sitting across the room are suddenly upon us. A foot lands on the back of one of my sandals, causing me to trip. I'm just behind Eric when I fall, but no apology comes; a crowd of shadows step over me and disappear into the distance. I suddenly feel hands grip my arms – thick hands, fingers that look dark and carry individual little muscles of their own. I realise they belong to Austin, who picks me up and slowly dusts me down. He smiles and for a moment I forget where we are and what is happening. Behind him I see the horrified faces of the other guests. Their shoulders knock against his, but he doesn't retaliate, he just calmly stares at me. Eric soon appears and grabs both of us, forcing us to run. The clashing of bodies soon causes obvious brutality, as people forget our common humanity. We all run, one big crowd of scared individuals; our fear has boiled away any loyalty – our only cause is survival, and we all head outdoors.

I realise that it is Eric who is leading the way, pulling our small human chain towards the beach. I let him lead, feeling strangely safe, thinking of his acute mind looking forward, and a tough guy at my back. They're like a sandwich of safety, taking me to wherever these screams don't yet exist.

It doesn't take long before my feet sink into warm sand. It slows us down a little but still feels strangely comforting; the soft grains cover my skin, wrapping me in the warmth which still remains from earlier in the day. We keep running until we make it to the shore, along with many hundreds of other fellow holidaymakers, all strangers who I'm shaping in my mind as survivors of whatever has just happened. I turn back to see more of them leaping onto the sand, the men helping the women, and the odd child in the arms of a watchful adult.

I look back towards the complex, towards what was our temporary home, now a ghostly backdrop of dark windows and a few flickering candles, along with the odd beam of torchlight. I close my eyes and picture the brochure, remembering a photo taken from the beach; what the photographer saw then and what I see now are entirely different. You don't hear the horrified screams when you turn each page of that glossy magazine, and you don't imagine fear in the eyes of your fellow tourists when you picture your peaceful week away.

Everyone soon forms into several main groups, all huddled around large fires. Everyone looks around like frightened mice. This small island is now a cage, this dream holiday now a nightmare. I do the same as everyone else – I count the members of our group and I look around for options. The screaming gets louder, which I think means whatever is causing it is coming closer. The reactions are what you would expect to see: some huddle closer, some cry out; only a brave few walk back towards the hotel, determined not to be victims. I look behind me, but see only the sea, and realise that we have all put ourselves between hell and a barrier of water.

'Where's Jessica?' I ask Kyle and only Kyle.

He lets out a long groan, his shoulders shrugging. 'How should I know?' he says, looking genuinely surprised by the question, which I had thought was an obvious one to ask.

'You should know!' I say, prodding his chest. 'You should know because you're sleeping with her, which means you have some level of responsibility.'

He says nothing for a moment, and just stares at me, clearly processing something bigger than his brain normally has to cope with. 'You're jealous, aren't you?' he says and pushes me backwards, into Austin's welcome arms. 'You had your chance with me, and you blew it!'

Before I can think of anything to say, I realise I'm laughing. I shake my head but my mind tells me he is probably right. I try to answer him, wanting to deny that there is any truth in his unexpected observation, but that sharp, sickeningly keen feeling is already rising from the depths of my dark soul. Emotions come flooding into my mind, and still I battle to say 'no'.

An explosion in the main hotel brings me back this moment, back to the hell we're now in. 'I'm going to find her,' I say, quickly moving away, before I get involved in any further debate.

Kyle stays where he is, his head shaking, clearly showing that he isn't willing to be her hero, just her holiday fuck. I shake my head, wondering if he even bothers to hold her in bed, even bothers to stroke her where it matters most. It's Austin and Eric who live up to the images I have created of them in my mind; they both run towards me, not willing to let me go back to the hotel alone.

I stop and turn, then push them both back. 'Obey!' I say, moving forward again. I break into a run, weaving through the masses of people, sensing they are just a step behind me, and pleased they haven't actually obeyed me.

We don't stop running until we're off the sand and back onto wood and concrete, which offer a clear and open route to whatever is happening ahead of us. The waves of people have gone; we've fought our way through them, and now find ourselves on a crest of our own fear. The screams have stopped too, replaced with the odd moment of shouting and a few whimpers. Hearing a sudden noise I turn to look at a bush and see two people huddled behind it, their bloodshot eyes and shaking heads telling me they've seen something.

'The beach is probably more comfortable right now,' I say, looking down at them, waiting for a decision to be made.

They look at the three of us and then to each other, and they decide to run. I choose to push us forward, thinking of the TV and all those reports, and of the inevitable darkness that awaits us all. I run ahead, catching the other two off guard, as my eyes take in things that would never normally be noticed on a casual walk to the beach in flip-flops; the moonlights lined along the bushes, the shadows of the palm trees swaying in the dark of the night.

I notice someone ahead – a Thai woman. Her flawless skin has been scored by lines of anguish; her normally flat and shiny hair is now mangled and torn. I grab her but she pulls away. I pull her back towards me, forcing my arms around her; our eyes lock as I demand that she recognises me. 'Your name is Cherry, or at least that's what I've been calling you. You clean my room, don't you? Do you remember me?'

She nods, already pulling away from me. 'I remember you.'

'What's happening?' I ask, wondering if we will be laughing about this tomorrow as she changes my sheets and I sit out on the sun deck with my oversized shades on, both of us pleased that the natural order of things has returned.

She looks at me but doesn't answer, her face creased and her body pulling away again.

'Tell me!' I say, shaking her. 'I need to know what's happening!'

When she realises that she cannot break free she stops moving and stares at me. She doesn't say anything at first as she seems to take me all in, trying to figure out what it is that she wants to tell me. 'The devil,' she eventually says. 'He comes.'

I nod and quietly release her. She immediately runs away, like a dog let off its lead. I don't think she knows where she is going but she disappears into the darkness anyway. I wonder where any of us can run now.

'The devil?' I say, quietly and only to myself. 'Is that all?'

*****

We sit quietly in a circle, as if being able to see each other at all times will help the situation. Keeping each other in sight makes this feel real but it doesn't keep out the fear and it doesn't explain what is happening. I laugh at the fact that we're back in the bar, that even the chaos can only last for so long.

'Whatever they saw spooked the shit out of the locals,' Eric says.

'Damn straight,' Austin says from the other side of the bar. 'So, who wants another one of my special drinks?'

'Shouldn't we stop now?' Eric says, looking around for someone official for what must be the hundredth time.

'The management don't seem to give a shit so I think it's time for doubles all around,' Austin says, and winks at Eric. 'But don't worry, I'm keeping track.'

Kyle leans in, his head casting a shadow in the candlelight. 'They told us to wait in here for the boats and if they think we're paying for any of this they can go fuck themselves. And another thing, I want all my money back. Total refund with bags of compensation.'

'I think they'll be okay,' I say, moving the candle closer to Austin, so he can make my cocktail properly. 'They have much bigger things to worry about, believe me.'

'Do you think they'll have the power back on soon?' Eric asks, looking at me, obviously assuming that I would have an answer that makes sense. 'And when do you think the boats will get here? It's been over an hour.'

'You know what I know.'

Jessica suddenly lets out a whimper and Kyle grabs her again. This makes for pleasant viewing: she finally gets at least some of the attention she deserves. I move a candle towards her, keen to comfort her as well, and I'm also desperate to know what she knows.

'What the fuck is going on with you?' Kyle asks, shaking her, suddenly changing his tone, his big frame surrounding her small and fragile body. He clearly thinks that he can scare an answer out of an already terrified young woman.

She says nothing, just stares down at the drink, carefully crafted by Austin, which she still hasn't touched; her body is present, but it's as if her mind has been somehow removed.

Kyle lets out a long groan, followed by much loud muttering about how this thing of beauty has been nothing but ultra-high-maintenance since the moment we arrived. He moans at her, but fixes his eyes on me, and aims his feelings of frustration in my direction. The truth is known to everyone: I paired them together all in the name of a nice holiday. This was true, but it was an experiment that was too good to miss: to find out if he could cope with her, the girl who requires more upkeep in a day than I need in a year. I was desperate to know if he could use everything he had learnt, if he could last longer than I expected.

He finally pushes the table away and storms off, shouting that he could have been with his friends, his real friends, on a fun dudes' holiday.

'Tenderness over testosterone,' I say, loud enough for all to hear, although I'm not sure if Kyle is even listening. I kneel down in front of Jessica and gently touch her knee with one hand. 'Jessie, sweetie, what happened? What's going on in your head?'

She finally looks at me, but takes her time to realise that I'm here, that I'm with her in this place. She looks around the large room and then back at me, like she has just woken up.

I smile and clamp my hand tighter around her knee, trying to be reassuring, but not sure what I am actually offering her safety from. 'You can tell me,' I say.

She nods and then shakes her head, as if trying to show both that she agrees and that she doesn't know. 'I'm really not too sure but I definitely saw something.' Her face suddenly scrunches up, and tears start streaming down her face. 'Something is here.'

'What a load of shit,' Kyle says, who has by now returned to see if I have been more successful than him. 'All that crap on the TV and then a power cut has sent everyone mental.'

He keeps shouting and people keep looking; he is attracting a growing audience. We all want to agree with him, to believe that nothing sinister is lurking around the corner. I see people scattered across the tables around the bar, the whites of their eyes reflecting the candlelight. They look and they listen but they don't move, and each small gust of wind threatens to plunge us back into darkness, leaving us alone with our fears and our hopes of boats and daylight.

Kyle continues to rant about how much he needed this holiday, and the fact that he chose to come away with us instead of his football team, which I think means he is admitting in some way that he wants to change things about himself. No one interrupts, and no one challenges him – I don't think anyone cares that much.

I carefully listen to his confessions, trying to pick out the bits of this puzzle that are down to me to solve. I've been in his head; I spent several months fucking him like no one else ever has, as he so aptly put it. I believe this qualification from Kyle himself means I was that catalyst for the creation of this new man, the one who is now systematically screaming at each small group of frightened people, telling all of them that he really does deserve more. I think about my room maid and on some level I hope she is right. If hell is going to unleash all of its horrors I hope it starts on Kyle first. It's almost as tantalising as it is scary.

'Screw this,' Kyle says. 'I need a piss.'

Eric suddenly stands up. 'I'll come too. I didn't want to go alone.'

Kyle shakes his head and storms forward. He pushes his way past empty tables, kicking unused chairs out of the way. Eric quickly follows, only two paces behind, taking advantage of the path his brutish companion has created.

I walk away and sit back on my stool. Austin is still on the other side of the bar, and he looks at me and smiles, setting down two empty glasses in front of the two of us. 'I think I've found my new vocation in life,' he says as he starts to work his magic with the shaker.

I watch as it rattles. His muscles tense and get bigger as his shaking gets faster. I want to jump up and hang off what bulges through his tight T-shirt; I want my legs on his forearms, my hands around his neck, and my bum resting on those pecs that look like firm pillows wrapped in tight sheets. I curse myself for what I must do and for what I know I can never have, no matter how hard I try to manipulate his strong mind. He's too powerful, too strong for any of my tricks, and I know he deserves more.

I sit back and watch. I always find beauty in the things that I can see but not touch. I think this shows the true difference between love and lust, and is concrete proof that once you have one you cannot have the other. They are simply too much to have in the same space and time. As I start to wonder which one of those Kyle and I both ended on, I turn around and see Jessica. She is still staring at nothing, her body curled up in the small seat as she slowly rocks to some rhythm the rest of us can't hear.

Austin pushes a glass towards me and holds up the other one. 'To random shit.'

I laugh and take hold of my new drink. 'To whatever this night hides.'

'Girl, that don't sound good,' he says, his head shaking but a smile still on show.

'I don't think any of this is good, but there is one thing I'm sure of and that's if this is our last night on earth then I will most definitely need to see you naked.'

He smiles, looking around the room and then back at me. 'You just don't quit, do you?'

'Never quit, Austin. Even when time runs out and the tides change, and you have nowhere to turn it's important for me to know that you will never quit.'

His head still shakes. 'Time and tide never run out. They always come back.'

'That's deep for someone so young.'

He knocks back his drink, already grabbing the cocktail shaker. 'I can do deep. Just as deep as you.'

I laugh. 'You'll never be able to go as deep as me, I promise you that.'

His eyes narrow; it's like he's taking me all in, the good and the bad. 'Why do you have this exterior of... you know?'

'A bitch?'

He laughs, his head mindlessly nodding. 'I was going to say tough girl from the ghetto.'

'I like that,' I say, liking him more by the minute. I wonder how much I would like Austin once we finished fucking. Would I want to cuddle and lie on his ample chest, those solid rocks of stability keeping me calm and warm? Or once it was over for both of us would I want his dick out of me and my devious intentions out of his head? Having taken all I could, would I want to move on, or would he be able to remain be a person who kept me interested on many different levels? I look at him and wonder if he has enough layers to occupy my busy mind.

'You like being a bitch, don't you?' he says.

'I like princesses, too, but I don't want to be one.'

He shakes his head, still smiling, but his energy is going into the ice bucket, his mind only on the task. 'You talk in riddles.'

I smile and grip his arm. 'And yet you still get me.'

He nods. 'I get you; I just don't get why I'm here.'

'But you still agreed to come, still agreed to spend some of your parents' hard earned money, still got on the plane with us.'

He holds up a silencing hand. 'I earned all this myself and I wanted to come. I needed the break, but now I'm here I don't get where I fit in, or how I match with any of you.'

I laugh, looking around at Jessie and wishing the other two were here to prove my point. 'None of us fit in as a group – surely you've realised that by now? We are all hiding things; none of us are as we seem.'

He nods. 'The only constant in this entire group is you, and you have fucked all of them. Am I right?'

I crease my face, offering a smile. 'Fucked is such a crude term but, if you must know, I am indeed one of the many girls Kyle has fucked.'

He shakes his head. 'You haven't been fucked by him. I get you enough to see how your brain works.'

I smile, loving Austin even more, this feeling competing with the lust that has been there since the first time I saw him strip off by the pool. 'It all started last year when I realised that I had wanted Kyle for a while. He's the typical football captain and I wanted to take him away from all the cheerleaders who were begging him to pick them. The thought of luring him away through ways and means that were incomprehensible to them turned me on so much, and if I could take him from them it would prove that blonde bimbos cannot rely on their looks alone, especially against an intent and focused mind.'

'You wanted to fuck the football captain? I expected better from you.'

'Oh, no, I didn't just fuck him. Believe me, Kyle is experienced but not talented when it comes to the bedroom, and as deep as I taught his cock to go, I was able to get deeper into his mind. I dominated and rode him like my prize stallion for weeks. The day I found his prostate was the day I realised I could do anything I wanted to him, because once you understand that a man is ruled by his cock then you can get him to bend to any demands you have. The first couple of times, I gave the impression that I was letting him take charge; that was until I realised his set routine was never going to improve. You could say that he brought the body and I added the creativity, and for quite some time he was my greatest lust – the one who performed best after I had trained him. If there were awards for this sort of thing then Kyle would have won "best improved in bed."'

'You evil bitch,' he says, giving away nothing.

I wait for a smile, a laugh or any sign at all that he still gets me. But he continues to say nothing, and I quietly reflect, wondering if I've said too much, if I have revealed a monster that even he didn't expect to see.

'And what about her?' he says, looking over at Jessica. 'Do I want to know?'

'What are you asking about her?'

'You know what I'm asking.'

I nod and look over at Jessie, trying to sort out all of her endless complexities in my mind. 'You have to take your time with a girl like Jessie. She's a tender thing who had become too used to the quick and rough penetration of simple men. The first time I kissed her down there she first begged me to stop then begged me never to stop. People always want things that aren't easy to get, and I wanted her. There are things hidden in the depths of everyone's minds, just waiting to be unlocked, however much they promise themselves it won't happen. I think I unlocked something within her and she did the same within me, and now I can't put it away, no matter how hard I try. Even getting her the best jock-on-the-block, the newly trained football captain with an improved appreciation of women, hasn't helped either of us.'

I turn back to Austin to see him staring at me. 'People leave your company a little bit fucked in the head, if you don't mind me saying.'

I can only offer him a silent nod.

'I'm wondering if I'm next on your list,' he says, leaning over the bar, edging closer towards me. 'You know I'm not going to be that easy to crack.'

I stroke his arm and look into his dark eyes. 'We met because we share a love of gin and we are old souls who want more.'

'You're saying I'm like you?'

I shake my head. 'You're better than me, Austin. You won't try to chase what you can't have. But I can't help myself. I will always want the impossible. And yes, I would love to lie myself down and spread my legs, feeling you deep inside me, even though I know it will never happen.'

'Damn, you are one sexy kitten.'

I slowly nod my head. 'I might be, but not for you. I know what you really like and you might not believe me but I promise you will get it.'

He nods back but I'm not sure he understands or even believes me. 'What about you and Eric? What's the deal with you two?'

I down my remaining drink. 'Eric is yours. I made him for you.'

He spits his drink out, and for the first time I see his mouth fall open.

'When he comes back you two are going to the beach. You are going to take him to the edge of the shore and you will make tender love to him.'

'Just like that?' he says, stepping away from me, making himself busy whilst fussing over the remaining liquor, our realities no longer the same.

'He will obey me and he will embrace you.'

He leans forward, close enough for me to taste the ice-cold gin on his breath. 'You can't just take what you want in this life.'

I quickly grab his T-shirt, pulling this hulk of muscle halfway across the bar, pinning his ear near to my mouth. 'Time is running out and you will do this, both because you want to and because this *is* going to be our last night on earth.' I keep my gaze on his face, my heart beating faster and my breath giving away the loss in my normally controlled exterior.

A tear eventually trickles down my cheek, and he gently holds my head and wipes it away with one calm flick of his thumb. It makes me shudder with unknown passion, before filling with jealousy, which must be obvious to see. I wish that there was more time to figure all this out. Maybe it would take months, maybe years, but eventually I would have seen his love for Eric grow at the same time as he proved his passion for me. A threesome would never have been out of the question, not for me, not with Austin involved.

But as much as I want it I know that I can't have it. My love for Eric tells me that I shouldn't, and the lack of time tells me that I cannot. I grab Austin by the neck, squeezing tight, my behaviour contrasting completely with his tender touch. 'You will do this and you will give him the pleasure he deserves,' I say, watching him, looking for any sign of doubt. I keep my hands firmly on him, doing all it can to stop his head from shaking. 'And if it all goes bad, as I think it's about to, then you pull him into the water and drown him. Do you hear me?'

He pulls away, as far away as he can get, until he clumsily bumps into the back of the bar. 'Listen to yourself – you've totally lost it.'

I look at him, and only him, wanting those big eyes and those perceptive ears to be ready. 'Jessica,' I say, my eyes still on him. 'Did you see the devil tonight?'

I turn around to see her looking at me, at both of us, her face still silent, her mind still calculating. And then she screams. She screams so loud that half of the people in the bar stand up. People huddle close to the walls, close to candles and closer to each other.

Jessica looks around, as if she has spotted the many people she didn't know were here; or maybe she didn't realise where here is, anymore. With nothing to say she starts to run; her frame is slight, but she still manages to knock over a table. She makes it to the doors, pushing them open and releasing a chill into the bar. But it lets in more than the cold air – it also brings more screams from the distance as she quickly disappears into the night.

Kyle and Eric return, both of them running towards us, the same fearful glazed look in their eyes as the rest of us. 'Something is coming this way,' Eric says.

'Where's Jessica?' Kyle says as he looks around, looking more frantic than I have ever seen, showing more concern than I would ever have thought possible from him.

'You just missed her,' I say, standing up and pointing to the path she has just fled along.

People start to run out of different doors, following different escape routes, all of which lead to nowhere. Austin leaps over the bar, putting himself in the mix of whatever decision we make.

'Where the fuck has she gone?' Kyle says, pinning his stare on me.

I look back at him. 'She's gone to a world of fear.'

His face scrunches up, and he shakes his head at me for what I vow will be the last time tonight – possibly ever. He pushes me, physically and deliberately, enough to make me step backwards and thankfully enough to put a space between us.

Austin fills this new void but Kyle ignores my new protector, and leans around him to get a proper look at me. 'You know that you're so full of shit. You're just a pretty girl with fucked-up ideas that you want to dump on everyone else.'

I don't say anything, but it turns out Kyle has nothing more to say anyway, so we all stand for a moment in our strange, little formation, as crowds of people run around us. It's like we're in our own slow-motion, silent movie, all of us waiting for the next scene to begin.

It's Eric who breaks the peace, as he calmly taps on my arm and slowly finds my gaze. 'What do we do now?' he asks.

I look at his precious little eyes sitting on that adorable face and then I kiss him on the forehead, taking my time to properly absorb his presence. I'm trying to pluck that last shade of doubt from his mind, leaving behind the braver and bolder Eric that I have worked so hard to create. 'I love you,' I say, as I pull Austin closer to him. 'But now you two are going for a walk and I want you to promise me that you will enjoy it.'

Eric shakes his head, seeming to know what my plan is but not willing to accept it. I join them together, forcing them to touch hands and join fingers. It's somehow symbolic, somehow like I'm selling one of them into slavery; I'm just not sure which one. The cream and brown, little and large, cute and sexy; they contrast so well with each other. I stare at them both, at their flesh and at their faces, and I know that I have yet again created something new and unique.

They are both shaking their heads as I push them towards the door; it's like I'm trying to launch my creation out into the open sea, where it will forever sail and send back hopeful thoughts through the wind and the tide. 'Please obey,' I say, as I keep pushing.

Eric is shaking his head, his body anchored to the same spot.

I focus all my physical energy on Austin, as I find him to be a little more willing to listen than Eric. He moves his body, and their arms tighten and pull against each other. I look at their hands, hoping the knot will hold. I keep pushing Austin but I look only at Eric. 'If this is all some stupid practical joke then what have you got to lose?'

Eric is still shaking his head, listening but not hearing. 'I'll lose you.'

I kiss him on the mouth, forcing our lips to join, and then I pull away, always staying in control. 'The boats aren't coming, so if this is something more, something bad, then our end is already decided.' I push him again; I push them both. 'Go and enjoy love before the end, before it's too late. You said you would obey me, so please obey me now.'

Tears stream down his face as he kisses me, and before I know it Austin is doing the same. I cry too, I can't help it. I push them again, needing them to leave now, before I change my mind and keep them here, forever stuck with me.

They finally obey, Austin pulling Eric along as he still looks back at me. I watch them for as long as I can, until I see Austin put both arms around Eric and almost carry him out of here. I'm glad they listened but I realise I have forced myself to lose something; this was a selfless act, one that can never offer me a reward I would want. It feels good and bad in equal measure, but I decide that my emotions can fight it out later.

I turn to Kyle who is still staring at me. 'What the fuck?' he says.

I walk towards the door that Jessie fled through, determined to follow, desperate to find her. I turn to him, signalling that he should tag along for as long as he can. 'Are you ready?'

'What the fuck is going on, and what the fuck are you talking about?'

I walk and talk, picking up anything that can be fashioned into a weapon, quickly making my way into the unknown. 'Have you done it all? Have you prepared your speech, your excuses and all your meaningful reasons?'

I stop and turn. 'Well, have you?'

He looks down at me, his simple face full of unlimited uncertainty. He's not ready, never will be. Kyle is one of the masses of the unprepared, no different from the hundreds who have already run past us, screaming and crying, but not truly sure what they're scared of. We're all in a club, with millions who have literally done nothing – require no excessive judging; part of the world of billions – to be judged for everything.

And then he starts crying.

'Good luck, Kyle,' I say. I'm not sure if it's enough, not really sure what you say at the end of all things. He drops to the floor, and I pat him a couple of times on the head, rubbing a hand through his golden hair, behaving as though he is a dog rather than my ex-lover.

I leave him now. I leave him to judge himself, like he is preparing to check-in to his own personal hell he never knew was waiting for him.

*****

She lets out another whimper as I tighten my hand across her mouth just a little more. We're both looking through the small gap in the wooden panel, both looking for whatever is still lurking out there.

It's quiet now – another period of silence that will likely hold for only a few minutes. The last scream was close; a lonely scream that had a fear all of its own, not shared with others. The small groups had passed several hours ago; the time when hundreds were yelling at once now a distant recollection; this dream holiday a memory that was no longer worth having.

I see people stumbling into the open – there are a handful of them, which is far more than I expected. This could be the largest number of people I have seen in hours, certainly since daylight broke, but I'll never be sure. Some look around and a few cower around bushes and boxes, but the one thing I think they all do is hope. They hope they will survive, they hope they're not being hunted.

They start to run, all looking the same way, screaming and falling over each other. They know it has found them; we all know it has tracked them here. Jessica whimpers as it slowly appears. The fur of a wolf, the eyes of a shark; it stalks its way forward.

'Sssshhh,' I say, one hand turning her around to face me and the other hand teasing its way into her skimpy thong, slowly pulling it down. I kiss her all over her lips and then her neck, teasing and distracting in equal measure.

I focus on her neck so that I can look over at the people. I don't call them to us. I tell myself that I don't want to invite them into our moment, that this is my time of selfishness. I barely acknowledge the lurking truth that I don't want to attract what they have. I don't want to meet what follows them. It hasn't noticed us yet and that gives me hope: survival may still be possible. But they have looked into the eyes of what has come to take all hope from them.

They all turn and now they are fleeing, as it willingly gives chase.

I say nothing, letting her kiss my neck and ride my fingers, the interruption very welcome. But even while she whines and slobbers all over me I keep looking out there. I just can't help it: the sensations of lust and fear are causing a clash of new, strong emotions.

I watch as the others quickly fall, the terror sucked out of them, leaving only a lone man to face the horror that has found him. It takes a moment for me to realise that this man is Kyle. His T-shirt has been almost totally torn off, and his left arm is sliced from shoulder to elbow.

He staggers forward and taunts his nemesis with a stick. It's not enough to fend off judgement, but I wager he'll give it a go. He slashes into the air, the effort of his one good arm accompanied by the puffs and pants of an exhausting night. I can't help you, Kyle, I think. If I had ever felt more than just lust for you, something more than what rests on the surface, then I would act. If it was Eric or Austin out there then I am sure things would be different. But it's you, and you are alone.

It doesn't take long before the cloud of torment, fangs and fur swallows him up. Flesh is spat out as Kyle screams his last scream. A big part of him lands near us – the torso and head of the man of our mutual lust but no single love.

I fall back, pulling Jessica with me. She turns to see what I have been keeping from her and when she looks at him she cries out in horror.

He is looking at us, his eyes still moving. They flicker when he sees us in the remnants of our hidden fumble. In those last few moments I think he truly sees what should never have been allowed to lurk in the shadows, and as we share the revelation, it becomes obvious that what was secret is no longer out of sight. We are all free now; what has been hidden for too long has been exposed, and that's just the way of it.

The creature sees us too and moves closer, clearly seeing no need to be cautious. It sees the end; we all know what's coming.

I nod at it and slowly stand up, looking down at the remains of my best lust while pulling up my worst love, still half-naked and just as confused as she always has been, as I knowingly greet my own judgement with all that I have to offer.

Thursday 18th August – Florence

What is truth if not real?

I will always remember that the pain came first.

Before it there was only darkness, the absent kind that only comes from the deepest of sleep. I don't even remember dreaming but, if I'm honest, I don't think I have had a proper dream for a long time. I can only recall the pain gripping my entire body, pulling me from that quiet place into what I convinced myself had to be hell, all of my own making. I could sense the bright lights all around me and shining into my face, my body being moved and contorted. I couldn't see the ungodly shape it created, but I will always remember how it felt.

The shouting came shortly after and once it started it didn't seem to stop. It was joined by questions like 'can you hear me?' and 'can you look at me?'

When I didn't answer they shouted my name, and it took me a moment to realise that they really had found me; that they knew who I was and what I had done. 'Adam, do you know where you are?' someone asked. It was a woman's voice, and it was somewhere in the distance.

'They know my name,' I kept repeating to myself. I soon had to admit what I didn't want to: that I was still alive. I was in hospital. I had actually survived, but how could that even be possible?

I suddenly felt weightless, like I was being lifted. It was enough of a jolt to make my senses return to their awakened state, one by one. I soon realised that I was now on a different surface, one which felt a little more comfortable. It made me wonder what I had been on before, but a sudden sharp pain in my wrist distracted me from any more thoughts. Something was being pumped into my veins but I still hadn't found the strength to look at anyone, or see anything that was happening. Opening my eyes was simply too much, too hard in such extreme circumstances.

I could tell that the woman was still around, still making her demands. 'Adam, can you hear me? I need you to open your eyes,' she said, and I felt her hands on my head, pulling at my face, like it was playdoh to be moulded into whatever hideous creation she wanted.

I had no interest in opening them, and so I decided that I wouldn't. I didn't want to see these people, didn't want to know what this version of shame looked like.

Just as I was telling myself for the tenth time that I didn't want to be here my eyelids were suddenly pulled up, and I was forced to look around. There were bright lights everywhere. I couldn't see much that made any sense but I could see many sets of eyes staring back at me.

Then I heard someone say: 'Adam, can you look at me please?' I could tell that it was the same woman as before.

I couldn't see where to look, even if I wanted to, but she didn't give up. 'Can you tell me how many fingers I'm holding up?' she asked, as if it would ever matter.

There was too much going on; it was more than I could handle, more than I ever wanted. My head was spinning, and I lost the ability to focus. My body felt like it was on fire. I barely felt it coming as it quickly flowed up from my stomach and out of my mouth as though I was releasing years of fiery pain and neglect at whoever was now trying to care for me.

'We have started the procedure,' she said, although I wasn't sure if she was telling me or just informing those around me. She didn't force my eyes this time, and so I decided that I didn't care who she was addressing. Maybe she didn't want to see me anymore – perhaps the disgrace was too much for her to witness. It didn't matter anyway, because I didn't want to see any of them; I didn't want to see anyone. That was the whole idea and so I kept my eyes closed as the depths of my stomach spilled themselves into this world I was stuck in.

I realised I was lying on my side but I don't know how I did it. Maybe they helped me, I'm not really sure, but either way, they had allowed me to curl up. I could sense something coming from my back end and so I stayed as quiet as I could, my body scrunched up and my mind praying that no one noticed or at least made comment of it. Most of all, I prayed that this would all be over soon.

I could only hope they were too late, could only hope that I ultimately succeeded and that they would soon fail. Everything felt numb, as if my body was no longer my own. I felt myself slipping and I let the darkness take me away from – away from the pain and the shame.

Please, take me forever.

*****

Air. It's all I can think about – I desperately need some. I gasp, long and deep, inhaling as much oxygen as my lungs can take in one go. It feels like what I imagine my first breath, thirty long years ago, was like. It must be like a new-born baby's first entrance into the outside world, when they declare that they are here, and when their lungs finally have a chance to work – to prove themselves – to celebrate all that life has to offer and all that is still to come. After all, they have something worth celebrating and so much to look forward to.

I open my eyes, this time of my own free will. It's bright again and at first I only see light. This place could be heaven but I really doubt it. I couldn't have been that lucky. I look around, slowly letting my mind figure things out as the light fades, just a little. My brain seems to be bringing me back to the rational world, telling me that it's brighter when I look towards a window and darker when I look away from it.

This thought makes me look around and I notice that the surroundings appear much more civilised than what I saw earlier. Everything I see brings me back to normality and the simple cream walls and the shower curtain next to my bed seem almost boring compared to all the drama I have experienced of late. Am I back in my bath? And since when did my bathroom have a window?

Get a grip, I tell myself. I'm not in a bath or in my house, or anywhere else I should be able to remember. It's a hospital room: I can tell that from the red string hanging from the ceiling, the tasteless picture on the wall – art by no one, only one per room. Everything around me is economical, efficient and sterile. I remember it now; a stark reminder of basic reality. I'm back in that world.

I try to sit up but I'm too dizzy. I'm sure I could fight against it if I really wanted to; somehow force myself up, like they always do in the films. It looks so much easier when someone else does it, especially when they don't actually have anything wrong with them. Life is easier when you only have to act out living. After all, I did it for long enough.

I lay my head back down but that one small movement exhausts me. I prepare to close my eyes again, hoping my new best friend, darkness, will take me away. 'Don't bring me back' I mutter.

'What did you say?' a voice asks. It's a voice I recognise easily.

My eyelids crank open again and I look around to find what I clearly missed just a moment ago. And there he is, sitting in a chair opposite the bed, his legs folded and a magazine in his hand.

'How did you get here?' I ask, needing to know how he found me, when he found me and where he found me. Was it *him*? Did *he* catch me at my lowest?

He stands up and comes closer to me. 'The more important question is how did *you* get here? That's the question I've been dying to ask, as you can imagine.'

I don't say anything but close my eyes and pretend he isn't there, begging the blackness to descend upon me quickly. I know he is still talking but I don't hear anything specific as I feel the pressure building on my weary eyelids. I want no more questions, no more demands, and so I slip away, quietly and without any more drama.

Just as I had wanted.

*****

I didn't want to come back, so why do I keep waking up? This wasn't what I wanted but I don't know what I can do to fix it, to make the endless hum go away. I feel cold, and there is this constant droning noise in my ears; it's like I'm in some sort of chiller. I immediately wonder if I am finally dead. I'm not lying down so perhaps I'm hanging up like meat in a cold room?

I want to sleep but I'm too uncomfortable and so I open my eyes. I need to know how I can fix this; how can I leave this place and drift away into that world of forgetfulness.

I soon see that he's here again, sitting next to me, still reading a magazine. We're on a plane and are both sitting still. He doesn't look at me; I don't think he realises I am awake. His trimmed beard is as neat as it always is; his shirt crisp and tight. He carries his age well: a man in his mid-thirties, with the lifestyle of someone in their mid-forties, yet graced with the look of mid-twenties. All of these masks he wears fit him so well and I think it is handy to have someone like that around.

He moves a hand to turn the page and I quickly shut my eyes, worried that he will look over. I'm not ready to meet him, not ready to talk or to answer. I want to know nothing and share nothing and so I wait for the drift, the pull away from here. I soon feel the heaviness of my eyelids as they find their favourite resting position. I don't know why I'm floating away so often, but it must be because of whatever medication I'm taking – this cocktail of chemicals that keep me away from reality as much as possible. Whatever the reason, in this moment, I am always happiest.

If only I had the whole bottle. I know for sure I wouldn't plan on coming back.

*****

I can open my eyes whenever I want to. By keeping them closed I'm just pretending – pretending that I'm asleep when I'm actually awake, just thinking and wondering. I have so much to think about but so little that I want to discuss with my tortured mind. I'm not sure how much longer I can keep quiet for; I know he won't buy it forever, and besides I've run out of things to distract my scattered brain with. The truth is I am not sure how much longer I can be alone. It drove me insane before and it's doing the same now.

I feel the light again, the sun crashing against my skin and forcing a reaction in my eyes. I see a slight tinge of colour where there was only blackness before. I know that I need to eat; I can't think when I last had proper food, or when I last craved it so much. It somehow feels good to feel hungry: I need sustenance and my body needs me as much as I need it. If I don't eat, don't feed it, then we both die. Our co-existence depends on it – our mutual deal for life, as long as we both accept it.

He must need me too, must feel pure agony at my continued failure to offer him any answers. He needs to know that I'm here, he deserves that much. He actually deserves a lot more, but I need to start somewhere. I decide that I'll take just a few more minutes. It feels good to be in control for once, to know that I can open my eyes whenever I want. Actually, this entire morning feels so very special: just to know that light is coming from the window and to be able to picture my surroundings – the desk, the sofas, the bathroom, the other bed.

The hotel I could never afford and the best friend I have never deserved.

I hear him now, somewhere in the room, as I try to keep a mental picture of where we are. I imagine him moving around, talking to himself out loud, directed at the both of us. I hear the curtains moving on the rail, the balcony doors opening and the summer breeze drifting into the room. The cool air tickles my skin and I realise that it's a positive sensation. I'm appreciating something simple for what it is and how nice it can be – it's been such a long time since I have acknowledged things like this. Despite the cool breeze I actually feel warm, warmer than I have felt since before it all happened.

'You can't still be asleep,' Mike says, with a hint of sarcasm in his voice. He knows me too well, and has had the time to watch me whilst I continue to be absent from this place he has brought me to. 'If you're still asleep then I apologise profusely for what I'm about to do,' he says, as he rips off my bed covers.

I open my eyes as I feel the quilt leaving me. I hear it scrunching up on the carpet and then look to see that one corner of it is still clinging onto the side of the bed. I feel a slight chill from outside and wonder if I have any clothes on. It's enough to make me look down at my flat body, thankful to see that pants and a T-shirt are covering my withering skin and bones.

'You managed to dress yourself last night. It was a significant improvement on the last few days,' he says, as he shakes his head. 'Oh and good morning for what must be the tenth time. I do hope you're going to stay with me this time, otherwise there is a chance that you'll miss out on your dream city.'

'We're really in Florence?' I ask. I can only partially remember the last two days, and I am not truly able to believe that we actually got here.

'Yes, we are really in Florence,' he says, gesturing towards the balcony. 'The city, in all its eternal glory, patiently awaits you.'

I sit up in my bed, looking out towards the balcony. I can see the blue sky, the scattering of clouds, so few and only fluffy with no threat of bad weather. I can hear the birds singing in the nearby tree, such a contrast with the traffic and hustle of this small city.

He sits down on a chair, staring over at me. 'We have already been here for 12 hours and have seen nothing. I know it was night time and you needed sleep, but that's no excuse, because whether in the day or at night, this city is a marvel, as you well know.'

I nod, agreeing completely, and feeling very happy to be here. When I was feeling that I could cope with nothing more, this was the place that came into my mind – the one place I knew I would miss. I look between him and the city below us and its constant air of possibility. 'I can't believe we're here.'

'And I can't believe you're actually smiling,' he says.

I stop for a moment before I agree with him, knowing it has been a long while. I look around the room and realise just how lucky I am. I notice extra detail in every corner, from the oversized television to the minibar with a cabinet all to itself. 'Thank you,' I say, knowing it's all I can offer him right now.

He nods but doesn't seem to care. 'So, are you thanking me for getting us on a flight when the prices have tripled since only last week, for checking us into a five-star hotel, or for getting you out of hospital and out of the country after you took a jar of drugs strong enough to kill a herd of elephants?'

I look at him, his face serious, my experience telling me that I'm in deep trouble and our long friendship telling me that he won't let this drop. 'Probably all of the above,' I say, wincing at the thought of everything I have put him through, despite my so very different intentions.

He smiles. 'Yes, they are all quite interesting topics for discussion, which I will happily discuss over breakfast. But when I'm done telling you about what fun we have had, and when we're done seeing all the sights, at some point you have some explaining to do. Feel free to take your time but by the end of this holiday I will need to know everything.'

I look down, hoping this holiday won't ever end, that perhaps they will shut all the airports and we will never have to leave here. If that happens then Mike will get no argument from me; just a plea for us to stay in this hotel permanently. His credit card would have a lot of stretching to do but I know it's a better alternative to returning home. I laugh to myself – I haven't thought that far ahead in years.

'Get showered and dressed,' he says, throwing clothes onto my bed. I don't have anything to say, don't know what the point would be in checking what other clothes I have. He obviously packed them all and I have little interest in making sure than anything matches. 'It's time for breakfast on the sun terrace and then we have a day to see all our favourites.'

'Only one day?' I ask, slightly disappointed, although it does feel nice to feel something about anything, even if it is disappointment.

He's already shaking his head. 'Oh, we're here all week and I tried to book ahead but the concierge insisted that there is no reason to book anything. Tourist visitor rates are down 75%, so the queues will be virtually non-existent. Only the bravest will be here. It should be interesting but the good news is that we will be able to see all of our favourites, each and every day for a whole week.' He throws a towel at me and his head motions me to the bathroom. 'As usual on our little trips all of my stuff is on the right, yours on the left.'

I get up and think of all the problems, of all he has told me and all the things that are happening that I know about. Most of all I think of a Florence without queues; just another reason to believe this place really is heaven in the midst of hell.

*****

'You were right about the queues. It's like the start of the season – totally unlike any other August day I can ever remember here.'

He nods and brushes his hair back, scraping a hand through the long strands until they are resting on his forehead, just where he wants them. 'The queues are always shit but now they're not here I somehow miss them. It's strange but I also miss the crowds, the way there is always someone in the background of every photo, no matter how many you take.'

I laugh, knowing just how many times that has happened. We're both pros at the travel thing, the Italy thing and the Florence trick of perfect photos – get here very early and then spend the afternoon sleeping by the pool. 'I don't miss the tourists but I do miss having a VIP pass and walking along the long line, knowing that we will be in and out before they even get to the front of the queue.'

He laughs and edges closer to me, leaning into my ear. 'Everyone has a job in this place. The concierge gets his tip, the doormen do a little more and get something extra back, and basically everyone is happy. If there are no masses of tourists then none of these people have a purpose, and so they will disappear.'

'You think that everyone's roles are changing?' I ask.

We both look around the half-empty square, taking it all in. I think we both imagine that it's really a cold day in January and not the supposed peak of the season. I try to pretend the sun isn't really beating down on all these cobblestones and the lack of thousands of footsteps isn't really an issue. 'They're not just changing. I think they're falling apart. You forget that you've missed a lot of news lately. All I'll say is I'm glad we live in England.'

I take my turn to listen to him as I watch and observe. I still see the touts outside the restaurants, the street sellers still trying to flog all manner of cheap plastic and overprinted art. I see determination in the eyes of everyone around us: they want to continue, to act as if nothing threatens our existence. The class system seems to have remained place so far: the workers do the work, the street sellers do the selling and the tourists do the buying. No roles have changed and no one has challenged the expectations society has silently placed upon each of us, but I do see the issue. As I look around I see very few families and a lot more older people than usual. Maybe they have less to lose; maybe those of us who are here are on a pilgrimage rather than a holiday; all of us together, and all of us happy to see our end in a place like this.

I start to think that this is where I should have done it. I would have been surrounded by all that I love – centuries of astonishing creations to admire, all in one place. But then I look at Mike and I instantly know that it wouldn't have been fair. Even if he wasn't with me at the time he would have been the one to come over to identify my body, taking it back to England and burying it next to my parents – his last and loneliest job being to rest me in a place where I would never find peace.

'Perhaps we shouldn't be here,' I say, my deepest thoughts somehow being vocalised before I have a chance to understand them myself.

'Oh, not that again,' he says, pulling me forward towards a very short queue. 'You're really worried, aren't you?'

'It's like you say, the news reports are getting worse. Something has happened in parts of Asia and most of Africa, which that means it isn't far from the rest of Europe. If it comes by land then it might take some time, but what about travelling by sea? Italy is an easy landing spot, such an easy country to invade.'

He laughs – typical Mike, not worried about anything. How many people would have had the bravery to take a friend out of hospital and onto a plane after what I did? It's a wonder they let me go but priorities seem to have shifted in the last few weeks. When the needs of the masses change, the wants of an individual are difficult to process, and I think that bespoke care might just end up as a thing of the past. The reality is that Mike probably did them a favour by taking me out of the hospital, thus freeing up a desperately needed bed.

He catches me thinking and stares back at me, ignoring our surroundings, oblivious to the few people around us. 'We're here now, in Florence, your favourite place on earth, so you need to get with it. This will be a good break. We will not be killed by some virus and we will not be eaten by zombies, or whatever they reckon is lurking out there. You will find a way to move on from whatever happened, which will include telling me what actually did happen, so that I can help you to rebuild your life. Then we can both cheer the fuck up.'

I take a deep breath and nod. This could be the right place for me, a chance to be renewed. After all, around every corner is a church, a statue – a picture from the past just waiting to be found. How can something from the depths of time, frozen for so long, give so much so freely? How could it not stir up powerful emotions? 'This is the right place, I'm sure of it – just maybe not the right time.'

'Perhaps we need a disaster looming in the distance every summer, if it means that the Galleria dell'Accademia is emptied!' Mike says, pulling me into the large reception area. He dances through the ticket hall, then passes far more notes than are necessary through the small plastic hole to the solitary figure sitting behind the booth. 'We won't need the audio guide, we're professionals!' he shouts, as he drags me towards the main hall.

He's right about the audio guide: it's been a long time since either of us found any use for it. I can recite the background to every individual piece of art and tell every magnificent story from memory, without the need of a book or any other kind of assistance. But this trip is different – in more ways than I can count. This time, Mike pulls us left when I want to go right. I always start with the works of Giambologna and snake my way around the many Florentine paintings, all of them a teasing prelude to the main event. I don't want to see him until I have settled in, reminded myself where I am and truly savoured the moment. Mike is different this time; he's in some sort of hurry, dragging me towards him before I am ready, before I have had time to properly prepare myself. I sigh and pull back, telling him we should go right first, but he doesn't listen. He keeps dragging me, laughing as we cross the threshold. 'It's good to be different, to spice things up, just a little!'

I am still shaking my head, my mind saying no, when he suddenly stops. I collide with him, my brain confused by a simple change in the routine that has held true for a decade. I'm busy telling him off, telling him that this isn't what I wanted, not how it should be done, but he only looks forward.

'Ah, David, there you are, and how I have missed you,' he says.

I turn to face forward, allowing my gaze to rest upon what he has found. We both nod as we look at the simple beauty, amply detailed in only marble, no more than twenty paces ahead of us. I stare over at him and find it so easy to believe that he is staring back at only me. All of my frustrations disappear and my despair scurries into some dark corner, knowing that it cannot defeat me in this place.

'He is as beautiful as he always is,' Mike says, not looking away from the grey god standing before us.

I'm distracted for a moment by counting the number of people present: there are around 50 people in the room, far fewer than I'm used to seeing here. We once got into an exclusive after-hours exhibit and even then there were more people than I can see now. Any other time we have been in here I have had to fight my way around, but not today. With just a little patience I will get a great picture, one that will join the many others, but perhaps this time it will be the best I have ever taken. I look at Mike next to me and David before me and I feel the energy to go on, but also regret for what I did. I'm almost glad it didn't work and as I watch Mike walk away I wonder if maybe I should have confided in him, if he could have somehow helped. It all happened so quickly and I'll never understand how I could have spent so long being frustrated at all those unanswered questions. I never turned to my best friend; instead, I chose the comfort of online forums, of people who felt the same, who would only tell me what I wanted to hear and that I wasn't alone, which, deep down, I knew to be true.

I walk forward and linger for a while. Mike does the same. We separate, neither of us feeling any need to share this small experience, since we are sharing all of Florence together. I eventually sit down behind David, opposite his ass, where many go but few stay for long. The essence of his being is based on eternal intimacy, and while I admit that this isn't the most glamorous part of him, I think it's just as revealing as the rest.

I realised some time ago, on one of our many trips here, that I don't think of him as just a creation, delicately forged from solid marble with the most basic of tools. I'm amazed by what Michelangelo created but I'm also in awe of David and all of his perfection. I don't stare at him in some perverted way, although I like what I see more than I care to admit. I wonder if he was actually real, and if so, if he really looked like the god towering above me, or if he was simply a creation of the mind? The detail is captured so perfectly that I can't imagine him not existing, not being a real, flawless specimen of a man. I wonder if he realised that he was not just being copied and carved, but also immortalised, and that his image would live for far longer than his physical being, that he would be appreciated by many millions for hundreds, or possibly thousands, of years.

The odd person moves past me as I sit and reflect, but I'm too busy tracing every curve on his body to notice anyone. I'm not really here anymore; I'm in Michelangelo's workshop, observing his absolute dedication, watching hammer and chisel in the hands of an expert, carefully bringing this marvel to life. We will never know how much his work was truly understood or appreciated in his time, but the one thing I do know is that he had a sense of purpose, even if only for a short while. I feel entirely confident that he created more in a year than I have created in my lifetime, and he had so many things to call his own.

By contrast, I have nothing. I have no skill, no purpose and no right to be here. I have wasted my life until it has become truly pointless. I don't want to fill it with endless distractions. I know enough to realise that this kind of existence isn't enough for me, but I don't know how to change it. I have these thoughts often, and with more intensity over the past few years, to the point where escape has become the only option; the unthinkable gradually becoming the answer.

I feel the presence of someone else near to me. It's enough to break me out of my thoughts but not enough to make me look. I know it's not Mike and I know they will go away soon. People never stay in this bit for long; it's almost as though they feel it's wrong to linger here. I have more time and I know that I can have this small bench to myself for as long as I want it. I soon sense the person moving, but they don't seem to be leaving, as they shuffle closer towards me instead. I take a deep breath and sigh, wanting them to know what I'm thinking: my irritation that they have chosen to sit so near, even though there are so few people in here. They keep coming closer until they are next to me and I'm about to turn so that I can tell the beggar, the ticket tout or whoever they are that there is plenty of room for both of us.

'This is a funny place to visit when you should be dead,' this voice says. I don't recognise it but I know that this question can only refer to one thing, and I feel a horror building in the depths of my stomach. I turn to see who is sitting next to me, to confirm that it cannot possibly be who I think it is, not here and not now. I look at his head, the rest of him unknown to me, but the moment I see his face I know it's him. I take him all in, desperately trying to prove that I'm wrong, but everything I see confirms the unthinkable. I see his balding head, his beady eyes and his thick beard with the grey patch just above his chin. I shake my head, not knowing how this is possible and not wanting it to be happening. I have never met him but have seen him online, so real but still far away, and now he is sitting next to me. I only know that his name is Vance, if he was honest about that.

I stare at him and he stares back at me, as I try to remember when we last chatted. I think it was no more than a week ago but I'm not sure any amount of time will make a difference. Despite my intentions, he was always genuine about himself and the others. It put me at ease, made me feel like it was right, but now I don't want any part of it. I made agreements that cannot easily be broken, and now he has found me; he knew where I was and now he has tracked me down.

'I have changed my mind,' I say, flatly, as if it's as easy as that. It's like when you get to a checkout and decide you don't something that's in your basket – you put it down; maybe the boldest of us hand it back and make it someone else's problem.

He smiles back at me, his head tilted as he examines my face. He suddenly stands up and I flinch, wondering if this is the moment when I'll have to fight to survive. It wouldn't be the first time, except this time I do want to survive.

'Okay, I hear you,' he says, still standing in front of me. 'We would never have expected you to back out and let us down, but there is your answer.'

I stare back at him. He is standing in front of David, barely reaching the height of his buttocks. 'That's it?' I say, somehow relieved, still very cautious.

'Of course that's not it!' he shouts, standing over me with his eyes burning into mine, like I have stolen everything from him.

Someone else steps behind David and into our space. He's a young guy but still tall, still a third bigger than Vance, but that doesn't stop my worst nightmare from pushing him away. 'Go look somewhere else,' he says, his gaze following the guy until he disappears behind the other side of the statue, making only a hushed and insignificant protest.

I know that this confrontation isn't something I can win and so I get up, heading to the other side of David, knowing that I will have to be quick. I need to find Mike and get the both of us out of here before Vance tells him what we planned to do and what I failed to carry out.

He must see this coming as no sooner have I stood up and starting moving than he appears in front of me, having rounded the giant marble sculpture to head me off. He has to look up at my face but I know that my extra height will be of no help to me – my skinny frame stands no chance against his solid bulk. He takes a deep breath, clenching both of his fists. 'Agreements have been made which cannot simply be amended or ignored.'

I shake my head, not wanting to deal with this, not knowing what I can say to explain my actions or make him go away. I can't believe he has followed me here, from the depths of my nightmares to this place, which I consider to be my absolute sanctuary. 'You need to leave me alone!' I say, somehow hoping it will be enough to actually make him leave, but deep down knowing this is only the beginning of the end, an end I no longer want.

'Do you think it's that simple?'

I stare back at him, both of us waiting for an answer. I was so sure before, so entirely confident that I was making the right decision, and he made it easy to face up to these darkest of thoughts. He freely accepted my request to join them, to find a way out together, and in return for his confidence I told him things that I never wanted Mike or anyone else to hear. I push myself forward, determined that the new me will not be bullied, as I manage to get past him and into the small trickle of people.

He follows me, as I figured he would. His movements are still civilised. I wish this place was more crowded; then there would be more people to lose myself among. I feel his eyes burning into me as he stays by my side, mirroring my movements as I weave through the few tourists.

'I have already told you that I have changed my mind, but it doesn't mean I didn't try to go through with it,' I say, explaining myself in a rush, speaking not much above a whisper, not wanting anyone else to hear my excuses, which I know should not even exist.

He nods in answer and we continue to walk, as if we're friends and he has an obligation to listen. Anyone looking at us would think we know each other – the only other option would be that I'm being pursued, stalked, possibly about to be attacked, and that would lead to a very different reaction from the passers-by. I'm not shouting or screaming; I know that I cannot risk drawing attention to myself or risk bringing Mike running into this room.

I speed up, trying to test his resolve, but he continues to mirror everything that I do. I think about my limited options, knowing that I will need to do something soon. My only obvious advantage over him is that I know my way around here; I've been so many times that I know every corridor like the back of my hand. I can think of many exits and I know where Mike will be. We are both creatures of habit, and since this is our favourite museum, I know the route he will probably take.

Vance must sense that I'm about to run because he grabs my arm, sealing his vice-like grip around it as he pulls me closer to him. 'You made an agreement that cannot be undone. I wish we had more time to debate this but things have already been set in motion.'

I stop and look down at him. My heart is thumping wildly in my chest but my breathing remains mysteriously slow and firm. The fear is starting to leave me, replaced with anger at the fact he has found me and is making demands that no human should ever make on another. 'I have paid you the money, and I don't want it back. So you can leave. If you go now I won't call the police.'

'The police?' he says, as he stares back at me, his body anchored to a spot next to me. 'You seem to have changed your views somewhat in the last few days, which is very disappointing, as you were one of the keenest to move things along. You should know that the group wanted to wait for you, but as you can imagine, time is precious these days.'

I gasp involuntarily, remembering what was agreed, sad images of nice people flooding into my mind. 'They're all dead?'

He nods. 'We did our job and they did theirs. I have to say I was very pleased because there wasn't a peep out of any of them. It was one of my best yet.'

I feel my legs shaking, and I try to deny what I'm hearing. 'You can't talk about them like that, like they were animals for slaughter.'

'I can and I will because you made a pact, which is something that mattered to all of you, meaning that I'm pleased to say you will finally have your wish. I believe in many things and I'm entirely convinced that they will be waiting for you in whatever place is next.'

I push his arm off me, refusing to listen or give in to his demands, refusing to give up the life I now want to claim back. 'They can wait because I went through with it four days ago, in my bathroom. It clearly didn't work and now I have changed my mind.'

He stands still whilst staring at me; it seems that nothing I am saying is registering with him, as he slowly shakes his head. 'You poor thing, I can't imagine how awful it must have been to do that on your own. I can only promise you that it will not happen like that again. I always use the correct dose and you won't feel a thing. Like I said before, it will be like falling asleep, except that you won't ever have to wake up.' He gently but firmly grips my arm, pulling me along with him. 'You have hired the professionals and we will now finish our contractual obligations. Shall we go now?'

'No! I'm not going anywhere with you!' I shout, brushing him off me and then pushing him backwards. I push him again, still shouting, thrusting my hands into his chest repeatedly. With every step I take towards him, he takes a step backwards. I can only hope that he realises how serious I am. 'I chose to stay alive, so leave me alone and go home.'

He shakes his head again, proving that he really isn't interested in listening to me. 'You have entered into a contract and what you paid for will happen tonight, I can assure you of that. Your life will end and your possessions, as per your recently updated will, are to be transferred to our trust, as detailed in the agreement.'

I'm getting dizzy from constantly shaking my head but I don't know what else I can do. 'That's not going to happen. Don't you get it? I have changed my mind.'

He rubs his temples, the frustration he feels with me is very obvious now. 'I don't think you quite understand the gravity of this situation, or your place in the bigger picture. You were asked to sign and to verbally agree to this on several occasions. This gave you a total of three days to think about it and to make sure you made the right decision. You have signed the agreement and now I'm afraid that you are just a number, and that number has to pay certain fees.'

'You can't do this! You can't just make me do it!'

He leans closer, a frown spreading across his face. 'Did you not say that you wanted to die? Were you not telling the truth?'

I walk towards a bench and he follows, allowing me to sit down without any attempt to stop me. 'I was telling the truth at the time but now I don't want to do it,' I say, putting my head in my hands, trying to make sense of all of this, of a decision I made in a different time, when I felt a very different way. 'I can't believe this is happening and that you are real.'

He sits next to me, taking his time to look around. I'm not sure if he has been here before; either way, he doesn't look at all interested in renaissance art, history or culture. 'You meant it at the time and I remember how certain you were, so what was that truth if not real? You had tried to do it yourself before and failed, so when I talked about a collective of like-minded individuals all ending their lives at the same time you were very keen. I really do suggest you find that person again because one way or the other this is real and it is happening.'

I look at him, at the mass of blind determination that is sitting next to me. 'Why can't you just leave me alone? You can take all my things, all of them, and I won't say anything.'

He shakes his head. 'I wish that was possible but it isn't, because there are things you cannot give to me whilst you're still alive.'

'I will give you all my money, my flat, everything. We can check online right now so you can see how much money I have. I will transfer it all to you if you just leave me alone.'

He takes a look around this place, as if he finally cares about where we are and who could overhear our conversation, let alone understand it. 'I don't think you are listening. The fact is that you are now worth significantly more to us as a dead person. Your possessions might pay the bills but your identity will bring us much more.'

'You're talking about murder!'

He shakes his head and I wonder if he has ever heard this before, or if I'm the first person to back out and throw in that card. 'You agreed to this, as I have already said. It's too late to change your mind because you have already been allocated to someone else and considering everything that is now happening, we need to speed things along. They are already in the air and will take up your life as of first thing tomorrow morning. The truth is that you have to die, at least your physical being. Someone else will take your life from here – the life you didn't want – and hopefully they will make better use of it.'

I stare open-mouthed at him as the truth unfolds. When I made the decision that I didn't want to live anymore, I hadn't thought about what I would be leaving behind, and when I found Vance in a chatroom and learnt of his organisation's professional services, I hadn't thought about what would happen when I was gone. He answered all of my questions about my things and the need for my will to be accurate, in order to ensure fair payment for the services his secret organisation offered. He never told me what would happen after, once my body was laid in the cold ground, and I never thought to ask.

He moves closer to me, looking me up and down, like he's sizing me up for a coffin, or perhaps I'll just end up in a body bag. 'Your replacer would like to see your body before you are laid in your final resting place, which isn't very helpful that we're already in Florence. Unfortunately you already paid for your transfer and even though you have got yourself here there are no refunds, as per our contractual agreement.'

'I don't care about the money, you must realise that by now,' I say, shaking my head. I don't want to hear any of this. I hadn't thought beyond the arrangements that had been made for my body. An exact plan had been made, which would have resulted in it resting in a small cemetery just outside the city. It is a perfect place, in the hills, looking down towards the city that I have always loved. I didn't think further than that, beyond these material arrangements. I never believed that after my passing anything would happen. For me, the end of my world was the end of everything and now that I know otherwise, that my death will not be the end of it, I feel angry and strangely jealous, desperate to hold on to what I have been given.

This is perhaps my final chance to declare to the universe that I want this life, that my previous feelings of despair and desperation are gone, or have at least subsided. I will take what I have now in lieu of whatever is waiting for me in the afterlife. 'I'm staying alive,' I say, staring at him, waiting for a reaction.

He immediately shakes his head, as I knew he would. His determination is predictable. He then reaches into his pocket, and shows me a piece of paper that I quickly realise is a copy of my contract. 'You have made your choice and what will follow for you and the rest of us are the consequences of your actions. We have to do this tonight because there is so much to do afterwards.' He starts tapping on his fingers, mentally calculating things. I'm sure that this is just one job in many for him. 'We have to get you viewed and then buried – the tombstone will be under a different name, of course. And then I really do need to get your replacer back to London and settled into his new life. They always have so many questions. The last one even asked how the boiler worked – as if I'm ever going to know that.'

I lean forward, still not believing what I'm hearing, desperately trying to spot flaws in his plan, trying to think of any reason why he should just forget me. 'Why don't you just leave me out of this? It will save you time if you just take this person to my place in London tomorrow. I'll build a new life here and you will never see me again. Let this new person take whatever they want from me; I promise I will not contact the police or interfere in any way.'

He shakes his head, as I wonder if he has heard this story before, or if I am the first to ask all these questions of my after-life, and to ever back out from this kind of decision, the one that felt so right just a few days ago. 'We have a contract with your replacer, which guarantees that you will be dead and buried. That's why so many people ask to see the body. I think they want to be sure but they are also always curious to see if you look like them, which invariably you don't.'

I shake my head for the hundredth time, silently telling him I still don't want this.

He tuts, showing his open frustration. 'I have a life too, I hope you realise this. I need to get back to my family, to my wife and my little girls. They are petrified by everything that's happening right now. My wife won't let my girls watch TV anymore because the other day, *Peppa Pig* was interrupted in the middle by a BBC news broadcast. I mean, in the middle of a kids' programme, can you believe it? This world is fucked and you are my last job.'

He stands up; I stay seated. Even now, his head is only a little above mine. 'If it's any consolation, a quick and painless death might be the best way to go, especially if the reports are right. All of the United Kingdom is under curfew and it's doing better than most places. My counterparts in the United States have mostly disappeared. It's a blood bath out there.'

I listen to him talk, realising that I have not given enough credence to the stories of distant worries that might actually be true. When you haven't seen something for yourself, it's hard to process and even harder to believe. He's still talking as I try to face the idea that all of this is true, that what he plans will happen and that, unless I escape now, I will not be able to stop him. I know that I have to take this chance to get out of here and as far away from him as possible. He raises his arms to reinforce whatever point he wants to make, but I choose not to hear it, not to be a victim to my own poor decisions, and I kick one of his knees.

I've never kicked someone before, not properly, and I'm surprised how much damage I seem to do: he immediately falls to the floor and cries out. I watch him for a moment as he grabs his injured knee with both hands and wriggles around on the floor. It's only when he looks at me that I get up. He takes a hand off his knee and attempts to grab my ankle, but I'm quick enough that I move away in time. He starts to crawl towards me, then uses the bench to hoist himself up. I start to make my escape, running away, realising that he cannot possibly follow me. After a few strides I turn to see him shouting at me, telling me that I will never be able to hide from him, no matter where I run.

I take one final look at him and then up to David, wondering if I will ever see either of them again. The stone man gives me nothing. I wonder how many goodbyes I have said to him in my short life, and whether this will now be the last.

'Mugger!' I hear from Vance. He is now hobbling forward, obviously knowing he will not catch me without help. He must know that if people intervene and the police are called then his cover will be blown, but he points at me nonetheless, screaming that I have taken something from him.

People stop and stare at me, the absence of the usual crowds making me easy to spot. Vance is shouting that someone should stop me. I look around, wondering whether anyone will be brave enough, considering how uncertain these times are, and I suddenly feel a hand grab my shoulder. I turn around and raise a hand, no longer willing to be a victim in my own nightmare. As I turn, I feel someone grabbing it. They restrain me and tell me to calm down. It takes me a moment to realise that it's Mike, his blue eyes, still full of energy and hope, staring into mine.

He manages a smile and says 'calm down, it's only me.'

'Mike!' I shout, grabbing him and trying to push him away. 'We need to go now, so don't ask, please just run.'

He doesn't move, and looks around at the spectators, then finally towards my accuser. 'Who the hell is he and what's going on?'

'Why don't you tell him?' Vance shouts, starting to hobble towards us, becoming bolder and possibly more desperate by the second.

'Yes, why don't you tell me? Don't you think it's about time I knew and especially before everyone else in this room?'

I look at Mike. He's so close; his breath is brushing against my skin. He's always been there, always been willing to help me, even when I have not wanted to ask or tell him anything. 'I've been quiet for too long,' I say, knowing that my ample silences and regular disappearances have given him many chances to walk away, but despite this, he has always chosen to stay by my side. 'We need to get out of here and back to the hotel. I can't tell you now, but I promise if you get us there then I will tell you everything.'

He stares at me, then gazes over my shoulder before looking at me again. I know Mike, and I know he will think that Vance holds some of the answers he wants to hear. His keen mind quickly comes to a conclusion, and he grabs my arm and pulls me away. We run out of the main hall and away from David. I hear Vance's screams echoing down the corridor behind us. I can't really see anything else as I trust our escape and my future life to Mike. It's probably something I should have done years ago – maybe we wouldn't be in this mess if I had have done just that. But now I have no choice. I feel a rush of air when we burst through a fire exit and back into the outside world.

I turn to see Vance still following us, two security guards catching up with him. It doesn't take long for them to look over and see me, then make their way over towards us. I'm busy preparing my explanation; I decide that I will demand for the police to be called immediately, knowing that the only crime that has been committed is my assault on Vance. I'm so preoccupied with contemplating my lack of understanding of the laws and morals of this country, and just how powerful his organisation could be, that I barely realise that I'm being bundled into the back of a car. I turn away from Vance and his new allies to see that we're in a taxi. Mike pushes his way in next to me and shouts all manner of instructions to the driver.

We manage to start moving just as one of the guards bangs on the side of the car. It's enough to distract the driver and make him slow down, and he puts his window down and starts shouting. I keep a hold on the handle as the guard starts grabbing it from the outside, now shouting back at the driver. It's Mike who intervenes, waving a wad of notes in the driver's face, telling him not to ask questions, but just to drive and take his reward. For a moment I don't think he is going to accept it but it seems that the offer is too good to turn down, as he hits the accelerator and we speed off. At the best of times I wonder how well bribery works, and in these worst of times I wonder when it doesn't.

Mike throws the notes into the passenger seat and shouts to the driver not to stop until we get to the hotel. He nods and starts speaking in an odd mixture of Italian and broken English, telling us not to worry and that no questions will be asked by him. Mike eventually nods and turns to me, sweat dripping down his face as he shakes his head. 'That's fine with me, because I will be asking all the questions from now on.'

*****

Mike stares at me as I lie on the sunbed. He hasn't said a lot since I told him, just the odd question to confirm the darkest fears I think he already had. I didn't hold back, telling him everything, right from the start, a whole decade ago. I laid myself bare for him to see, to understand and hopefully accept what I can only now explain. My feelings of despair and – ultimately – defeat have been years in the making and Mike has been around for all of them. He already asked me if it was him, if he had caused all of this. It took me a while to reassure him that he wasn't the issue and that having a friend like him has probably kept me alive for longer. He didn't like that and told me to stop talking about death in this way as though it was some sort of transaction.

'The Police won't attend, not without any crime being committed, which technically he hasn't done yet,' Mike says, perched on the edge of his sunbed.

I barely move, not able to find the energy to give him some panicked response. 'Did you tell them about the contract, about what I agreed to?'

I see his frown reappear, which happens whenever I go near the subject that has been hidden in the depths of my tortured mind for so long, and which is now out in the open and on show for him to see. 'No, I didn't mention that. I figured it wouldn't help our case, as they are barely interested at the moment. The guy in charge spoke English as well as I speak Italian, but I managed to get some information out of him. He said a lot of police have been dispatched to Pisa and other places along the coast, but he wouldn't tell me why.'

I nod back, not knowing what I should do with this new information. I know it's probably relevant but I don't know how. I lie still for a moment as I try to think things through, to sort things out in my cluttered brain. The problem is that I'm trying to sort through years of fogged thinking – decades of haze – just to find where the real problems are lurking. 'Are you sure it's not a crime? Didn't he try to abduct me?'

Mike shakes his head and I know that his patience with all of this is running out. I think he was okay when he got me out of the hospital, even though he must have known more than he's letting on – the doctors must have told him what I had been trying to do. He clearly knows as much as I know, but it probably seems even worse when the graphic details of my failure are detailed by an experienced medical mind. 'You signed a contract, so I think you'd find it difficult to argue that it was kidnap. He was technically coming to do the job you paid him for or – more accurately – to finish the job you couldn't do yourself.'

I lean forward a little, knowing that this is an argument I will never win, one that will never be over. 'I changed my mind,' I say, for what I think is the hundredth time.

Mike stands up and paces around, his tall frame temporarily putting me in the shade whenever he passes by. I want to ask him to move, to tell him that I haven't felt the sun beating down on my pale skin for such a long time and that I'm finally enjoying one of our trips to the pool. For years I hid in the shade, only tolerating the outdoor bit of the holiday for Mike's sake. I would always look around at all the tourists spending hours baking in the sun, as though the whole planet was one big revolving oven, turning them around until they were a distracted shade of golden brown. I didn't see the point and I never wanted to be one of those people, because I was always convinced that it would be me who died from the consequences – and it would be truly ironic for the pale guy running from one patch of shade to the next for days on end to get skin cancer.

He stands over me again; his face has changed back to how it looked in that taxi. 'You should have talked to me, Adam. You should have come to see me a long time ago and I could have helped, or at least I could have got you some help. Instead you bottled all this up until you actually thought this Vance guy was an option.' He keeps staring at me, his body shaking, waiting for me to explain something I don't think I will ever be able to.

'What if he gets in here?' I ask, looking around at the high walls and locked gates.

'Are you listening to anything I say?' Mike shouts, attracting attention from our fellow guests. There are a few other sun bathers, but far fewer than there would normally be at this time of year. The pool area always used to be packed, and I would always get annoyed at how close the sunbeds were to each other, even a whisper could be overheard three beds down. But on this holiday things were very different.

I nod as I sit up, tucking my legs under my body. I'm on the one bit of the bed which still has a glimmer of sunlight on it, and I'm staring up at Mike. I look up his body, past his shorts and up to his chest; I have to squint through my sunglasses to be able to see him properly. He's still wearing a T-shirt despite the heat, a clear signal that he hasn't found settling into an afternoon of sunbathing as easy as I have. I look up at his face. His eyes are hidden by his black shades but I can still see lines of anguish painted across his skin.

I don't manage to answer before he walks away, shaking his head. He turns back and stares at me for a moment, before taking a step back towards me. 'The hotel has increased security, at my request, and we have moved rooms, which was my idea. They have hidden our details in the safe and kept our original room, which I'm still paying for, empty. I think you'll agree I have done my bit.'

'Where are you going then?' I ask, already missing him, already feeling vulnerable. I know that if I don't have Mike then I only have myself, and I know how quickly I will revert back to the helpless shadow that I allowed myself to become.

He doesn't answer and disappears into the main hotel. The waiter who has been keeping an eye on me nods at him and then turns his attention back my way. I lie down again and start to get comfortable, wondering if I should apply more lotion. We've only got Mike's bottle of Factor 15, when 30 would normally be a minimum for me, but he probably packed so hastily that he didn't think about that. I look back towards the hotel, knowing how many other things he did think about, all because of me. I know that I don't deserve someone like Mike but I desperately need him. I stare at the waiter, who is standing to attention in his tight white shirt and black waistcoat. I want to shout over to him that he should focus all his energy on my friend, and that he should be the one to watch, because I can't lose him and if it comes to it I know I want to go first. It's a selfish thought, but I've always been like that, never wanting to be the one left behind, never the one left to suffer.

*****

I feel someone touching my leg, which jolts me back to life. I scream as I awaken, my mind telling me that it's Vance who has finally caught up with me. I look around and realise that I'm still in the hotel grounds; the water from the fountains is still trickling into the pool and the birds are still chirping high up in the trees. I quickly catch sight of Mike and feel thankful he is still here. I have no idea how long I slept, but judging by how low the sun is sitting in the sky, it must have been a couple of hours.

'It's nice that one of us got to relax,' he says. 'It's just a shame it's never me.'

I shuffle around until I find my T-shirt. It feels chilly now the sun has gone down. I think I felt the heat fading even while I was asleep, but I didn't wake up – my mind needed time to process everything that has happened. I look at Mike again; he is sitting down next to me, a flustered, almost scared look on his face. This new mask doesn't suit him; it's not something I want to see. He's my rock and I need him to stay that way, for both of our sakes.

'They have closed all the airports,' he says, starting to pack up his things around him. I watch as he puts sun lotion, sunglasses and earphones into his neat travel case. Everything has changed so quickly today. I wanted us to spend this afternoon together, doing what he likes most after a day of sightseeing.

'Did you use any of them?' I ask, looking at his things as he packs them up, wondering if maybe he came back to lay next to me for a while. Maybe we both spent the long afternoon sleeping, enjoying being in the same place at the same time for the first time in a long while.

He sets his case down and takes a deep breath. 'Do you understand anything that I'm telling you? I just told you that the airports are closed, and I don't just mean the one in Florence, or even Rome. I am saying all the airports in Italy, Spain and the UK – have been closed, which means there are no flights out of here and no way home.'

I stare back at him, wondering how things have managed to get even worse, especially since I have only been gone for an hour or two. I look over to see that the waiter has gone as well. He's been replaced by the pool attendant, who is tidying up the few used sunbeds, glancing over at us occasionally, his job no doubt easier this summer than any previously. I see that everyone else is gone and so I look up to the balconies, to the rooms of the richer people who get a premium pool view. Normally I would expect to see many people retiring to their rooms to enjoy the sun going down, but this evening I don't see anyone. I shake my head, realising how everything has changed. From the other times we have stayed here, I know that this should be about the time the chef moves to the outside BBQ area and starts to prepare the evening meal. I look over at the equipment, which is all covered by green plastic sheets, not likely to come out tonight or any time soon. I finally look back at Mike, who has clearly been watching everything I have been doing.

'Don't you have anything to say? Perhaps something that would help right now?'

'I thought you said we would be okay?'

He buries his head in his hands as he lets out this long moan. When he finally looks up I see how red his eyes are, how exhausted I have made him become. 'Fucking hell, Adam, don't pin all this shit on me. How was I supposed to guess what would happen? And besides, we came here because of you, because of what you did and because I thought you needed a break.' He stands up and walks away, still shouting and still blaming me for what has happened.

I feel conflicted: I know that a lot of this is my fault but I somehow still feel that all these bigger things happening around us cannot be of my doing. 'I don't know what's real anymore!' I shout back as I start to follow him, desperate not to be left alone. He keeps walking away as I run after him, my desperation pushing me forward and forcing me to latch onto him. 'I know that I've done wrong but everything is changing so much. I can't figure out any of this in my mind and I don't know what's happening. You have to help me, Mike, because no one else can.'

He finally stops and turns, shaking his head. 'Maybe I can help you and maybe I can't, but I've done enough and the truth is that I don't know who you are anymore or what I can do to bring you back.' He comes closer to me, close enough that he only needs to whisper. 'You made your choices and you kept making them for a long time, so perhaps the universe is granting you your wish now. I tried to help, but clearly I have failed, so perhaps this is the time for us to go our separate ways.'

I take hold of his shoulder, trying to keep him in this place, keeping my anchor connected to me in case I quietly sail away. Even as I shake my head, I realise it might be me who's weighing him down but I still don't want to let go. 'You can't leave me, not now.'

He stares back at me, seeming to genuinely give this some thought. I have pushed him so far and silently asked for so much over many years; I have never thanked him for any of it and certainly have not given anything in return. It's a truth that I only properly accept now as I realise just how much I have taken from him.

He gently lifts my hand off his body. 'We have two rooms so I think it's best we split up for tonight. I'll look at the options for getting home and you should do the same. Hopefully we will be able to figure something out before we get stuck here forever.'

I look at him but don't say what I want to, don't dare tell him that I would be quite happy being stuck here forever. 'What about visiting the Uffizi Gallery tomorrow?'

He shakes his head. 'I don't think there will be any more sightseeing now, and I think you've forgotten that you're a dead man walking.' He hands me a key to one of the rooms and then turns away. I watch as he walks back to the main hotel, making sure he thanks the pool-boy, who is still standing and watching the only people remaining in the garden. He disappears from sight as I stand on the grass, somewhere between the sunbed and the shadows, in this nowhere space between the aspiring tourist and the cold truth.

I slowly gather my things and eventually walk away, nodding to the pool-boy, who will now be all alone. I wonder if he will go home or if he is as stranded as the rest of us. I don't have the energy to ask and so I leave him as he wanders around the garden, clearly taking his time to tidy up the last two sunbeds. These are the last of his jobs for today; what tomorrow will bring is still uncertain. I walk through the hotel and see that a crowd of fellow guests have gathered in the bar area. I watch them for a while and notice that they're not drinking, not celebrating anything. There are many nationalities present, many languages being spoken. I leave them and go to the lift that's just down the hall, trying to pick out words that I understand from the conversation; I catch snatches, mainly of people asking what will happen next and how will they get home.

Only when the lift arrives and I step into the compartment do I look down at the key in my hand. I look at the number and then up to the sign that says which floor the room is on. I press the button and the lift starts moving. I desperately try to figure things out, but realise that I have no idea if this is the key for the old room or the new one. I have paid little attention to what has happened for so long that it's almost like I have conditioned my brain to ignore everything around me. I have wasted so much of everything that I wonder if perhaps the best thing to do would be to start all over again. Maybe it makes sense to hand over this life to someone else; perhaps I should just quietly check out and let the next person enjoy it.

The lift door opens and I slowly walk along the quiet corridor, taking time to stop at the odd painting. The décor has always been to my liking, golden frames surrounding old yet bold-coloured oil portraits. I have always been more mature than my actual age, always hurrying along to get things finished, constantly wanting to know more than we are told. This place has always been an escape from that thing I called life, and the things we do each day that we consider to be living.

I stand outside the room, checking a couple of times that the key fob matches the number on the door. I'm fairly sure that I have been in this room before but I can't be sure. I think the other room is a couple of floors away and I have no doubt that Mike is currently busy on the phone, trying to secure a flight out of here. I wonder why he is so desperate to get home and I'm sure that if he only gets one seat then he will leave me behind.

I want to call him, to tell him not to bother with me, that I am best left here, that this is the only kind of life I have ever truly enjoyed. Leave me to wander these forgotten corridors, let me walk through the cobbled streets under the shadow of the great Duomo. Let me admire it every day and meet all those who came before me to create this amazing place. I want to tell him not to worry, that I have found what really matters. In a better version of this life I would have been born in Italy, somewhere in the colourful Tuscan fields. I would have grown up in the bosom of farmers, but desperate to do more. I would have been brave back then, leaving my parents behind to work the fields as I travel to the place that all artists called home. In that life I would have walked the same path as Leonardo, Masaccio and Raphael. Perhaps in that previous life I would have been Michelangelo and maybe, just maybe, David would have been my creation. That wouldn't have been a wasted life because I would have filled it with immense energy and with every ounce of purpose I could find.

But it's not the life that I was given, I think, as I open the door and quietly step into the room. I don't run; I have no intention to fight what is inevitable and what I now accept is right. They say all roads lead to Rome, but I say this path that I have wandered for so long has led me here and I will waste no more time, energy or whatever my world is defined by.

He looks up only for a second, barely even acknowledging I'm here, but then gives me a small nod. A little smile appears before he turns his attention back to the equipment. He is holding a needle in his hand and squeezing a clear plastic pouch which is suspended on a thin, wiry stand. After a few moments a jet of liquid spurts out of the end; this seems to make him happy, as he hangs it on the small hook.

I walk over to the bed and lie down as I quietly prepare myself, and when he is finished he starts checking my body, nodding when he sees that I have taken my shoes off. He absent-mindedly starts his work, turning my left hand over and slapping the underside of my wrist. I have nothing else to say, nothing else to think and so I leave my body entirely in his care. I take one final look at him; he is calmly working, doing what he has been paid to do.

Finally he notices that I am looking at him. Perhaps he thinks I'm feeling curious, maybe that I'm impatient – I'm not sure myself. 'Okay,' he says. 'Shall we begin?'

Friday 19th August - London

Do not disturb

She bangs on the door and shouts his name but there is no reply. There's no movement through the window, no noise in the hallway. She opens the letter box so that she can shout his name again. 'Blake!' she calls, sounding much more desperate than she did a few minutes ago. 'Please, you have to let us in.'

It doesn't take long before she stops shouting and levels her head to the only opening, catching a scent from her new plug-in air freshener just near the door as she does so – perfect for welcoming the visitors she never seems to get. Fresh jasmine and water lily, if she remembers correctly, not that he would notice such a thing – it's not like it matters now anyway. She's desperate to hear something inside the flat, some sign that she isn't negotiating with thin air. He has to be in there, otherwise how would he have left and put the latch on?

She looks in again; this time she thinks that she sees a shadow, a small movement in one of the rooms. She starts listening again, desperate to figure things out. She needs to see him, believing that she will somehow be able to appeal to his limited senses; to overcome his stubborn streak and find an ounce of her reasonable Blake she fell for at school so long ago.

She keeps looking through that small slat and listens, but she still doesn't see or hear him. She sees the hall table, the gorgeous lamp, the vase she saved up for, the beautiful wallpaper she took weeks to pick – all the signs that her home is as she wanted it. Then, suddenly, she catches sight of his fabric Adidas wallet lying on the table. She knows he would never leave the house without it, even though she could guarantee it would always have less than a tenner inside.

'Blake!' she shouts, not caring who hears, now far past about worrying whether her neighbours are getting a good show. 'I know you're in there. I can see your wallet.'

'Are they with you?' he shouts back, his voice coming from the living room.

Her eyes widen as she listens, looking for any sign of movement.

'If they are still with you, then you can be sure they ain't coming back in.'

She takes a deep breath, swearing that this will be it. She will get in and when she does he will be leaving within the hour. This time she will overcome those few remaining physical, emotional and sexual boundaries. Nothing is clearer to her now, and nothing will change her mind. She risks losing it all, because of him and his simple, selfish view of the world.

'No more, Blake!' she shouts. 'This is my home and they are my guests, my work, and my livelihood!'

'Then I believe you have your answer,' he calls back. It's not even an aggressive reply and shows no sign of a full-blown argument. She imagines him sitting there, exactly where she left him, laughing to himself at the fact they are stuck outside.

'If you don't open this door then I'm calling the police!'

'Again?' he shouts. She imagines him smiling as he sits on the sofa, his hands on the controller, his mind absorbed in that game – the only thing that gives him some distraction from his pestering girlfriend. He'll be topless, wearing only his jogging pants, with beer cans spread all around him. She wonders which part of that picture will be the reason she gets kicked off the child-minding register – something she worked so hard to get on. Everything about him is entirely inappropriate for her chosen path in life. She knows this now; it has just taken her too long to accept it.

She stands up, grabbing her phone, contemplating that call to the police, vowing all the while that this will not go on any longer. Sure, they might break the door down, and they might remove Blake for her, but then he would be on the outside, whining and shouting. He would involve the whole street in his drama, and that would keep the kids up all night.

Only then does she think about the children. She looks down to her left, seeing them both standing still, silently watching her. They look up at her and she looks down at them. They've been watching the weird events unfold very quietly, looking confused, having only limited experience of the world to help them explain all this.

And then Poppy starts crying. She screams loudly, her blonde, frizzy hair matted and worn from a day of fruitless travelling, her eyes wrapped in big, red circles of uncertainty.

Hannah leans down. 'Oh, Poppy! I promise it will be okay. Please don't cry.' She tries to take hold of her, to offer whatever comfort she can muster, but Poppy pulls away. Hannah knows she's a runner and gets ready to give chase.

'He's a monster!' Poppy shouts.

Hannah wants to disagree but she knows she can't, not today. 'He's not a bad monster. He's just protecting our home and once he knows it's us then he will let us in, I promise.'

Poppy shakes her head. The excuse is so lame that it doesn't work even on a five year old.

Hannah gets back up, looking at the door, the window, searching for any possible way in. 'Noah, please help your sister,' she says, not knowing what else she can say. Her time and patience are both running out.

Noah doesn't move and instead he stares at Hannah. 'If he's not a monster, then why won't he let us in?' he says, his hands resting on his hips. He has got double the experience of life than little Poppy has, and although it's not much, he's using everything he's got.

Hannah leans down a little, but not too far: he is growing taller every day. 'Oh, sweetie, it's a game. He's just playing a game and it's gone a little too far, that's all.'

He stamps his feet, his arms flapping beside him. 'He's not playing a game and when I tell Mummy and Daddy what he's been doing they will be so angry at you!'

'Really?' she asks, standing back up, feeling something rising within her. 'If you're going to tell your parents then where are they?' she says and stares at him, wanting an answer. She needs to know this more than ever and finds herself willingly making this demand of these unlucky kids who are unfortunate enough to have been left with her.

'I don't know!' he screams, his face scrunched up for the hundredth time today. She looks at him as he shakes; his long fringe is pulled back which reveals even more of his angry face. She remembers a time when she was little, when her grandmother would tell her not to frown, as if she did, her skin would settle in that position. She wants to tell Noah this now but how can she when he is entitled to be very angry, especially with her?

She kneels down on one leg, so that she can look up at Noah and across to Poppy, taking her time to see the whites of their eyes. 'If I knew where they are I would go around right now and let you tell them everything on me, I really would. But we can't, because they're not at home and they're not answering my calls.' She stops, just shy of declaring to a five- and a ten-year-old that their parents are missing, that they were due home three long days ago and that now she's running out of food and money, and her fuckwit boyfriend is doing nothing to help. When you then think about all the bad things that are happening, and how things are getting worse by the day, she thinks that maybe they should be told, that perhaps she shouldn't have to bear this burden alone.

Although she has all of these dark thoughts, she doesn't say anything, but only because Noah is now crying too. They both stand there in their own separate worlds, both sobbing. Poppy's long curly locks are shaking as she cries rhythmically; she is shouting that she wants only her mummy, ignoring everything Hannah has just said.

She turns away from them, partly to stop herself from crying, but mainly because she wants to vent all her frustration at just one person. She doesn't want to admit it but she has felt desperation lingering over them like a cloud for several days now. First the emails from their mum stopped, then the phone calls ceased, and at about the same time the amount of news of bad things happening abroad started to triple every hour. This desperate feeling, the feeling that control has all but gone, has by now started to sink in; she fears that something bad has happened and is still happening now.

She bangs the door one more time. 'Blake, please let us in!'

There is still no answer, so she waits as the children continue crying behind her. She waits for him to come to the door or for their parents to return home, whichever happens first.

Waiting. It's all she seems to be good for.

******

'Why won't you help me?' she asks, standing over him, a tea towel in her hand. She has finally got into her own home but she doesn't feel like she's got any further in dealing with all of the problems that have been thrown her way.

'Because they're not my fucking kids, are they?' he says, not actually looking at her. He moves his arms, sticks his tongue out and tenses his muscles as he frantically pushes buttons on the controller. 'And they ain't your kids, either. You do remember that, don't you?'

'They are my responsibility!' she shouts, demanding that he realise this, that someone take note of what an immense burden she has been left with. 'I'm their nanny, their child-minder, and I've been looking after them.'

'Yeah, for the odd day,' he says, finally looking up at her. 'What parents leave their kids with someone for over a week? You wanna ask for more money when you see them.'

'When I see them?' she asks and takes a deep breath. She remains standing over him, staring down at him as he plays his boy's game. She wants to ask if perhaps she should ask for more money so that he can spend more of it. She wants him to know she feels that there are three kids in here, and that the oldest is 22. She wants to ask when he's going to get a job, pay her some rent, contribute to the upkeep of this place and make her feel more than an intermittent lust for him. Deep down she knows that her longing for a reliable, life-long partner has been replaced with the shell of a man in front of her, but she doesn't know what to say, and so eventually she silently walks back into the kitchen.

'Bring me another beer,' he shouts. 'And when's dinner, 'cos I'm fucking starving!'

This proves to be one demand too many and she walks back into the room, deliberately standing in front of the television. Her television. The one that never shows her programmes. It comes as no surprise that he doesn't realise the issue, as he absently bends his body so that he can see the screen. Hannah moves to block his view again.

'Get out of the way!' he shouts, tutting and huffing.

She looks at him but continues to stand in the way, silently protesting about his complete absence of anything that doesn't interest him, coupled with her need to be listened to. She feels the tension grow between them, his face scrunching as he attempts to keep control of his game, her desperation finding new levels as she tries to get noticed.

Eventually he throws the controller across the room. 'Fucking great! I've just lost the level because of you!'

She moves closer, hoping her intervention has caught his attention but he puts a hand up to silence her. 'Sammy, you still there, bud?' he shouts into his microphone. 'You there?' He eventually stands up. 'Oh for fuck's sake, Hannah!'

'Now will you listen to me?' she says. 'Please, I need your help.'

'What?' he says; seeming shocked by the idea that anything could be more important than what he is going through.

She takes a deep breath and finally manages to make eye contact with him, although she is unsure how long it will last. 'If we can't find their parents and I can't go to the police, then I don't know what I'm going to do. They have already logged it and have said there is nothing they can do, so we have only one more option left.' She pauses to check if the connection between their eyes and their minds is still strong. 'We have to go to North London.'

He throws his hands up in the air, which is more or less the kind of response she expected. She knew this would be a tough sell, but as the days have ticked by and the hunt for their parents has dug up nothing, it has come to seem like the only option left. She prepares her sales pitch, her desperate plea for his help, but he's no longer looking at her.

'Yeah, Sammy, I'm still here,' he says, his attention gone. 'What happened?' he says, walking across the room to collect his controller. 'Fucking missus is what happened. She's having a benny, and yeah, it's all about those fucking kids.'

'They're in the next room,' she says, to the back of his head.

'Yeah, they're still around,' he says, then falls back onto the sofa – her sofa, which already has a sweat patch forming on it from all the easy days he has spent sitting in the same spot. And that's when it hits her; the future that is spread out before them. Fast forward two years and this scene will look exactly the same. He will have new pants but still no T-shirt – same arguments, same Sammy, same not listening. Fast forward five years and there is new wallpaper and probably a new console too. Same hard work from Hannah. Sammy got a job, found a life, realised he has to work for what he wants. It's now Levi. Slightly younger, the same age Blake was when she thinks he should have grown up. But Blake doesn't realise this, doesn't want to know, and so he's still exactly the same boy. He's gained a little weight – more of a burden – he really should wear a T-shirt now.

Fast forward ten years: Blake still wants to play all day but he's not allowed to now. He knows Hannah will shout a lot if he does. She doesn't want to nag but she has no choice, because if she doesn't moan then he won't move. The two kids she insisted that they had are their new burden and now she's properly weighing him down, except that he's lost his appeal.

The only thing he had ever had to offer was a decent body – his abs formed nicely but a brain never did. But there turned out to be nothing beneath them and now they're gone, covered by the ample layers from a decade of laziness. He can give her nothing but he knows that now, and so due to his inability to move on and her desperate love of their children they keep things stable, keep them safe.

She suddenly wakes up, snapping into real life. 'I don't want any of that,' she says.

'What the fuck are you talking about?' he says, gently but firmly pushing her bum until she's no longer blocking to his game. 'Totally lost it, Bruv,' he says.

She watches as he taps commands into the precious thing he is cradling in his hands, as the television – her television – makes various clicking noises behind her. 'Let's get going again, Sammy. This time she won't get in the way.'

She finally walks away, now determined to show the truth of his words.

'Hey!' he shouts, just before she reaches the kitchen.

She turns around, more from a natural courtesy than any actual curiosity. She immediately wishes she hadn't as she sees his joggers on the floor and his thick cock standing to attention. 'This will need sorting when you're done feeding them,' he says, as though he's doing her a favour, giving her a toy that she hasn't already had enough of.

'For God's sake, Blake, in the living room?'

He smiles. 'Sammy don't mind.'

She leaves, hearing him still laughing with his cyber-mate, or whatever he's called. 'Sure, Sammy doesn't mind,' she mutters. 'We'll see about that.'

*****

'Why won't you suck it?' he asks, whining like a little kid. 'You used to love sucking me off. Don't you remember? You'd do it anywhere and everywhere.' He's lying on the bed now, having finally lost his joggers but still not managed to take a shower.

'Maybe I've grown out of it,' Hannah says, keeping herself busy folding clothes. She sniffs the towels. She knows that they remain fairly unclean when washed by hand, but what choice does she have now that there is an energy suppression order in force throughout the neighbourhood? She looks down at him. 'Maybe I need more now.'

He looks up at her as he lies there, his legs spread apart. He strokes his balls and occasionally rubs his cock, keeping it hard, desperately trying to find new ways to keep her interested. She realises what this looks like; she has learnt all about this. They are now in a parent-child relationship and she's trapped firmly in the role of the bad girl with a sweetheart boyfriend from school. He hasn't changed; he's exactly as he has always been. Hannah won't accept that and so she is now trying to force him to be something he isn't, which he is actively rebelling against. It's clearly all her fault for ever expecting him to gain any emotional depth or maturity. When he finished school, he declared he would become a mechanic, a builder, a plumber. None of these jobs required him to remain at school, but as Blake is learning now, they did require further study, a lot of early starts and a significant amount of hard work.

When she started minding Poppy and Noah she thought that she would have these behavioural problems with Noah, as he was due to turn ten about six months into her time as the nanny for the Anderson family. It didn't worry her – it was just part of the challenge of looking after children. She had always known she would go into childcare and she imagined setting up her own child-minding business. She would have a few kids and a house, and then would slowly expand the business. It would be fine because the house would be big enough, with a large kitchen, big utility room and a separate games room. Her husband wouldn't mind either. He would be out working in the daytime, getting the tube to his busy banking job. He would leave early in the morning, safe in the knowledge that everything would be fine and that their children would also be cared for by Hannah.

Once her business had grown and he had been promoted a few times, they would get a bigger house with a plot of land on the side. By then he would be travelling to London by train, but the commute would be worth it, especially considering that they would be able to get a much bigger place outside of the capital and that this would mean better quality of life for the whole family.

She looks down at Blake and he looks up at her, his eyes pleading. He's still got hold of his cock, his fingers wrapped around the base. He jiggles it, slapping it onto his stomach, smiling at the noise it makes. She was never really meant to end up with him; at school, she just saw him as a bit of fun – entertaining his great cock together. They were both supposed to move on after that: his practical side and her childcare studies should have pulled them apart, and it wouldn't matter what kind of body her executive husband had, because it would be all about the bigger picture. She would always have the memory of Blake but that is all he was ever supposed to be. She sees now that where he is still throbbing for her, she has moved on and wants more, sees a different future.

She watches him, thinking that he's quite lucky that he has remained youthful. He was a slightly late developer at school – probably somewhere in the middle – his balls didn't drop early enough for him to be accepted by the coolest kids. Hannah was always happy about that because he never became a real tough guy, although he was never bright enough to be with the geeks. And look at the bright ones now – five years after leaving school they are the doing the best in life. At the ten year reunion they will be the ones turning up in Porsches, while the Blake's and Sammy's of the world will laugh about how those guys drink posh wines, go to yoga and would never cope down the proper local pub that real men go to.

He shakes it again. 'Oh, come on, babe. You know you love it!'

She looks at it, the simple bit of flesh, and she thinks about the sacrifice she has made and the life she really wanted. 'That isn't going to build me a house in Guildford, is it?' She walks towards the tiny en-suite, not caring about what his response is.

He quickly storms past her and slams the door; she feels the thin wall vibrate. 'I need a shit,' he shouts. 'Then you can suck it.'

She sits on the bed and thinks about the disrespect he shows to her and everything she has built. All those precious things that her inheritance went into making a reality, so she could have a better life until that cool city guy in the Porsche came along to woo her with tales of a better world. She wishes right now that she had stayed in the Andersons' home with the kids, but when their parents didn't return on time she didn't like being alone in that big house. She has watched the news enough recently to know she wanted to be at home. In her home. With a man to look after her.

She looks at the bathroom door and quickly realises how stupid that thought was. She hears what is spilling out of him, splashing into the bowl. He'll flush the toilet, if she's lucky, but he won't look around. He won't check the mess he's made. He will simply come back into the room and lie on the bed, his arse-crack stinking of shit and staining the sheets that she has just changed. He will never understand how much she has fought for what they now have; the shopping trips she made to see if her favourite things had gone on sale yet – her endless battle with the budget. She always knew what she wanted and would check, compare and wait, willing to compromise on nothing but her time. It's what her parents would have wanted, and what she has got so far would have made them proud.

Everything except for Blake, that is. 'What do you see in him?' they would ask. 'You'll need more than his legendary cock to keep you going,' her friends would say. It turned out to be quite true, but now she's stuck – intelligent enough to want more, stupid enough to have got herself trapped. And now she's got kids pinning her down as well, even if they aren't actually hers.

Those poor children are both scared and worried. Their parents somewhere in America – a trip they apparently couldn't avoid and one which has meant they have been added to the list of the many that are missing. They are now just a desperate memory in the minds of their helpless children and a hasty report filed with the police, who were able to offer little care or advice. 'Will the kids be okay with you?' the policeman had asked, already filing the paperwork away. In normal circumstances, they would have been referred to child services, and someone in authority would have come round within a day. She didn't even have any faith that what he had written would ever make its way into a computer database, let alone into the hands of someone relevant and obliged to intervene. There was too much happening: too much chaos – reports were being received of missing people everywhere, with little good news from anywhere.

Hannah knows that she is on her own and that something has to happen. Now she can either stay at home or go back to the Andersons' house to wait another day. She also had the third option, the only one that she hasn't really given much thought to, mainly because it is unlikely to do any good. Even though Mrs Anderson had written down their details she had repeatedly told Hannah it would be pointless. The police would be a better option, she had said. Look how that turned out, Hannah thought. She hadn't expected much, but had already tried the number and left messages. They are the grandparents we don't really speak to, Mrs Anderson had said. On his side of the family and always been a bit weird. Not interested in us and certainly never helpful.

They didn't see the children as their grandkids, apparently. It was his dad's fault, she had said, her eyes rolling as the story unfolded. Since he had remarried, both he and his new wife had agreed that she was never really going to be a dutiful mother or grandmother. Mrs

Anderson said that they never saw either of them, because his father had said that he had worked all his life for his two boys, and now he planned to see the world and achieve what he wanted. But since Mrs Anderson's parents were all the way in America she probably felt that it was wise to leave a family phone number. She probably thought it was more likely to be used if they died while they were away – something serious, something like what is happening now.

They were listed as "Mr. and Mrs. Grump (grandparents, apparently)".

Their entry was at the bottom of the page, after a couple of friends; almost an afterthought. She had tried the neighbours and these friends already but had got nothing but voicemails or permanently turned off mobiles. The ones she had managed to get hold of told her they had moved away, out of London, to somewhere safe in the country. 'It's coming your way,' they would say. 'Get out whilst you can.'

Hannah couldn't have agreed more, but she felt such a loyalty to the kids, at least enough that she was determined to get them to their family, whether they were welcoming or not. She had done her duty, been the diligent carer, but now she had to think about the future.

Blake walks out of the bathroom. 'Needed that,' he says, giving her a kiss on the cheek. 'And I even cleaned up because I know that bugs you.' He pulls himself over Hannah, knocking her head as he moves, and then lies down beside her. 'See, I can be an awesome boyfriend when you need me to be.'

She looks at him as she takes a deep breath. 'That's hardly awesome. Once past infancy it's assumed that you are capable of cleaning up after yourself.'

He frowns; she knows he is getting annoyed. It's the way he always behaves when she nags too much. He picks up the remote and looks at the television, still playing with his cock. His subconscious is teasing it, doing what she has obviously failed to do.

She picks this as her moment and curls up closer to him, stroking his chest. 'Since you're in the mood to be a dutiful boyfriend, could you perhaps do one more thing?'

He looks at her, his eyes unmoving, his mind unwilling to commit to anything that will take him away from the final level with Sammy tomorrow. 'I'm not watching those kids. I'm not bloody doing it. I've told you to drop them at the cop shop and let's both move on.'

'I've said many times that you don't have to mind the kids, but this *is* about them.'

He throws the remote down, his manhood shrinking by the second. 'Oh, for fuck's sake.'

Hannah grabs his arm, squeezing it tight. 'But it's about moving them on. The police can't help as there's too much going on but I have another solution.'

'And it involves me, doesn't it?'

She takes a deep breath, ready for the inevitable sulk. 'You and a car. Neil's car, if you can get it?'

'You want me to go all the way to Croydon? I need a lie-in tomorrow.'

'Blake, every day is a lie-in for you.'

He shakes his head. 'Neil ain't gonna just lend me his car without some cash.'

She nods; that's the least of her worries. 'It's fine, I'll pay.'

'And what you gonna do, anyway?' he asks, his head already shaking, his mind already denying the possibility that he might need to leave this flat tomorrow.

She figures that she needs to explain her plan in a way that will mean as little work for him as possible. She wonders how she can possibly sell him on the idea of driving to North London to track down these kid's disinterested grandparents, who will likely turn them away anyway, making it a wasted trip. Her thoughts turn to the help she needs, to Blake: he was almost sweet at school, but now he's a total waste of space. Perhaps she is wrong: perhaps he was never that nice and she only imagined it. Either way, she knows he will eventually help but he won't ever come quietly.

*****

'I'm getting really sick of this now,' he says, taking his eyes off the road for just a second so he can look at her properly. 'We've been driving for hours.'

She sighs, knowing this was a big mistake the moment he arrived with his brother's car. He has given her nothing but grief since then: for taking too long, for the kids not being ready, and for the state of the traffic. It was all her fault – all of it – including the shit that was going on in Central London. Protests were happening everywhere about the lack of information from the government, and whenever the police intervened, riots ensued, then killings, followed by more protests.

She wonders if the reason for his latest outburst was that he hated asking someone else for the use of a car, that perhaps he was embarrassed to ask his brother who was three years younger. Maybe it makes him think about how little he has achieved with his life and perhaps surfaces some vague feelings of shame? And then Hannah wonders if perhaps she is expecting a little too much from Blake, considering his obviously limited depth.

'I knew this would be a waste of time,' he says, this time looking only forward.

'Blake,' she says, as calmly as she can, giving him time to register whatever she is about to say. 'Please try to remember that the kids are in the car and we have only been driving for 2 hours. It's really not that bad, so please stop moaning about something you agreed to do for your girlfriend who you live with and share a bed with every night.'

He shakes his head, silently refusing to accept any responsibility for the burden she has rested at his doorway. 'Well, just you remember that Neil needs the car back by five and the traffic will be just as shit on the way back. You've seen how many roadblocks there were just getting here and we've got to go back through them all again.'

He continues to moan and Hannah continues to ignore him. She has said her bit; made her plea and found it has had no effect. She turns and pats both kids on the knee, one at a time. Poppy looks back at her with a longing stare, showing her need for only her mum. She looks set to burst into tears at any moment and Hannah knows this continual need to be validated and reassured is never going to go away.

Noah pushes Hannah's hand off his knee. 'I don't need *your* help. I'm fine as I am.'

As much as she knows that isn't true it almost makes her feel better; she has one less thing to worry about. Her whole week has been filled with anxiety and confusion and it doesn't seem likely to stop now. A cloud of doom has been hanging above all of London, but Hannah feels it's affecting her more than anyone else. She doubts this trip will make any difference – after all, the grandparents might not even be there. She doubts the kids will ever see their parents again, not with everything that is going on. All she knows is that she dreads the prospect of looking after these kids forever, never knowing where their parents are.

These thoughts instantly make her feel guilty and she turns around to tell them both that it will be okay, that she will find their grandparents and it will be good to be with their real family again. She doesn't wait for an answer, expecting only more tears from Poppy, and Noah insisting that she is their real family now. She continues her story, telling them both that if, for whatever reason, it doesn't work out then they can stay with her until she finds their parents. It's all she can think to say to stop guilt from setting in, and Blake immediately huffs in response.

Noah leans forward, tugging at his seat belt so he can get closer to the front. 'Poppy has never met them and I have only met them once. They don't want us, Mummy said so.'

Hannah turns around, fussing over him and gently pushing him backwards. 'Well, times have changed and no one saw any of this happening, but it will all be okay now.'

'Doubt it,' Noah says, folding his arms, giving her a frown far beyond his years.

'It had better be,' Blake mutters, looking only at Hannah.

The car is silent for a while and Hannah looks around the different streets, all of which are very long and lined with large, imposing houses. They are exactly as she had thought they would be, with well-maintained gardens and freshly painted fences. The few people she can see appear to be calm, as if life is continuing as normal, as if the prestige of living in St. John's Wood has granted them immunity from whatever is happening elsewhere in the world. Many of these houses survived a war, have seen bombings and recessions; some have now been converted into modern flats, while others are clearly still large family homes. She knows they all share one thing – the determination to survive this as well.

'Turn left,' the satnav says.

'Finally, we're really fucking here,' Blake says.

'Language,' Hannah says.

He ignores her and looks out the window, his right hand clenched around the top of the wheel. During the drive he had been masterly, clearly in control while weaving between the parked cars, through the narrow streets. Now he starts to make his way down this unknown street with ease, concentrating totally on the hunt for the right house. Hannah cannot help being struck by his confidence and the ability and passion he is now bringing to this task, however simple it is. He will start moaning in a minute, telling her to hurry up or that he can't find a parking space, but right now he's a better man than that – someone much closer to what she needs.

She takes a deep breath and imagines – just for a moment. She thinks of the future again, but this time it's different – this time she's with her dutiful husband in their big space cruiser, a vehicle which he handles with ease; they have their two children in the back, both of them obedient and trained. She wants this and now, looking at Blake's tilted cap covering his shaved black hair, his shoulders bobbing to the beats from the stereo, she remembers why she fell for him. She liked that he was a bit of a bad boy, his practicality and his ability to cope with things she doesn't find easy. She wonders if that was why she picked him.

Did she pick him? Despite the small amount of time that has passed, the memory of that decision is blurry. The one thing she does know is that his practical side has never really blossomed as much as she had hoped it would. He never used it to decorate her flat, much to her dad's dismay. He moved a few boxes, dumped his clothes on the bed and told her they would christen every room, but he failed to bring home the bacon or look after her dad's little girl in the way he should have. It was like he had fast forwarded from their teenage fling, and was now behaving as though they had been in a relationship for many years, as though their roles were now very clear, and it was totally acceptable for him to do very little.

'Result,' Blake announces. 'There's a parking space right outside.'

Hannah jolts forward, wondering if she is dreaming. She looks around, out of both windows, trying to figure which side he means. Her eyes flick between the numbers on the doors of the houses and the road until he pulls over to the left and reverses into the parking space with ease, leaning around as he does so. She catches him winking at the kids, giving a rare glimpse of his caring side, giving the impression, briefly, that he could be a good father. She sees a few exposed hairs at the top of his otherwise smooth chest. There is only a scattering but even so, they give hope that he can still become a man. She watches him carefully, his muscles tensed – her heartrate speeds up, just a little. He swings the car backwards, turning the wheel with precision as he looks around until he is happy with how they are parked. Her man got them here and took care of her and the kids, she thinks.

'Thank you,' she says, knowing how seldom she says these words to him.

He pulls his cap down. 'It's posh around here so you kids will do alright,' he says, looking at them in the rear-view mirror. He leans over and kisses Hannah gently on the cheek.

She feels a surge of emotion rising up within her, propelling her back to her school days, the memories of them sitting together in his old VW Polo. The first time she saw his car he had just done it up and made it his own. She remembers she had just got her A-Level results when he took her for that first drive. It was the first time they made love properly, on the back seat. It wasn't a quick, demanding blow job but proper and passionate love-making. She thinks it might have been that day that she chose him, and now she has been given a welcome, though rare reminder of what she had felt back then.

He blows air behind her ear, just where he knows she likes it. 'Dump the kids and we'll have time for a quick drive in the country before I drop the car back at Neil's. We can go back to our old haunts, relive those good times.'

She leans back, staring at him, wondering what is going through his mind. She wonders how he can forget the curfew, the darkness, the grid switch-off and the kids in the back seat. 'It might not be that simple. You realise that, don't you?'

He shakes his head, still smiling. 'You will make it simple; I know you will. See you around, you crazy kids.'

'You're not coming in?'

He quickly shakes his head. 'They're not my responsibility. I've done my bit.'

She reaches for the door, shaking her head, but knowing how easily his limits are reached. 'I won't be long,' she says, not wanting to push him too far, not wanting to make him so angry that he does something stupid.

She hears Noah lean forward, his thin coat squeaking as he moves. 'They won't want us. No one wants us.'

Poppy takes this opportunity to start crying again.

'Now, that's not true. I promised you both that if they cannot take you then you will come back with us.'

'*He* doesn't want us,' Noah says, his tiny finger outstretched and aimed at Blake.

She catches Blake looking back at him in the rear-view mirror. 'He's a clever kid.'

'Let's go, both of you,' Hannah says, moving out of the car. 'Don't go anywhere,' she says, looking at Blake who has already pulled out his handheld console, the portable extension to his regular mind numbing. She wonders what is so thrilling about it and why he wants to escape reality so often, but she knows she will never get an answer she understands.

He catches her watching him and smiles. 'We got two hours battery on this thing and I'll need some of that for the journey back on the bus from Neil's.'

'Come on, you two,' she says, shaking her head and backing out of the car.

'Just saying!' he shouts, not looking up, already absorbed in his favourite world.

She rushes around the car, making Noah wait on the pavement as she gets Poppy out of the road side, then escorting her to safety on her first new step of many in her young life. She tries not to look at the house but in the end she can't help herself, and it's then that she notices a curtain twitching. She checks one more time that it's the right place. She can't see a street name but the number is right, and if Blake has indeed been able to find the right place then they have struck lucky. The red bricks are dark and aged but still immaculately maintained. The white brick trim looks fresh and the gate that's central to the large porch has been touched up recently. All these people were probably getting ready for summer when things started happening; making sure everything was perfect for BBQs and dinner parties, as the chaos made this a different summer to all the others. The lawn on either side of the path is immaculately trimmed and the plants are well looked after, all signs that the good life wants to endure.

She sees another curtain move, this time downstairs in a large bay window that she imagines opens onto the dining room, or perhaps the first reception room. It's everything she hopes that one day she will have.

The gate squeaks open; it's almost as if the sound was included in the design. She looks back once more to see that Blake is still engrossed in his game; he could be almost anywhere – a teenager who has never had to grow up. She leads the children up the garden path, towards the big wooden door. Hannah wastes no time and presses the button as soon as they reach the door, since the occupants clearly already know she is here and must surely recognise the children.

She doesn't wait long before pressing it again. She is very keen to meet them, desperate to accelerate the inevitable rejection, with thoughts running through her mind of leaving the kids at the door and running to the car. After all, she thinks, this is a burden for the family to bear. She was only paid for a week's work and now she has all this responsibility for nothing in return. It's not fair, she thinks. What about me, she asks herself. Considering whatever is happening right now, she has many worries already – leaving these children with some rich family really shouldn't be one of them.

If she just slammed the gate shut, Blake would happily start the car and she would have a precious head-start on Noah. It wouldn't take much for Blake to speed off; he would happily tell her that she has done the right thing. He will help her numb any guilt she feels, and his inability to see that there might be anything wrong about it will help her to forget. She needs to focus on her needs – that's the right thing to do.

But then she starts to worry that they aren't the right family, or that she has got the address mixed up, or that Blake has driven down the wrong street. She knows that she could find another hundred reasons why she cannot leave them and so she presses the bell one more time, pushing those bad thoughts out of the way. She looks down and smiles. 'It's going to be okay,' she says, holding her finger on the bell.

*****

'It's not like we don't want them, she says, perched on an armchair. 'It's just not a convenient time right now.'

Hannah looks at her and although she has nothing to say back, at least she knows she was right: the window did indeed lead into a large reception room and a world of luxury. She wants to call it the living room, but thinks she might somehow be insulting it by doing so and she doesn't think it's the only one – it's just the first and only one they have been allowed into. She wasn't able to see into any other rooms when the front door was finally opened and they were allowed in. It wasn't a particularly welcoming greeting but Hannah was just pleased that it was them. Agnes and Simon barely managed a smile between them but they were family nevertheless. She didn't ask if their name was really Grump, she just presented the children to them, like prize trophies they never wanted, never asked for.

Agnes took her time to look them up and down, to ask a hundred times why they were here and where their parents were. Only after Hannah forced her way in, pushing Noah over the threshold of the large step, did this woman finally give in.

'Are you listening?' Agnes asks, leaning forward. 'I was just saying that this is not really a good time and perhaps you should keep them, just until Karen and Alistair get back. I'm sure it won't be long now.' She smiles, showing off a row of perfectly white teeth. Hannah wants to ask if they have been whitened or if they are dentures; she wonders at what age people usually get them fitted. Agnes looks too young to have false teeth; she looks as though she is at a point where retirement is still not overdue, although it would be welcome. Her grey hair is immaculate, her green blouse a perfect fit, albeit not a shade that is fashionable any more. 'I even hear that they have temporarily re-opened Heathrow airport so that's got to be a good sign.'

Hannah takes a deep breath, brushing back her fringe, desperate for Agnes to see the bags under her young eyes and the lines that have appeared from nowhere in a matter of days. She needs her to understand a very different view of how things are going. 'They didn't fly out of Heathrow, and besides we have to face the fact that they might not come back at all and that means you need to face this with me.'

Agnes doesn't say anything, but looks around, no doubt hoping that her husband will appear and get her out of this mess.

Hannah takes the chance to look through the windows to the large doors that open into the dining room, where the kids and Blake now are. She's pleased that she managed to get Blake inside, even if he is still playing his little boy's game.

Agnes leans forward and touches Hannah's leg. 'Little one, they are both very resourceful adults and I'm quite sure they will find their way back soon. I do believe you can fly out of one London airport and back into another. Well, at least you can as a gold member, other classes I'm really not sure about.'

'I know that!' Hannah shouts and then stands up. 'I'm not that stupid.'

Agnes sits back and brushes her skirt, trying to remove fluff that isn't there, picking at anything she thinks doesn't belong. 'Oh, well, I'm sure you're not,' she says, staring over at Blake. 'It's just that you and your partner don't seem too used to flying, that's all. I know there are those cheaper airlines now, so I assumed their rules are probably a little different.'

'Whatever you think,' Hannah says, now pacing around the living room, or whatever it is. She stands on the rug, feeling how cushioned it is, wanting to ask Agnes where she got it but knowing that there will probably never be a right time to do that. She knows it's expensive – she almost definitely didn't pick it up in a sale. 'I don't care about flights, what I care about is when they will be back. And don't you think that if Karen and Alistair were able to fly then they would have been back by now? Or, if they could make contact, don't you think they would call to check their children are okay, either with you or me? I mean, have you not heard anything and are you not a bit worried?'

Agnes sits still and runs her fingers through her hair. She stares downwards, no doubt looking for any sign of dirt on the rug, but she doesn't seem to be giving the question real thought. After taking what seems like minutes to think of an answer that should take less than a second, Agnes sort of shrugs her shoulders. She should be able to offer more but she can't seem to find any words to put it in context.

Hannah watches in astonishment, feeling the tears build in her eyes as the wave of confusion somehow lifts. She has been exposed to the true horror of real families, and how having the same name and the same blood, can sometimes do nothing to keep them together.

Agnes eventually holds out her hands. 'You really do look like you are judging me so perhaps you need to ask the father, the one who is actually related to these children. You see, I'm not actually family and so I really have very little interest.'

Hannah steps off the thick padding to get closer to Agnes, and as she does she sees that her grey eyes are genuinely lacking in any emotion. 'Those two children have lost their parents. You're a woman, a human being, but you say that you have "very little interest"?'

Agnes stands up, pointing a finger at Hannah. 'Now, you can judge me all you like but I have children from my previous marriage. Simon and I both fell in love at the start of our second lives and since we had already raised our own children we both decided we were going to start afresh together.' She suddenly grabs hold of Hannah's blouse and starts leading her to the door. 'Life is about us now and I won't have you coming in here and railroading our happy retirement. There has been enough of that happening lately and we really do have far more pressing things to be doing right now. They chose to fly at a very strange time and now they are living with the consequences. I'm sure you understand.'

Hannah grips both sides of the doorframe, anchoring herself in position. 'No, I really don't understand. I want to speak to their grandfather, to Simon, your dear husband, who disappeared the moment we arrived.'

Agnes shakes her head, looking at Hannah's face and then at her fingers. They look ripe for picking off the frame, sending her flying to the floor. 'Look, he feels the same, so it's time you were on your way.' She suddenly grabs Hannah's hands, trying to pull them away from the doorframe.

They both struggle, both trying to say their bit while also outwitting the other, looking for any chance to win, any chance to physically injure the other without starting a proper fight. Just as Hannah contemplates head-butting this woman who is more than double her age, she hears a door open in the hallway and sees Simon walking in. At first she thinks this must be part of some plot; that he has been listening at the door, letting his wife do his dirty work. She soon realises he has no clue what is happening: he is walking towards them, a tea towel in his hands, talking absently. 'Sorry for taking so long but it was worth it, the rear windows and back door are now completely sealed. Nothing will be getting through those buggers.'

He eventually looks up to see Hannah and his wife at the doorway to the living room, still in their standoff poses. 'Agnes, is everything okay?' He stares at them both. His eyes look weathered but still young. The tissue around them looks healthy, and there are no bags: he obviously gets plenty of sleep.

Agnes lets go of Hannah and steps away first. 'Well, I was just saying that perhaps they should be leaving. After all, we have the Higgins and Laithwates coming around shortly to discuss the new security precautions across the street.'

Simon holds out his hands, pushing both of them back into the living room. 'Well, let's not be hasty: we need to check everything is okay first.'

Agnes moves closer to him, staring at Hannah as she grabs his arm. 'You know we don't have time. We had two choices and we chose to stay, which means we have to take the precautions that were advised to us.'

Hannah moves towards them. She can hear everything clearly, even the changes in Agnes's tone as she speaks. 'What's going on?' she asks, only a step away from them.

Simon ushers both of them towards the sofas, gently pulling Agnes off his arm and giving her a kiss on the cheek. 'I'm sure it's nothing to worry about, but as you can imagine with everything going on people are trying to make sure they are safe. We had a choice: to stay or be evacuated and a few of us, far fewer than I expected, have elected to stay in our homes.'

'Evacuation?' Hannah asks, sitting down without being asked. 'I didn't know anything about an evacuation.'

Agnes stays standing, her arms folded. 'Perhaps this is a lesson about the class system for you after all, young lady.'

Hannah stands back up, ready to show Agnes what she really knows about the class system, thinking perhaps she'll start her own little London riot, right here in this living room, or whatever it is.

Simon puts his arms out, taking a deep breath and trying to catch the eyes of both these women. Eventually he manages to usher Agnes to the door. 'Why don't you rustle us up some tea and check if the children need some juice.'

She looks at him, her eyes wide, her shoulders shrugging, making her thoughts clear about his deviation from the big plan very clear. 'We don't have time for this. They said to be locked down for when the energy curfew commences. We have talked all week about this.'

'We have time,' he says, calmly, giving Hannah hope that he can perhaps be reasoned with, that his moral compass will show him the right way.

'I'm sorry,' he says to Hannah, as he watches Agnes close the door. 'She gets a little panicked but, as you can imagine, it has been a tough couple of weeks.' He looks around the room and then gestures towards the suitcases in the corner with his head. 'We were supposed to be in the Maldives right now but with everything going on we were advised not to travel. We have left them packed, as the army have said they might consider a forced evacuation, and I'm sure you can already imagine how that would go down with Agnes.'

Hannah doesn't laugh, can't comment and hasn't heard anything about any evacuation where she lives. 'And I don't suppose you thought for one minute about your children, grandchildren or anyone else, whilst you have been busy debating how you would feel about getting an army airlift out of your little palace?'

He frowns and then shakes his head. 'None of us asked for this. Not you, not me and not my son or daughter-in-law. They chose to go to America at the worst time and I'm surprised, but I guess even a week ago things weren't as bad as they are now.'

Hannah nods, unable to disagree, and stares into space. 'They're saying that virtually the whole planet is affected.'

He nods back, offering the tiniest of smiles, the smallest bit of empathy. 'That's what they are saying. I wish I knew more, I really do.'

'But why would they choose to go at such a time? I still don't understand.'

'They had their reasons and I imagine it revolves around money, or at least wealth, like everything always does.' He looks around the room, catching sight of all the things Hannah has already admired. 'Many people will do whatever they can to preserve their way of life. Some will fight and others will use money to give them power. One thing for sure is that Karen's parents were not short of a few precious heirlooms.'

'They left their children to fly across the world to collect valuables?'

'Those valuables might help them to survive in the months and years to come. Maybe they went to get her parents and bring them back over. Whatever their reason, they deemed it important enough that they decided to travel without the kids, but the fact that they did leave them means they *are* coming back.'

Hannah leans forward, practically at the edge of her seat, the answer falling off her tongue. 'When they come back you could pool your resources together so that you would have more power, and you could—'

He holds up a hand. 'We will do no such thing, young lady. They clearly planned to come back and that's why they left their kids with you. The best option open to you is to return home and wait for them.'

Hannah stares at him, waiting for something, desperately needing more. 'You really don't care, do you? Your grandchildren are next door and you've barely paid them any attention. All you've done is get them some fucking juice!'

He suddenly stands up, towering over her. 'I have already raised my children and done my bit. I worked hard to put them through good schools, ensure they attended solid universities, and I paid more than my fair share for an extremely extravagant wedding.'

'Oh, poor you,' Hannah says, looking over at the pair of large suitcases.

'But I did all of that. I stayed in a loveless marriage until I was 55 – constantly being nagged not to leave, not to break us up and always to do what is right for our children. You get less for life!'

Agnes walks back in, a tray in her hand – tea in mugs, no biscuits. Hannah instantly knows not everyone gets treated this poorly. 'You really do get less for life,' Agnes says.

Simon rests back down in the seat and takes a deep breath. 'We both did our time and now our lives have changed – for the better, I must add.'

Agnes hands her a mug. 'I took the liberty of adding milk and sugar.'

'It will clearly speed up my departure,' Hannah says, thinking of spilling it all on that nice rug just to see what reaction it gets from these two.

Agnes moves closer, staring at her, showing she is ready for their next round. 'Look, we have a different set of priorities now and people shouldn't judge us on our lifestyle choice.' She sits on Simon's lap and kisses him, a proper kiss that goes deep beyond the lips, something Hannah thought was reserved only for the young. It is the kind of kiss that she knows she should be experiencing on a regular basis, but seldom does. When they are finished she looks back at Hannah. 'We each had very good jobs and when our children were still with us, we worked hard to give them everything we could.'

'And settlement payments when we moved on,' Simon says.

'We really have done our bit and will do no more,' Agnes says.

Hannah sets her tea down. 'So that's it? You don't care what happens to your grandchildren?'

They both shake their heads in unison as Simon speaks for them: 'I'm sorry, but we don't see them as our children anymore, and we certainly don't see those things next door as our responsibility any more than we would a homeless person. We made this clear when we divided up the family.'

'They're only children!' Hannah shouts. 'You would see them out on the street?'

'What can we do?' he says, looking to Agnes and then to Hannah. 'This neighbourhood is already at risk and you know we are planning to stay here to defend our home.'

'And perhaps even our lives,' Agnes says, finding a tissue from somewhere in the depths of her sleeve and dabbing her dry eyes. 'We built this home as a symbol of our new and exciting life together and now look at what is happening.'

Simon takes hold of his wife, his true companion and lover. Despite hating them for their open lack of humanity, Hannah can tell they were meant to be together, with everything that happened in the decades before their meeting just destiny's silly games. If only they had met earlier and not settled down so early in life, they could have had many wonderful years together – perhaps their whole adult life. They could have had children together, developed their careers together and travelled the world as one, enjoying their bodies in their prime. Hannah sees their past mistakes, as much through her own choices as theirs.

Agnes looks at Hannah, her mind seemingly focused. 'We really do have our own problems and we asked not to be disturbed.'

'So you really don't consider that you have any commitment to those children in there?'

They both look at each other and shake their heads.

'We have both started new lives,' he says.

'We made a commitment to each other to build this new life,' she says. 'We even had my dog put down.'

They quickly embrace as one, wrapping their arms around each other, as Agnes's eyes finally show a liquid glint. 'Nothing from before carried through into our new life.'

Agnes suddenly stands up. 'I wish you'd never given them the address.'

Simon nods, then takes a white envelope from his back pocket and pushes it towards Hannah. 'Here is £1,000. Use it to look after them until Alastair and Karen return, which I'm sure won't be long now.'

Hannah keeps her hands down, refusing to take anything from them that will lead to this meeting ending. 'Let us stay here, please.'

He shakes his head. 'You and your boyfriend will be fine. You are young and far more likely to survive, as long as you adapt to the situation and keep your wits about you.'

Now it's Hannah's turn to shake her head, to share a secret or two of her own. 'He doesn't want them,' she whispers, looking over at the door.

Simon takes a deep breath and stares at Hannah, twisting the ring on his finger. 'Well, then, it's lucky they have you.'

'No,' she says, shaking her head and edging towards them, desperate for their help, hopeful for their understanding when her own parents are so far away. 'Please, help me. I'm begging you.'

He steps away from her, still holding out the envelope, but Hannah keeps her hands held by her sides. 'I need more than money.'

He forces it into her hands and then lets go, no longer willing to argue. The scrunched-up envelope falls to the floor. She looks at it and then up at him, still unable to believe what she has had to witness. 'I can't do this,' she says.

Simon gives her a stern look, as though he's a parent telling a child that their first day at school will be fine, that the fear and anxiety will ultimately pass. 'You can and you will.'

Agnes starts fidgeting, looking at the door and then over at Hannah. Her body is shaking now. 'Make them leave, Simon!' she shouts. 'I don't want them here and I don't want any of this. It's not the life we agreed to and I want you to make them leave us alone!'

Hannah looks over into the other room and sees two small shadows against the glass doors, and is immediately struck by the absence of a bigger shadow that she so longed to spot watching over them.

'There's enough hell out there without letting hell in here too, so make them leave!' Agnes shouts, before rushing to those doors, frantically pulling them open. 'Get out! It's time to leave! We don't want any of you here!'

'Calm down, Grandma,' Blake says. He is still casually sitting down, unwilling to be either a help or a hindrance.

It is Noah who steps forward, his finger pointed towards Agnes. 'You've never wanted us and you're the most horrible grandma in the world!'

'I'm not your bloody grandma!' she hisses, with a hand raised up.

Poppy starts crying and runs towards Noah, but he doesn't seem to want back down. He faces the horror in front of him, full of new-found anger after his weeks of neglect.

Simon moves towards Agnes and grabs her arms, telling her to relax and that all of this will go away, that all these people will leave. He tries to calm her down, to silence everyone, as the voices, screams and cries of a very lost family echo throughout the room.

Blake walks past all of them, snaking his way around the ongoing feud. Time stands still for a moment as he makes his way towards Hannah, the only one who is silent, mesmerised by what she is seeing, witnessing the true horror of what a reconditioned human mind is capable of.

'They are only children,' she says, still looking at them. 'Any adult's instinctive reaction would be to protect them, especially now.'

'Let's go, now,' Blake whispers in her ear, unwilling to debate anything he has heard. 'While they're distracted we need to sneak out and get into the car. By the time they realise we have gone, we will be speeding down the road to freedom.'

Hannah immediately shakes her head.

'Look, I've heard all the shit that was being said between you and the Grandparents and I've been watching the news. There have been more killings and more random shit going on, especially in London. We have to look after ourselves so I say we get to Neil's and grab him and Arianna. Then the four of us fuck off out of London for a while. We also need to get to a bank and get out as much cash as we can.'

Hannah takes her eyes off the fight, looking away from the crazy woman being held back by her husband, and the boy now hitting the monster before him. It would be a scene from some family drama if it wasn't happening against the backdrop of a floor-to-ceiling mahogany stand, the wood as polished as the ornaments it holds. 'As much as I can get?'

'Yeah,' he says and stares at her. 'You know I haven't got any and they didn't hand out any dole money this week.'

'So what are you bringing to this little trip?' she asks. 'The entertainment? And will that be electronic or penis-shaped?'

He scrunches up his face, shaking his head. 'Oh, what are you on about now?'

'Should I pack your bags for you too? Because, let's face it, you can't even bring your own car to the party.'

'Enough!' he hisses, looking over at the ongoing feud. He realises that they have attracted the attention of Simon, who is now looking over at them while leaning down and trying to talk some sense into little Noah, as well as holding back his frantic lover.

Hannah watches the battle she has created unfold before her eyes, listening to Simon try to explain his lifestyle choices to a ten-year-old.

'I did my job,' Simon says.

'These kids were just a job,' Blake whispers.

'I did more than I should have,' Simon says.

'You've done more than you should have,' Blake whispers.

Blake starts to pull Hannah away. 'They are with family, like it or not, and it's time they got into the real world and we fucked off. Do you think their parents are coming back, with all this shit going on? Where will these kids be safer? Stuck in your poky two-bedroom flat, or in this palace that's probably got the army watching its back.'

Hannah looks over at them as Blake's voice rings in her ear. 'But they won't be loved,' she finally says, looking at him, desperately wanting to hear him agree.

'It's now or never,' he says, already stepping away.

Hannah feels him leave, his breath no longer tickling her skin. She is trying so hard to sort all these things out in her mind, remembering the parents who have disappeared and the threats that have surfaced all around the world. What matters most is where these children will be safest, and clearly it will be here, because what these two can afford is safety and security, and surely that is more important than love. If they survive, they can look for love later; they will have a roof over their heads and each other for company.

'Okay,' Hannah says, pulling him back towards her. She turns to him out of a desperate need for reassurance but this is something which Blake cannot give her; he can only show her what is right for him. He pushes her towards the door.

A few seconds later they're in the hallway. Blake is at her back. 'Faster!' he shouts.

'Where are you going?' she hears Simon shout over Poppy's crying and Noah calling out her name.

She says nothing, but grabs the door handle. It won't open.

'Bottom handle!' Blake shouts.

She nods, genuinely trying her best. Both her hands shake as she tries all the handles and locks, pulling the door and begging it to open. She knows they are coming and the thought scares her – especially if he is with them. Please, she thinks, any of them but Noah.

'For fuck's sake!' Blake shouts, pulling her out of the way. 'We are *not* staying here!' He tries the handles for himself; the seconds tick by slowly. She can't watch him anymore and she knows she must turn to face her enemy. She prays, desperate for him to get that door open and set them free, but he's doing no better than she did. They are both too slow. She takes a deep breath, ready to face Simon, hopeful that it's only him.

It is Noah that turns the corner first, just a second before. She sees his small body overshadowed by his reluctant grandfather. 'Hannah,' he says, tears streaming down his face. 'Where are you going?'

'Yes, Hannah, where are you going?' Simon asks, as he towers over the boy.

She can't say anything in return, doesn't know where to begin. She hears the door open, and sounds of celebration from Blake echoing across the hall. He pulls her backwards.

'You're taking them with you!' Simon shouts and lurches towards them.

She ignores him, knowing only one person truly matters right now. 'I'm sorry,' she mouths to Noah, with tears rolling down her cheeks.

Blake puts the keys in her hand. 'Fucking run!' he shouts, pushing her down the path.

Simon gives chase. She thinks about all the experience of life he has: his decades of festering bitterness, the few precious years he has spent living for himself – it's vast in comparison with Blake, the boy who has literally done nothing.

Hannah reaches the car first and throws herself into the passenger seat. She leans over and puts the keys in the ignition, her hands still shaking. She looks up to see that Blake and Simon are halfway down the path. The kids are running past them and towards the car. 'We're coming!' Poppy shouts, her small legs trying their best to get her to where she desperately wants to be.

And that's when Hannah does the unthinkable; the one action that undoes all the good work she has done. All those months of care, all those recent nights when they crawled into bed and she held them tight, they mean nothing now as she locks the doors.

It's a step too far. Noah starts banging on her window and Poppy stands in the road. No one thinks to help her; everyone is too occupied with their own needs to find the time to care. Hannah looks over to see Agnes watching from the door, her face full of shock. Her sense of shock is nothing compared to the boy's.

Hannah is about to open the door, to put them in the backseats and tell them to get down low so that Blake will not see them until they are miles from here, but she is quickly distracted, as she looks up to see Blake punch Simon on the nose. 'Blake!' she shouts, as he curls up his arm, cradling his wrist; the in-between boy never quite learnt to fight in school.

Despite this, he still hit him hard enough to make blood spurt from Simon's nose. He grabs his nose and blood spills through the gaps in his fingers. It's enough for Blake to make a run for it and leap over the gate.

He's too quick for Poppy. She tries to reach for him but when she fails she screams, then desperately looks around for someone to comfort her. This life isn't something she knows, not something she should ever have been expected to cope with.

Noah seems to have a better idea of what to do and starts to chase after Blake. Hannah watches him move around the car, then she realises Blake is now banging on the driver's window, his face up close to the glass.

'Let me in!' he shouts.

Hannah quickly unlocks the door, looking over at Simon who is now running down the path. Agnes is chasing after him with that dirty tea towel. She turns back around, feeling Blake leap into the car. His screams of 'fuck, fuck, fuck!' ring in her ears as he tries to start the car, leaving the door wide open.

She can hear the voice of the other boy as well; his whining, his begging. 'Please, Hannah!' Noah shouts, standing next to Blake. His little hands claw at the plastic seat as he tries to clamber into the car. She turns to see him: that blond fringe, those red eyes. 'Don't leave us!'

She wants to say something in return but she can't. The words won't come out and she somehow finds it easier to say nothing, to blame someone else. Maybe this is just how her life is now. Blake certainly won't object to leaving them. She looks at him as he gets the car started. Suddenly, he realises that the boy is there and moves to close the door. Blake pushes Noah away, forcing him to the floor and out of Hannah's view. She hears his cries, the screams of terror, but the slamming of the door quickly drowns them out and numbs her pain. She can't believe he has done that and will never believe what she has failed to do.

She jumps again, this time at Simon's angry face at her window.

He snorts blood over the glass. 'Open this door and take these children! I'll leave them in the street if I have to. At best they will be picked up by an army patrol. You cannot imagine the terrible things that could happen to them and remember it will be all your doing.'

'They are your grandchildren!' Hannah shouts back. 'Your family!'

He looks at her now, finding the whites of her eyes and smearing a crimson line down the window. 'I told you, blood doesn't matter to me, but will you be able to live with yourself?'

'I think we'll find a way,' Blake says, hitting the accelerator.

The car speeds away and Simon follows for a second, still banging the window, still shouting out what she has caused.

'What have I done?' she asks, looking at Blake.

'You've returned them to their family, that's what you've done,' he says, his driving erratic and his damaged hand resting on his knee. 'Bunch of fucking freaks, if you ask me.'

She turns to look out of the rear window, needing to see the horror that she has caused. She sees Poppy chasing them and Noah rushing to catch up with her, both of them in the middle of the road. Stop, look, and listen is a thing of the past now, a lesson not worth learning. When Poppy realises that she will never catch the car she stops. Noah soon reaches her and immediately wraps both his arms around his little sister.

Family take care of family, Hannah thinks. But that's when she turns to see them – the grandparents who didn't want to be disturbed. She sees Simon, those kids' flesh and blood, walking back to the house, being pulled by Agnes. She imagines her telling him to hurry, to rush back in and close all the curtains. Shut the gate behind you and maybe they will forget which house it is. They are only young, after all.

Hannah wants to say it; what she thinks. 'They're only young.'

'Bollocks,' Blake says.

She knows they can't fend for themselves and that the world is changing by the minute. Bad things are happening everywhere and no one deserves to be alone. She can't let it be them. She can't allow it to be her.

'Stop!' she shouts.

Blake shakes his head. 'What the fuck are you saying that for?'

'Stop now.'

'No fucking way.'

Hannah shakes her head. She knows is better than this and will not go along with the standards of those she shares her time with. She grabs his left hand, pulling one of his fingers back. 'Stop or I'll break it, and let's see you play your stupid games with two broken hands.'

'You silly cow!' he shouts, slamming on the brakes.

She lets go of him and the car stops. He takes it out of gear and then takes his time to pull up the handbrake. He looks ahead, only ever forward. 'All these years since we chose each other in school. It was fate, you know? And now you want to pick them over me.'

She shakes her head, thinking of that boy she fell in love with. The few facial hairs he had then have somehow turned into a decent beard; she remembers those beautiful blue eyes that once had such energy. That cap, always tilted to one side.

'I can't leave them,' she says. 'And I need you to be more than that boy I fell for in school. I need you to grow into the man I have always wanted, and I need you now more than ever.' She takes hold of his arm, gripping him in the same way that she has thousands of times before, but this time it feels so different, so desperate.

'I need you, Blake, and *we* have to do the right thing. We can get through this. I know we can.'

He turns to face her and she can just about recognise the old Blake. She picked him and he picked her; after that, neither of them was supposed to look back. She doesn't know if it was a big mistake, but she doesn't think she has the luxury of time Simon and Agnes had.

'Okay,' he says, actually nodding. 'I can't see you changing your mind on this.'

'Really?' she says, smiling, half-laughing and squeezing his arm tighter, just where a muscle bulges.

'Go get them.'

'Thank you,' she says, kissing him all over his face and neck. She leans back and laughs, then leaps out of the car and is soon running towards them. 'I'm so sorry!' she shouts, her mind full of excuses and her heart filled with new hope of a bright future. Both of them run to her, their faces smiling and their arms held out. She grabs them both, pulling them closer and shouting how sorry she is, knowing she will shout this for all eternity.

'I will never leave you again!' she promises, kissing Poppy and grabbing Noah. 'I'm so sorry but we will protect you, we really will.'

She walks them forward, still kissing their heads and reassuring them. 'Come on, let's get out of here.' She faces forward, not willing to look back, seeing no point in being rejected again.

That's when she sees a hand come out of the passenger door and pull it shut.

'Blake?' she shouts

The car starts to move forward, not stopping, and soon it's far away from her and the children. She imagines that Blake is shouting in the car, telling himself that she made her choice and these are the consequences. She feels around in her pocket and soon discovers that the keys to her flat are no longer where they should be.

'Blake!' she shouts again

'Where is he going? Noah asks, as Poppy starts to cry. She realises they both have a firm hold on her coat and that both of them are now looking up at her.

'I chose you, Blake,' she says to no one. 'We chose each other, didn't we?'

She watches until the car turns a corner, soon out of sight. She knows that this whole thing will soon be out of his mind. He will get his brother and together they will search her flat for anything valuable that they can take. She senses darkness is falling, and she knows that they will never get back there in time. She turns around and the children turn with her. She looks at the house, where Agnes and Simon should be.

She's just in time to see the door closing. She imagines several locks turning, and she soon notices movement in the first reception room. She sees Agnes at the window but she doesn't look out; instead, she removes the tie-backs, gently sorting them and carefully unfolding each layer of the curtain until she is ready to close it.

They stand in the road, and Hannah watches each light go out in the house. Agnes does the same thing again and again until the house is dark, quiet, and not to be disturbed.

She turns back around but Blake hasn't returned. She spots the envelope of notes on the ground and picks it up, suddenly seeing realising that it could have much value in the future.

'What will we do?' Noah asks.

She moves them along the path, keeping a tight hold on both of them. She looks at the other houses, but all their curtains are open and the lights are off. There is no movement and no one left. They wait for a while as the sun goes down; she counts how many lights come on and how many curtains are drawn. She only sees a scattering of lights across the entire street, maybe at three or four houses, and she wonders if maybe some of them are automatic. It's obvious that those who wanted to leave have already gone.

The streetlights don't come on: the energy curfew is just as strict up here. And as she looks around, she realises that she is now alone with her decision, and she notices how few cars there actually are on the street. In all the rush of the hunt earlier her mind painted a different picture of this leafy suburb she had always wanted to live in. She counts all those empty spaces now; there is ample parking, since so many people have fled to family members or to second homes. She thinks of the journey here, of Blake, and how he did it. He finally achieved something, eventually got them here against all those apparent odds. Maybe those odds weren't as she imagined, not as tough as he made out, that he can do things when he wants to. She thinks of him now – the boyfriend he could have become, the stretch to a father figure not as impossible as the thought – as she realises the power of a choice and the possibility of a decision. She sees everything now for what it truly is, as she realises that it really was very easy for Blake, after all.

Monday 22nd August – London

In all but the darkness

I think it all started when I watched this couple filling up the boot of their car. What was unusual is that they had only bought water. Bottles of every kind, all stacked neatly and with as little empty space as possible; it was like a game of life-and-death Tetris, only played by the prepared. Still or sparkling – I don't think it mattered. They were methodical and calm. You could easily have missed it, this small clue to the chaos that was yet to come. I remember standing still, in the middle of the underground car park, watching them as they emptied the contents of two shopping trolleys into the boot. They were so well-organised about it, that I wondered if perhaps they had already made many other trips weeks before the rest of us thought that might be a good idea.

She saw me, I remember that much. She looked over at me as her husband, partner or whatever he was closed the boot and rushed into the driver's seat. As she stared back I thought for a moment that she was going to help me, perhaps give me a subtle hint as to what she thought was coming. They were still young, or at least just into whatever middle aged means these days. Anyway, they were old enough to know something about our world and young enough to want to fight to stay in it. But she didn't say anything, just got into the car, and so I decided to move on, to do my shopping and to continue my usual weekend routine – shopping, eating, crying and forgetting.

That was weeks ago but I still think back to that moment every single day. I think of those two and I wonder where they are now; I wonder if they got away and if they have found sanctuary, wherever and whatever that could be. Most of all I wish I had been more than a silent observer. I wish I had asked, taken heed – seen the subtle signs that all is not well in this world.

The news has not been kind and I should know as I've been writing half of it. The reports were isolated at first: tales from across the ocean, accounts of horror and fear, stories of impossible things that could only be happening on another part of the planet. It's funny when you watch people's reactions on seeing the news. They talk openly about what it means to them, and only then they sometimes wonder if they can possibly help. Charitable donations normally do the trick; they pay and forget, somehow feeling that they have made a difference. The issue will surely be fixed by someone far more capable; someone in authority.

But it didn't happen like that this time. It just wasn't that easy to forget. When the strange occurrences started happening a lot closer to home, in France, for example, that's when people took notice and thought it might take something more than donating by text to fix this particular problem. As the stories continued and more tales were being told face-to-face, people started to move from denial to open shock, as the truth quickly unfolded that all these bad things were actually happening. Whatever you read in the newspaper or see on the news, it never quite lives up to the real thing. I wonder now if television was invented only to numb us – to put the minds of millions into a constant anaesthetised state of never quite believing. After all, the daily dose of news is usually sandwiched between everyone's favourite soaps and a film, so who can tell what is real anymore?

When the country moved from a state of shock to sudden panic I think we actually moved forward as a nation. I think most people were angry at the government for not doing more and just a little pissed at themselves for not being more prepared. I feel eternally thankful that I'm close enough to the news to know more than most. It means that I know that the government has done a good job, whatever anyone else says. Yes, there have been riots, but there are also police everywhere and soldiers stationed all over the capital – like the Olympics defence plan on steroids. I think it has helped to maintain order in more than one way, because if you can keep many thousands busy policing millions then they aren't adding to the problem. It is a plan that has kept us all busy, but I don't think anyone thinks they will actually get paid at the end of this month. Despite this fact, many of us have kept going to work – after television, work is probably the next best amnesiac.

I intended to do the same today. I thought this grey and misty Monday would be just like all the others: that I would trudge down the escalator at Pimlico, wondering if at the end of the day I will return home to the flat I love but can barely afford, or if Western civilisation will finally enter the brink of collapse. Perhaps if it does it will be a good thing, because maybe then I won't have to pay the mortgage anymore. Instead, I'll continue being this perpetually single girl living in central London, but now I'll be fighting off the daily barbarian hordes who want to use and abuse me.

I always knew it would get to us, especially after many other capitals, from Bangkok to Berlin, went dark. I'll never understand why we ever thought we would be any different, especially as the stories started to creep across Europe. When the Defence Minister confidently pointed out on *Newsnight* that we are an island, and perhaps slightly more defendable, someone in the audience quite rightly pointed out that Australia is an island, although a much bigger one, and that didn't particularly help them.

I never thought I would say it, but I miss *Newsnight*.

I look at that blank television on the wall and I think back to just a few months ago when my dad mounted it up there. Just like every other man-task in my flat, he tackled it with ease. He spent longer listening to the demands of two women, Mum and me, while we decided just exactly where it should be placed, than he did installing the brackets. And once he had put it high up and tuned in all the channels, they both kissed me goodbye and wished me well in my first apartment, funded by their savings and my first bonus, ever-hopeful that this would be a new life for me, and a happy one at that.

I look at my watch and I know I don't have time. I can hear people shouting outside; it sounds like today is different from other days. There is a slight sense of panic in the air, even more than usual. I pull up a chair below the television and stand on it. I can't bear the gloom any longer and so I start putting pictures all over the screen, covering each bit of black with a different, happy memory. Within a few minutes it is covered with snapshots of crazy nights out, of my loving parents and of my childhood pets. I step down and stand back, already knowing that this is a better than the dim, lifeless object it had become.

I know that I could leave the television on and in the first couple of weeks that's exactly what I did. I left it playing all day, even when I wasn't in. I would come home to broadcasts of only bad news. The presenters were too familiar to me, their scripts of doom created by my hand several hours earlier. I had written so many reports on countries that had stopped functioning, world leaders who had been confirmed dead and the impact all of this has had on our crumbling society and ruined world economy. The favourite kind of story with our viewers was usually about dead celebrities found in the streets; their bodies mangled and their faces just about recognisable. The faces might have been familiar but the wounds and accompanying stories were normally hideous, although often made up, but I think that maybe this helped others to connect more strongly with what was happening around the world.

Even those stories dried up, as there were fewer people around to spot the odd famous person who had been seen recently mutilated, and levels of global communication dropped off when the internet was restricted to government use only. So, as the news got worse the updates from around the world got less, and the number of channels still broadcasting was reduced each day. Now it's only the good old BBC left. Some say this is the government taking control but anyone with half a brain knows they have bigger things to worry about.

I give my television a triumphant nod and then look down at the three pictures I am still clutching in my hand. I look at my parents and I decide that this is the weekend I will go home. Apparently, two-thirds of Londoners have remained in the capital, seemingly to keep things going, but for many people it is their one and only home, so they cannot leave, even if they wanted to. The fact is that refugees stuck in the middle of a crisis in a civilised society don't fare well, because people are too concerned with protecting what they have to open a door to strangers. But for people like me, who call this place home but also have an alternative, it's something that has been weighing heavily on my mind. Perhaps the countryside will be safer, as my dad constantly insists, or perhaps it's just more appropriate for me to leave this life, which I will never manage to protect, to be with those who matter most. I flick to the second photo, which is of my girlfriends, all of whom have stayed in London. Defiant until the end, that's what we agreed.

It's the third photo that makes me wonder, makes me yearn. I hold up the picture; it's of a man I have never met, a world I've never known. He's just a man from a magazine, someone I'll never meet yet he has still earned his place in my small collection. He's the unknown someone, just like one of the many I see every day and wish could be single and mine to hold. My one regret is still being alone at the age of 30. Despite living in a city of millions, I still spend every night on my own; even the impending collapse of the last pillar of the western world hasn't led to me having any nice, young and talented men in my cold bed.

I tuck him away, into my small purse, where I keep pictures of my family and friends, as well as a scattering of other small treasures and a wedge of notes that make up all that is left of my limited wealth. I start to wish I had kept more money hidden in the flat; I should have seen the restriction on cash withdrawals coming from a mile away. It's funny that the things you tell people and the things you do don't always end up being the same. I was too busy writing news stories about how money will soon lose all its value that I forgot to count up what I had and hide it somewhere safe, just in case I survived and just in case I was wrong.

The sudden noise of a siren in the distance jolts me back to life, back to my small world of big worries. I look out the window to see smoke rising up in the sky, joining the grey clouds and casting a shadow over the view I once loved. Whatever is happening now is new and different and, in my tortured mind, it becomes something entirely more sinister. It looks to be a few miles away, but it's not like I could ever know for sure.

I grab my day-pack and my coat and head for the door. I look in the mirror, still evaluating and offering myself some everyday criticism. My skin looks tired, my makeup application half-arsed at best. I ruffle my hair, pulling my fringe over as much of my pasty skin as possible. I manage to find some praise for myself – my choice of skinny jeans and a tight jumper seem appropriate for the dangers of today, in being entirely unattractive, although they do add a post-war drama feel to my attire.

I take one final look throughout my apartment and wonder if I will see it again. Everything here is a symbol of my progress towards the life I desperately wanted – the yellow cushions that match the sunny weather, the pictures covering nearly every wall, all deliberately chosen from the year I spent travelling the world.

I look around at all the things I could never fit into a suitcase, let alone my small survival pack. This isn't supposed to be happening because this is supposed to be my happy home – my place of sanctuary where I await my man. He would come in and smile at the ready-made woman for him. He would have his own place, too. The weekends would be ours to fill as we pleased, but the odd evening he slept here would mean the most. He would choose to add interruptions to his weekly routine; he would give up a gym session, post-work drinks or a meal with his dearest friends to spend his time with me. It would be our time and it would be the midweek boost I would need. And in the morning, when he clasped a silver watch around his wrist, getting up early to make into the city in time, I would start my countdown to when he would next wrap me in his solid arms.

'Get a grip,' I say, out loud to no one but myself. I'm still shaking my head at my own desperation when I finally find the courage to open my front door. I'm still looking into my flat, into the world I so desperately want but that's now being taken away from me, day by day. I take out my phone and get a picture, taking a snapshot of this place exactly how I left it. I do this every time I leave and I look at the photo several times a day, each time reminding myself of what I have to come back to. I also take this daily photo so that when I get home I can check the exact detail of the image against what is in front of me, looking for any signs of a disturbance. Mass looting might not be taking place, but burglaries are up 500%, as I reported in my editorial feature last week.

I drop my phone deep into my coat pocket – out of sight but close to my heart. Don't leave anything in your backpack: that's the current advice from the Metropolitan Police. I pull my backpack around to my front, hunting for my keys, openly laughing that this advice doesn't quite cut it for this urban, end-of-the-world city girl.

Just as I find them, I feel something grip my arm. The hold is tight and I can feel another hand making its way around to the other side of me. I scream and pull myself away, frantically shouting until I trip over and fall down. I'm still yelling as I hit the floor and turn over, hoping to somehow use my feet to push the door shut. I'm already seeing visions in my head of some crazed man scratching his way through the gap, trying to slice me up.

No sooner do I get my mind sorted do I then realise that it's Carla, my one remaining neighbour.

'Emma!' she shouts, her hands held out. 'It's me, it's just me!'

I lie still for a second and my heart continues to beat in triple-time. I look up and I let her stare down at me, wanting her to realise how close she caused me to come to a heart attack. 'Carla, what the hell was that?'

She smiles and then laughs, her frizzy hair almost vibrating along with her body. She offers me a helping hand but I ignore it, in order to prove just how little I need her. The truth is that I would rather do without her – she does nothing but infuriate me. She has this incessant squeaky voice and she can go on for hours about things, freely sharing her frankly uninformed view on what is happening in the world.

As the last few days have unfolded and more of our apartment block has emptied out, she has suggested several times that we sleep together, or at least stay in the same flat – preferably mine because it's higher up. Each time I have politely declined, telling her that it's best that we keep to our normal, day-to-day routines for as long as possible. The truth is that as much as she scares me I also refuse to have her as the first person to share my bed, my personal space or any part of my life. It's just my luck that the only remotely attractive single guy abandoned our block a week ago, as it turns out, heading back up north to find his last girlfriend, the apparent love of his life. I told him she's probably a zombie by now, but it did nothing to make him stay.

As I stand up she can't help but fuss over me, straightening my jacket and padding me down. 'I'm sorry I scared you but if we were staying in the same flat, as I suggested, there would have been no need for me to rush up the stairs, would there?'

'I've told you we're not doing that. The world hasn't ended, yet.'

She lets out this high-pitched squeal, her arms suddenly flapping all around me. 'Haven't you seen outside? Something bad is happening, something very different to yesterday.' She grabs hold of my arm again, forcing her crazy gaze upon me. 'That's why I came up to see you, to warn you to stay here. You see, I really do look after you. We have to look after each other now and there's no way you can go to work today, it's just not–'

I grab hold of her, mirroring her pose so that we're both holding each other. 'What the hell are you talking about? What's happening?'

'Haven't you heard? What have you been doing all this time? Some people are saying that whatever happened in Paris has made it through the tunnel and is coming up the river. Water won't stop it, nothing can. But I personally think it's those vigilantes from the south coast. They have finally got past the army barricades and are working their way to London, raping and pillaging as they go. The army won't stop them – why should they? They have bigger things to worry about, don't you think?'

I shake my head, openly refusing to accept her explanation. I can't believe what I'm hearing, not because I'm in denial, but rather because all the reports we received yesterday said there had been no activity near the tunnel. It also said that all the army barricades were still holding strong. The government made the decision weeks ago to recall every warship, every soldier and every fighter plane in order to protect our homeland, and while they were criticised for not joining the short-lived Global Defence Force, the safest place to be right now is England, particularly the south. I remind myself of all these facts that I have read for myself and of the presence of thousands of soldiers around the coast, and then I look to my frantic neighbour. 'Carla,' I say, gently shaking her. 'Please slow down and tell me what you know, not the gossip you have heard, because it's very different to what I reported just a few hours ago when I left the office at midnight.'

She shakes me off her, taking a step back and folding her arms. 'You know, Emma, you can be quite cutting at times. I was just starting to get to like you and then you get all judgemental on me.'

I ignore her and find my keys, taking my time to turn all three locks, but the whining continues in my ear. She doesn't seem to notice what I'm doing. I turn each lock to a certain point and then pull the key out, memorising exactly which position I left each lock in, just in case someone decides to pay my flat a visit.

I push the door one more time, reassuring my later-self that I did lock, check and double-check it. I turn around and she is still standing there at the top of the stairs.

'Haven't you heard a word I've just said?' she says, her arms folded and my escape route blocked.

'No, I haven't,' I say, moving myself forward, quite willing at this point to push her down the stairs. The police would never turn up, even if called, and no one would ever know, except for me. I have visions that she might not be the first person who gets in my way who I deal with like this; I know that the element of surprise would be my biggest asset, hopefully compensating for my unfortunately slender frame. Even high heels don't help, and besides they are most definitely a thing of the past, which is one thing at least that I am thankful for.

'Oh Emma,' she says, her head tilted and this smile on her face. 'You're too independent for your own good. You're just the type of person who will do well in whatever wasteland awaits us. And that's why we should stick together, because with your survival skills and my organisational talent we will make it through this. I know we will.'

'I'm going to work,' I say, pushing myself forward, now only a single step in front of her. 'And you'll need to move out of my way for that to happen.'

She shakes her head, a hand on each side of the banister. 'There is no more work, don't you see? It has finally caught up with us and now we have to take steps in order to survive.'

I take a deep breath, not knowing where to begin but very clear in my mind that I will be going to work and today is not the day that we all give up, making hiding the only option.

'Now, while you have been wallowing in self-pity and still going to work in the vain hope that you will get paid, I have been busy stockpiling and collecting what we will need. So, I say we do one more trip to Sainsbury's – the big one, I mean – and see what final bits we can get there. Once we've done that, we need to barricade the downstairs door. We're lucky it's solid oak – that should help a little bit. We will use the furniture from the other flats to help reinforce it. I doubt they will mind and we will never see them again, anyway.'

I silently shake my head, which only serves to make her eyes wilder; her whole body quivers. The thought of barricading myself in this block with her would be very like encasing myself in my own personal hell, and it's not something I plan to do.

'I don't think that you're taking this seriously, Emma,' she says. 'You have to realise that this is the end and we need to prepare. Please, don't worry, because I will take care of everything. And just so you know, the nice couple over the road are doing the same. We have plans to stay in our separate houses and communicate through the windows. Whoever or whatever comes down the street in the depths of the night will hopefully think the houses are deserted and will move on. I bet we will see that lots of people have done exactly the same.'

'I'm still going to work,' I say, pushing forward again. My body comes into contact with hers, and my eyes look down, ever hopeful that she will move without a struggle.

Her body tenses and I feel nothing but a solid bulk of determination in front of me. She wants to keep me here, keep me trapped. I know that right now she is scarier than whatever waits for me outside, but if I leave her like this I'm not sure I'll be able to get back in later.

'Look, Carla, why don't we just treat today like a normal day. I'll go to work and see what is going on out there, while you start the preparations. Perhaps we could have a chat with those Australian guys over the road. I think they're still here and if they are planning on doing the same, maybe we should all put our supplies into one block. Don't you think that would be the best idea for everyone?'

She doesn't speak, but her eyes probe mine. She looks at me, then around me. Her gaze finally finds the door behind me. 'Give me your keys, then.'

I shake my head before I've fully processed what she is asking and what she could possibly be planning to do with my things, my home and my life.

'If we are truly a team, then you should trust me and give me your keys so I can prepare, but I can see straight away that you don't actually mean what you are saying.'

'Look, Carla, I'm not giving you my keys. This is my flat and it's full of my things.'

Suddenly she pushes me, hard enough to make me fall to the floor. She stands over me, her fists clenched and her body trembling. 'You plan to leave me, just like she did. I only went out for an hour to get some food and when I came home she was gone.'

I know that Carla is referring to her flatmate, who walked out a week ago and never returned. I remember watching her leave. She got into a car with two full bags of luggage. She looked all around the street and then frantically threw her things into the backseat. I had thought she knew something was coming but now I'm starting to realise that she simply wanted to escape from this crazy girl. That night had been horrific: Carla shouted and screamed into the early hours about how she had been abandoned. She banged on my door several times but I didn't answer. I just curled up in my bath, in the part of my flat where her desperate cries were faintest, as I waited for her to finally tire and go to sleep.

'She didn't even leave a note, not one fucking word! And how do you think that made me feel, Emma? All I do for people and this is how they repay me! Well, I tell you that you are not doing the same. If you leave now then you will not get back in tonight.'

I get up, knowing that I must be stronger than I look if I am to survive. This is my first test, and it's nothing like I thought it would be. 'Carla, enough!' I shout, getting back up for the second time in just a few minutes. 'I am going to work and when I come back tonight I *will* be getting into my flat and we *will* continue as normal, do you hear me?'

But I can tell she doesn't hear me. She reaches into her back pocket and pulls out a flick-knife. She shakes her head as she moves towards me, a look of disgust on her face. 'It's different out there today. I wish you would listen. We could have got all this sorted, got ourselves prepared, but instead you've turned out to be quite the liability. I can't have this. I can't feel like second choice.'

'Second choice to what?' I ask, not knowing what I'm competing against, apart from the deadly contents of her imagination. 'Second choice to the end of the world?'

'You'll leave me, too – I know you will! You will find someone or someplace better and never come back.'

'I'm not yours to decide what to do with. You realise that, don't you?'

Carla twists her wrist, and the blade flicks out, the silver shiny and bright. It's new and unused but in the hands of this mad girl, it's deadly. 'You are staying, Emma. I don't know how long we're going to be trapped in here and I can't do it alone. I'll go mad if I'm left by myself any longer, I really will.'

I think about asking her if keeping me here at knife-point is the right way to win me over, and I even think about asking if she plans to live with me or eat me. In the end I decide that I am not going to be stuck night after night with this thing; I am more worried about the horrors in my home more than the ones outside and that must change. I've seen enough reports to know what is coming and I know my world is now all about survival.

'So, what's it going to be?' she asks.

'I pick freedom,' I say and push myself forward, forcefully enough to dislodge her. She topples backwards. I think about what I will do once she lands halfway down the stairs but then I realise she has taken hold of me with her spare hand. The other hand starts to rise up, the blade coming back into view. I know that it is now or never and so I push the palm of my hand into her face as hard as I can.

She screams as blood starts to flow from her nose but this isn't enough to make me stop. I do it again, as she starts to scream wild threats back at me. She seems determined not to let go, and she swipes the knife at me with her free hand, missing my face by only inches.

The desperation to escape surges through me now and I bite her hand as hard as I can, until I feel my teeth sinking through the flesh and I taste the warm blood flowing through her angry veins.

I hear the knife drop as she grabs her bleeding hand. 'You total bitch,' she says, a hand gripped over the wound, blood trickling down her arm. 'I'm going to get you for that and you'll never leave now. I'm going to tie you up and leave you for the monsters to feast on your bony, little corpse!'

I shake my head, determined that she will do none of these things. Enough has been taken from me already. The life I was promised has been picked apart piece by piece and now there is nothing left to celebrate, nothing left for me to aspire to. I feel the rage rise up within me as I think about the life I will never have. I feel myself move forward, stretching an arm out to punch her. I think she sees it too: she grasps the bannisters again, but it's too late for her – I'm too angry now and she is too weak. In this moment I finally understand that I will die alone and so with all my hatred for what I have become I smash into her body, the force lifting her into the air.

I watch as everything happens slowly. She screams but it doesn't mean anything; it won't change what will happen now. Her bum lands on the edge of a step and her face wrinkles up. Those angry eyes are still angled at me as her head hits the back wall and there is the inevitable cracking sound, seeming to freeze every bit of her in time. As her body finds its final resting place it becomes scrunched up like a ragdoll, all twisted and deformed. The small patch of blood on the wall is the only clue as to what has happened. She fell; it was just a nasty accident – that's what I'm telling myself, although I'm quite sure I will never have to tell anyone in authority about this.

I step down towards her. Her vacant stare tells me that she is most definitely dead. My first bold decision of the new world has resulted in me removing a significant obstacle to my day and life in general. This worries me, not just because of what I have just done, but because of how unaffected I feel by it. I don't look at her as a human anymore, but rather an issue that had to be resolved; maybe I murdered her, maybe I didn't, but I know that I don't feel guilty about it.

It doesn't matter now because she has gone to another place, leaving me to pick up the pieces of what remains and to try to survive just a little longer. I think about dragging her down the stairs and into her own flat and leaving her there – a problem to deal with tonight or tomorrow, but when the shouting on the street gets louder I decide that I should leave her. I decide that if I do survive the day then my reward to myself will be dealing with what remains of my life and this new, bold me.

*****

As the station entrance comes into sight, I see the big metal gates being pulled shut. The noticeboard outside the station is barely visible through the crowds but I am briefly able to catch a glimpse of it, with its big, pronounced writing that declares: 'Station closed.' These are such bold words for so early in the morning, as if someone has finally dared to break the routine that has kept London together this long. I think about how far I will need to run to get to Victoria, or any other station, and how they might be shut too. It makes me run quicker, determined that I will be one of those last few to squeeze through the closing gates.

I know that I am not alone, not the only one rushing towards something and away from something else. Most of the people around me are running now, their hands outstretched as if they are trying to pull themselves past the next person. It has truly become every human for themselves. There are women with children, and a few older people, but they stand no chance. It becomes obvious that the few winners past this line will be the younger, alpha males and maybe a few unimportant hopefuls like me.

Sweat is streaming down my face, and my coat is smothering me. My bag is so heavy that I feel like it is trying to anchor me to the same spot, whilst everyone else seems to be getting ahead in this new fight for freedom. My legs get heavier as I keep pushing myself forward, now certain that this is my only chance of escape. My walk from the flat had quickly turned into a light jog, as I overheard people telling each other that the barricades had fallen. I listened to them, hearing that despite the sheer numbers of our brave soldiers, they were overwhelmed within minutes. I heard someone else shout that the newly built city defences had been breached and all remaining troops were being airlifted out, so that some resemblance of an army still remained. That's when I knew that I had to make it out of here. I didn't know where but since everyone was running towards the station I did the same, figuring it was time to catch that train to the countryside, to my parents and whatever fate awaits us all.

As I see the tube staff step back behind the invisible boundary that will soon become their only safety, I already know in my heart that it's too late, that these gates will shut for good. I wonder if going underground is the right thing to do. It will mean my phone is useless and will perhaps deprive me of my last chance to tell my parents that I love them. I feel my phone vibrate again in my pocket and I know it's them: my mum will tell me to come home, my dad will tell me I should have done it days ago. I don't stop now; I don't even think about answering it. I think only about getting into the tube station, getting up to Euston and catching the train, any train, out of London and closer to them. I will call them later, when I can, and that call will tell them that I am on my way home and that we will not be defeated.

I focus every ounce of my being on getting towards the entrance and the few police officers who are trying to calm down the onslaught that approaches them. When I am ten paces away I see that they are giving up, as they retreat into the station and take hold of the two metal gates. They start to push them shut as the people who approach and squeeze through become the lucky final few. The rest of us are clearly destined to become the mob, an ever-growing onslaught of flesh against these gates of freedom.

I take one final look around and see the masses that are gathering behind me, crowds of people funnelling down every street that lead to this one last place of apparent safety. As I look forward again I see the paint has been scraped off the metal gates; I see the shock in the eyes of the police officers, who must be wondering if they will ever be able to hold back the tide of bodies that are lapping against them. Behind them I see a few more officers with cylinders of pepper-spray drawn, threats to unleash their contents filling the air and openly warning everyone as to what will follow, should we not stand back and leave.

The gates are nearly closed now as too many people try to force their way into the tiny space. I see a man smash into the gates, his screams distinct. Several other people start to push at his back until his voice can be heard no more. 'Let us in,' they shout, a mixture of pleas and demands, all wanting to be the one who is heard.

When I reach the front of the crowd, I think about what to do next. I know that I will be crushed if I don't do something soon. I put a hand on each door, as I look through the small gaps to find the young man who has the keys to my survival. I catch his eyes and he sees me, before his concentration turns back to the bundle of metal jingling in his hands. The other around him are shouting now, demanding that he finds the right one and that he does his duty. Behind them, the officers with pepper spray release it into the crowd. There are screams all around me – the yells of those caught with pain in their eyes. They have nowhere to move, and I hear the cries of those who are being crushed against the metal slats, their skin pushed through any small space until it turns red and raw.

The man with the key's failure may well be my salvation, as the two big men either side of me prove to be stronger than our uniformed foes on the inside. They manage to get the doors open, just enough for a few people to squeeze through. Two younger guys push past me and make their way in, their bodies twisted sideways, so desperate that they contort and bend themselves until they are successfully through. The police fight them back at first, until they regroup with the obvious realisation that their aim must be to permanently seal this station from the endless masses of desperate invaders.

I push and I fight but I still don't seem to get close enough to get through. Those men inside seem to regain control as the doors come closer to joining, which will seal the fate of those outside. I think about giving up, and about how I can escape this nightmare and find some space to rethink my plan, maybe even find some like-minded people.

I'm about to turn away when a thick, hairy arm comes out of the mess of limbs and bodies. I look up past many tattoos, each one seeming to have a story behind it, eventually finding the face of a man the age of my dad but with the determination and bulk of a sailor, and a week's worth of stubble that's about to become a beard. 'Get in there,' he says through gritted teeth in a deep, Irish accent. He pushes me forward, and I pass through a gap so narrow you would never have thought it possible.

I look into his eyes; they are dark and determined, like he's seen a few of these battles in his time. He looks back at me as he tries to withdraw his arm and I realise that I'm now in another place from him. I'm inside, the dim lighting of the underground station entrance starkly different from the world that's now a whole foot away from me. I grab his hand, feeling the thickness of his warm fingers. I pull him, somehow willing my saviour to join me, but it's too late. The gates close, and over the clanging of metal I hear the cries of my man, his forearm trapped as our worlds are separated.

I quickly let go, realising the pain I have caused him. He falls to the floor and I fall with him, making repeated tearful apologies to my hero and to all those who are with him. Big, black boots soon surround me as the officers unleash their spray on him. He screams in pain and pulls his arm out and back towards his body. Blood flows down his leathery flesh as I see this new wound has cut to the bone.

People push against his head as he rubs his eyes and tries to focus on me. I reach my hands through one of the gaps. I know that I am risking getting my fingers chopped off, but I'm determined to hold him. I stroke his chin as he grabs my hand and pushes my fingers against his stubble. 'Are you an angel?' he shouts, his head banging against the metal, his face covered in tears, blood and oil.

The boy with the keys returns but he's still shaking too much to work the lock. One of the other men grabs them off him and pushes him across the floor. He lands a few feet away and I soon hear that the keys have been successfully turned in the lock. The police stand back, and I hear the flick of batons, as I sense that horrific spray filling the air ahead of me. They fire indiscriminately into the crowd, trying to make them withdraw, determined to make them realise that staying in this place is no longer an option. I don't think they understand that those at the back can't see this; they haven't realised what is happening and they are pushing further forward, impatiently demanding their turn at the front of the queue.

I look at my man and see that his head is falling. I grip his hand harder, reminding him that I'm still here. He suddenly comes back to life, as he smiles at me through all that pain. I see blood flowing down his forearm and tears streaming down his face. 'I'm so sorry,' I say, starting to cry at what I have caused.

His head hits the metal gate again. He reacts by pushing the people back with whatever energy he has left, for what might be the last time. 'Don't say sorry, angel, say thank you.'

I reach further out, deeper into my despair, until I can run a finger through his black hair. 'Thank you,' I say, several times, until he finally responds with a smile.

I suddenly feel hands on my back, reaching under my arms, and I'm quickly pulled to my feet. I turn round and see that one of the officers is shouting at me. It takes me a second to find his voice amongst the hundreds, and then I realise that he is telling me to get down the escalator. I ignore him and turn back to my hero, my man who was fresh to the fight. I try to kneel down but the officer still has a hold on me and is shouting from behind me.

I look at this eternally brave man and he looks up at me. His face is covered in new gashes, which have been caused by the wild crowd in the few seconds since I left him. 'Run now, angel,' he says, his battered face looking defeated, but his spirit somehow still with me.

I shake my head, tears still streaming down my face. 'Thank you,' I mutter.

I can't see what he offers back or witness the pain he will now endure in the name of my safety. My body is spun around, until I'm pointing towards the escalators. I feel dizzy when I try to turn back, but I'm met with the yells of the officer, for what I think might be the last time. I obey and run through the ticket barriers, which have been open for days now.

I don't dare turn around, and instead I join the back of the small crowd of the other lucky ones. They funnel themselves into a line, and I push my way onto the escalator. I move over to the left side of the escalator, hopeful it will be slightly quicker, and that once I get down there I will feel better. I see the tracks and look up at the board, thinking only of the future, knowing that salvation in the form of a long metal cylinder will soon speed into sight to take us all away. If I can get on that northbound train, I will know I can make it, and if the tube is working then the trains might be running too. I keep telling myself this, remembering the regular briefings I have had as a lucky member of the press. The human urge to keep things regular, to protect our way of life, will ultimately save me, I know it will.

But today there is no quick movement, and no chance of pushing in. The people on both sides of the turned-off escalator remain totally still. I try to look past the man in front of me. He's wearing a black coat, his briefcase still in his hand and a thin line of dandruff runs across his shoulders. I wonder if he realises what is happening – how far the depths of his denial go, and if they make it all the way to a tie still wrapped firmly around his neck.

I can hear shouting ahead, 'Move down the platform, now! Just fucking move!' It makes me think of how busy it is down there. Perhaps it is just as chaotic down there as it is outside, where my hero still hopefully fights to survive. The shouting doesn't stop. People seem to be shoving their way forward, pushing everyone else deeper into the tunnel.

'There are severe delays on the Victoria Line,' the computer announcement says, swiftly followed by the tube staff saying the same thing, shouting down the platform, trying to make sure everyone knows just how screwed we really are.

I squeeze past people, fitting through spaces so small that you wouldn't think it possible. I don't know where I'm heading but I figure that the further I go the more space I might find, as though despite everyone huddling together on one part of the platform, there might still be a lot of space that no one has spotted yet. I keep moving, trying to get to the same spot I go to every morning. I look down, trying to find the chewing gum caked into the floor that marks my regular personal space where I always stand.

I get near but I'm not as close to that spot as normal. I see two members of tube staff, all snuggled up in their bulky silver and blue coats, and I figure being next to them would be a good place to wait, certainly as safe as anywhere else. The boards have no times displayed on them and these two are frantically talking to each other whilst pinning their radios to their ears. They stop for a second to give each other a look; it's at this moment that time literally freezes and all the drama and people demanding around them means nothing.

I move closer, ready to ask something.

One of them starts talking into their microphone and it takes me a second to realise that what he is saying is being announced across the PA system. I can see and hear the choking in his voice and the fear in his eyes. 'There are no more northbound trains, I repeat, there are no more northbound trains,' he says, much to the shock of everyone standing with me on the northbound platform.

Someone grabs him, pulling his arm and demanding his attention. 'It's only 7:15 in the morning so how can this be?'

He pushes them off him and his colleague comes closer. They stand side-by-side, as if safety in numbers will ever help them. Their uniforms make them targets for questions I don't think they can answer. They huddle together, their attention back on their radios and the secret things that only they know.

'Control room, come in please,' one of them says, tapping his radio whilst staring at his partner. 'Control room, say again.'

They suddenly look at each other. That kind of gaze has become too familiar to me now. 'It's down here, on the tracks, in the network,' one of them says, his eyes bulging with horror.

The other one grabs his mouth as those around them start to ask what they mean. 'Everyone needs to board this next train,' he shouts. 'This train will be heading back south.'

People start grabbing them again. They try to pull away, but they don't know where to go any more than the rest of us do. They hold onto each other as questions, demands and pleas come in from every angle.

'We need to get to Camden,' this woman says, staring at them through red, worn-out eyes, whilst cradling her two young ones nearby. 'My husband is there and we need to get to him.'

'There is nothing northbound,' the man says again, turning away from her as soon as he has finished his answer, her face probably not even registering in his mind.

She must need more, must be desperate for someone to help, because she pulls at his coat, then taps on it with a skinny finger. 'Please help me,' she says, her face scrunched up and tears streaming down her face. 'He didn't come home last night.'

The man brutally pulls her hands off him without any of the emotions any human would normally feel in such a situation. His exhaustion and confusion has conditioned him to this new way of life. 'I just told you: there is absolutely nothing north of the river.'

She turns to me, her face begging. She can't hold things together now, not even for her children. 'What does he mean?'

I shake my head, unable to speak and unsure of what any of this means now. I think of this woman and her obvious troubles but I don't really feel anything for her; all I am really wondering is what this means to me, what has happened in Euston station and whether my shiny train will still be waiting for me in the abyss of a demolished and desolate skyline.

A welcome noise echoes down the tunnel and this means that I don't have to answer, don't have to try to find words of comfort, which would only be lies anyway. Everyone hears it and we all stop shuffling for just a moment. I see some distant lights coming through the hole. At any other time I would be able to hear the train properly, would be able to feel the grinding of metal against metal as it approached. Normally, the mass of seasoned travellers on the platform would remain silent as the train enters. But not this time; this time the desperation in the air is overwhelming. People push along the platform, all thinking the same thing, all praying that it isn't already full.

It makes it halfway into the station when the first person falls onto the tracks. I look over and hear the screams of those who must have seen them fall, and of those who are about to witness a brutal death. No one leans down to help; everyone just pushes back against those behind them, desperate not to suffer the same fate. Some women scream, as do some men, while others look down silently. Perhaps they pushed them, perhaps they know them, but all I see is a hand reaching up from the track, then swiftly disappearing as whoever it was is swallowed up by the machine that cannot possibly stop now.

I see at least three more people fall to the same fate. I imagine the driver shutting his ears to the terror of others and closing his eyes to the blood that has stained his window. Those who are lost are quickly forgotten as the two-thirds-full tube comes to a halt. The doors don't open immediately. The announcements demand that we get on in an orderly fashion, and that this tube will be heading back down to Brixton. The automated announcement of 'let passengers off the train first, please,' echoes throughout the station but we all know that no one will be crazy enough to get off and there are more people squeezed down here than could ever fit on, even if the train was empty.

I look up at the board to see that it is still blank, and I curse myself for not having lined up next to one of the doors. I start to count the huge numbers of people in front of me, and then I push my way left, towards the door at the end of one of the carriages. I can only hope that most people around me will have put their bets on the double doors.

I look through the windows into the tube train, and see that the many people inside don't look like they feel safe. They are all looking out, staring into the mass of frantic people who are about to bring their savagery into this travelling haven. I wonder if they know more than we do, if they know what has happened.

'This station is closed, you must board this train,' an announcement says. It comes from the tube staff who spoke earlier. I see that he has only managed to make it a few feet since I last saw him. While he states the obvious, he moves forward, slowly squeezing himself past everyone else, making it clear that he plans to board this train along with the rest of us.

It forces me to move forward and as the doors open my shuffling turns into blatant pushing, as those behind me make their intentions quite clear. My eyes dart between the small entrance ahead of me and the windows, as I see how quickly this precious space is filling up. People are spilling into the tube train like water set free from a dam into a quiet river, quickly pushing further into the centre of the carriage. They must be happy to be one of the few to have made it on because once they have passed the threshold and found a place for themselves, they look out, suddenly thinking of the rest of us. A man looks at me, and seeing that I am still stuck on the other side, while his position now secured, his expression turns to something that looks like sorrow, but not sorry enough to help.

As I reach my turn I realise how close I am and how far I still have to go. The carriage is full – my eyes tell me this and the voices of those lucky enough to be on board confirm it to me. In the fight for air, their manners get pushed away to some distant place, far from the reality of this long tunnel. I frantically look for a space, realising that I'm shouting out loud, telling everyone just how small I am, as those behind me are still pushing. They're not trying to push me further in, but rather trying to get me out of the way so they can get a chance to shout, beg and sell desperate stories of their own.

'Board this train now,' the announcement says, which I think is a little pointless. 'This is the last tube. Leave now... get on board now!'

The doors bleep as they start to close and I make my attempt. I push against those who are blocking my way, determined that I will fit, whether I have to climb above them or crawl under them. I make it at least halfway onto the tube before the doors close. The one single door hits the right side of my body before pulling back, doing its duty to protect a human from harm. I realise that I am back onto the platform and hands are grabbing at every part of my body. I look over to see that beside every door are people who have pushed their luck and ultimately failed.

I hear the bleep again and make the same move, this time with even more determination and just a little hope that my last push has cleared some space among the bodies of these ample strangers. I move through the door, my head passing the threshold first. I think I might just make it, as I push against the tide of disjointed limbs, until I'm met with the forceful hands of another. This woman looks down at me, her makeup smudged and her blouse half-ripped. 'There is no more fucking room!' she shouts, as she pushes me back.

The door closes again, forcing me to stare at my attacker through the dirty, sweat-stained window. She stares back at me; she doesn't even mouth that she is sorry or offer me a tear of pity. I shake my head, feeling unknown levels of anger at what she has done to me; this entire month-long saga now seeming to be all of her making, my fate now entirely her fault.

Just as I start to imagine what I would do to her if the doors opened, they do as I had hoped and slide apart. I thank the makers for this automated safety, not able to leave someone trapped in between the doors. I look up at her; my anger has been replaced with hope, but I have also realised that I will not make it through the wall of bodies without help.

She shakes her head. 'You can see there is no room so what the fuck should we do?'

I'm unable to answer her. I see the closing door sign start flashing again. I'm about to give up, to fall back into the crowd and let someone else take over this fight, but just as the bleeping starts again a hand stretches out from within the carriage. As it takes hold of me I hear someone declare that there is room. I can't see who said it but he sounds young. Instead of trying to pick him out from the tightly packed crowd I instead look at the hand that has taken hold of me. As I'm pulled into the mass of bodies I look only at his outstretched forearm. He seems very different in appearance from my last saviour: I follow a scattering of dark hairs up a pale forearm. I gently take hold of it, feeling the warmth and hoping that our connection will be strong enough to get me on. But if it isn't, if I'm cut off by the brutal woman and the power of the door, I will forever remember holding what I have wanted for so long. I imagine myself being held in these exact arms, as I explore each and every fine hair while he slowly makes love to me all night.

When I'm snapped back to reality I find that my head is buried in the cleavage of the woman who hates me, and I immediately realise that I've made it on board. The door tries to close again and I see that someone else has made it on with me. It's another young woman who has managed to piggy-back on my success, but she is only half in, as I was before, and has fallen victim to the same tuts and pushes that I received from my fellow humans. I try to pull her further in but there really is no room.

'Please help me!' she screams frantically. Her eyes are on me but her plea is directed to all of those around us. She is begging for an answer from anyone; for someone to move back, just a little.

I feel a shuffling behind me as I realise that my saviour still has hold of me, but this time he is gripping my arm. 'I won't let go,' he shouts through the wall of bodies. His face is still unknown to me but his voice is so entirely welcome.

'This tube is leaving, whether the doors are shut or not,' the driver shouts with such determination in his voice. 'I repeat, all the safeties are off and we are leaving now.'

'Oh, God, please help me!' the young woman shouts, as the train starts to move. It accelerates slowly at first, struggling to pick up pace with so many extra souls on board.

She pulls at me, somehow managing to drag me further towards the door rather than getting herself any closer to safety. 'I'm only half-way in,' she yells. 'Oh, please, it's moving now! You have to let me in!'

I pull. I pull with everything I have, but the space is too compact and no one has enough room to manoeuvre. I realise that he is pulling too, still shouting that he won't let go of me. But it's not enough; I realise that not everyone agrees with our plan: some are refusing to move and some seem incapable of understanding the consequences of our group inaction.

'Let go, it's too full!' the angry woman shouts and spits towards her new target.

'We have to get her on,' I shout, still pulling, still begging. I realise that we're getting closer to each other, but it's not because she is fully in, but rather because my hands are making their way up her arm. My levels of effort are not in question, but my ability to save her is limited. My eyes meet hers. I know how desperate she is, but I don't see a choice or a way out of this. 'You have to let go.'

She shakes her head. 'Please,' she says, her begging face telling me that she clearly sees this train as her final chance to escape this hell we are in.

'We're nearly out of the platform,' I shout, starting to push her towards the door. I want her to realise that it's for her own good. 'You have to let go!'

She doesn't listen to me, doesn't see the danger and so a long scream signals her departure from our train. I close my eyes as she is dragged away into the dark tunnel. I shut off all my other senses and focus only on the screams of the unlucky; those who never quite made it. And with every door that passes the concrete entrance to the tunnel, a new scream travels into my head, horrible sounds caused by our obvious failure.

Once the unanswered cries stop, all we are able to hear is the calm of the tunnel, and I finally open my eyes. Everyone is silent, as I look at the people around me, each of us covered in the blood of the unlucky. The bitch pushes me, just a little, into the small space that the woman just occupied, so that she can clean herself and remove the bits of guts from her white blouse. I see a bit of flesh fall into her cleavage. Her hands dig down deep, following the trail of blood, trying to remove every memory of the one we just lost.

Someone else vomits and I start to cry. Peoples' faces show wrenching emotions, horrified by what has happened to those we just lost. I can't see straight anymore, or get control of myself. My vision fades. My legs start to quiver as I realise that I am going to faint while standing up. It's most likely that I will awake in the same position, in this same nightmare of strangers.

I feel those around me shuffle; for a moment I think someone is trying to help me, but then I realise that they are tutting at something behind them. I keep hearing 'excuse me,' as the owner of that familiar, heavenly voice makes its way towards me.

I keep myself awake somehow, determined to stay with him as I realise that I'm slowly being turned around. My stomach touches his, the space between us nothing but intimate, as I feel a hand on each of my arms. 'Thank you,' he says, as I sense him looking around but he gets nothing back.

I take my time to study him, to feel him holding me. I slowly let my eyes follow his tight shirt upwards; he has no tie on and I look at his neckline – one button undone, an untrimmed rug of experience on show. Just the right amount, I think.

'Are you okay?' he asks, sounding friendly and genuine. It's almost as if he is smiling as he speaks.

I realise that I haven't yet dared to look at his face and so I nod and take a deep breath, then look at his chin, which is perfectly shaved. I wonder if he intended to go to work today, or if he just planned to look this immaculate when meeting his doom. I stop for a moment, entirely forgetting where I am, but sure that the eyes will make this moment. I keep looking and then smile at finding these bright blue rings set against thick, dark hair. I look at him, feeling nothing but safety. Then I suddenly feel angry; I'm angry that I have only found him here and now, on what could be one of my last days on earth.

I don't hear what he is saying to me now, even when the man next to us, who can't help being a part of our moment, offers a smile as he waits for our next move. I realise that I need to start being a glass-half-full kind of girl and thank the stars that I have finally found someone who could tick all the boxes that matter. These thoughts only lead me back to my endless misery and so I quickly thank him, squeezing up closer and feeling his firm stomach tense with my touch. I feel somehow liberated, distanced from the crowd and the horror of the moment. I am no longer afraid of making my move. I'd normally be paralysed with fear before going up to a guy, let alone openly touching him.

'I'm Scott,' he says, leaning closer to me, trying to create some privacy for us.

I laugh again, still shaking; I'm nervous, but aroused and curious. 'I'm Emma and I owe you so much for what you just did.'

He looks at me and then turns to the bitch who has managed to stay just behind me. He has a big smile stretched across his face and his gaze quickly returns to me. 'Well, some of us still remember our manners.'

I feel the woman try to move, most likely getting ready to defend herself and her actions. I'm thankful to see him put up a hand; none of us seem willing to hear her excuses. They're all pointless now and I know it will be a long time before we all process what has happened here, let alone get to judge, to properly remember or truly understand.

He quickly turns his attention back to me, offering a small smile and tilting his head as he seems to take me all in. 'I've seen you before,' he says, taking hold of both of my hands.

'You have?' I ask, knowing that I have never seen him before, sure that he is someone I would remember. Even if I saw him sitting with his girlfriend, or after a drunken night out, or in the supermarket – back when shopping used to be normal – I would remember him for all eternity.

He calmly nods, still smiling down at me. 'You always get on the second carriage from the front and I always get on the third carriage, one stop before you.'

I lean backwards, as far back as I can, until I hit the person behind me. 'You've seen me that often?' I shake my head, not believing it, not able to imagine someone has ever noticed me in the haystack of daily travellers.

He nods again. 'You're quite the creature of habit. You always get on the tube at just after seven and you always get into the same seat, writing in the same journal and generally looking down at that same floor.' He looks below me, to the carriage floor. 'I was starting to wonder what you'd found down there.'

I look up at him, finding one of my hands tracing up his shirt, my fingers soon teasing their way along his cheek. 'I never found you.'

He laughs, loud enough for all to hear but he doesn't seem to care. 'That's so cheesy. You're clearly practiced at this.'

I look around, soon finding my way back to him; back to the person I already never want to leave. 'I'm never good at this and today isn't the day I thought I would start.'

He nods, his eyes making their own journey around our small space before coming back to me. 'Well, if it makes you feel any better, I had been planning to move into your carriage. That was until all of this started and everyone's lives got a bit screwed up and I didn't see you as much. But I'm kind of glad I got on this tube today.'

I nod and smile, not believing this is real. I'm about to answer him and to ask more questions, all in order to confirm to myself that this really is happening to me. Before I can speak the desperate voice of the driver spills through the speakers: 'We will not be stopping at the next station, or at any other one, for that matter. We are going all the way back to Brixton and you should all hold on real fucking tight.'

I feel the train speed up as I take a firmer hold of Scott and he wraps his arms around me, this level of intimacy not intentional but necessary. The tube jolts forward as people gasp and whimper. None of this normal and all of it is difficult to process. We seem to speed up but then we suddenly stop, all of us packed in so tight that I don't know who I'm touching, other than Scott. Everyone looks around, trying to get a glimpse through the window, all waiting to see what will await us when we get out of the tunnel. I expect to see hundreds of people all banging on the glass, desperate to get on, happy in some way just to touch what could have been their freedom. I think of how this must be happening all over the city, in many different these stations and about how many people must be trapped in these desperate places.

The driver knows more, he must do. What he doesn't say out loud he reveals in his tone. We all look at each other and I think we are trying to somehow convince ourselves that we will be okay, but deep down we must all know that this simply isn't the case. Something bad is happening, something far worse than a person jumping in front of a train or a multiple signal failure. This is a whole new level of bad and I don't think it is something those in charge ever planned for.

The train edges forward again, as I keep looking between the black tunnel outside and Scott's crystal-blue eyes. He spends all of this precious time looking only at me; the world of caverns and other people don't seem to be of any consequence to him. It makes me smile and even though it's only a reflex born of years of waiting, it still makes me feel good, if only for a second. The train judders again and I let out a whimper, as all those around us take deep breaths. I think the air might be running out and I wonder how long we would be able to survive in a place like this.

'So, Emma, can I ask you something?' Scott says, leaning his face close to mine, like we have been in this embrace for a decade or more.

I look at him and I feel my heart beating faster. I feel faint from exhaustion and hunger – I didn't eat much for breakfast and now it's taking its toll. I feel the grip on me get tighter, as though he is mine and I am his, and always have been.

'Do you have a boyfriend?' he asks, and then stutters, perhaps wanting to say more. He looks around and probably realises that there are twenty-or-so people listening, having no choice but to witness our first meeting. 'It's just that you always seemed so quiet, so uninterested in those around you, that I assumed you were probably taken.'

I smile and wait, trying to find genuine excitement from the scariest of places. 'No, I don't have a boyfriend. I *never* have a boyfriend.'

'I see,' he says and then nods, finally looking around the carriage, almost as if he's got bored of me, as if picking up single girls while society is collapsing is something of a hobby for him.

I push a finger into his chest, desperate to see how solid it is, imagining how many hours I would spend doing this if we were in my bed. 'Do you have a girlfriend?'

He smiles and turns his attention back to me, moving his mouth close to my ear. 'That's better,' he says and blows soft air behind my ear. 'It tells me you're interested in me and not just this bunch of miseries we're stuck with down here.'

I can only offer him a half laugh in between my frantic panting, a smile forming in a place I never imagined possible. I study his neckline, gazing at his smooth, creamy skin, which looks good enough to eat. I look down his white shirt, seeing what bulges out of it. 'You haven't answered me yet,' I say.

He nods and pulls his head away slightly. 'I used to have a girlfriend. We split up just before all of this started but we should have ended it long before then.' He puts his arms around my waist, pulling me up, moving my face closer to his. 'I should have sat down in your carriage, in the seat opposite you, a very long time ago.'

I feel his arms struggling to hold me, the space is not big enough and his back is taking the strain. Before he lets me go I take my chance and move my face closer to his. I approach slowly, distinctly aware of how little time we have and how his energy is draining away, but my eager mind is trying to capture this moment forever. Our lips finally touch, slowly at first, just teasing each other. We both know that time is not on our side, that the option of a slow build-up is not a luxury that we have today, and so his warm tongue is soon in my mouth, slowly teasing and exploring its new home. His passion flows through me, reminding all the time me of just what I have missed, of all the men I have rejected in favour of continuing to search for my personal definition of perfect. And now that it has found me I realise both the lost opportunities of denial and the reward of the wait.

The train suddenly jolts forward again, forcing Scott to put me down. He still manages to do it gently, and his eyes quickly find mine again. 'That was nice,' he says, with a smile, a smile that I only hope to see in a hundred places, in a thousand moments, until the day I die.

I want to keep looking at him, taking it all in, but we're both drawn away from each other as the light of the station starts to shine into the carriage in front of us. I brace myself, waiting to feel the battering on our train from the many hysterical people waiting to be rescued. I wonder if the tube will do a few more journeys, trying to all collect those who have been left behind.

The much-expected banging doesn't take place; instead, I hear screams from the people slightly in front of us. Whatever this new horror is, it reaches them few seconds before us. I look through a space between some people, focusing on the windows between our two carriages, until I see those in front yelling and crying at whatever it is that they have just seen.

It is soon our turn to enter the station platform. We all look through our own long windows into the station. I stay silent, quietly witnessing the hell that is spread out before me. Those in our carriage join the others in crying in fear at the unknown terrors separated from us by only a thin layer of glass.

The door is still open. Scott grips me tighter and I can do nothing but try to catalogue every horror that is laid out before me. I feel his breath against my neck as I trace the blood that has stained every wall in the underground cavern; the splatters of red seeming to spell out a pattern, a reminder of many painful deaths. Across the concrete floor bodies lie scattered everywhere, their flesh sliced open and many limbs severed from their now dead owners. I look closely, forcing myself to see all of this, my mind quickly realising that the bodies don't seem to match the parts left around them. People must have run and fled whilst they were still being chopped apart.

The people in the seats try to move backwards, desperately hoping to escape the evil outside. The sounds of the dead and dying find me now, as I realise just how close I am. We're packed so tight and I'm still at the front of the crowd and so I edge closer to the open door, needing to look, to see and to understand. It's the reporter in me, something that will never leave – my need to help others know what is happening somehow overrides the fear of what is spread out before me.

Scott must feel me stretching away, because he starts to pull me back. I feel my body moving, as I realise he is trying to rotate us so that he is closest to the door. I turn to look at him. 'I need to see what is happening,' I say, not having the energy to explain why.

He immediately shakes his head but I move quicker than he anticipated. 'Just keep a hold of me,' I say, leaning out of the door. The lingering smell hits me first; it's as though it was just waiting to catch me off-guard. I look along the station and see that the bodies of the fallen stretch all the way along the cold, stone tiles – the corpses of the mutilated take up a lot less space than the living bodies of the humans who were once here. I make myself look to the end of the platform and I see others doing the same, the brave few who are willing to stick their heads out and get a proper glimpse of this very real hell. I look at the formations of corpses, the pile of bodies at the end of the platform. The victims must all have run the same way, all clambering over each other to get out. I see nothing but red flesh and faces painted with the horror of a gruesome end.

'What can you see?' someone shouts from somewhere behind me.

'Why aren't we moving?' says another.

I'm about to turn around, to try to explain what I can see and describe horrors I never imagined when something pulls at my leg. I scream, pushing myself into Scott as his grip tightens and he pulls me backwards. My panic seems to spread throughout the carriage and others do the same; our primal instinct to share our fear with others seems to take over.

I look down at my feet and see a bloodied hand is trying to take hold of me. I follow the trail of the arm until I see the mutilated face of a survivor, his skin covered in blood, his hair matted with sweat. His back has been sliced open and blood still flows from it, telling me all of this happened very recently. I can only shake my head, as though I am apologising for all that has happened down here.

I think about reaching out to him, trying to help, but Scott pulls me further back before I can do anything. 'You can't help him now,' he says, seeming to know what I was thinking.

I take one final look at this man as I wait for the life to drain from him. It won't take long now and I'm hopeful the train will start moving again, ending my need to share his last few agonising breaths. I curse myself for somehow becoming this evil, this uncaring, this utterly selfish, but I'm at a loss to know what I can do for someone who barely resembles a human being, and who will pass over before the help that no longer exists could ever reach him.

I look ahead, back to the front of the train, starting to wonder why we're still here. And that's when I see it – the reason for all of this horror. It's only a flash, a flicker in the corner of my eye, but it leaps into the front carriage, clearing its own space, throwing bodies out of the way using its long claws. Those who cry out as they fly through the air look dead even before their bones crack against the far wall.

I try to pull myself in; the fear that swells through me more intense than I ever thought possible. Just as I retreat inside I see another flash in the corner of my vision; something is tearing a path into the carriage at the rear of the train, much closer to us.

Screams are echoing from every angle now. Scott looks into my vacant eyes and demands to know what horrors I have just witnessed. People try to move, some even jump off the train and onto the bloodied mass of corpses. They slide on the fluids spilled by their fellow man, slipping onto the floor as they scramble to get up and to get out.

I think about doing the same; my eyes carving out a path across the floor, thinking of jumping across the few spaces of clean concrete, as though they were stepping stones to freedom. I'm about to pull Scott with me but he doesn't move. I turn to see that he has become trapped between the masses of people who are struggling and moving in all directions. I try to keep a hold of him, thinking about who is in my way and who I can use as a shield, but as they push we are suddenly pulled apart. I fight against these people, my new enemies, thinking only of survival for Scott and me. I know that have to get to him; I have to get us out.

The lights start to flicker on and off and an announcement comes from the driver. 'Hold on, we're about to move,' he shouts. Any fear he once had seems to have been replaced by determination to get his remaining passengers to safety. I start to like him, to have faith in his ability, until I remember what has boarded our safe haven.

I keep shouting Scott's name and find that I suddenly have space to move, thanks to the few people who have already fled. I want to do the same, to get out of here and back to the surface. If the tube train moves then I hope it will take this evil with it, giving those who are willing to run a fighting chance of getting away. Find Scott and keep moving, I think. It is my only possible future now. I keep telling myself that we will get out and make it to the countryside. I picture my parent's faces when they see that I have not only come home, but also finally brought a man back with me, and how proud I will make them both.

The tube moves forward, then jolts to a halt again. The driver starts to speak but whatever reassurance he once offered is now replaced by his own screams; our one hope of escape has now been obviously been butchered before he ever got to save any of us.

I look around, desperately trying to find Scott in the midst of the moving bodies and frantic shouting. I shout his name, my anger at losing him seeming to drown out my fear.

The angle of those left seems to suddenly change as something new makes its way into our carriage. I hear the slamming of a door and the screams of the people who can see what has been waiting for us down here.

I look ahead and see jets of blood travelling over the heads of those about to meet their maker. I look through the window, seeing that the passengers who have jumped off have not fared any better; blood splatters across the train, making it look like a crimson canvas; the guts of those who had thought they were the lucky ones are now on show for all to see.

The number of people remaining in the carriage is quickly dropping; we have become one long line of victims. A few look like they are putting up a fight, but most simply fall back like they have already lost a battle they never saw coming. They collapse into the seats, slowly retreating towards those who are bundled around me, cries for mercy and screams of pain all muddle together. My own doom is now only a few feet away.

The lights go out, plunging us into near-blackness as the shadows of those around me claw for survival. Something suddenly takes hold of me and arms wrap around my waist. I don't scream or try to flee, but I soon feel the welcome touch of the man I have always longed for. I feel his breath on my neck; his embrace is warm and he gives off a faint, primal smell of sweat mixed with his aftershave. It's some new world scent – such obvious effort to prepare for this moment, our moment, this short space of time we have together.

He turns me around, wrapping me tight in his arms, then slowly steps backwards, taking me away from this place. The endless screams around us seem to fade away and we become a silent movie – black and white, except for his blue eyes which shine like an ocean of calm, despite the chaos we are in. We reach the end of the carriage and he presses his back against wall. I try to turn, to see the evil that approaches, but he doesn't let me. He faces our fear while making me bury myself into his chest. I feel his heartbeat, thumping a million times its normal speed. I'm not sure if it's only my body that is shaking, or if it's both of us, but it doesn't matter now.

'Ssshhhh,' he says, as he holds me tight.

I can feel people still scrambling around us, the number of screaming people diminishing with every step forward that it takes. The crowd pushes against us but he doesn't let go, he just holds us in together in the corner, in this little world he has carved out for us.

I start to cry as the inevitability of what will happen is overshadowed by the pain and suffering that will precede our deaths. I want this to end, and to end quickly, for us to both be welcomed to the next life: a place where I will be with Scott forever, always in his arms.

He places his head on mine and wraps his arms tighter around me. He doesn't say anything; we must both know that words are pointless now. He slowly rocks us both as my face stays joined with his chest. I want to be brave; I want to turn around and face our enemy together, but the simple truth is that I cannot bear to see it. I know what it is and that is enough for me; I want to keep all that I have seen as a vision somewhere in the distance.

There are now only a few desperate cries from the handful of people still shielding us. I can feel them drop one by one, their hard bodies hitting the floor with such regularity that I count them as they fall. Through all of this Scott doesn't move, as I wonder if he has his eyes shut too. I focus only on his beating heart. I never want it to stop; my eyes stay closed and our bodies join as one.

And when all the crying finally ends, when that last prayer for mercy goes unanswered, I wonder if I'm already dead. Nothing seems to happen; only the silent smell of death surrounds us as I convince myself that I have already been sliced open. Time seems to want to make me wait, as does the beast, as I feel something lingering behind me. I sense its breathing; think I feel the lashing of its tongue against my neck.

I don't scream now; I'm no longer willing to beg. I have what I want, can still feel the beating of the heart of someone I could easily love and I refuse to ask for more.

And so, in all but the darkness, I hold on tight to what is finally mine.

Tuesday 23rd August – The Caribbean

The Enduring Inevitability of Corporations and Cockroaches

After what seems like an eternity the tie comes off.

I knew it would. I watch as he throws it onto the chair and it joins all the others in a strange pile of overlapping patterns. The colour combination was not bold enough and so it lands next to the dark green one with white spots, and the blue and red one, which I thought stood a chance, but which apparently makes him look like a schoolboy.

'Not enough red,' he says and then continues to tell me how important today is. He has told me this a hundred times before, citing countless reasons why today is more important than any other day; it's even more important than the end of the world, because it will be the beginning of a new world. I nod and listen to the endlessly repeated lecture. I get that today is totally important, like in a crazy way, but it's no more or less important to me. It's just another day in this hellhole we're all stuck in.

'Perfect!' he announces, as he finds what he believes is an exact match, forcing me to turn my attention back to him just at the moment he pushes the knot up to his throat until it's almost choking him. Sadly, it's still not quite tight enough for my liking.

I nod back at him, not really knowing what to say. I think it makes him look like one of Virgin Atlantic's finest, although he's clearly a few too many kilos past what would be a respectable flying age.

He doesn't seem to want anything in return, just to have his own voice echoed back to him. He starts to comb back his hair, that combination of black and grey which seems to capture the essence of where he is in his life. He licks a finger and then focuses on a few stray hairs, putting them back in their place, forcing compliance where none is needed. When he finally turns to me he stares in complete shock. 'Henry!' he shouts, the look of horror blazing through his black, thick-framed glasses. 'You will have to change your entire outfit because we look far too similar. What were you thinking?' He fixes his cufflinks while his reflection judges from the mirror, watching to see what I will do next.

I look down at myself and then over at him and can't help but shrug my shoulders, although I quickly see what his issue is – the younger version of him looks better, healthier, a little less burdened.

'Sometimes I think you do this deliberately,' he says, his head shaking. 'You are my executive personal assistant but that doesn't mean you should try to outshine me. You just need to do as you are told. That was our deal and yet you often try your best to undermine me.'

I shake my head, openly denying his accusation but not wanting to bring this argument to life, not again.

He turns around so he can glare at me properly. 'You are not me and you never will be. When I think about what I had achieved by your age, it's clear you will not become an entrepreneur, even if the world was as it should be.' He makes his way towards me, placing a hand on each of my shoulders, his eyes digging deep into mine. 'You must realise your place and try to learn from me. You have the potential to go far in my organisation, providing you keep your head where it needs to be.'

He pulls down hard on my tie, forcing me to bow down to him. He keeps a tight hold on my reins and leans in closer, so he can whisper into my ear. 'We have no time for mistakes today. They arrive in less than an hour and I need everything to be perfect. If it isn't then we risk everything. We have all to gain or all to lose on this deal and it's your job to make sure I am focused on one thing and one thing only. Do you understand me?'

I cough, barely able to move. He eventually releases his grip and we both straighten ourselves up and look at the other, neither of us refusing to give in. I am the junior, the servant to my master, and a vulnerable servant at that. But as he looks at me I know that deep down he is the small one – the little boy in the body of a relatively successful man.

That's what my dad had said when he told me that an internship at SkyCloud Industries was the right thing to do, that it would offer me a future that he never could. From the moment he said it I didn't believe him but I knew I didn't really have a choice. My dad owed so much and it turns out the only thing he had to give was me. And so I've been made the whipping boy, the verbal punch-bag. I'm at his mercy and we both know it.

'You need to be 100% on your game today,' he says, his attention back on his reflection. I wonder what he sees – perhaps a cat who thinks he's a lion, or a boy who thinks he's a man. Or maybe he sees a different truth that he doesn't want to accept. 'If we lose this investment then we lose everything. The world has changed and we are now behind, which means we need to adapt and we need to do it quickly, before it's too late. My plan will only work if everyone plays their part and yours is to support me in making this deal happen.'

His eyes don't leave the mirror as he straightens his shirt, fussing over himself. 'My plan *will* work,' he mutters, as he tucks the shirt deeper into his trousers. He suddenly turns, almost walking into me. 'What are you still doing here? Go get changed and then check the room is ready to receive our Chinese guests.'

I nod and do as I'm told, walking away as he mutters something about never having asked for an executive lap-dog, but that's what he got.

I walk calmly out of the room, conducting my final affairs with the ultimate of dignity. Only when I get outside and close his door do I allow my most obvious of frustrations to show as I behave like the young guy I actually am. I storm down the corridor, scrunching up my face and pulling at my hair, allowing myself to be angry, to be entirely fucked off. I'm dizzy, lost and mad, all at the same time. I know that everything will be my fault if today goes wrong, because if we don't get the resources and the investment then we won't be able to launch the Sky Cities, and if we cannot launch them then we will not be able to deliver what we promised to the new world citizens. What gets under my skin is why any of this is my concern. I should be in college, in lectures, in a bar – anywhere but here, with the burden of a megalomaniac and the end of the world conspiring against me.

I'm not worried about the fact that if we don't launch in time all these people will be stuck on this small island, and if that happens, the country will eventually fall into chaos. I'm worried because these people, the apparent top citizens of planet Earth and complete bloodsuckers, have paid a lot of money and now we are risking a furious reaction from a several hundred angry members of the elite who are accustomed to only a five-star lifestyle. Telling them we spent all their money but never managed to get anything off the ground would not be received well. I imagine telling them that they should return to what's left of their decadent mansions and try to reconstruct their privileged lives that fate so abruptly stole from them.

I storm into my room, ripping off the tie from around my neck. I feel the burning sensation through my shirt as I picture the few other ties that I have. My limited funds only stretched to very basic colours. When I walked into Lawrence's suite this morning I looked my best; I had saved my favourite outfit for today, and now because of one small decision I find myself lost.

'You took the thought out of my mind,' a voice says from the other side of my room. I recognise it and I only look over out of instinct.

'Great minds always think alike,' she says, her naked body spread across the crisp, white sheets of my freshly made bed. She moves and stretches like a cat lying by a fire, taking her time, knowing that I'm watching. I stop still, my mind immediately mesmerised by the curves of her body. She lays flat, running a finger along her back and onto her firm ass before pointing at me and motioning me to come to her.

I shake my head, my sense of duty is waning, but somehow it still overrides every instinct pumping through my veins. 'Destiny, you can't be in here,' I say, turning my attention back to the wardrobe. I focus my entire mind on hunting for an outfit that matches, something that won't make my boss feel I'm challenging him and one that I haven't worn a hundred times before. It somehow helps, as I forget where I am and think back to the day I left home. My mum did her best; bought the best she could with what money they had. She smiled when we laid the ten shirts and ten ties out on my bed. There was just about enough for two weeks and they were varied enough to stop people thinking they had seen me wearing the same thing, and discovering the pattern of how poor I really was.

'Henry, I need you!' Destiny shouts, still pinned to my duvet. 'Please come to me.'

I take a deep breath as my loneliness takes over any sense of control and I slowly move to the bed. I soon realise my mistake as she lashes out, trying to pull me back into our endlessly complicated web of lies. I pull away, my mind unable to comprehend what will happen if this precious creature is found in the executive assistant's bedroom, in this wrong place – in any room at all with me. I move too slowly, my reaction too late as a hand catches my shirt, creasing it as she grabs hold. My hands are soon all over hers, grappling and pulling her away, all the time shouting that she is damaging my shirt, wrecking my day, ruining everything.

She hears them too, the words that I cannot retract. 'You sound like my fucking father!' she shouts as she lets go and lies back down, choosing to finally cover herself with a sheet. 'Why don't you lighten up? It's not like he will ever come into the room of one of his minions, is it?'

I sit on the edge of the bed and run a finger along her leg. 'I know that, of course I do. But you don't seem to get how important today is and how much is resting on us reaching an agreement with the Chinese.'

When she doesn't answer I walk over to the window, looking across the beach and out across the ocean. This complex used to be one of the best resorts in the Caribbean, and until recently I could only have dreamed about coming here and taking a girl to this place for a summer vacation of sweet love and crazy nights. This place is probably all that remains of luxury life on Earth; it's also empty, lifeless and so utterly incomplete. The only time it will mean anything again will be when all our guests arrive for a couple of nights ahead of the launch. Some are already here but many more will follow, and I'm sure it will be two days of partying and champagne toasts to the new world, as we send off the lucky ones who are getting to escape. They will most likely suck the final few drops of life out of this island and leave it with nothing, meaning that for the sake of my own survival, I hope I'm with them and not with those who must remain behind.

We all know that the people who call this place home will get left the landfill and a hangover from the special few. They will have to live off whatever remains, from the cast-offs of the super-rich. I find it ironic that those elite few will still need those on the ground to send up food and supplies, all of which will be locked away from those down below.

I turn to her, hoping she will at least listen, if not understand what troubles me, what should be troubling us all. 'The world has changed a lot, but we don't see it when we're on this island. We're sheltered, cut off from all the bad things that are happening. I heard earlier that the United Kingdom is now in big trouble. It was the only country still transmitting from that part of the world; we're getting nothing from more than half of the planet. Iceland disappeared yesterday and no one knows why. The world is collapsing, Destiny, do you get that?'

She says nothing as I stare out the window at the people who are enjoying the beach. They are early arrivals from places that have already lost hope. Lawrence claims they have good reasons to be in the final few – they are the scientists, politicians and doctors who will be needed in the new world, and while I question their qualifications I am ultra-confident of their ability to pay the entry fee. I turn around, checking the reason for her silence, expecting to see that she is listening, reflecting – maybe even realising that what is happening may well be something that even her father cannot protect us from. She's still on the bed but she's not heard anything I've said. She is lying on her back, her legs in the air, gently teasing herself.

She lets out a long moan. 'Forget world collapse. Get over here now and shove your big stick inside me!'

I shake my head, much like I do every time she makes this demand. Sometimes it's coupled with a smile, nudging me to appreciate Destiny for the primal beast she is, but this time it comes from a place of genuine disappointment. She cannot see what is happening; her refusal to look beyond the moment and the simplest of pleasures proves that she doesn't deserve what she will automatically get – passage out of here and a privileged life of luxury for as long as her precious daddy lives and leads us all. As much as I want it for her, I know she doesn't deserve it, and if he doesn't survive for as long as he hopes then it's anyone's guess whether her whining will be tolerated, or if she will simply be thrown overboard.

'Fuck me now, Henry!' She pushes her finger deeper inside herself and lets out a loud moan. 'Fuck me now or I'll scream so loud! I'll scream until they all come running into your room to see what we're doing together!'

I move towards the bed, pulled closer by a mixture of desperation and anticipation. The threat is not registering in my pants and only my mind wonders if perhaps I have let this go too far, that this once simple girl has now become my crazed lover. By the time I consider my choices I'm already on top of her, softly kissing her neck; her moans are subdued as she forces our bodies into an embrace.

She pulls my pants down and rips my shirt open. I sigh, wanting to tell her off for ruining one of my few perfectly good ones, but before I can say anything she's got hold of my cock and is forcing it inside her. She jolts our bodies together, forcing us both to move to the rhythm of her constant moans and her desperate need for my attention.

I don't spend this precious time in the realms of lust; in fact, I'm not really in the same place as Destiny at all. I think of her working both of our bodies towards a joint purpose but all I really care about is everything that must be done today. As she forces me to go faster, to reach the climax she's been teasing herself to reach all morning, I wonder which shirts I have ironed and ready to go, and which ties will match. I think to myself that this isn't how the morning of the pitch to launch the salvation of mankind should have been, not from my perspective anyway.

******

'You've changed into blue now,' he says, looking me up and down, trying to find fault in the most obvious of places, never knowing the layers of blame he often manages to place on me.

'I changed into a grey suit, blue shirt and blue tie, something plain so I would look nothing like you, because I didn't want to outshine you in any way, sir.'

He adjusts his glasses, like he always does when he is deciding if something is worth a fight. 'Good,' he finally says, much to my surprise. 'You're starting to learn but you need to remember it's not about outshining me but rather about knowing your place. Do you know your place, Henry?'

I nod, only enough to satisfy his need for control. I have still not truly got to know where my place is in all of this. I haven't had somewhere I could call home for weeks and no one to trust since I left my parents. The absence of both makes me feel more alone than I had ever thought possible. I'm in a cage with a cobra I thought I used to know. He used to be someone I trusted; I remember him from my youth as being a decent and kind person, but then I grew up and found out the truth.

He smiles back but doesn't say anything – a clear signal to move on.

But I don't want to move on. I have things to ask, more that I want to know. I want that decent man back, the one who would give me a few bucks each time we met, telling me to save it, to be wise – to be everything my dad wasn't. I followed his advice, it seemed pretty simple but I never knew at the time that his generosity had such powerful messages attached: I was constantly being conditioned to think of my parents as inadequate. I think of them now but no bad thoughts come into my mind. Our separation has only served to remind me of how much I miss them; my dad's reckless energy to achieve his next big thing and my mum's grounded smile – they both worked together to mould me into who I am today.

These thoughts make me desperate to succeed, to feel like I have somehow paid them back. My determination to find a way makes me take a deep breath. I wonder if this is the moment, if I still have enough in our mutually worn-out bank account to pull this off. I watch him going about his business, shuffling folders around his desk and checking figures on papers as if they hold the lost key to our future. Maybe they do but I can only think of my future, of what I want, and so I cough loudly, enough to make him look up for just a moment. 'So, I've been meaning to ask you something.'

He stares at me, his eyes narrowing, his keen mind no doubt already working this out. He could probably ask the question for me but he won't. He won't give me any help or mercy – it's simply not his way.

'I was wondering when my parents will be flying out here?' I ask, watching for any reaction. 'They still haven't been told anything and I'm worried that time is running out.'

He stops moving and stares at me. This isn't what he wanted – not today, not now. 'Henry, for heaven's sake, how should I know this detail?'

'I just thought–'

'You thought that just because your father is my brother that I would pay him special attention for something as important as this project? And with everything going on today, with the entire fate of this project and thousands of people's lives resting on these next few hours, you pick this moment to ask me?'

I keep quiet, unable to answer, my mind finding it impossible to think of any reason he will understand. My entire purpose in being here, in becoming a hopeful survivor, is thanks to my parents and their love for me. It's the only answer I can give, and it just happens to be the only one he will never understand.

He moves around his desk so he can get closer and look down at me. 'You know that my brother and I have never had a good relationship and now the world is falling apart he somehow wants to latch onto my success? I made it clear from the day you arrived here that this isn't about family and that you need to prove your worth as my assistant, which doesn't mean a place will ever be guaranteed for your parents. I will not allow emotions to get in the way of judgement and this outburst reminds me that you have as much to learn about family as you do corporate affairs. I'm glad your father gave you to me: I can at least try to fix you.'

I want to shake my head to tell him he is wrong, that he will always be wrong to believe that family loyalty is not a part of who we are and where we come from. But I cannot say that, not to him and not right now, and so I nod and look down, not wanting to start another argument. 'I just hope they make it onto the island.'

He takes his glasses off and sits on the corner of his desk, taking a few moments to reply. This is uncharacteristic: normally, he would strike like the snake I know him to be. 'The truth is that the list is still being finalised but I'm struggling to find an adequate reason for them to be a part of this. You know that in the new world everyone must have a purpose and useful abilities. The reality is that your mother is entirely unskilled and your father cannot pay a fraction of the cost for transport and entry.'

I refuse to hear his words, how inaccurately and unfairly he is portraying things. 'You weren't there. You didn't see how hard my mum worked to look after my sister until –'

He holds up a hand, already shaking his head. 'Please do not even start to play this card with me. What happened to your sister was very unfortunate and we all feel her loss but you cannot let the past control your future, and I will not be forced into making a rash decision.'

I feel my mouth gaping open as the tears build, caused by both his bite and the memory of Jessie and her journey from health to hell. 'You have no idea of the pain we went through and the sacrifice my mum made to look after her at home until the end.'

He nods, almost like he is agreeing, as if he could know anything about this: he never visited and never offered to help. 'That may be the case but we have little call for dedicated housewives in the new world, and add to this the fact that your father has failed at pretty much everything he has ever done. You can really see my dilemma about letting people up into paradise if they don't have the skills to enable them to pay their way.'

'Or the bags of money that are also accepted as payment?'

He suddenly leaps from the desk, pushing and forcing me backwards, before grabbing hold of me. He grips my body tightly with both hands and drags me to the window, making me look outside. 'My passion and singular understanding achieved this and just look at what I have created. I have not had the time or the energy to worry about what I cannot change or those who will burden the project. With my vision of an overcrowded planet and the need for something new, I have made it possible for us to create a better life for those who are daring enough to reach out and grab it.' I choke for breath as he squeezes tighter. 'Answer me this, Henry, will your parents ever be daring enough to reach for the sky as I have done?'

I want to say yes. I want to argue that in their own way they have reached for the moon and more, but their reach was as limited as most people's; they could only stretch a little considering the background: a dying planet full of clueless caretakers who never took their jobs seriously. I look into his eyes and shake my head, rubbing the burnt area on my neck against his tight grip. I want to tell him that he's right, or is at least as close to it as anyone I have met. We need to do something different and his is the best option I've heard yet.

He releases his hold on my neck and embraces me lightly, pulling me closer to the window. 'Just imagine what we can achieve with all these likeminded individuals working as part of a bigger team in a small and co-operative town. And, yes, they need the money to pay for it, but doesn't the fact that they have acquired wealth indicate that they are more successful, better educated and more equipped to cope than most people? It will not be perfect and it will be hard and that is the reason why we must have the right people, people who can work together to achieve this vision of our new world.'

I don't answer. Instead, I look down, distracted by a cockroach scuttling along the floor, finding free passage into areas that would normally have been off limits to its kind. It worries me how quickly their numbers have grown. Pest control became a thing of the past when the army of gardeners deserted this place. The thing is large and seems adventurous; no longer caring about what humans will do to it. I've always hated them and as it comes closer to my shoes I instinctively pull away. I feel sweat dripping off me now, caused both by the heat of Lawrence's body coupled and the mid-afternoon sun beating through the windows, now that we can no longer afford air conditioning.

It's just about to reach my foot when Lawrence finally sees what has distracted me from his latest sermon. He doesn't hesitate for a moment and stands on it; the crushing sound echoes in my ears and I see its guts spreading out across the floor. He looks down at me, his face expressionless. 'We don't have time to clear piles of ironing; we can't promise that the next job will earn enough to pay back a debt that never seems to end. This isn't about families or feuds. This isn't even about me, this is about our collective legacy.'

I nod, trying to prise my way out of his hold, knowing all too well what is coming next. He will explain in much detail the failures of my side of the family. This will be followed by threats that I will be sent back to experience the last days with my parents, which would be something I would cherish if it wasn't for the fact they have sacrificed everything to put me here. I imagine turning up at home, desperately trying to find my abandoned parents. Their faces would be a mixture of relief and disappointment. And then there is Destiny – how can I leave her?

'My company and my creation will live on long after I am gone. The new world will remember what happened here. An organisation that operates correctly must never think about just one individual. We are all just small cogs that allow the whole unit to survive.'

Another cockroach crawls along the floor. It continues over the grey tiles until it finds the other cockroach's remains. We both look down at it, both watching where it goes, knowing there will be another thousand where this one has come from. It sees its friend, or perhaps its brother, up close; it must somehow know that it's dead. The insides are spread all around for what would seem like a battleground measured in many metres if they were human beings.

Lawrence's foot moves, ready to strike another blow to the crawling kind, but instead he kicks it away and looks at me. 'Henry, never forget that both corporations and cockroaches are able to endure. Both can adapt and both can grow rapidly, and both think about the whole, rather than just one or two or ten. Humans will always think about themselves as individuals but bring them together under a religion, a dictatorship or in a corporation, and then suddenly they find they have a collective purpose. If your parents do not make the final list then you must find a way to appreciate the bigger picture, to understand that space is limited. You need to take an objective view of these strange times we now live in.'

I take a deep breath and nod, knowing there isn't much else I can do. 'I hear what you're saying, Lawrence, I really do. So I assume that feeling includes Destiny, as well?'

He stares out of the window, not dignifying my question with a look. 'Don't test me by talking about the thing most precious to me, Henry. Not today.'

*****

'The helicopters are about to land,' Tyrell says to Lawrence.

He nods in return, then grabs Tyrell's shoulder, shaking his hand and looking down at him like he does with most people. He squeezes it tight, as though he wants to force his thoughts into the mind of his poor subject. 'This is the moment we have been waiting for, my dear friend. The time is fast approaching when everything will come together, with my technology and the ability of the Chinese to build anything quickly and efficiently.'

Tyrell nods. 'This will be a special moment in the history of man, of that I am sure.'

'It will indeed,' Lawrence says, then pulls away, all too soon for my liking. He never gives Tyrell the time that he needs, or the respect he really deserves.

But this time Tyrell seems to see this lack of attention and continues to shake his hand, his firm grip keeping Lawrence in the same spot. 'You won't be forgetting my little island in all of this, will you?'

Lawrence laughs out loud, looking first at me and then settling his eyes on Tyrell. He gazes at him with some sort of a hypnotic stare. It has been very clear that he is trying to keep control of what has been a delicate situation since the moment we landed here. 'Now, why would I do that? We need each other and all of us will be inter-dependent forever. Just think about how impossible it would be to launch the new cities without your island.'

'And my people?' Tyrell asks.

'Must we do this now?' Lawrence says, looking to the open sky, making it clear where his energy is focused. 'You will get the fair percentage, just as we talked about. There isn't room for everyone and you know that.'

Tyrell nods, knowing what we all know, having been given the same speech I have heard many times before. 'There had better be a balance, black and white, that's all I'm saying.'

Lawrence gives a slow and pronounced nod in return. 'There will be fairness, as I have always assured you.'

'I do not think that this is the same thing, not in the eyes of different men.'

'It will be in my eyes,' Lawrence says, pulling Tyrell forward. 'Now come on, they will arrive in a moment. We are going to build this new world, cloud by cloud. Look around you and think about what we are going to create in just a few weeks.'

I watch them, my eyes following them both as I look at what is already here. It's easy to take the hotel for granted, but I never do. I have never stayed anywhere like this place and even though half of the five-star resort is closed off this place still amazes me. It has more pools than I have owned swimming trunks in my short life, but it's when we turn 180 degrees and see what is behind us – what has replaced the acres of gardens – that I really feel my heart set on fire. A concrete platform stretches across the complex, white and solid with long steel slats running through it. It's like a patchwork design: more a piece of art than engineering. These slats all join together, woven into a complex pattern that houses the bolts drilled deep into the ground, all part of the plan to keep everything in the sky attached to the earth. To the left is the launch centre – a hastily constructed platform of scaffolding without any luxuries, not even windows. In this heat they aren't needed but when I see the rows of desks with computers sitting on them, all exposed to sun and sand, I wonder if the Chinese will think of us as a little amateurish.

We all step onto the concrete structure and start to walk along the red carpet that leads to the central building. The carpet feels soft under my shoes – one of the few luxuries still allowed. They walk a few more paces and then stop, both looking up at what has been named 'Cloud Reach'. It's one of the few prototypes that have already journeyed to the clouds and back, proving that Lawrence's vision can be realised. Measuring thirty feet in diameter, it isn't ever going to be big enough for no more than a lucky handful to fit inside, but it proves that this wild concept can work. Inside is a small control room, the engine area and a boardroom – the place where Lawrence has sold dreams to so many of those who are desperate to be permanent survivors.

Each group of hopeful delegates is treated to these luxury surroundings, with all the best the Caribbean can offer, furnished by top designers who already have a promised ticket. The first time I went up into the clouds, I have to admit that I felt a rush at knowing I was part of this, as well as knowing that humanity can achieve anything it wants when working together. The smiles of the sometimes skilled, usually creative, often super-rich people would always give me a warm feeling knowing that we were building something big.

I often look at the clouds and imagine 100 silver mushrooms in the light blue sky, all glistening from the solar panels running along their dome-shaped roofs. The finished structures will be bigger than Cloud Reach and will stretch for quarter of a mile in length, with the bottom half of the structure holding the engines for the on-board motors and living quarters. Imagine a giant hamburger: the bottom part attached to steel tethers and various power cables, while the top bun contains the balloon control area and individually maintained super-helium feeds that can lift the immense structure up into the sky.

People would often laugh at Lawrence, pointing out to him just how expensive helium is. This is so obviously true but imagine what you can get your hands on when it's not being protected, and besides he would just show them the next steel tether, which runs even further up into the clouds, far above us. This next structure reaches up towards the stars and houses the hydrogen generators and more giant balloon casings. At this height, with our precious citizens no longer at risk from explosions, this final dome holds the floating city in place, keeping us up high, safe from whatever lurks on the ground.

It took me time to accept the idea that something so big could be kept afloat by just a couple of different kinds of powerful gases and some giant engines. He proved it could work with Cloud Reach and he showed that air density, temperature and pressure aren't capable of stopping us. You just need a big enough balloon, as Lawrence often says. His team of geeks have even managed to find a home for water storage tanks and heating, insulation and waste removal, which does have a nasty habit of dropping on those left below.

When our visitors arrive we don't discuss this detail. Instead we let them look out of their hotel windows to marvel at the view; for most of them the experience seems to rapidly change from post-apocalyptic escape to simply viewing a new holiday home or a second apartment. They quickly forget the hell that will be inevitably unfolding in some other place, but I wonder if they will realise what awaits them in this new life. The opulent surroundings of Cloud Reach give a real view of the height of the project, but the sheer scale of what Lawrence plans means that most of the lucky ones will be in box rooms with no windows and only shared facilities, at least for the first launch. Although I always see shock on their faces at the end of each tour, I am invariably left amazed by Lawrence's ability to turn this around and to sell his vision of the future despite the probable harshness of the first year or two.

I think about this new vision for the future, and the Chinese who have come to hear this story and the ultimate selling job Lawrence has done on Tyrell, who must remain dedicated to the plan. As they walk forward I stay close to both of them, desperate to hear Lawrence's new twist. Once again, he wins over the simple man in front of him who will forever remain doubtful. He isn't a clever man but he is a powerful one, at least on this island.

Tyrell examines him. Questions and demands seem to be on the tip of his tongue, but they never quite surface. He doesn't really have any choice now: he has murdered most of the small parliament; the remaining people are on his side by brutal default. The police gave up their title the moment the world started slipping into chaos and this man now rules the island and everything on it. He doesn't really have a clue; he just happened to be the police chief at the time and was offered a way out by some guy in a posh suit and with a far bigger vocabulary. If world power still existed then the army, an army of some nation, would have landed on these shores and liberated the people and removed these madmen long before it was turned into a launch pad. But there are no armies within a few hundred miles and any organisation that is left in power has other things to worry about. Other problems have paled into insignificance compared to the dramas now facing each individual nation.

And then came along Lawrence, an egotistical but determined man who seemed to have an idea to save some of humanity. He's carving out a path to the future and bringing a select few with him. Tyrell will make the final cut – after all, we need him. We need his land and we need his people. But most of all we need them not to join us in the clouds and to keep their place firmly on land, to protect our roots and sacrifice themselves for our greater good.

Despite all Lawrence's outstanding sales pitches, this is one I'm still waiting to hear.

*****

'Launch sequence commencing,' a voice announces from the command centre.

It's the standard drill, a slightly over-the-top take-off procedure for something so slow and which will be travelling vertically upwards, with only the odd wind turbulence to disturb us. There's little to see at this stage but I still remember how blown away I was during my first few trips. Maybe I'm too used to the standard sequence now but one thing that strikes me as we're being served drinks, is that the Chinese delegation aren't smiling, unlike all the other guests we've had in here previously.

Lawrence talks as champagne is offered and declined by everyone but me. I encourage Roddy, our usual servant on these missions, to fill my glass to the top. Today of all days I believe it will be needed. I watch our new delegates but listen to the usual noises, hoping they will spark some interest. Below us I feel the roar of the engines, powering the motorised fans that will growl below us and carry us upwards. Above us, I hear the hiss of the pressure valves, doing their bit to regulate the helium flow, and above that the hydrogen generators are coming to life. When you put all these bits together I think it's the sound of hope – we engineered this creation and together we stand a chance of survival. When I say 'we', I include myself, but I don't know what my role is apart from following Lawrence around and accepting whatever abuse is required of me.

'The entire system regulates itself through a central computer system,' Lawrence says, leaning back in his oversized, leather chair and smiling as he spins his well-rehearsed and perhaps overused story. 'It might be a little clunky to start but once we're safely anchored in position the system really comes into its own. It can make up to 20 adjustments per second which, when you consider it is battling against weather, pressure and gravity, is something quite remarkable.'

'You really don't hear a thing once we're at target altitude,' I say, leaning forward, desperate to be noticed but even more determined for our guests to feel what we feel.

All three of the Chinese delegates turn my way, all of them staring at me through dark eyes, their mouths unmoving, unwilling to offer the slightest acknowledgement. I catch Lawrence from the corner of my eye; his scowling look tells me I've gone too far by daring to be heard.

The only sound comes from Tyrell, who is sitting to my left; he calls up a deep laugh from the pit of his stomach. 'Best be quiet from now on, little man,' he says, grinning and flashing all the gold he could afford. His eyes are on mine as I look to the floor, obviously defeated.

'We have set our target altitude to 8,000 feet,' Lawrence says, making turn back to him. 'At this altitude we stop moving upwards, although we may sometimes move up to 10,000 feet, depending on pressure and weather fluctuations.'

The lead Chinese guy, who goes by the name of Jin, leans forward, looking slightly out of place sitting in the fine leather luxury at a time of obvious austerity. 'At this altitude there will be some need for human acclimatisation, so how do you plan to overcome this with such a large number of people?'

Lawrence smiles, having heard this amateur question a hundred times. 'Actually, there are about 140,000,000 people who already live at this altitude all year round. We reach our optimum altitude slowly and in the main super-structures this will take even longer, so it should give everyone the chance to adjust.'

Jin nods back, his eyes narrow; he has been gazing almost exclusively at Lawrence. 'I appreciate the engineering triumph that launching this small object into the lower atmosphere represents, but how exactly will you launch and keep a giant platform afloat in the sky?'

'And keep it there for hundreds of years?' one of his men says.

His leader looks at him and gives a nod. It's a small gesture, but it shows that he agrees – indeed, that he almost appreciates the opinion. It's simple yet I realise it's everything that I don't get from Lawrence.

'I'm glad you've asked, gentlemen,' Lawrence says, as his glass is refilled. 'We have the technology and the idea, but what we are lacking is the labour and building expertise. That's what I hope you can bring to this project. I'm going to explain our remarkable story so far, so may I ask again if you would please join me with a drink?' He grins, adjusting his glasses and crossing his legs, getting himself comfortable.

I feel it's a little short-lived celebration as the Chinese delegation shake their heads in unison. 'Just the facts will do, Mr Lawrence,' Jin says. 'We will not waste the luxury of time when all we need is knowledge.'

I watch Lawrence uncross his legs and take a deep breath. I really hope he will succeed, because if he cannot convince these men then his dream will not work. He has continually prided himself on not bringing his design team up here with us, on the fact that all the technical and toughest questions he will answer himself, as our leader and our self-appointed saviour. But there are too many pieces missing to make this happen without help, and despite how inspired his vision is we all know it won't take off without a lot of help.

*****

'Let me explain this again, gentlemen. It really is not difficult,' Lawrence says as his glass is refilled for the fourth time by the ever-helpful Roddy. He fills up mine, too, knowing I have the same needs as my master even if I don't deserve to have them fulfilled quite as much.

'The platform will be built on land, starting with the tallest structure – the hydrogen container, which is designed to be significantly higher than the rest of the city. Once the generators are active, the pull will help to drag the rest of the city upwards, while still keeping a safe distance from a gas which is obviously highly flammable. The other parts of the sky city are the helium containers and the living quarters, with the motorised fans below us. It's just like launching a regular hot air balloon but on a massive scale. Please remember the giant balloons will be individually woven, with their own helium feeds, so that even if one is damaged there are many more. There will be no need to repair any balloons, as new ones can be launched from the centre of the structure, meaning they can always regenerate themselves.'

'What about storm damage?' one of the doubters says. 'Even at your proposed altitude there will still be weather factors to contend with.'

Lawrence takes a deep breath and nods. 'Weather will affect us to some degree but we will not experience storms of the severity of those felt on land.' He looks around and then smiles. 'Please remember that there will be two types of giant gas feeds, both pulling us upwards, so life in the clouds really will be utterly safe and very different from life down here.'

None of them laugh or smile; there's not even a nod of agreement. 'Storms below will make your land-based operation vulnerable, of this you cannot deny.'

'Yes, the anchor centres will be affected by storms, but remember that these islands have been chosen due to their stability and the predictability of their weather. The steel ropes cannot be broken and any turbulence will be reduced by on board motorised fans that will automatically stabilise us and keep movement to a minimum, just as they are doing now. It will feel no different from being at sea or on a plane.'

Everyone stops and looks around, all of our guests suddenly realising that we are no longer moving. In fact, we stopped a while ago, in the heat of the debate, and now we are simply hovering 8,000 feet above the ground.

Lawrence suddenly stands up and opens his arms, as if embracing the silence, seeing the break in the conversation as representing a change in our fortunes. 'Gentlemen, perhaps it's time to stop discussing and go smell the clouds.'

This is his favourite expression. It's more appropriate than "smell the roses", as we're a long way from where they grow. I'm thankful when all three of them stand up. They are handed their coats as they head towards the door to a small balcony. We all step out into the cold air and take hold of the railings, as I remember just how chilly life will be up here. I look around and feel like time has stopped; there is nothing here but a vacuum of sky.

Lawrence stands next to Jin, watching carefully as we all look over the edge and they finally break into a smile, no doubt marvelling at the fact we are looking down at the blue sea and a scattering of land. I peer over too, taking every chance I get to enjoy this view, still aware that if I don't make the final cut, I will need to keep hold of this vision until the day I die. The day may yet come when I look up and think about what Destiny can see as she stares down.

'It's a thing of beauty, isn't it?' Lawrence says, looking down as well. 'We can adjust the height of the sky city depending on weather conditions. If it's going to pour with rain we go higher and if it's going to be a scorcher of a day we can drop down lower. The temperature will be a lot lower, but the natural heat from the engines and generators will combat this.'

Jin looks up at him and finally gives a nod of approval. 'You have created something quite remarkable, but you must know that there are too many variables to contend with to make this a viable option for the masses of survivors.'

Lawrence smiles back at him, looking like he has finally won the ultimate accolade, even though it comes with a side dish of scepticism. 'And that's the beauty of big businesses. We're not constrained by government funding or rules and regulations. We simply get on with things. We have already sent this baby up high enough to know what the coldest temperatures that man and machine can withstand, and we have learnt the hard way what happens when the engines fail.' He looks back out into the open air and then down to the ocean below us. 'This isn't our first sky city and this isn't our original crew, but what we have lost in resources we have gained in knowledge, and now all we need is your engineering expertise to build this on a much larger scale. The principles of gravity, density and flight do not change. We saw that when the first commercial super tanker hit the open sea and the first jumbo jet took off.'

'You talk with much passion, Mr. Lawrence,' Jin says. 'And you bear the loss of your people like a true leader.'

'Thank you,' Lawrence says, smiling down at his new, potential subject.

Jin bows his head in return, for the first time since they have arrived. 'But what I would like to know more about is your passengers. How many you propose to put up here on one platform, for example, and how do you plan to pick the lucky few?'

'Each sky city will have one thousand residents, and once we have established an air transport network we will allow people to transfer between them. Imagine a future where you wake up every day a little closer to the sun than we are now and where you can board a transport shuttle to take you to another sky city – maybe to see a friend or perhaps for work? These people will pay a survivors' fee to join the city but after that they will be required to add genuine value to our community.'

They all stare at him quietly. Their silence is partly because they are mesmerised by his ideas and partly, I think, because they simply don't believe him. I don't think they doubt the engineering possibilities – after all, we're standing on the crest of his achievements – I just think they have the same doubts as the rest of us.

'And these happy residents, what will they do all day? What will their jobs be?' one of the men asks.

Jin's hand goes up, silencing the others. 'Before we discuss what these inhabitants will do all day, I still want to know exactly how you will pick the few from the many.'

Lawrence nods quickly, because he has heard this question more than any other, far more frequently than people asking if it is actually possible to send a thousand tonnes of steel into the air. 'They must add value to the future world. We cannot have people who are simply along for the ride; we need researchers for future technologies, repair teams, maintenance, teachers, scholars, food technicians and many other skilled individuals.'

'And will all these people be residents of America?'

Lawrence shakes his head and points a finger at Jin, the man who was a welcome guest and our hopeful saviour just an hour ago. 'If you're thinking that I am only planning to do this for my people then you are mistaken. Tyrell has occupied these islands, I have the idea and we need your engineering speed and ingenuity to make this happen far quicker than we originally intended.'

'So you propose an equal third split?' Jin says, all too quick and all too clear on the hand that he wants dealt to him and his people.

'I wasn't quite thinking that. You must remember that hundreds of people in my organisation have been designing these sky cities for many years. We saw them as an alternative place to live on an already overcrowded planet. They were a commercial venture but since the world has fallen into chaos, I believe they are now man's best hope of survival. We all know that our best chance lies in getting off the ground and this project offers us a chance to do that.'

'And you need us to build them? So we should technically get at least half of the spaces available, especially when you consider how big our population is.'

Lawrence is shaking his head and behind him Tyrell is doing the same. Both of them know that the more people they allow on, the less they get for themselves. 'No, I'm sorry, but I cannot do that,' Lawrence says. 'An equal share is a fair deal, gentlemen. The journey will start here but we will inevitably build many sky cities that will house more people, and the more we build, the more people from *every* continent get saved.'

Jin is nodding now; he seems almost sold on the idea. 'So we can use this technology to build more of these sky cities?'

'Of course, we will enter into a deal to share resources and expertise. If we build and float this first Sky City then many others will follow.'

The Chinese look at each other. They are huddled tightly together, talking amongst themselves in a language that I guarantee none of us know. They are difficult to understand, not just what they're saying but also what they mean, but their harsh tones and loud words seem to indicate more towards negative feelings about everything that has been said so far.

They eventually stop talking. Jin looks at Lawrence and then at Tyrell. 'What we have seen today is truly remarkable. You must trust my word on that. But we do have concerns about the quality of the people who will reside in these cities.'

'Quality?' Lawrence says, shaking his head. 'What do you mean?'

'These cities will be small when compared to the mass of land people are used to. There will be little space and far fewer resources. To this end, I believe we would be better suited picking those who will cope better with being economical. I mean people who are used to having limited space and scarce resources, as well as those who can remain focused and actively contribute for the duration of their lives.' He looks over the edge and then back up at Lawrence. 'I am sure you will agree that these structures cannot carry passengers and the question we keep returning to is what will you do with the mass of undisciplined, overweight and inevitably older people?'

'Are you saying what I think you're saying: that Americans are not the right people?'

Jin nods, not trying to hide his thoughts. 'We have carefully observed those who have landed on your island so far and judging by the amount of suitcases and other baggage we can only assume they are passengers and not engineers, builders or other active contributors. They may have bought a place in your new world but how can you possibly convince them that they will need to leave behind the luxury that they have become accustomed to, and live a new life of frugality and hard work up in the sky?'

Lawrence mumbles his words. 'But they have paid their way and they understand that there will be a new way of life up here.'

Jin shakes his head in response. 'They have left the paradise they lived in before and moved into a five-star hotel until the Sky City is ready to carry them off into the future. I believe your idea will work but I do not believe they are the right calibre of people.'

I step forward, determined to help. 'We will have a sky citizens' charter which they will live up to,' I say, the words falling out of my mouth before I have checked that they make sense and that they're appropriate to this brutal world of business.

Everyone stares at me again, probably wondering why I'm speaking and why I have chosen now to contribute to the discussion. Only Lawrence doesn't scowl at me this time, and I wonder if he really appreciates my help.

'I'm sure that you will, young man,' Jin says, with a small smile. 'But we believe a much better location is the Himalayas. When you consider all the variables of land and people there, as well as the easy access to significant resources, it is a much stronger proposition.'

Tyrell is shaking his head and looking at Lawrence; he clearly knew what was coming. This is the moment of tension in their relationship that I have been waiting to see, desperate to witness the strain in what others view as the perfect partnership. As long as they have had an island and an idea they are safe together, but now something is threatening to pull this apart, and I'm not sure Tyrell will ever be enough to keep it together.

The Chinese stick to their resolve: they walk into the reception area and sit back down, as if they had simply been viewing a house. The rest of us are left with no choice but to follow them back in, as Jin tells Lawrence that we can start our descent.

Lawrence follows them back in. I can tell he is angry. He sits down and looks at the floor and then back to our guests. 'The deal was to build the first sky city here, above this island, and for there to be any deal I must insist upon this.'

Jin stares at him for a moment, perhaps sizing him up or perhaps not remotely interested – it's difficult to tell after all that has been said. I wonder if all they needed was the inspiration that they have been given today to go and create their own version – one that's better, faster and has the right people living in it. I wonder what Lawrence would do if that happens. He won't be able to copyright it, not now – not with everything else going on.

'There has been no hostile activity in that region and the geographic barriers to the threats advancing on other countries are quite immense. When you couple this with a significantly more advanced workforce, it really does show how ill-advised it is to use this location for a project of this magnitude.' He leans forward, towards Lawrence. 'You clearly have a grand dream, but do you really want it to die in such a small place?'

Tyrell bangs the nearest table to him and stands up, looking over at Lawrence. 'What are they talking about? We have had no activity on this island or anywhere nearby and we have water all around us!' He drawers an invisible circle in the air as if we needed help to see what he is saying.

The Chinese don't move; all of them remaining still like seated statues, until Jin finally leans back. 'Mr Lawrence, I think we should take a break and then continue this negotiation once we are back on land – perhaps minus your colleague, Mr Tyrell.'

'What?' Tyrell shouts, his arms raised and his eyes blood-red. 'I will not have this on my island! You are in my home and in this place that has already been built as a visitor centre!'

'With all due respect, a visitor centre does not build sky cities. This island is too small and the threat is very real and likely to be close. What is left of the United States is on your doorstep and water has been proven to do very little to stop the advance.'

Tyrell points at his adversary, his new tormentor, as he makes his way around the table, his big arm outstretched, today's drama now taking its toll. The visitors start to fidget in their chairs; it's the first action that has provoked a physical response from them.

Lawrence quickly moves to stop him, his height making him a dominant presence, despite his more slender frame. 'Tyrell!' he shouts. It manages to get a reaction: the bulky islander stops still at his master's call.

Lawrence looks around at the others. 'Gentlemen, we cannot argue like this, not at such a crucial time. If we are to do this for humanity and make a commercial activity from it then we will find fair terms with which to sign this agreement. We will build the first sky city on these islands because we can make the launch centres secure to protect the anchors, and Tyrell has guaranteed that we can make them safe from whatever threats are lurking out there. We have control of a substantial number of weapons and many men who can use them.'

'You can believe me on that,' Tyrell says, both of his hands on a table, looking more like a gorilla than a leader of the remaining inhabitants of this island.

Lawrence starts pacing. 'If we need to build more then we will do so, but through fair and equitable corporate terms. We must remember that we are to become new world leaders and we cannot start by arguing on the eve of such great success. Man built and sailed the first boat and a man built and flew the first plane, but it was corporations who took these ideas and made them commercial, scaleable and permanent. We sailed super tankers around the world when many people argued that tonnes of steel would simply sink to the bottom of the ocean, and we put winged metal birds into the sky, when people thought that all they would do was fall. So is it too unbelievable to think that we can work together to put many square-mile cities into the air and keep them up there?'

The others look over at Jin, all waiting for an answer. I catch Lawrence doing the same, his success or failure in the balance. His eyes don't leave him until Jin stands up. 'You have said a lot and some of it makes total sense but much of it, if you pardon the pun, is up in the clouds. You are not alone in being creative in such extreme situations: both the British and the Japanese did a good job of fortifying many of their islands, not that it has been successful in the long run.'

'Just as we will fortify this one, which will work,' Lawrence says, gripping Tyrell's shoulders, keeping him in the game with one simple yet unenviable task. 'The world is in chaos and none of us know what is happening but we can make a success of this.'

Jin nods but he doesn't look convinced; he looks like he's done with Lawrence's motivational speeches. 'We all need to pick sides. I believe you are right that from the ashes will rise stronger corporations, willing to work with whoever survives, as well as demanding value from each individual who remains alive. What is in question is whether yours is the most effective plan and if these islands are the best overall location.'

Tyrell screams and bangs his hands against his head as he runs over to a map on the wall. 'My islands are perfect!' he shouts, pointing at the map. 'Look how much water there is!'

The Chinese leader shouts something at his subordinates, who all stand to attention, before he turns his attention back to Tyrell. 'You will excuse me if I perhaps think you are a little biased in your assessment. We must consider the feasibility of bringing so many workers and resources to this part of the world, when they will ultimately not make it up onto the platforms. Our people are not stupid.'

Tyrell rushes back to the table, looking neglected and full of a need to be understood. 'Many of my people will not make it up on the first sky cities and that is why we will build strong defences.'

Jin smiles in return. 'That, Mr Tyrell, is the choice you have made. I believe we have landed so you will excuse us as we take time to make ours.' He walks out, followed by his men. I watch as both Lawrence and Tyrell also follow, just for a little way, until they realise they have not been invited to join. This deal is still far from being accepted, leaving them with only each other and their leaking dreams.

*****

Get me a fresh shirt and make sure it's white,' Lawrence shouts as we walk into his room. 'They need to realise who has all the ideas, the plans and the patents. We didn't just design this overnight. It's been years in the making and we risk losing it all at the last hurdle.' He throws his used shirt across the room before coming towards me. 'We can build them ourselves if we need to,' he says, a pointed finger aimed in my direction. 'There will be enough skilled labour still left in the USA, and they will have far more spirit than those bastards could ever show.'

I shake my head, almost without realising.

'You have something to say?'

I take a deep breath. I know that I shouldn't say anything but I don't have a choice now. 'Well, I'm not sure patents will stop them if they want to build something similar.'

'Whose side are you on?' Lawrence shouts, spitting all over me. His arms are waving frantically in the air; his dream is clearly breaking apart before his eyes and it's so easy to lay the blame on me.

'I'm on your side but I have also had the benefit of observing them and getting an idea of what they think. It's obvious that they have other options available to them.'

'What?' he says, his face creased, denying what is clearly true.

'They could build here with us or perhaps they could replicate our technology in their own country. You picked here because it's surrounded by water, but they probably think their remote land is surrounded by a vast amount of emptiness, so they can do the same thing. And they're probably in discussions with Britain and other countries as well as us.'

He pushes a finger into my chest. 'By *us* you mean *me*, and what you're telling me is that they flew all the way here just to consider their options? This project isn't just an option, it is a lifeline to the people we have chosen.'

'Do you mean the people who have paid or the people you have chosen?'

His eyes widen, as I realise I have perhaps pushed him too much this time. 'Might I remind you that I picked you as one of the chosen people. You cannot afford the payment so you are here only thanks to me, and don't you ever forget that.'

I gulp and I nod.

'Now get out of my sight and go make sure lunch is ready. Can you at least do that?'

I walk away, wondering if all that I will ever be good for is something between the menial and the hopes that never were. That place between chores and dreams that will never be enough to get a ticket into his new paradise.

I close his door and start making my way down the corridor, but I don't get far before a hand comes out of nowhere. I realise it is Destiny as she pulls me into a room.

'I was wondering where you've been,' she says as she closes the door and smacks my ass. 'My busy boy has been negotiating hard with all those powerful businessmen.' She sniffs the room. 'I can smell the testosterone. It's oozing from you!'

'I'm not sure I've done a lot of negotiating.'

She stares at me and I look back, wondering if she understands any of this. I try to see through those fluttering lashes and those big, brown eyes to spot something of substance, some glimmer that she gets the gravity of our situation.

I shake my head, deep in my own reflection. 'We have a lot to do if we are ever going to make this become a reality.'

She paces around me, her eyes stalking my every move, what she is seeing and what I am seeing are two entirely different things now. She says nothing, although maybe she just has nothing to say.

'Whose room is this anyway?' I ask, realising that I have no idea.

She lies herself on the bed, looking up at me. 'Does it even matter? It's just a room. Everything is everyone's and I am yours, so take me now.'

'Destiny, this really isn't the time. I mean, do you even understand what's happening?'

She leans forward, staring up at me and then she laughs. 'Not really. I've never really understood what the big issue is. I see everyone is getting so upset but we are still alive, so why get on such a downer?' She suddenly gets up and runs over to me. 'I don't want to live in the clouds. Let's run away to somewhere deep in the country. Let's just get off this island and travel the world!'

I shake my head, blocking out the multiple impossibilities of what she has suggested. It wouldn't work on so many levels; so many reasons for how wrong it would be.

'Why not?' she asks, trying to understand my doubting thoughts.

'Because the world is fucked. Where would we go and what would we do?'

She takes her turn to shake her head. 'The world is different and it will always continue to change. Whatever happens next, do you really think living up there with my dearest daddy as the emperor of everything will help us? For one thing, we won't be able to be together.'

'Why do you say that?' I ask, already knowing the answer.

She grabs my tie, pulling me closer. 'You probably won't even make it into his final list. The only thing that's keeping you here now is his duty to his brother. You know that, don't you?'

'I don't even want to think about that right now.'

She moves me closer, pulling me towards her, forcing us against each other. 'Because it makes you think about us and how wrong we are together?' She kisses my neck and then my ear, slowly, carefully. 'And how right it feels to be so wrong.'

'Please, Destiny, I don't want to talk about this right now.'

'Well I do!' she says, stamping her feet. 'Every time you take me I think about what Daddy would say, me being shafted by my long-lost but utterly gorgeous cousin.'

I prise her off me. 'It's best not to think about that.'

'Why are you so paranoid?'

I sigh, knowing we will need to go over all of this again – her simple mind asks for explanations but the reasons that would matter to most people won't matter to her.

She grins, carefully stroking my cheek. 'You do know that none of this would matter if we just ran away and left this place.'

'It's not that simple, you know it's not.'

'It's very simple,' she says. 'Let's just leave and take our secret with us and bury it somewhere on our way to paradise. You know that I'm sick of this and sick of my father.'

I look at her, the girl who has got me so obsessed. At times she makes such sense; moments when all those serious and adult ideas mean nothing to us when we're together.

She brushes a finger through my hair, filling the silence with her boldness. 'You know he won't let me go willingly, don't you? We will have to sneak out of this place in the dark of the night and keep running until we are far from his reach.' She bends down and starts unbuckling my trousers, still looking up at me. 'Would you run away with me? You know I'd make it worth your while. After all, I'm your Destiny.'

She stands up and puts her lips onto mine. I know somewhere deep down in my core that she's right, that our paths have crossed for a reason. I think that maybe they have crossed before, over and over again for an eternity. We have been different beings but have the same essence of life, regardless of the image we are recreated with, and are always meant to find each other. When our eyes meet and our tongues wrap themselves around each other I feel an overwhelming urge to love her, to remind myself that we are meant to be together for all time.

But she moves down low too soon, long before these calming thoughts have travelled throughout my body, ready to protect me from the reality and fear of what is actually happening. She kneels down and pulls at my pants, quickly finding what she wants and wrapping her lips around it. That's when all of this starts to feel really wrong, when it starts to feel that what we're doing is forbidden by both logic and law. In the silence, while her mouth is occupied and my mind has time to think, I start to question what I have allowed us to become.

She works quickly, obviously knowing we don't have much time, her angry mouth determined to finish its mission, whilst one of her hands holds on tight to my shaft, as if she will never let go.

I grab her hair, trying to pull her up or maybe away from me – anywhere but where she is now. 'Don't go too fast,' I whisper.

She resists me, working harder, more fluid, more tongue, more lashing of my manhood. I beg her to stop, to leave me at this point and go no further. But she doesn't listen, in favour of pushing my desperation towards a limit I don't yet know, before swallowing it all and looking up to me with a giggle and then that look of wanting reassurance.

It's something I cannot give her, because after my release comes the anxiety. I look down at her and I know the haze has been removed and reality has returned. It leaves my mind clear that what we are doing is wrong and that what she is planning for us can never happen. I can't nod or smile but neither can I share these darkest of thoughts with her, and so I silently reach down for my pants, feeling embarrassed and alone with my guilt.

She stays kneeling down and looks up at me as I look down at her, but neither of us says anything. Maybe there is nothing to say and maybe there is everything still to say. Our silence seems to make me oblivious because the next thing I hear is the door opening. I don't even try to put my clothes on, to cover my shrinking manhood. I simply stand here, knowing that fate has brought Destiny and me to this point.

The door swings open and he stands there, not really even looking shocked. He smiles and nods, as if he knew this was happening all along.

*****

The status bar moves slowly; it's like a clock ticking towards better times. I cannot take my eyes off it. It will lead to a new world, I am sure of it. We were caught and now I am committed to a different cause, one which I cannot back out of without consequences. I mentally run through my next steps, from pulling out the memory stick and removing any trace I have been in this room, to my journey through the hopefully abandoned corridors of this once lively hotel. I mentally choose the best route, the one that is likely to attract the least suspicion. Destiny will have packed up her clothes by now and whatever she has not already taken from her opulent wardrobe will have to be left behind.

The green bar is by now around the 90% mark, the memory stick still flashing as it absorbs all this priceless information into its belly. I take a deep breath, feeling hopeful that I have completed the first stage of our escape.

Just as I allow myself this small victory I hear someone on the other side of the door. A code is being inputted into the keypad. I look back to the screen, desperate for a solution. Despite all of my hastily put together plans I hadn't given enough thought to getting caught again. The answers need to be on the tip of my tongue – logical excuses that would give me a reason for being in this secured room.

I take a deep breath and pull out the memory stick, clearing the screen as the door swings open. I figure that having 90% of the sky city schematics is better than having none, especially if I get caught by the wrong person.

'What are you doing in here?' Tyrell asks, standing in the doorway, his ample girth blocking any plans I have for a quick exit.

'I'm just updating the master server with some files for Lawrence,' I say, turning my attention back to the screen, acting as if this is a regular occurrence.

He doesn't say anything at first, but I feel his eyes probing me. He moves forward, into my space, sniffing like a caveman around a place he doesn't belong. I hope these are things he doesn't fully understand.

I turn towards him, figuring that assertiveness is more likely to win the battle than silence. 'Do you have a problem with my work as Lawrence's executive personal assistant?' I ask, staring into his eyes. As I watch and wait, I study the thick red blood vessels that surround his dark pupils – they tell me of age, recent desperation and of much sacrifice.

He grins back. 'I do not care about your position with Lawrence. You forget that this is my island and around here it is my rules that matter.' He stares up to the corner of the room, forcing me to look with him. 'The camera begs to differ on what you have apparently been doing in here.'

The door opens again and this time it's one of Tyrell's men. He gives his boss a nod, but remains standing in the doorway, doubling the odds against a simple escape.

'Hand it over,' Tyrell says, has thick arm outstretched, clicking his fingers, full of new-found power and obvious enjoyment.

I shake my head, not knowing what to say or do. I think of Destiny waiting in her room with both of our half-packed suitcases. The TV will still be playing loud music and she will be painting her nails, innocently waiting for me to fulfil my end of the plan. She will have no concept of my failure, no understanding of getting caught. To her this is a simple stroll out of the building. I told her to write her dad a letter but, since I have been away for a longer than I planned, she is more likely to be dancing around the room or straightening her hair; anything but taking this seriously. My failure will be obvious when her father enters the room without her hearing him, her clothes not packed, our grand plan still strewn across the bed.

'Do not test my patience any longer, little boy,' Tyrell says, taking a step closer to me.

I shake my head again, trying to preserve the impression of innocence for as long as possible. 'This memory stick,' I say, holding it up like a prized trophy. 'The one I have been using to upload new files. Your conspiracy theories are getting ridiculous. My network connection isn't working again, because of your people.' I raise my arms, flapping them around like I'm an angry guest in his chaotic world. 'And I have had to come down here myself to do such a basic thing!'

His eyes narrow but he says nothing. I know he is giving my excuse genuine thought. You have to give Tyrell credit: he's been a police chief in such a straightforward world all his life and now he's trying to turn detective in a new place of constant lies and hidden meanings.

I move forward boldly, towards my freedom. 'I'm done here, so unless you intend to confiscate a memory stick that I use every day, on an island that I cannot leave, then I suggest you let me do my job.'

Tyrell says nothing as I start to believe I have succeeded and that I will soon have Destiny in my arms, our new life starting without delay. But as I reach the door I find Tyrell's man blocking my way, his gun pushed in my face. I stagger backwards, my heart racing, as I realise I will have a steep price to pay if I'm caught trying to rob Lawrence of his most prized possessions. I stare down that barrel; the black steel offers me a void in which to send my thoughts, as I wonder which of the things I plan to take will result in a longer sentence – the data or his Destiny.

I suddenly feel Tyrell's hands on my shoulders; he pulls me around and throws me across the room. I land on a desk, sending the equipment flying onto the floor. I hear the crash of things that cannot easily be replaced in the coming months and years, and for a second I feel protective of the world we are trying to create.

Before I have regained my balance and calmed my thoughts I see Tyrell appear before me, his hands reaching around my throat. I feel his rough skin join with mine as he squeezes tight. 'You are a liar and you plan to sell this information to the Chinese. I have watched you for a long time and I know what you have been doing.' He releases his grip, only to throw me to the other side of the room.

I feel my back crunch as I land on yet more precious items. He quickly follows me and spits in my face. 'You are Lawrence's problem and when he hears what you have been doing I hope he passes you back to me for punishment.' He bends down, wearing the widest smile I have ever seen on his face. 'You have no idea about how the rule of law works on this island. On my island.'

He shouts something I don't understand and then his man is suddenly on top of me, pulling me off the desk and putting my hands behind my back. As he puts my wrists in cuffs I feel Tyrell's hand reaching into my pockets. He soon finds the memory stick.

He holds it up, smiling at his own work. 'Your fate is sealed.'

'Please,' I mutter, shaking my head, my mind empty of options. 'We can work something out. We both know that Lawrence is not going to get this deal.'

I feel his fist crash into my jaw before I see it coming. For a moment I don't feel any pain, my brain still trying to figure out what has happened. It's my first punch since high school and my first one from a real man. My jaw feels different. My mouth has filled with blood, which I have to spit out. I look down, expecting to see my teeth scattered beneath me but all I see is a small, red puddle on the floor. I know there will be more to come.

'You have given up on your master so easily, little man,' he says.

I lift my head up; my arms are still held tight by my silent captor. I stare right back into Tyrell's dark, judging face. 'He gave up on me and my family a long time ago and I promise you he will give up on you too. Do you really think your people will ever make it into the sky city? You will be living on this island, forever fighting for scraps of food like a dog!'

I see Tyrell's right hand rise, as the other one pulls me tight into his body, bracing me for the impact. I feel his man grabbing my hair from behind, pulling my head back and putting me at the best angle for his boss to completely silence me.

'You know I'm right!' I shout. 'This island will be worthless if the deal is lost, so let me help you talk through the options.'

'There are no options that involve you any longer,' Tyrell says, his approaching fist clenched.

I close my eyes, ready for what will inevitably be only the start of my torment, as I wonder how much I will be able to endure in the selfish aim of creating a better future for myself and the girl I love. But the pain never comes as I hear a muffled sound from behind me. I open my eyes to see blood splattered across the wall and Tyrell's body lying on the floor in front of me. The guard releases his hold on me and I feel myself falling, my knees crunching against the floor. As I struggle to hold myself upright with my hands still cuffed, the only consolation is Tyrell's dead face, as I try to figure out what is happening.

I hear another muffled sound as my frantic mind tries to piece everything together. I force myself to turn around, but stop when I see the guard's leg, motionless and with a stream of blood covering the floor around him.

I look up, hoping to see my saviour, but instead I'm met with the barrel of another gun, this time longer, held more steadily, and undoubtedly more deadly. The man staring down at me looks Chinese but he is not a member of the negotiating delegation. He's taller, bigger and even calmer – clear of the part he has to play and the purpose he serves for this organisation.

'Where is the memory stick?' he asks, his eyes darting around the room and then back to me, the gun not moving.

'He has it,' I say, indicating Tyrell with my head.

He nods and continues to survey the room, before resting his gaze on me. He sees the handcuffs, seeming to genuinely survey my situation, before our eyes properly meet. The gun doesn't move as we both examine each other. I soon realise how I am worthless compared to the knowledge contained on that one small piece of plastic.

'The memory stick doesn't have all the data,' I say, looking at him with pleading eyes that somehow hope to appeal to his sense of logic, if not his guilt. 'I got disturbed before the transfer had finished.'

He doesn't say anything and so I close my eyes, waiting for my inevitable muffled end. I figure at this close range it will be all I hear, and the pain will be far less than what Tyrell would have inflicted upon me over many hours or even days. In my final few moments I'm almost thankful, until thoughts of Destiny come flooding into my mind. I think of the future that could have been and of the path that was laid out in front of me, if only for a brief moment. I put my mind to rest, pleased in some way that she is a problem and solution I will never have to trouble myself over again.

'Who had the keys for your handcuffs?' he asks, still seeming no closer to finishing me off. I notice that he is using the past tense, as if each of these men is now gone and no longer relevant.

I open my eyes, looking up to see the gun has gone. He's looking around, clicking his fingers. I nod towards his second killing and this is all he needs to start searching their pockets. He eventually finds a bunch of keys and I'm quickly set free and put to work on gathering all the files.

'Which are the main servers?' he asks, dragging both bodies into the middle of the room, a trail of blood following them from where they originally fell.

I nod to the main computers and turn around to see that the door is closed and both of us are sealed in this tomb. I know that once I give him the complete set of files I will be expendable, and so the same question runs through my mind as before: how do I get out of this room in one piece? I watch as the status bar fills completely and a countdown to my demise appears on the screen, flashing proudly that the end is near.

He's standing behind me now and it makes me think that he will be kind enough to finish me without any real knowledge of what is going to happen next. I close my eyes again – anything to stop me from fainting, although I can't see that being a bad thing if it does happen.

'I'm not going to kill you,' he says. 'Your passage to Beijing is still guaranteed. You and that girl you're with, and your parents are being located as we speak. You made a deal and my employer will honour it.'

I open my eyes and look at him, a smile forming across my face. We will make it out of here and I will be with Destiny. We will build a new world, one that is meant for us to be together, and one that knows nothing of the past. I realise what a price I am willing to pay for the freedom of those I care most about; nothing else matters.

As soon as the memory stick is full I pull it out and quickly hand it over to my new protector. I feel happy to be a passenger on whatever gets us out of here: happy not to be making decisions anymore, not to be taking responsibility for so much.

'You keep it,' he says, without turning around. He's busy attaching small boxes to the various systems. It doesn't take a genius to work out what he's doing: each of them starts to flash as soon as they are in position. I realise now the true meaning of my decision, in that Lawrence will be left with nothing but a dream and perhaps some residual determination. I'm taking it all and I'm leaving him with very little but rubble and regrets.

He leads me out of the room and down the hallway, tapping something into his phone as he charges forward. We step over bodies and pools of blood: people I knew, people I talked to – decent people who simply bought into the best vision that came along, wanting to do what they could to survive. The world changed and they tried to change with it. They left their homes, moved their lives and lost loved ones, all because of hope, and now they're dead – crushed by someone bigger than them, all in the name of something even bigger. The higher it goes the more nameless each act becomes.

'She's already in the helicopter,' he says, pulling me down a different corridor. We move quicker now, fighting against time and fate. The two guards at the end of the corridor don't even see us coming before they fall by the hiss of that gun. When the paths of this man and me separate, I realise that our individual skills will give us very different chances of survival in the coming years. As he stalks his way around the corner I contemplate the very obvious fact that he has adapted far better to what will be required.

Two more hisses and a reload of the gun find us outside and on the roof, both of us running towards the waiting helicopter. He covers me, constantly turning around and then running to catch up, pushing me forward towards my liberation. I see Destiny in one of the passenger seats, waving hysterically at me with both hands, her giant shades covering all but her smile. The other Chinese delegates are on board too, calmly waiting to leave.

I reach the door, shouting that I have completed my mission, ever thankful when they pull me in. Destiny unbuckles her seatbelt and wraps her arms around me, frantically kissing my neck. She scrambles around the small seating area, hysterically screaming my name and getting in everyone's way.

'Get your seatbelts on, both of you,' Jin says. He looks straight at me, his face void of any emotion. 'You have all of the data?'

I throw myself into a spare seat as the force of the helicopter lifting up pushes me downwards. When I can finally reach into my pocket I pull out the memory stick and present it to my new employer, proud of my work and wanting validation as much as safety.

One of his men quickly grabs it from me and puts it into his laptop. It doesn't take long before he is nodding to his superior, which I take as a good sign. I grab Destiny's hand, partly to make sure that all this is real, but also to make them feel somehow guilty if they chose to throw us both out now.

'You have proven yourself very useful, Mr. Henry. This information is what we lacked and with your knowledge of these schematics we can build our own sky cities, but they will be far bigger and much safer than what was planned for this island. If he thinks we will ship our resources halfway across the world for such a small project then he really is as narrow-minded as he is arrogant.'

I nod, thinking of how Lawrence's big vision has ended up so small. It makes me think of when I was a child. I always told my mum how I planned to build a robot and full of nothing but hope I would try to bring a few bits of plastic and an old battery to life – always dreaming, never quite succeeding.

'I'm not a bad person,' Jin says, looking at me and only me. 'This is not the usual way we do business and in any normal time we would have signed a deal, come to a valid agreement or simply bought out Lawrence's little business. But with none of those options available to us and time running out I'm sure you will agree that different measures are required.'

'Do you want me to blow the servers,' Jin's hitman asks, a finger on his phone.

It's at this moment that my phone rings, causing everyone to look at me. I look at it and see that Lawrence is calling. Without thinking properly, I tell my new boss that my old boss is on the phone, the option to speak to Lawrence clearly in his control, to which he nods.

I answer, immediately hearing Lawrence shouting at me. 'Where are you?' he says. 'The Chinese have attacked us. Tyrell is dead and the server room has been compromised.'

I sit quietly for a moment, wondering what to say, not knowing if it is worth saying anything. 'We've been attacked?' I ask.

'Yes!' he shouts. 'Where are you? We need to stop them before they get away. I'm heading to the roof. If those bastards think they will escape then I'll blow them out of the sky. They cannot leave with the data they have taken.'

I quickly unbuckle my belt, looking out the windows until I can see both the complex and the new threat to us. 'They are going to fire on us,' I say to Jin.

'Blow the servers,' my new boss says without hesitation.

A return nod and a single reflex later, we all feel the vibrations of an explosion. No sooner has the hitman accomplished his task then he grabs a sniper rifle from the side of his seat and adopts a position near the door.

I finally put the phone back to my ear, waiting to savour the moment of our final goodbye. 'You're with them, aren't you?' Lawrence says.

'Yes,' I say, flatly, bluntly, as if it is such an obvious answer. 'I have taken the schematics and the server room has just been blown up.'

'You little bastard!' Lawrence shouts. 'You have betrayed me and taken what doesn't belong to you. I knew you were just like your father and yet I still gave you a chance. I will destroy you for this. You and your parents will pay dearly for this, I can promise you that.'

'Speaking of family, aren't you going to ask me anything else?'

He's quiet for a moment and I think that maybe it's the noise of the chopper. We bank to the left so we can get a good look at the complex and I wait for him to say something. 'Destiny,' he says. 'She's with you.'

'It took you a while to ask. I wonder if you really had thought of her at all?'

'I'm not going to argue with you so just give her back to me.'

I look over at her, to the one we both want, but she's busy looking out the window. I follow her line of her sight until I see him; he is standing in a suit with several of Tyrell's men around him. They are heavily armed, with machine guns and a few rocket launchers, and he isn't stopping them from taking aim. I start to feel vulnerable again, wondering if he would dare shoot us out of the sky now that he knows she is with us.

My fear quickly vanishes as I see those men start to fall, one by one, as each feel the systematic blows of a true killer. Lawrence suddenly realises what is happening and runs for cover, as the remaining men flee towards the stairs and away from the roof. When the shooting stops I see him stand up and put the phone back to his ear, as he straightens his thick glasses and looks up to the sky to find us.

I feel her soft skin as I take hold of her hand and look at her. I know that those eyes are the only place I will ever find comfort. 'Can we go now?' she says.

'Lawrence, she doesn't want you and she will always be with me from now on. I can't change how we feel for each other but I want you to know that I will always take care of her.'

'That's not good enough,' he says. 'Return her to me; you know she's all I have. Land now and we can discuss this and agree a fair exchange of knowledge.'

I laugh, feeling a huge wave of relief rush over me, knowing my life will never be the same again. 'There's really no need. They have all they came for and you have nothing left to trade, but I have to know something,' I say and look down at him as the helicopter circles. 'If you had a choice what would you pick – Destiny or the data?'

I watch him as he walks to the edge of the roof, looking up at us, his body turning as he follows the helicopter's movements. 'If you knew me properly, like you should, you would already know the answer to that.'

'Humour me and I'll see what I can do to help.'

I watch him shake his head, endlessly disappointed in me. He's no longer my employer, my mentor or even my miserable uncle. 'If the cause is just, the corporation must rule over the individual for the greater good.'

I watch him for a moment, wondering if he is truly brave or if he is just a cheap coward wrapped in an expensive mask. 'If it's not for her, then why do all this?'

'You'll never understand the answer to that question,' he says, his head still shaking. 'Just put Jin on the phone.'

I nod but say nothing, intending to do exactly as I'm told. 'He'd like to speak to you,' I say, holding the phone up to my new boss.

Jin shrugs his shoulders and then shouts in Chinese to the cockpit. The helicopter starts to move away as his personal assassin leans out the window again.

'You taught me well, Lawrence. I believe you when you say that corporations and cockroaches may both endure, but right now I am picking what excites me, and what my heart is telling me is right. You should know that I will always love her, this one simple individual.' I switch the phone off and sit back in my seat as I let Destiny take hold of me, my eyes closed and my mind only on this happy future that is finally unfolding.

And with a final hiss of the gun, I allow myself a smile.

Thursday 25th August – Los Angeles

That secret slice of life

I bang on the door again. 'Come on, you son of a bitch, I know you're in there,' I say out loud, not caring if he hears me. I need to be careful, I know that. I can't push my luck and I can't fight my way in, either. The only choice I have is to get him to the door and somehow make him help me, no matter how much he doesn't want to. I bang again, shouting out his name. I hit the door loudly, desperately. This place is my only lead, the only place that I stand any chance of finding her.

I'm still banging when he slowly opens the door. I see his disapproving face through the small gap, and then he frowns and sighs, telling me all I need to know. 'It's you again. This is starting to become a bit of an annoying habit.'

'I'm sorry, I know I shouldn't be here again, and I know I start with an apology each time I come knocking.' I lean a cautious hand on his wall, near the doorframe, trying to force some sort of connection where none exists. 'I really don't know what else I can do.'

'There would be no apology needed if you stopped bothering me.' He starts to close the door, even quicker than he did during my visit yesterday. I expected this but I still don't know if he's shutting me out because he knows something or if he has simply had enough of my regular visits.

I don't have the luxury of time and can't afford to offend him, and so I place a foot in the doorway.

'What do you think you're doing?' he asks, repeatedly pushing his door against my foot. His black eyes only give off anger, which is all directed at me; it's like he's the victim in all this, the one who is unfortunate enough to have me banging his door each and every day. I look at him: his belly overhanging his jeans, his hairy arms having stolen much from his thinning head. He looks tired but no more than the rest of us; his sleeves are rolled up, and his face is coated in a thick layer of dust and sweat. He's probably been packing all night, running around and preparing, just like everyone else. Perhaps he is the genuine model citizen of these times; doing what he can with what he has left, but I just can't be sure.

'Carlos, I'm sorry, I have more questions that I need answered. You're the only one who can help me and I think you know that.'

He opens the door a little more so he can come closer to me. He steps on my foot and points a stubby finger at my face. 'Look, I'm getting real sick of you coming around here. We've been through this a hundred times – I don't know where this Lucy of yours is. The police have searched my place, you came in with them. They have asked me all the questions you could think of and they told you that they have more important things to be doing right now.'

I don't want to hear this, not again, not when I'm out of options. I push him backwards, stepping into his place, the home of a man I don't trust and yet cannot prove why. 'Nothing is more important than Lucy!'

He doesn't take long to gather himself together, his deep voice growling as he pushes his hands into me. I fall out of his house and onto the floor, with only my feet still in his doorway. He starts kicking them, trying to remove me completely. I rush to get up, knowing this is my last chance. Deep down I know he won't open this door tomorrow, and the police will only tell me again that I need to drop this and move on with what is left of my life.

He bends down and grabs my ankles before I can properly get up. He takes hold of them and pushes me along the floor, my back scraping against the cement of his porch. 'Please, Carlos!' I shout, as I scramble to get up and find enough dignity to be able to ask for help that he clearly isn't going to give.

'I don't want to hear it!' he shouts back, as he throws my legs onto the floor. 'You are one weird kid. Go and play your games with someone else.'

I manage to get up and find myself level with him again. I stretch out my arms, hoping my pleading eyes will somehow get through to him. 'The recording has been cleared up. It makes more sense now.'

He puts a hand out, stopping me from coming any closer. 'What?'

'Lucy's cell phone message, you remember? I thought that if you just listened to it one more time you might be able to help me figure some stuff out.'

He takes a deep breath, his head slowly shaking. 'Look, I'm sorry you lost her, but I don't know anything. You keep coming around here with your accusing stare and random questions. The police told you she probably got grabbed into a van and it's not like she would be the first. You need to stop coming around here and laying your guilt on me.'

'My guilt?'

'You fucking left her alone!' he shouts. 'I've got my own problems and I'm getting real tired of hearing about yours! If you come around here again I'll take the law into my own hands, and we both know the cops won't bother to come looking for you now.'

'No, wait!' I shout, but it's too late. He slams the door shut as I hear several bolts closing and chains scraping into their holders, sealing him in and locking me out.

I don't want to leave, can't face going home, and so I sit down on his step and take out my cell. I turn the volume to its highest and press play. I know that he won't hear it from inside but I hope that this enhanced version of those last few agonising moments will help me to relive it in some way, maybe help me hear something that I keep missing. There has to be a clue, something in the background that I'm not getting. Those twenty long seconds; I listen but don't think I'm hearing them anymore – I already know each word and every scream.

I look around his street but see nothing different to the last time. The houses all look the same with their darkened windows and a scattering of open curtains – all signs of the indecision of a rushed evacuation. I don't even need to look at the pictures I have already taken to know that they are the same as when they were abandoned. The families fled days ago, leaving only Carlos and a brave few in the homes they have built.

Her cries for help suddenly flood my senses, and as her pleas for mercy get louder and more desperate, I feel as if she is here with me. She shouts out my name: 'Harvey!'

I press stop, unable to hear the rest. Those last few seconds are only a memory now, the recording always stopping at that point, leaving me just on the edge of knowing the true nature of the horror that found its way into my Lucy's world.

*****

'Oh God, Harvey! Where are you? They're still following me, and I couldn't see you, and I didn't know what to do... I ran and now I don't know where I am... I'm knocking on doors but all the lights are off. This one has a light on but I can't see the number. I can see them now... they're coming! I'm on Chesterbrook Road, opposite Number 12... You need to stay back! This is my friend's house and he's phoning the police right – '

I jolt upwards and I know I'm still screaming, my heart pounding quicker than I can breathe, my body drenched in sweat. I look around the room, remembering where I am and who I am. I've had this same dream every night since Lucy went missing. I can relive her abduction as though I was there myself; my mind does an amazing job of piecing together her recorded account and my mental memory of where it took place. Every night I feel her fear and experience her horror, but I do not know the true faces of those who approach to take her. In my version of Lucy's nightmare it's Carlos who advances towards her, taking short, quick strides, a determined look across his face. The other man is blank – a nobody – just a random person thrown into my nightly terrors.

I wish Lucy had described them, given me more detail to go on. If she had just told me heights, builds, features – anything that would prove it was Carlos. I picture his face now and I think of everything that would make him stand out: the thin tufts of hair that do their best to cover his scalp; the potholes in his tanned face; and his accent: he must have spoken and shown his Mexican roots. Maybe he didn't speak and she didn't see what I have seen and maybe, just maybe, it wasn't him. I know she did her best. I wish the police had answered her first call, come to her rescue – sent a squad car to a respectable neighbourhood where I thought we would be safe and where order still remained.

More than any of that I wish I hadn't left her. I thought it was the right thing to do. Cars are constantly being looted or stolen and if they can't break in quick enough they can take the gas in just a few seconds. 'Watch it from here,' I had said, so that she was under the light and protection of a camera. How was I to know it wasn't working, on a long repair list that the chain's head office said they will no longer get to? One small video would have answered so many questions, like why she didn't run into the store and who it was that dared to take her away from me.

I pick up my cell, pushing myself to listen to the next instalment, her final terrified message. It's nearly 5 days old; time and fate are working together to push us further apart. I press play but then immediately stop it again, wondering why Carlos didn't want to hear it. He didn't seem that flustered – no more or less than when the police played him the original. He shook his head that time, wincing with the rest of us when she screamed and shaking his head when she shouted where she thought she was. I remember he looked at the detective when he paused the fuzzy recording, his eyes blank, maintaining that he had seen and heard nothing. When they played it to the end, to that last part that will haunt me forever, he finally looked my way and a tear fell down his cheek. 'I'm sorry,' is all he said.

I think of his face; it seemed genuine enough. The look he gave me earlier, when he had to kick me out once and for all, also seemed honest. He was angry, frustrated, and probably felt harassed by my constant calls. Maybe he wasn't involved, maybe he doesn't know anything. He said he was in the basement most of that evening, which is totally believable. That basement was searched twice – I watched them do it and then I searched it again. I looked and looked, turning over every corner of his home until the detective came down and told me I had been there for over an hour. All the other officers were gone and Carlos was patiently waiting in his living room, waiting for me to finally leave him alone. He didn't say much as I left, he just apologised for my loss and gave me a pat on the back, wishing me luck for my future, whatever that looked like.

The detective, Marius was his name, calmly led me out of the house. He told me they had gone door to door knocking but hadn't had any success: they didn't find many people home and none of the houses had been disturbed. He offered to escort me home but I declined in favour of searching the neighbourhood myself. I grabbed a torch from my car and shone it through every window as I checked every lock on any door I could find. I'm sure Carlos was watching me as I prowled around his neighbourhood until the early hours. I'm sure he woke up to see my car still there, my curled-up body asleep in the back, just in case she came running past in the night.

He knocked on my window early the next morning and quickly told me that I should go home just in case she was there. We swapped cell phone numbers and he assured me that if he remembered any new details, or if he saw anything suspicious, he would call me straight away. He never offered anything else, didn't ask me to relive my story. I never expected him to be my counsellor but he didn't seem at all bothered by what had happened directly outside his home, as if it was just a normal occurrence in these strangest of times.

That morning I thought he might have brought me some coffee, at least offered to witness my torment. I would have told him what I knew, about a trip to the store that couldn't be avoided, even that late at night. How I had seen a few dodgy guys in there, which meant it made more sense for me to go in while Lucy waited outside. I didn't leave her in the car – I'm not that irresponsible. But I did leave her – the love of my life – alone in the dark of the night in a place that clearly wasn't safe at a time when bad things could happen, and were happening.

I thought that if he listened to all that then I would get to the point where I confessed what I had done – my worst decision: leaving her alone – but he never did ask, so I didn't tell. I didn't even tell the detective. I was too ashamed; realising now that we should have stuck together, even if it meant the car was stolen.

I wondered what Carlos would say in return, if he would tell me that anyone would have done the same thing in my position. He would take the empty mug from me and offer me the chance to freshen up at his place, making sure I knew that he was comfortable for me to be there. I would use his bathroom and he would shout up that in these times you have to work together to survive.

He didn't do any of that; instead, he left me to drive away, never really knowing what he thought. I think of him, I think of Lucy, and then I think of my guilt.

I jolt forward, throwing the bed covers off me as I search for my notebook. I'm shaking as I rip through the pages, desperately trying to find everything I wrote down last night. I quickly find the page and scan to the end, to just before I describe him slamming the door, to the last words he speaks before making the threat, the only real opinion he expresses throughout: 'you fucking left her!'

I read the words again and again, my mind beyond any doubt as to what he said. He told me something I haven't told anyone else, a confession that had never left my lips, that I did leave her, and that only someone who was there would know how I failed to look after her as I should have. As I put last night's clothes back on I wonder how he could have known that without me telling him, and how he now cannot be guilty.

*****

'Carlos! Let me in! I know she's in there!'

He doesn't answer; none of the curtains move and the door holds firm. I think about how far I am prepared to go to get into his place. Breaking and entering no longer bothers me, and the thought of him taking the law into his own hands doesn't scare me. What worries me is if she isn't in there. What if I get into his place and she is nowhere to be seen? What if she's already suffered some horrible fate, all because I couldn't rescue her quick enough?

A bedroom window suddenly opens and Carlos looks down at me. 'I told you what I would do if you turned up here again!' He leans out of the window, holding a bowl with both hands. He tries to pour its contents over me.

I move out of the way as the liquid splashes all around me, catching my shoes and trousers, the scent of gasoline charging up my nose. I look back up to see him holding a flaming torch in a bottle.

'Leave now or you'll burn right here on my porch. I swear to God I'll do it.'

I don't move at first, somehow figuring that I'll be able to outrun a flaming rag, or maybe I'll be able to rip off the burning clothes before the flames get to my skin. Whatever the answer, I know that I cannot leave her. 'She's in there, you bastard! I'm going to get in and I'm going to find her.'

'You've really lost your fucking mind!' he shouts back.

I ignore him, looking around for something to smash his windows with. He's willing to burn me until I become a cindering corpse on his lawn, so I figure it's fair game to break my way in to his place. No one will stop me; no sense of moral order will hold me back. I grab a metal bin and tip the trash onto the ground. The smell immediately hits me and makes me want to vomit. Waste has been piled up over weeks and the baking heat has long since turned it to mush and liquid. The remains trickle their way down the path until they reach the road. I cover my mouth as I drag the bin up the path until I find the strength to pick it up by both handles. I hold it over my head as I take aim at the living room window, flaming torches landing all around me as though we're in some sort of siege battle.

'You think that's going to get you in?' he shouts, as he lights another rag.

I ignore him and throw it with everything I have. The metal container hits the glass, causing it to shatter but not break, and then it hits the ground. I run forward, hoping to see something inside, but I soon realise how hopeless my attack has been. 'Bars,' I say out loud.

'That's right, you fucker!' Carlos shouts, looking down at me, ready to launch another flaming torch at me. 'I've been preparing to defend my home. I'm not running away like all those other scared people. I'm staying right here and I'll protect it from whatever comes this way. You're not the first to try to get in here and you won't be the last.'

I stare up at him, wondering how I can get in, if not physically then through his mind. 'Let her go and I'll stop being one of them. I'll take her with no questions asked and we will both leave you alone, I promise.'

'Why won't you listen to me? She's not in here!'

I watch him for a moment and then drop to my knees. 'She has to be.'

He lights what I think will be the final rag. I'm out of options and I cannot be without her. If it hits me then fate will consume me and I will pass freely to the next life. It feels like it's the only place I haven't looked, and so I close my eyes and wait for the inevitable.

The consuming pain never comes; instead, I hear sirens from what I hope is a police car getting closer. I open my eyes and watch as two cars come tearing down the empty street. Their rapid approach changes everything, as we look at each other and he hides his weapon, and I step away from the stinking pile of waste.

They pull up at the house, the only obviously inhabited place left on this street, and I walk towards them. I want to tell them everything, my words flowing out of my mouth quicker than I can organise them. They start shouting back at me but I don't listen properly. I keep pointing to the house, telling them in every possible way I can that she is definitely in there. My Lucy is alive, she is trapped and we can all save her. They don't seem to want to listen; one of them smacks his night-stick across the back of my legs. I immediately fall to the ground and feel my arms being pinned around my back. Two of the officers press their knees into my body as they put cuffs on me.

'You need to calm down,' one of them shouts while making sure I'm restrained. I watch as they fuss around me whilst the others head to the house. I hear one of them on his radio, telling despatch that it's only civil unrest – only one individual this time and he has been easily detained.

'It's not civil unrest, it's kidnap!' I shout back, hoping they will listen, or the person on the other end of the radio will hear my plea and at least ask them to investigate. 'My partner, Lucy, has been kidnapped and I can prove that this guy did it!'

'You need to calm down, I've told you once already,' the cop shouts. He's the one with his knee still pressing against my back. My wrists are cuffed tight and pushed up, the extra pain an obvious incentive for me to shut up.

I decide to follow his instructions and I stop shouting in favour of looking around. I see the officers are now near the house, talking to Carlos, who has made it to his front door. I watch and listen as he shouts at them. Their hands are held out and their guns are drawn. They clearly are not taking any prisoners right now and I'm relieved that they are willing to treat him as badly as they have me. He doesn't seem to want to listen any more than I did. He shouts that I have been coming here every day, harassing him and leaving him no choice but to defend his property. The cops both nod, and even though they still look defensive, they know they cannot charge him for protecting his home against looters. The raft of new congressional orders was intended to simplify the work of the police and army, so that they can focus on keeping civil order. It's obvious they don't have the resources to arrest and charge every crime now committed, so defence of your own property with any force is now accepted as a matter of survival in every remaining state.

'I can prove she's in there,' I say to the guy holding me. I speak quietly, calmly, knowing the only way I can save Lucy is by conducting another search of the property. 'Don't let him go back inside. Don't give him a chance to hide her away again.' I arch my body around, twisting like a snake until I'm able to look into his eyes. 'Please, you have to help me.'

He takes a moment to look at me, examining my body, studying my clothes and my mannerisms, clearly trying to judge whether I am a mental person or a genuine citizen in need. 'Okay, where's this evidence?'

I look around for my backpack and nod towards it. 'There's a journal in there.'

He looks down at me, his eyes surrounded by rings of fire that have been weeks in the making. He looks exhausted, his stubble unkempt; I don't think he was planning to look like this. 'We have new orders and unless a crime is in progress that will cause immediate civil unrest then we are instructed to leave it alone.'

'My girlfriend is in there, taken and trapped by that man. Since when wouldn't that be a crime?'

He nods slowly, quietly, clearly torn between doing what is right usually and what is right at this moment. 'She isn't the first and she won't be the last. Your evidence needs to be immediate and very compelling for us to stay here any longer.'

'Just get my journal,' I say.

He finally lets go so he can walk the few paces to get my backpack, but as I watch his feet move I see someone else pick it up. I look over to see it's the detective, Marius, holding up my backpack and looking directly at my only ally.

'You don't give up, do you?' Marius says as he walks towards me.

'This guy says he has evidence of the kidnap of his girlfriend, who is allegedly being held in this house,' the officer says.

He picks me up so that I can see Marius, or perhaps so he can look at me properly, even though he doesn't seem willing to acknowledge the allegation. 'We've been through this and we've searched this house, and yet you are still here,' he says.

'I have new evidence. I know she's in there!'

Marius looks to all the other officers. 'Gentlemen, is there a crime in progress? I don't see that there is. In fact the crime that has alleged to have taken place is nearly a week old.'

'He told me something yesterday that no one knows!' I shout back, trying to make sure it's audible to Carlos, who is still waiting at his front door. 'He told me that I left her but no one knows that.' I put my head down, knowing what I now freely admit. 'I left her to watch the car while I was in the supermarket. I left her alone and he took her.'

Marius shakes his head and drops my backpack to the floor. 'That is your compelling evidence to prove she is inside the house?'

I shake my head, knowing he's not listening, not giving me the time I deserve to explain my case as a genuine citizen in need. 'I didn't tell anyone and he used those exact words yesterday. He told me that I left her, but how could he have known that?'

I look at Marius who gives me nothing back and so I look at the other cop, the only one who briefly felt anything for me, although he does nothing but shake his head.

'No crime is happening and no evidence suggests any more time needs to be spent here. All of you ship out now. We have bigger things to be dealing with.'

'No!' I shout, struggling in my cuffs, fighting my new chains. 'You can't do this. You're the police and you have to help me!'

My outburst gets me another jab below my knee, making me fall down again. This time I'm supported by the officer holding me up, so that I land softly and am able to pay proper attention.

Marius kneels down and takes off his sunglasses, looking straight at me. 'This district is just a number now and it's not a good number. Citizens have the choice to stay and hide, or to leave for another district, anything above number 15 will do. Everything is organised by numbers and the crime you allege to have happened no longer has a number. Only crimes in progress get a response and from what we have seen you are the guilty one. I'm going to let you go but you need to move on, get your life back together and get out while you can. There is nothing here for you now, do you understand me?'

I look at him, my mind never more determined. 'Lucy is in there.'

'If you truly believe that then you will die here,' Marius says and stands up. 'Let him go and get out of here.'

The rest of the cops head towards their cars as Marius walks towards Carlos, no doubt to apologise for my insane actions. I wonder if he is going to ask him some questions and do his duty as a detective, perhaps see if there is any glimmer of hope that he doesn't obviously want to show me.

I feel a grip on my arm and I realise it's the nice cop. 'You seem like a decent guy but whatever has happened isn't a crime that can be solved. No one will come here again and no one will fight for you.'

'Then why did you come this time, bringing two cars and a detective?'

He looks around and then back to me. 'Look, you need to wake up. I have no idea why he showed up as these guys aren't solving crimes any more. They are going around and issuing orders with lots of reporting back to those above. Two cars turned up because this neighbourhood was classified as off-grid.'

'Off-grid?'

'We can't patrol everywhere, so places that now have limited residents have been taken off the grid for police and all other public services. When we got the call we thought something was here and if it was, then things would have been easier to deal with, with fewer people around. This entire district is being prepared as a potential battleground area, so the guy in this house will bunker down and hope to survive, and your best chance for your own survival is to get the hell out of here.'

'You don't understand,' I say, shaking my head. 'I'm not leaving her.'

He leans closer as he takes the cuffs off me. 'I bet you've seen the news and you should know that this place goes under complete military rule at midnight tonight and we are *all* shipping out. You either join the queue on Highway 55 now or you go up against that guy. No one will come here again and no one will stop you. If you think she's in there then you do what you have to do. There will be no laws to break on either side.'

My hands suddenly feel free as they fall to my sides. I instinctively rub my wrists, feeling for any damage. 'I know what I have to do.'

His partner calls him to the car as Marius walks back down the path. He takes one final look at me. I think to myself that this could be his last humane action he carries out as an officer of the law: the days, weeks and months ahead will be governed by that numbers game and I don't think he will have the luxury of empathy for some time to come. 'If you get her then escape to Highway 55: it's the only one that will be kept open for civilians. The army presence will be high so don't shock those guys and make sure they know you're coming.'

I take a deep breath, remembering all he is telling me, knowing how much I still have to do, as I offer my hand up to him 'Thank you.'

He shakes it but doesn't say anything else, has no further comforting words. He gets into the car and I watch him drive away. I turn around to see Carlos shut his door, no doubt putting all those bolts back on as he seals himself inside with my Lucy.

I see Marius standing in front of me as he lights a cigarette. 'It's obvious he isn't coming out until all of this is over, and there's no way you will get in, so the best thing you can do for everyone is to move on with your life and get out of here.'

'And what if I don't?'

He walks towards me, opening his jacket and giving me a flash of his firearm. 'I declared this neighbourhood as safe, low risk, no activity. So you can imagine my frustration when I get a call to say that precious resources have been dispatched here to stop civil unrest in progress. So to answer your question, you will move on from here now. What you do after that is none of my concern, but you needn't come back here again.'

I take one last look at the house and then head towards my car, figuring the only thing I can do right now is drive away. I say nothing as I pull away, thinking only about when I will return. I wonder about what will happen after the sun sets and I wonder when I will get my Lucy back from that man. I don't know how I will get into his fortified prison; I have no idea where she is and I can't imagine how we will get out of this warzone in one piece, but somehow I vow that I will make it happen.

*****

Most people would say, if asked, that they are scared of the dark. It's easy to understand, because we spend almost all of our waking time in the light, whether it comes from the sun or is somehow man-made. The time we spend in actual darkness is normally when we are asleep, when our minds are taken elsewhere, to a place of colour and imagination.

The first few hours she spent in this true darkness were terrifying for Lucy. She couldn't see anyone but heard every little movement. The room wasn't just dark, it was black. There wasn't even a little bit of light unless he opened the door, which now only happens twice a day – or at least that's what Lucy thinks. It's difficult to judge how much time has passed when there is no way of distinguishing light from dark, or day from night.

When they first took her she was convinced that he was in the room with her. She awoke from some strange, chemical-induced sleep, and found herself bound to something, her body laid flat and her arms and legs tied down. She could hardly move, could barely wriggle. The noises from the shadows had terrified her, with every part of her body exposed to things she couldn't see, her very being trapped in a nightmare she couldn't begin to understand.

After what seemed like hours she realised that she was alone and the room was some sort of cell. She didn't know how far she had been transported, where they had taken her, or even how many of them there were. As she lay there, her other senses became sharpened but her precious sight could offer her nothing. She eventually managed to calm herself down and stopped screaming, as she thought it was doing nothing but heightening whatever pleasure her attackers were getting from this. The first thing she did was to control her breathing and start to think through what she knew. Okay, she had thought, it's a dark room so what can I see in this darkness? She had looked around for any red lights, any sign that this was being recorded, but could see literally nothing. She didn't give up and tried compartmentalising each question as a small problem yet to be solved. She soon realised that she was no longer clothed, and that her left-hand restraint was slightly weaker than the right. She stored these small facts in her mind, as she thought they could turn out to be crucial over the coming hours and days. Just as long as she could stay calm, these little victories had given her hope.

It was in this darkness when her remaining hope quickly fled, and that was the moment when she finally cracked. That small hero inside her who took charge didn't last as long as she had hoped, when she felt something moving up her thigh. Her scream was loud and long, as everything she knew and every mental image she had created in her mind quickly fell apart.

This thing had been in the room with her all the time, enjoying every moment of her initial capture. She was probed and touched for a long time, her exposed body being examined from head to toe. He didn't speak through any of her first ordeal and, after a while, neither did she. Begging him to stop, asking who he was, or offering any amount of money didn't do anything. He had all that he wanted and he silently reminded her that the only power resided in the darkness.

She has learnt a lot since that first time. He wore infra-red goggles and he deliberately made the first few hours as terrifying as he could so that she would break more easily. He has given her little bits of freedom over the last few days, such as a daily shower, although she has to take it while blindfolded. She gets more food than she did at the start, sometimes even a pot of chocolate for dessert, and has almost become accustomed to the routine he has given her. She knows that after each shower she will be given a pill, washed down with vodka, and when she awakens she will already be tied down tight to what she now knows is a table, and that those restraints will only be released when he is finished. After that he will allow her to get off and scurry into a corner. During each assault he whispers to her that she is his favourite, but she never says anything back, she makes no moan or cry. He is taking all he wants but she will give him nothing freely in return. Lucy thinks she isn't alone, that others might be going through the same thing, and although she wouldn't want anyone to suffer this, she admits that it's better than thinking she is truly alone.

She still hears things deep inside her frantic mind, mainly the little hero who whispers to her from somewhere in the dim recesses of her failing spirit, telling her to remember all that happens here, to catalogue everything he does, to somehow find a way to use it.

Now she awakes to the sound of movement on the stairs outside; he's right on time like always. The two locks are undone from the outside; they are only ever bolted, never locked with a key. The door opens now and light floods into the room. She knows just where to sit these days, the exact angle at which her eyes are able to adjust quick enough to get a proper look at him. All those features – she would always be able to recall them even if she never sees him again. Her mind pictures every pothole and every thinning patch on his head each time he mounts her on that table, but she reminds herself to keep looking. She knows that in order to spot the way out of hell you need to look the devil in his dark eyes.

'Blindfold on,' he demands, as he throws it down to her.

She does as she is told, knowing that he will lead her to the bathroom, to that lukewarm shower and that inevitable pill that brings on the sleep that edges her closer to the torment, and a little bit further away from the Lucy she remembers.

'Hold on,' that voice within her says. 'Remember who you are, remember Harvey, and know that he will be looking for you. Those sirens earlier, they had to be him.'

*****

If there is one thing the chaos allows, it is for things a normal person would see as unthinkable to suddenly seem acceptable, permissible, and even necessary in order to survive. I hold the shiny object in my hands. It's heavier than I expected and completely terrifying. The guy didn't take long to show me how it worked and it wasn't because he was afraid of the cops or anything, it was just that he really didn't care. He had somewhere else to be, he said. A war is coming and he wants to be a part of it. I didn't dare ask whose side he will be fighting on and I didn't think of haggling with him. Dollars don't do a lot these days, he said, and so he took all the jewellery I had and told me to fuck off before he shot me and took my car as well.

I left quickly and so did he. Both of us went our separate ways, going to very different battles. Now I'm sitting in the car, parked several houses down from Carlos's place. I pulled in as soon as it went dark and turned the lights off, the absence of any streetlights having hidden my approach. A regular helicopter flies over and shines lights all over the district, close to this neighbourhood and then further away – looking for something it cannot seem to find. I'm almost grateful to see it flying overhead, to know that some resemblance of government power remains, even if it won't come to my aid. I think of that cop from earlier and I wonder where he is now. He must know I'm coming back here and I would like nothing more than for him to come around the corner and get into the passenger seat, telling me his master plan for our attack.

As I accept that no one is coming to help me I look down at the gun – the only plan I managed to come up with. I have to get Carlos to come to the door one more time, then I can shoot him. If I kill him where he stands, I can get in, taking all the time I need to find Lucy. And if I have to shoot him as he leans through the window, then that is what I will do. As I plan all of this and think about what will happen, I realise that my choices are entirely limited, yet completely inevitable.

I put the gun into my backpack, not comfortable with having it stuck in my belt, never really convinced that I will be able to fire it. Killing a man has only just crossed my mind, and as I step out of the car I remind myself that the bigger worry for me is that Carlos may also be armed. The thought that I might be wrong, and that I could be planning to shoot dead an innocent man, only enters my thoughts at the last moment, when I have already convinced myself that I am right. And if I am somehow wrong? I have already decided that finding Lucy is worth every bit of his soul and I'll walk over a hundred dead Carlos's to find her.

I hate everything about him but I know deep down that I myself am a monster, created by this changing world.

I stalk my way over lawns and through bushes, until I find safety in the shadows of a house on his side of the road. The helicopter circles overhead again, its light on the road. It shines over a few houses but doesn't stay for long and clearly doesn't see any threat. Sirens sound in the distance and it quickly pulls away to whatever is happening over there. I kneel down for a moment, trying to steady my thoughts. Only the image of Lucy is in my head, as her blonde hair and big smile both offer me comfort; the thought of holding her close distracts me from the impossible task that awaits me. I don't know how I will get in but I know what I will bring out. I am sure of it.

I'm soon outside his house, and I slowly start making my way around to the back. I duck down low as I crawl under the windows. I know they are sealed tight but I don't take the risk, cannot let him hear or see me coming. I survey his house, looking for any signs of vulnerability but I see that he has sealed up the front pretty well. I get into the garden and look at the back of the house, figuring he might not have had time to fortify it as much. I position myself behind a large bush, thankful his home preparations didn't stretch to pillaging the wood from out here. I look up at the house as I inspect each window from this safe distance. They all look sealed: all are covered with bars or large, wooden boards.

As I start to think about how much noise I will make if I take them off, I start to wonder if any lights are on. The windows with bars make it easy to figure out, but in the dark of the night I cannot see the slightest bit of light shining through any gaps. He's either in the basement or somewhere else in the house and running the power at a very low level.

I get up, my body still hunched, and I start to make my way towards the back door, hoping it is not as sealed as it looks from here. Halfway across the lawn I stop as I hear a car door slamming. I didn't hear any noise from a car engine but the hum from the helicopters in the distance probably hid it. I run back to my hiding place, although I'm not sure what I'm hiding from or if I even need to bother. I reach for the gun, pulling it out and holding it down to the ground. I try to listen for voices or noises and I know that if I was braver I would find a way to get closer, to be able to find out what is happening at the front and back of this house. I stroke this thing in my hand, trying to remember if I have put the safety in the on or off position.

I drop it on the ground when I hear someone coming through the gate and then I hear a man talking on the phone as he heads to the back door. I recognise the voice but I'm struggling to place where I heard it before. It's not Carlos; the man is a good foot taller and his voice is not as deep. I lean forward, just a little, trying to get a closer look.

He still has his back to me as he starts to unlock the door to a house that I don't believe is his, yet he has all the access he needs and enough confidence to know where he is going.

I move a little, hoping to catch a glimpse of the man's face, but I'm not careful enough and I tread on a fallen branch. It easily snaps under my weight and the noise is enough to make him turn around.

I quickly crouch down, as low as I can go, hoping I'm shielded enough for him not to see me, or that he is in enough of a hurry that he will not want to investigate further, and will just assume it's the noise of some animal. I look through the thinnest part of the bush, through a small space in the leaves, just enough to notice the gun that's pinned to his belt and the police badge that sits on the other side. He looks around for a moment, saying nothing as he scans every part of the garden for any threat that might linger.

The sirens in the distance suddenly go off again and it's enough to bring his focus back to the door, and just as he turns I see that it's Detective Marius. He doesn't turn around again; instead, he goes inside and closes the door. I run closer, suddenly finding courage, knowing this might be the only chance I get. I'm soon at the wall of the house and my heart is beating faster than I ever thought possible.

I'm about to push open the door, to storm in and try to catch him off-guard, when I realise that I have left the gun behind the bush. I curse myself, knowing I've blown my only chance, but as I consider my limited options I realise that I haven't heard any locks turn.

I quickly run through the garden, snaking my way around the edges, trying to be invisible, just in case he has found a gap through one of those windows.

Before I know it, I am back and standing opposite the door, my weapon held up to the moonlight so I can check the safety. I'm still not totally sure but I convince myself that it is loaded and ready to fire. I realise that I'm finding any reason I can not to go in, not to face whatever horror is awaiting me. Only the thought of Lucy pushes me forward. I put my hand on the handle and I think of her now, alone and desperate, and somehow it gives me the strength to do what I must. I push down on the cold metal, take a deep breath, and slowly creep into the unknown.

*****

'You're sure it was him?' one of the men asks from somewhere outside her room. Lucy can make out each of the voices, although she only recognises one of them. Her man – her regular tormentor – says very little but she knows it's him. Each and every time she awakes from that forced sleep, her body aching and her head spinning out of control, it is his voice she hears. And every time she wakes up, she knows that he has already started. He seems to get a kick out of realising she has woken up, his cock getting obviously firmer as she realises what is happening to her, and only then does she remember the horrors he has already inflicted and is about to repeat.

She knows that he always grinds slowly at first, almost tenderly, as he lets her ligaments adapt to the restraints and he kisses her face. The infra-red goggles almost always bang against her temple as he slobbers all over her – it would almost be laughable if she didn't know what was coming next. The last time is the one that she remembers the clearest: he was preparing for his final onslaught when he leaned in closer to tell her she would never leave him, and that she was, and forever will be, his secret slice of life. He promised that what had happened to the other women wouldn't happen to her. She was safe but his always.

Lucy knows he is coming now but she also knows something is different this time. She has never heard any of her jailors speak before, but now they are freely talking to each other outside her prison cell. She should be fast asleep right now, the shower and the pill doing their usual thing. But not this time, not with that hero inside her gathering all those small victories and putting them together into a plan. Lucy's mind is working overtime now – from her chemistry degree she knows that alcohol destroys most of the potency of the sedative, especially when held in her mouth for a minute or two. He was careless this time, not following his usual routine, not checking her mouth properly, something making him rush.

She's awake when she should be asleep, able to hear every word from outside. 'He was in the garden, I'm sure of it,' the unknown man says.

She wonders if they are talking about Harvey – she hopes with every ounce of her remaining self that it is him. She knows there are others here; she knows it could be another saviour for another prisoner. She wastes no more time thinking of men as her thoughts turn to the other captive women, and how she will be the one to make this right.

'I knew he would show up again,' her man says. Her man? She curses herself for having such thoughts, for allowing herself to think of him as more than a rotten piece of meat. She vows to show him what he is to her when he comes in. He will mount her and she will take her time as much as he takes his, waiting for the moment, knowing this will be his last ever defiling of all that she is.

She tells herself to be quiet, wondering if she is speaking out loud. She sits up, just about to undo her last restraint, still eternally blessed that the left one just a little too loose; something in the knot, never quite doing its job. When she hears them still talking she finishes her work, gets down from the table and starts feeling her way around. Even the blackness cannot hold her back now and she moves around with relative ease. She hasn't spent the last few days being idle, however many of them there have been; she is a long way from being that girl who cried in the corner. She has observed, planned and above all got to know her way around this room. In some ways it now feels like her home; in fact, it's more hers than his and she knows every groove and crevice. It's her biggest asset and she plans to use every bit of it.

'You know that we don't have any more time. I say we leave him and let the monsters have their feast. It's the perfect distraction. We have enough of them left to trade, so now we just have to sit back and let this storm pass.'

She listens to them talking, the other one clearly convincing her man of whatever this plan is. She pictures him nodding and knows that she doesn't have long. She finds what she is looking for and checks it will still do its job, before making her way back to the table.

She is about to jump back onto it and do up her ankle restraints when she catches her foot on something. She stumbles and wants to scream but quickly puts a hand over her mouth, trying to steer her thoughts away from this new pain. What was it? A nail or something? She sits on the table, her fingers finding the moist patch on the sole of her foot. She rubs it, feeling what is flowing out of this new wound. She licks her finger, the taste telling her what she already knew. She senses dripping onto the floor, can tell it's bleeding more than she had hoped.

She suddenly looks up, hearing the conversation as it seems to come to an end: 'Come help me seal up the door and let's have a drink to celebrate all that we have achieved.'

No, she thinks, not now. She is torn: she wants to have time to fix her wound but doesn't feel able to endure another hour in this silent hell. She lies herself back on the table, unsure how bad it is but knowing she must ignore the pain. She needs it to happen now; he must come in and finish what he started. He knows the drug will wear off soon and she knows it must happen now, before she is trapped in whatever tomb these monsters have created.

'You go seal it and I'll finish up here.'

'Can't you leave her just the once? You know we have more important things to do.'

She gasps as she tightens the binds on her ankles, aware that she may be pushing more blood down her leg and out of the hole that she cannot see, as she starts an agonising wait for him to come in.

'No, nothing is more important than what I do every evening and what I will do every evening for as long as we are in here. It is my release and it gives me purpose. Remember that I have worked hard to create all of this while you were speeding around in your car, doing your apparent detective work.'

There's a pause, a moment where she imagines her man and this other once facing off against each other. 'Remember that it's my *apparent* detective work that got us all these women.'

'And I intend to enjoy this one more than all the others. She will be mine each and every day until the end of this stinking world.'

She hears him laugh. 'You'll split her open if you're not careful.'

'Never you mind what I do to her and just remember she is mine and mine only.'

Lucy waits, her head lifted up and her mind frantically telling her to relax into position. Thoughts run through her head. She struggles to believe that one of the men outside is a detective. Still shaking, she thinks of her captor; she is terrified at the thought of what he is going to do and the lifetime he plans to do it for. Remember your place, remember you are asleep, that little hero tells her. She takes hold of each of the ropes wrapped lightly around her wrists, hoping that through his infra-red lens they won't look different from usual. She knows that he pays them no attention when she is awake and only releases them when he is done, quickly leaving her alone to fall off the table and find those rags in the corner of the room, which are her only comfort after every ordeal. But she doesn't know what he does at the start, when she is asleep. Does he touch her there? Does he check that the restraints are still tight? She has no time to worry about that, and she tugs at each of the knots on her feet, which are as strong as he usually makes them. If it all goes well she won't need her legs, but she worries about the wound, becoming convinced that she can hear blood dripping onto the cold, hard floor.

'We agreed she is yours, so don't worry about me. But you know she might be better in the basement with the others. If we have to hide for a few days you won't be able to get to her up here. They can sense the blood moving through our bodies.'

'I have insulated this room just as you showed me, so she stays here, okay?'

Lucy doesn't hear the answer, if there is one. She thinks of the distant news reports she heard before she was taken and can only imagine what horrors have emerged since then. Only when she hears the door open and shuts her eyes, playing as dead as she can, does she realise that she is on an upper floor – maybe an attic? It doesn't matter now and will never matter if she isn't able to defeat the terrors on the inside first; after that, she can start worrying about those on the outside.

She keeps her eyes closed and her body limp; her senses heightened as she hears the steps of her enemy in this quiet place, and she thinks of only her freedom that's edging a little closer. Just climb on and give it to me, she thinks; waste no time with your usual torment. Do your worst, and do it as quickly as possible, she prays, and then I will do mine.

*****

I can't hear him and I don't know if he is waiting around some dark corner to pounce on me. It's obvious that he has a lot more training than I do; he will be far more conditioned in the use of a gun. My only advantage is surprise and I try to remember that, even though I've been left no choice but to use my torch. The dark house is full of obstacles that I don't remember from my one previous visit here. I've searched downstairs and found nothing and so he has to be up there, I think, as I look up the stairs.

Helicopters are flying overhead with such regularity now that they almost seem to be timetabled. I'm pretty sure I've heard some of them firing weapons; masses of bullets spraying towards something in the distance.

I suddenly hear movement upstairs and the creaking of the floorboards above me. Maybe he has been spooked by the choppers; he will know more than I know and I expect him to come running down the stairs. I wait for a few seconds but hear nothing more. I think of Lucy trapped in a room with him as he does all manner of unmentionable things to her, and I know I can't wait any longer.

I move quickly up the stairs, my gun pointed forward and the end of the barrel following the lead of my torch. As soon as I reach the landing I look around and see several doors, plus another staircase. I pick the first door, the room I thought I heard noise coming from. I take hold of the handle and push the door open, almost falling into the room as I try to process everything I see and register any threat quick enough to fire before he does. I see a bed and a woman lying on it – blonde hair, as light as Lucy's – her back to me. I spin my body around the room, pointing the gun into every corner, making sure he isn't hiding somewhere.

I suddenly think that I see him hiding behind the door and so I fall to the floor, my arm extended. My eyes confirm it's just a shadow; just a fraction of a second more and I would have fired. I stay lying down and push the door closed with my foot, figuring it's better to keep a barrier between Marius and me.

I then turn around, crawling the short distance to the bed. 'Lucy?' I say, barely a whisper. 'I have finally found you.' I kneel at the side of the bed and put the gun on the floor, close enough to me but out of sight and risk of going off. I call her name again, gently sliding one arm underneath her body as the other one prepares to embrace her. She groans as I slowly move her and then turn her body to face me.

She says nothing in return as I lay down her body in a new position. Now I am able to look at her properly and as I do so I gasp and fall backwards. I keep looking, my mind struggling with what I see, trying to understand what has happened. 'You're not Lucy,' I finally say, looking at the young woman before me. Even despite the mask of matted blood, sweat and obvious pain I can see that she is beautiful, but she is not Lucy. I look at her arm, which is covered in marks – scars caused by the things she has been forced to endure and the way she has been kept restrained.

I try to touch her as she turns over again, but even when I shake her I get only the slightest groan. I know it won't be easy to get her out of here. 'I will help you, do you hear me?' I say, as I stroke her exposed cheek.

She says nothing as I stand up. Before I can do anything I know that I need to find Lucy. I think of asking if she knows anything and if she saw anyone else, but I know that she cannot help me now. I grab the gun and head to the door, my thoughts on the rest of the house and if I will find Lucy in a similarly terrifying situation.

Once I'm out of the room things move quickly, as I start to search everywhere. I follow my standard pattern, launching through each door and pointing my weapon at every dark corner, determined to fire on anything that moves – almost willing myself to release it on someone or something.

Despite searching every room, I don't find my lover or my enemy; only three young women, spread across the different rooms on this floor. With every door that I open I find a new nightmare, but not one that holds Lucy. I look up the next set of stairs, knowing that I only have one option left. I know that I haven't been quiet but he still hasn't come down here to fend me off.

I look at the woman standing next to me; her clothes are torn and her body is bruised. Her eyes are surrounded by red craters and I can only imagine what she has been through, but I'm thankful she is half-smiling and grateful that at least one of those I rescued was awake. She looks up those same stairs and takes a step forward, as if nothing in this place can truly scare her anymore.

I take a gentle hold of her arm and pull her back towards me. 'Get the other two out and wait for me in the garden. Try to hide somewhere.'

She looks at me for a moment, perhaps no longer willing to obey anyone, perhaps wanting to grab the gun off me and carry out her own form of justice.

'What's your name?' I whisper.

'Terry,' she whispers back, in a raspy voice that probably hasn't been used for days, maybe even weeks.

I nod, silently acknowledging her. 'Whoever is up there, I promise I will make them pay. They have taken my girlfriend and I want her back. We don't have much time so trust me and focus on getting the others out.'

She finally nods and tiptoes to the first room. I wish I could go with her, help her through the obvious trauma of seeing how she must have looked to me, but I know Lucy must be on the last of the floors, and I have to find her. Terry says that she didn't see any other women, doesn't know any Lucy, and so the empty room must have been hers. I can't bear to look in it again, to see the pain she has gone through since I left her, and so I follow the only path left open for me, up the stairs and into the attic.

I don't even check the safety on the gun, but I feel entirely ready to use it, to end the lives of these two men, to see their guts spread across a wall of my choosing. The thought of taking Lucy into my arms whilst carrying her down the stairs and into my car is the only thing I need, and as I shine my path ahead, I think only of how I am going to win this war.

I finish my climb and stand outside the only door on this level. I have no other choice but to go in there and face my fear. I was as quiet as I could be climbing the wooden steps, although nearly all of them creaked as I made my way up. I figure they must know I'm coming and will have set some sort of trap. A sudden wave of relief falls over me; it's so inappropriate, but the presence of these abused women has validated my suspicion. I may not have my Lucy but I have my convictions, and although it's not much help it gives me the strongest purpose I have ever felt.

I put one hand near the handle and the other one held up to shoulder height, the gun poised, ready to fire, knowing that I must face Carlos and Marius together; two strong men against just me. I burst through the door and do my usual routine, pointing my gun at each corner of the room as my brain tries to process what I can see. My assault is accompanied by a loud scream and I spin around as quickly as I can. I soon find I'm turning again, as my scattered mind fails to locate any threat. I calm myself down, looking for another door, another bed, another place Lucy could be.

I soon accept that she isn't in this room. There is only one bed and it looks as used as the others – a pattern of sinister stains covers the once-white sheets. It looks that whoever was here suffered the same treatment as all the others, but they have since been moved on.

I sit on the bed and touch one of the red stains, tormenting myself by wondering if it came from under Lucy's tender skin. I put my head in my hands, the gun clashing with my forehead, as I wonder where she is, and where Marius and Carlos have managed to hide themselves. I start to cry. My tears flow freely as I think about what I have allowed to happen; those I have rescued are just not enough.

It's all too much – everything happening out there, all that's happened in here – and so I take a firm grip of the gun. I have to be with her and wherever she goes I will follow.

'Where are you, Lucy?' I ask out loud, as the barrel of my new friend finds the side of my head, presenting me with the only real option I have left.

*****

He closes the door and that's enough to make her shudder. Every small noise and every subtle movement feel like an earthquake to Lucy's crumbling mind. She doesn't know how she will do this, doesn't know if she really can. She imagines him coming closer as she uses everything she has, desperately trying to play dead, to not move, to make sure he suspects nothing. Surprise is all she has got and it can only help her the once.

She waits for that first touch. It will be a test for the both of them – can she really pretend to still be asleep, and can she make no move and no sound, even though she wants to explode with a mixture of pure fear and absolute rage?

She knew it was coming but his one simple stroke still takes her by surprise, distracting her whilst she plots and schemes. Her foot instantly moves, an involuntary twitch that she didn't see coming and could never have stopped. It was such a simple test; such a clever way to check if his prisoner was actually awake.

She immediately feels his tight grip around one of her ankles as she imagines him looking through those infra-red goggles, inspecting every part of her body. She knows it's over, that she has lost the only thing that could have helped her win – the element of surprise. She doesn't feel any more touching; she knows he's not on the table and that's where she needs him to be. Close, but not too close. He's too in control of the situation, too balanced – both of his feet are still firmly on the floor.

Lucy doesn't know what to do and cannot believe that her one chance has come to an end. She waits for his questions, his shouting and his swift punishment. And as she waits and wonders, that is when the thought comes to her, as she gently moves her head and lets out a short groan. Her only hope is that he will think she is rousing from a peaceful slumber and that it will be enough to appease him, enough to entice him to do what he always does, what he plans to do to her every night until fate, or some luck on Lucy's part, forces them apart.

He doesn't appear to move, his stillness giving nothing away as she tries to remain calm. She lies still, as if in her dream state she is far away from him. The agonising seconds tick by. She waits for his hands to grasp her throat, a punch to her ribs, or worse – a needle entering her veins and returning her to the state she should have been in. She is just moments away from sheer panic and doesn't know how to stop it.

'The medication grows on you, dearest,' he says, as she feels him climb onto the table. 'We will have to increase your dose from tomorrow.' She feels his sudden warmth against her face, his moist tongue running up her cheek, his rancid breath penetrating her nostrils. 'We can't have you joining the party before it gets properly started.'

She says nothing, her eyes firmly closed as she lets out another short moan. It's all she can do to breathe in and out properly, enabling fresh air travel into her lungs. He moves away from her face, his full weight resting on her stomach as she struggles to hold her breath. This is what happens when she sleeps; her limp body and absent mind somehow cope with it, but when she is awake she has the experience of this overwhelming pain without any of the anaesthetising effects she desperately needs. She moans again, which is the only way she can get control of her body, as she wonders if he has spotted something very different to every other night in this week of hell.

He moves further down her body, his pelvis lined up with hers. Lucy knows what is coming next but she still feels relieved when his crushing weight is removed from her chest. It is clear that he suspects nothing, remaining focused on what he wants. She feels the rough fabric of his clothes against her soft skin as his body grinds against hers.

She wants to scream; she's desperate to push him off, but instead, she just talks to the hero inside her. Be calm and be ready, that brave voice inside her says. It won't be long now, although she really can't be sure how long all of this will take.

Her patience starts to pay off: she senses him taking off his clothes, layer by layer, scraping his hairy stomach against her at every opportunity he gets. The moment must be coming but she can't feel it, wants to feel it, wants all of this to be over.

He's naked now; she can feel their skin touching as he kisses her all over and shuffles around. It's so uncoordinated and not at all what she expected. The silence seems to have taken her scary captor and replaced him with this shaking, shell of a man.

She can still feel nothing where she thought it would be worst. He is still grinding on top of her but nothing is growing and the darkness now makes more sense to her. His ample weight, horrid features and feeble girth of that thing below now reveal him for what he is. Behind every man is a little boy and Lucy sees this one. She wants to leap up, to grab him and tell him he's less than half the man her Harvey is, but she stays still, not wanting to provoke him, not dare reveal her fully awakened state.

'You are losing your appeal, dearest,' he says, as he huffs. 'You're becoming very ugly to me. Very ugly indeed.' She feels him moving, ready to climb down and give up at a time when she desperately needs him to stay and continue the torment. 'We need to start this over again because this is all wrong.' She feels a slap to her face. 'All of this is because of you! If you were asleep, then it would all be fine, but you are not, are you?'

She wants to scream, wants to shout and plead for her life, but instead she lets out some sort of whining noise. She takes all that anger, frustration and fear and channels them into a long and playful groan. Time is against her and Lucy cannot afford to sleep, cannot afford to miss this moment because she knows she will not get another.

She tenses her body against the straps as much as she can, teasing with whatever she has left, hoping that he will somehow find the energy to carry on. She keeps her eyes closed, her head moving as she fakes a stirring, a longing for impulsive love-making; the kind that comes from nowhere and consumes a couple for a short time in the middle of the night before they fall back to sleep in each other's arms.

She can sense that he is still watching her; he hasn't moved since she faked this new-found interest in him, this desire for him to touch her, to tease her and to do what he came here to do. She imagines him looking through those goggles, his senses torn between trying to understand her sleepy motives against believing any genuine desires his prisoner could ever harbour for him.

He finally runs a hand up her stomach until he reaches her breasts, and as he takes a firm yet clumsy hold she lets out a deliberate gasp. She pushes her body upwards, subtly begging him to follow through on his primal urges. He lets out a moan of his own as he runs both sets of fingers down her body and then pushes two of them inside her. He doesn't tease, doesn't offer any love, just brutally takes what he wants. His sharp nails tear into yesterday's still-fresh wounds and Lucy knows all she can do now is beg.

'Don't stop,' she says, her eyes open, although she can't see anything.

'You're fully awake,' he says, his deep voice sounding shocked.

Lucy knows how dangerous it is to change his rules but she doesn't stop, doesn't fear him anymore. 'Take me now,' she begs, her body moving up and down as much as she can without giving her game away.

He lets out a long growl, his manhood stabbing where his hands have just been. His thighs are pinned on top of hers, and he tuts and moans as he tries to find the right angle to get in. Whilst he is doing this, Lucy takes her chance to get ready, her hands slipping out of the fake knots tied around her wrists. She pulls back, her legs stretching against the restraints, knowing she needs to make him work a bit more, just to be sure his focus is on this moment and on this most evil of tasks.

'Stay still!' he shouts and smacks her across her face. She feels the pain and yet somehow thinks she is the one who has gone too far, pushed him over the edge of what he will tolerate. Her defeated mind anticipates the next slap and the ten more that will follow it.

When it doesn't come she feels relieved. Both of his hands brush against her inner thigh as he tries to push it in. She imagines the pressure mounting with every moment that goes by, and her lack of encouragement could cause a quick shrinking. More than anything, she knows that if he loses his erection she loses this night.

She knows that this is her time – it has to be – and while he is focusing both his hands towards the centre of their embrace, his body the most unbalanced it will ever be, she shifts all her energy and any power she has left to her stomach. She doesn't shout, doesn't scream, as she silently pulls herself up. At first it feels like the most painful pull-up she has ever done, with every part of her body aching at this brutal heaving. But with every ounce of energy she has left she pushes herself all the way up, and as she starts to move she summons all this power that's being carried through her arms and shoulders by nothing but pure determination, because she will not remain her, at his mercy, for a moment longer.

She collides with his body in exactly the place that she wanted to; the palms of her hands dig into his chest and push into him with everything she has. With his body off-balance and his mind occupied, the force of her push makes him fall backwards and off the table, his initial shouting soon replaced by welcome silence.

Lucy remains sitting upright, her heart pounding and her head turning and jerking as she tries to listen for what she cannot see. She waits for a moment, wondering when he will grab hold of her neck and start to strangle her, or batter her head with his angry fists until she is no longer a problem.

When nothing happens she finally finds the courage to untie her ankle restraints, and then slowly lowers herself off the table, her foot hurting the moment the open wound touches the floor. She lets out a whimper but continues to limp forward slowly, her arms held out as she reaches for something ahead of her. She takes a couple of small steps but can't feel anything yet. She thinks that maybe her plan didn't work and that he is silently watching her from the other side of the room, getting a kick from her obvious failure, planning her next punishment.

She lets out another moan when she finally touches something. She hears him cry out in pain, calling her a bitch and a whore; he starts graphically describing what he will do to her but is clearly unable to follow through with any of these threats. Lucy takes this as a good sign and fumbles around until she finds what she is looking for.

Once she has taken the goggles from him and put them on she finally lets herself breathe again. After taking a moment to adjust, she is able to see the dark green image before her. His shouting is combined with snarling and teeth gnashing; his face is half-hidden by an overgrown beard; the whites of his eyes move frantically around. He has been plunged into a dark world and is trying to see. Trying to move, he cries out in pain; the wooden stake that passed through his back and out through his chest still has him pinned to the wall.

Lucy watches for a moment, seeing the result of the agonising hours of preparation that has turned into barely a fraction of the justice she deserves. She knows that he cannot move, that his body is impaled on the floorboard she battled to get up and placed delicately where she hoped he could be pushed into it. She thinks of taking her time now, of slapping, beating and strangling him. She even thinks about poking both of his eyes out, leaving him in the permanent state of darkness that he so freely exposed her to.

Her thoughts quickly turn to Harvey, to the other women and maybe men, all of them needing to escape this place where at least one more captor is still here. She quickly ties his ankles and wrists together and gags him so he cannot scream, before standing back and taking one final look. His head is already bobbing up and down, the loss of blood causing him to drift away. She smacks him, just the once, so that she sees him come back to life.

She moves closer, putting her mouth next to his right ear. 'You are not a man – you never have been – and you will die in this darkness. This secret slice of life, as you call it, will be your tomb, and I will be free to live my life away from you and this hell-hole.'

She quickly heads for the door, knowing she should have said something even worse, wishing she had the guts to push her thumbs into his eye sockets and hear him scream through the dirty rag she has stuffed deep into his mouth. Instead of any of that she thinks about Harvey, about him looking for her, and how she will not change who she is, will not become like them.

And so, thinking only of those who really matter and how she can escape, she opens the door and feels the welcome light of freedom flood through her goggles, an immediate reminder that the darkness is no longer her home.

*****

After I had faced down the barrel of my gun nothing else seemed to scare me. I wasn't able to end it, not without knowing what had happened to her, and so I moved back down through the house in some sort of trance. The weapon was hung by my side; I didn't point it at anything the whole time. I didn't seem to care if I made it out alive, or if I suddenly found Carlos or Marius hiding around the next corner. As it happens I made it out unharmed, yet clueless about where they are.

I walk around the house and find Terry and the other two women on the front lawn. The other two are starting to wake up; they are still disorientated but at least able to stand. They remain huddled together, their few clothes barely covering them. I end up stopping Terry from breaking into Marius's car: she seems to have found her balls from before I met her, before all this happened. 'You shouldn't break into a police car,' I say, risking starting some big discussion about why there would be a car here without any policeman. I tell her not to think about that now, not wanting to risk telling her about who her jailors really were.

There's a sudden bang in the distance which makes us all jump onto the ground. I look up to see several flashes, followed by more loud bangs, as the skyline of many miles lights up with its own special pattern of destruction. I watch as buildings I have often visited now burn and collapse, and I city I have called home all my life, slowly falls to ruins as the army launches things at an enemy I don't even dare to imagine. I follow the lights and picture the explosions as realise that they are not too far away – maybe only a mile in the distance.

'What was that?' Terry asks, a fearful look returning to her eyes. It's the same look she had when I found her, when I shook her awake; she naturally thought I was one of the bad guys, back for another round. 'We need to get out of here,' she says.

I nod but I don't really agree. I have to find Lucy; have to figure out what is happening. I was so preoccupied with getting into the house that now that I have searched it I don't know what to do next. I look at these three women; they are people I have saved from certain death, yet I couldn't feel more confused and angry. I sit down on the lawn and look around the neighbourhood, knowing there has to be something I'm missing.

'Did you hear me?' Terry says, shaking my arm. 'We need to leave.'

I don't answer her, looking only at the house straight ahead – the house that's opposite and the one that Lucy identified in the last few moments of her call. I grab my notebook out of my bag and flick through the pages, all the time trying to block out Terry's very fair demands.

She is still shaking me when one of the other women starts to cry. 'Please, we have been through enough, you have to get us out of here!'

I say nothing, but reach for my car keys and hand them to Terry. I look into her eyes, knowing it is the only freedom I can offer her. 'I have to get my girlfriend.'

Terry shakes her head, tears forming in the giant craters where her eyes once shone, now looking only hopeless and defeated. 'There were other girls, you know that, right?'

'She's not dead.'

'But she's not in the house, either.'

I push my keys into her palms. 'My car is down the street,' I say, absently indicating with my head where they will find it. 'I know you want to get far away but please wait for us because I promise we will be coming. Wait at the corner of Moorland Avenue.'

'Thank you,' Terry says, nodding repeatedly as she tries her best to assure me that they will wait. 'But how long should we give you? The helicopters are getting closer.'

'Give me thirty minutes. It's all I will need.'

She nods and starts to motion the other two women to get up, her protective instincts taking over. 'I don't know what else you can do,' she says.

'I do,' I say, looking at Number 12. 'I know exactly what I'm going to do because I know Lucy is in that house.'

We both look at the house over the road; all the lights are off and the front door and bottom windows are boarded up, just as they were last time I was on this road.

'I don't understand,' Terry says, although I'm not sure she really wants me to explain.

'Every time I have been to this road over the last few days that house has been empty and all the lights have been off. The owners had apparently abandoned it weeks ago.'

Terry quickly nods. 'It looks abandoned.'

I nod back, showing her a page in my notebook. 'If it's abandoned then why are the upstairs curtains, which were open yesterday, and the day before, and the day before that, now closed?'

Terry smiles, showing the fight that is still left in her, even though her brown mouth is full of the stains and troubles of such a tormenting week. 'Two houses, even more trapped women. But you can't go in there alone,' she says, and then holds out the car keys, freely giving them back to me.

I nod, feeling relieved, immediately thankful for the help. 'Get these two into my car and then meet me in the basement of this house.'

'This one?' she says and frowns, as she looks back at Carlos's house. 'But it's empty.'

I nod, looking at the road. 'It's also our way in, because I think he built a tunnel between the two houses. Maybe they planned to use both or maybe one of them is the decoy, but I know Lucy is trapped in Number 12.'

'We're helping too,' one of the other women says.

I only nod, not even asking her name. The look on their face says they want revenge; they want to storm the keep and kill the demons and end this nightmare once and for all. We all walk back through the garden and into the house, all with our own axe to grind.

As we walk I rummage through my backpack and find the other tool I brought today. I didn't know how I would get into Carlos's house but I figured there would be a need to force my way through a door. I didn't know what I would do if he launched his missiles at me, shouting all manner of threats, as I finally got through the threshold. I had never thought that far ahead, but one thing I had thought about was how strong those doors must be, and how some explosives would probably come in handy.

I hold the dynamite in my hand, wondering if it will even work, or if that thug sold me a stick filled with sawdust. All I know is that it's my last hope, my only way in, and all we have to do is to find is the right door.

'Help me search this basement,' I ask them, hoping they will be quick, praying they will be thorough; knowing we need to do a better job than before and in a fraction of the time.

*****

Lucy hobbles down the stairs, knowing she needs to move quicker than her wound will let her without making her screaming out in pain. She pushes a hand against the wall, letting it support her as she takes each step one at a time, her good foot constantly bracing her injured one. There is something stuck in it, something digging further into her skin, but she can't worry about that now. It's already gone too deep for her to be able to get it out herself and so she continues on her mission of escape.

She knows there has to be at least one more of them somewhere in the house, but she wonders if there are several of them spread throughout this place. It's a horror story she needs to find the answer to, despite how scared she is. As she makes it to the landing she figures she has to be at least one more storey above ground level. She only has a stinking blanket for warmth and wraps it tighter around her, almost feeling some sort of connection to this bloodied and stained rag. It has been her only comfort for as many days as she can remember; it has seen her through more trauma than she has ever known before. She holds it tight as she looks at each of the closed doors in front of her. She needs to go in, needs to find someone, but hopes with every ounce of her that it isn't one of her captors that she runs into.

Lucy thinks about moving on, heading downstairs and finding a door, but something stops her. The thought of anyone going through what she has been through makes her want to break down in tears, but it would be even worse to know that she had left other innocent people behind – people who didn't deserve this any more than she did. She can hear thunder echoing outside the house, somewhere in the distance, and she knows time is running out.

It's enough for her to grab the handle and push the door open. She stands in the hallway, waiting to see if someone comes running out. When nothing happens she walks in, immediately checking behind the door. The room is empty but she can tell it was not always like that. She looks at the walls, the furniture and the bed, and realises that this must be a child's room. There are pink decorations everywhere and forgotten dolls all over the floor, which clearly shows that this was once a girl's room, but there are marks on the bed which show her that whoever was the last to live in this room witnessed many horrors of their own.

She moves closer to it, her eyes fixed on the large, red patch in the middle of the mattress. Maybe there was once a sheet over it and maybe there was a happier time before all this suffering, but right now this room reeks of only pain and misery. She steps back, not wanting to know any more, not able to think that there was someone in here while she was upstairs. The small number of screams she has heard over the last few days have almost helped her, proving to her that she was not alone, but now she wishes it had only been her, that she had been the only one to feel the pain of this place.

She checks the other rooms but finds them all empty. One of them looks like it was recently lived in and also seems like a master bedroom, the bed a mess and the en-suite tiles still damp, with a musky smell and clothes thrown on the floor. It has to belong to a man and Lucy wonders if this is her captor's room, and perhaps his wife is locked somewhere in the building. She keeps moving, determined to get out before she learns any more brutal truths.

She quietly shuts the door, determined to leave things as she found them, and then starts to walk down the next flight of stairs. She presses her hands against both walls to help her move but the pain gets worse with every step. She reaches the halfway point and stops. Just a minute to catch my breath, she thinks.

As she is counting the six steps to go a man appears beneath her. He reaches the bottom of the staircase, his attention focused on his cell. Lucy freezes like a statue. She knows that he isn't going to simply walk away, but she's not strong enough to lunge towards him or run away. She frantically thinks through the options in her mind but hasn't thought of one before he finally looks up. He takes a step back when he sees her. He clearly finds the sight of someone escaping as surreal as being a captive has been for Lucy.

She starts to hobble back up the stairs, thinking that she will have to find a weapon of some sort – anything to fend him off. She wishes she had grabbed something on her way down; cannot believe she didn't think of such a basic requirement in this new reality.

'Come here!' he shouts, as he runs up the few steps to get her. He's on top of Lucy within moments, his thick hands grabbing her hair and pulling her back down the stairs. She screams as the pain bolts through her body, but it's not enough to make him stop. He drags her along the floor, shouting threats and asking where his friend is. He calls out 'Carlos,' which she realises is the name of her tormentor. She can't help but think how much the name suits him.

He doesn't stop pulling her until they reach the kitchen, when he finally throws her into a chair. 'What have you done to him?' he asks, slapping her across the face a couple of times.

Lucy doesn't say anything and looks around the room, trying to spot something she can use as a weapon, still hoping to make a quick escape.

He sees that she is looking, not paying him a fraction of the attention he wants, and so he slaps her across the face again, this time harder than Carlos ever did. 'He might have idolised you but you'll find I have far less interest, so tell me where he is.'

'He's upstairs, in my room,' Lucy says, looking her new attacker in the eyes.

He nods and then grabs her throat. 'He had better be alive up there because I'm not staying in this wretched place alone, I can assure you of that.'

Lucy spits in his face. 'Well then, you had best be quick.'

Her insolence gets her another slap and before she realises what is happening she feels her hands being bound behind her back. Her wrists are tied together and then attached to the chair. He leans down to look at her, his face as calm as ice. 'There is no hope for you other than my mercy, so I urge you to stay where you are and not struggle. If you don't obey me then you'll end up outside and I assure you there are far worse things out there than in here.'

She doesn't say anything as he walks away. She can only look around the kitchen, planning her next escape. She has done it once and she can do it again. She needs to be much quicker and even quieter, but she can do it.

*****

'Well done!' I say, as I look up at her and smile.

She looks back at me, the youngest of the three, the one who still hasn't managed to properly speak. She could only shout and point when she spotted the small piece of string which enabled us to find our way in.

'How long have you three been here?' I ask.

They look at each other, as if trying to count up the days. I'm not sure if they are trying to work it out, or if they simply have no idea how long their torment has lasted.

'I got here yesterday,' one of them says, looking around, still unsure where here is.

The quietest one nods, tapping her new friend's arm. She doesn't say anything but I can tell that her story is the same.

I look at Terry and her face tells a different tale of pain. 'A week,' she says, wiping the tears that are flowing down her cheeks.

'About the same time as Lucy,' I say, gently rubbing her arm. 'Do you think you were moved at any point?'

Terry quickly nods. 'I think I was moved a few times but I was always drugged up so I never knew what was going on. I could tell that I was in a different room, but mostly because the beds were different. Why do you ask?'

I nod, holding up this small bit of string. 'I searched this house a week ago with the police and we found nothing. The detective was really helpful. He let me search the house and I spent a lot of time down here, because I thought this is where Lucy would be being held.'

Terry looks around the dark room. 'But you obviously never found her?'

I nod. 'It turns out the detective was in on this whole thing and I think the reason he was so happy for me to search this place is because I don't think this trapdoor was here. I think Carlos, the guy who apparently lives here, tunnelled from the other side, using Number 12 to store the equipment and do his work. Detective Marius could never tell his men not to search a property without raising suspicion, but he could easily keep all of you in the abandoned house over the road. No one would ever know because there are many empty houses now.'

'So, he kept me over there first?' Terry says, as she looks away, her mind quickly elsewhere. I think she is probably trying to remember what was going on when she was taken: the inner city areas were still safe, the world was still okay, apart from what was happening around the edges – in the places most of us didn't really know about.

'I think they put whoever they took first over there, and I hope that includes Lucy.'

'Of course, Lucy too,' Terry says and eventually smiles. She's not as enthusiastic as she was before, but right now I'll take anything she can offer me.

'He couldn't risk creating suspicion while the police were still responding to calls, but in the last 24 hours things have got a lot worse, so they have probably found it easier to capture more women.'

The other two huddle together, stepping back from the small wooden door when I pull the string, checking how easy it is to lift up. 'Why don't you both go grab some blankets and towels, or maybe find some clothes? If there are others down there they might need it.' I hand one of them the keys. 'And then bring the car up closer to the house.'

Terry nods at them, telling them it's okay, before looking over at me. 'We don't have much time.'

'You lift the door and I'll go in first,' I say, handing her the small piece of rope and then taking my gun and flashlight in each hand, ready to face whatever comes crawling out.

Terry watches until the other two are gone before moving over and standing opposite me. Her eyes are on mine as she wills me to open it and face our mutual enemy together. I take a deep breath but don't experience the same trembling feeling I've had every other time in this place. Terry somehow gives me the confidence to go on.

'On three?' I say.

Terry nods back. 'Let's give them hell.'

She counts and I point, and when she reaches three and pulls up the thick wooden board, I point the torch into the tunnel, the barrel of my gun following the light. When I find no immediate threat I lower myself in, my gun and torch balanced on the basement floor as I crawl my way through the dirt. It's basic, drilled with some sort of small machine, something I think that could be worked by just one man. There are no wooden slats, nothing to hold it up. It's simply a thin vein that has been carved through the earth, leaving behind it a trail of soil and debris, and a smoky tunnel of floating dust.

Terry hands me the torch and gun and I nod to say I'm going further in. 'You figure out that dynamite,' I say, as I disappear into the darkness. I crawl along with the torch held in my mouth and the gun tucked into my pants. The structure goes down a few metres and then levels out. It's not wide enough to stand up but it is big enough to move and turn around in. There are no lights but I imagine that he plans one day to run cables through here and thus make it a proper path between his two dungeons.

I shine the torch on the floor and see a trail than extends along the ground; two long runs that stretch ahead through the soil like sledge marks. I'm sure that's how he transported the women between the two buildings, moving them as he needed to. I follow them for several metres – a length that must stretch under the entire road – until they reach an abrupt end, their trail blocked by some sort of yellow foam.

I suddenly jump as I feel something touch me from me behind. Trying to turn around, I fall down onto the gun.

'It's only me!' Terry shouts, holding her hands out and touching my knee.

I lie back for a moment, almost hearing the beats of my overworked heart echo through this small passageway. I wipe the growing sweat from my brow, all the time wondering how much more of this I can take.

'What is that?' Terry asks, looking at what I have found up ahead.

'I don't know,' I say, crawling forward so I can get closer. When I get near enough I touch it and feel how waxy it is. 'It's some sort of foam,' I say, turning to see that Terry is right behind me, the stick of dynamite in her hand.

I rub my hands along the strange material, seeing that it seems to join exactly with the soil, creating a seamless and tight finish, as though nothing was meant to get in or out.

Terry stretches her hand out towards me, still holding the dynamite. 'Shall we blow it?'

I gently push the stick away. 'That might not be necessary,' I say as I focus on the substance and push my hand into it. It immediately gives way to the force of my fingers, giving me the confidence to go deeper. Nothing burns as I slip my arm through it, and so, since time is not our side I start digging. We move quickly, working as a team. I excavate big chunks with both hands and Terry piles them up behind us. After wading through about a foot of foam I feel new, slightly fresher air. It makes me move more quickly. I know I need to get more than just my arm through, in case there is something lurking on the other side.

Once I have cleared enough out of the way I push myself into it, soon seeing that the tunnel follows a similar pattern up to the house. It snakes its way back upwards and the incline in the soil also has the same two-track pattern running through it.

I waste no time as I quickly crawl forward and then heave myself up. The trapdoor on this side is still open, so I quickly push myself into the basement of Number 12. As soon as I am inside I scan every part of the room, pointing my gun around nervously as I turn. It doesn't take long before I see the first movement in the shadows and I'm about to pull the trigger, which would end the life of whatever is lurking there and signal to anyone present that I'm here, that we have made it into the lair.

Something stops me from firing, a whimper in the darkness telling me that this isn't the threat I was expecting down here, and that my hours of searching demand that I'm careful for just a little longer. I keep looking, trying to make out the forms in the shade.

'Help!' a whisper comes from the far side of the room. It's the voice of a woman – not Lucy, but clearly someone who is also in need.

I move closer, my gun still pointing ahead of me. I look around the room, wanting to make sure that Marius isn't waiting to pounce. As I duck under beams and step over boxes I notice that all the walls down here are also coated with the same yellow substance. I touch some of it and it feels hard to the touch; it seems to have has set – clearly designed for a long term purpose.

When I get to the furthest part of the basement, where the plea came from, I stop and stare. I look at the row of large wooden structures – which, from a distance, I thought were boxes, but which I now think of as cells, each of which have a small hole at the front.

'Please, you have to help us!' the voice says again, from one of the structures closest to me. I am leaning down, trying to trace the voice, when I suddenly see an eyeball appear at the small hole. It flickers, clearly trying to find me. After it catches sight of me it immediately disappears, quickly replaced by a finger, which pokes out of the hole.

I move closer, touching it, desperate to show that I am here and will not hurt her. 'It's okay,' I say, barely a whisper. 'We're going to get you out of here.'

I turn around, knowing that I need Terry's help. I don't have to go far before I find her standing just behind me, staring in disbelief at the makeshift cells, all numbered in chalk. I watch as she appears to count them. Both of us can see that there are 12, all of which have numbers on, except for the last one. The number has been rubbed out, which shows it is no longer of any importance. The door has been left hanging open.

I soon think of Lucy, knowing that she must be in one of these, although I pray that the deleted number wasn't her. 'Lucy,' I whisper, walking along the row of wooden doors, desperate to hear her voice as she shouts back. I look up to the door to the house and I know that we do not have long, not long enough for me to inspect every box for only one person.

'We have to get them all out,' Terry says as she slowly unbolts the first door.

I nod, unable to believe that I hadn't already thought of that. 'We need to make them be quiet and we need to do this quickly.'

She nods back and the first woman falls into her arms. I already know she isn't Lucy – I could tell from the voice, but it makes me wonder how I will cope with opening every door and each person inside not being her. They will all want to fall into my welcome arms but I will want nothing but to move to the next, my search never ending until I find her.

I take a deep breath and unbolt the next door, opening it quickly and confirming what I already knew, that Lucy isn't in it. The woman inside, who is barely out of her teens, runs into me the moment I come into sight. She had been waiting, desperately pushing against the door, and now cannot stop thanking me and holding onto my chest, desperately squeezing every ounce of attention from me. I don't know what else to do but I know that I cannot face doing this a dozen more times without finding Lucy, and I know that if I find her then the rest will not matter to me.

I try to push her off me, telling her that there are many others to save, and Terry slowly prises her off and puts an arm around her, kissing her forehead and telling her that she is safe.

I look at the two of them, and the first woman we freed, all of them barely clothed and covered in the scars and stains resulting from their captivity. I know that this is going to take too long and that it's going to get too crowded for us to keep quiet. 'Lead them down the tunnel,' I say to Terry. 'We need to get them out of here and quickly.'

Terry nods – she clearly has the same idea. She leads the first two to the trapdoor, quietly explaining what they need to do and that there are others, more prisoners from different places but all suffering the same fate, just waiting for them on the other side. The first two nod as they listen to what they are being told. Terry touches them to reassure them as she calmly lowers them into the hole. 'Get the others,' she says to me.

I nod and turn, remembering the task ahead of me. I open many doors, each with their own crying wrecks inside, some more like girls than women, all equally scared and confused. I get to the last door and I am already convinced that Lucy isn't in there; the voice coming through the hole tells me not to forget her and to hurry, but doesn't sound anything like my girl. I open it, but I don't even look, don't even take the girl inside into my arms. She has clearly been watching, waiting for her turn, and I get only a whispered thank you before she runs to Terry and starts listening intently to the instructions for her escape.

I turn my attention to the staircase into the house, knowing that no matter how many I rescue I will still be forced to go deeper, my resolve pushed to levels I never knew I was capable of. I decide to make one final sweep of the basement, just hoping to find another set of wooden structures, or even just one – anywhere where Lucy could be. I notice a box in the corner and run over, knowing that it's shaped more like a coffin than a cell. When I get to it I see that it is made of steel and is some sort of chest, mounted on a wooden pallet. I lift the lid without hesitation and I'm pleased to see that it's full of cement bricks. It makes no sense but at least it's not a body.

Terry walks over to me and pushes against the chest to see how solid it is. 'You think this is how they plan to seal the trapdoor,' she whispers.

I nod, looking over to the pallet truck. 'Once it's in place nothing would be able to push the trapdoor up.'

'Nothing, you think?'

I don't get time to answer when I hear a voice coming from upstairs. We both turn our attention back to the stairs that lead into the main house. I recognise the voice as belonging to Marius and I figure that he must have crawled through the tunnel, and then set the foam substance in place. He's shouting threats at someone but I can't make out what he's saying.

As we both move closer to the door I hear someone else moaning. Marius tells them to stay still and asks how they could have been so stupid. 'I'm going to need to stitch you up,' are the last words I hear before the screams of another man echo through the house.

It's enough to make me move towards the door, my heart pounding as I wonder where Lucy is in all of this. I look back to the trapdoor and see all the women are gone, but I know there is still more to do; time is racing by. With Terry just behind me we start to crawl up the stairs, hoping they won't creak and give away our approach.

'Seal the basement first,' a voice says, which I recognise as belonging to Carlos. 'You said that we don't have much time before they come this way.'

'The foam will set within minutes now,' Marius says. 'And once it does they won't be able to smell anything in this house.'

There's a pause in which no words are spoken by either man, whilst my mind battles to understand all that they have said. I try not to think, not to connect their words with the frantic and scattered images I have seen on the news. 'What about my wound?' Carlos eventually says.

I don't hear any answer as I think about how Carlos could possibly be injured. Maybe one of his captives fought back; maybe it was Lucy? I start to worry if she is okay, which makes me tap Terry on the arm and point to the next room. She nods and we both run through the hallway and into the dining room, next to the kitchen. Terry immediately places herself behind me, her body pressed up close to mine as she leans her head over my shoulder, listening to the sounds coming from next door.

'Your wound was a stupid mistake on your part,' Marius says, as I imagine his cold face staring down at Carlos, his calculating mind considering what he will do with him next. I don't know if they have always been in on this together or if Marius discovered what Carlos was doing and wanted in, but either way it sounds like the detective is the one in charge.

Carlos suddenly screams, which causes both of us to jump backwards. Terry takes hold of my arm as I tighten my grip on the gun, the moment when I will inevitably have to use it creeping closer.

'Hold still,' Marius says, his voice barely audible above the constant moans from Carlos. 'The wood has gone right through but I don't think it has ruptured anything serious. Your bigger concern will be any remaining splinters, which could cause an infection, but as I'm not a qualified surgeon you will have to take that risk. I will seal the basement and then do my best to patch you up.'

'I need a hospital,' Carlos says.

Marius laughs. 'You know that's not going to happen, not for a few days. If you survive the storm outside, then we can look for one afterwards. I doubt there will be a functioning hospital left in the surrounding districts but maybe we will be able to find a doctor who is willing to work on you for a price. Perhaps we will have to trade her for your survival.'

There's a pause for a moment and I wonder who they are talking about, as well as what he knows about the threat that is approaching. Marius will know more than anyone and it makes me think of the secrets he must be holding, and how little time we have left in here.

'No trade, only hospital,' Carlos says again, his voice trailing off. The screams have gone, along with any sense of energy from him.

'There's no point in looking at her for help. She did this to you and I will certainly make her suffer for it.'

I step out of the dining room, as close to the kitchen door as I dare, as I try to listen for any sign of who else is in there. I hear a ripping sound, following by shouting. It's the voice of a woman, and she's threatening him, telling him what she is going to do to him. She is confident, taunting Marius with a story about what will happen when she gets free. She is describing it in graphic terms, totally unafraid; she is Lucy. I put a hand to my mouth, stopping myself from gasping out loud as I realise I have finally found her.

I hear a slapping sound and I imagine the palm of his hand striking her tender face. She shouts back, asking him if that's all he has got, which gets her another slap. But she continues to shout, as does Carlos, both of them telling Marius to leave her alone.

I wonder why Carlos would defend her and why he would not want Marius to hurt her. I need to know these things, to stop this once and for all. I turn around to Terry, silently telling her that I'm about to storm the kitchen. I know she will follow but I don't know what she will do. I need to shoot Marius – he is my one and only target. I assume Carlos will be too wounded to put up any immediate fight, but the detective, with all his training and experience, will be a different story.

I'm about to run in but the sirens outside start again, the sound echoing in the distance, and I hear helicopters flying over the house. The sound of the revolving blades is distinct, even from inside, and the fact that the sound doesn't fade tells me that the helicopters are now nearby. I hear a voice coming from some sort of loudspeaker, telling anyone who is still alive and able to hear that they should leave the area immediately.

I hear Marius make a tutting sound and I can easily picture his face as he does it. 'We don't have much time. I need to seal the basement and get you into a bath, because that's the only way we will hide the stench of decay coming from you. If I don't, then we will all die.'

'I don't see how giving him a bath will help,' Lucy shouts. 'Why don't you try drowning him? I'm sure that will work.'

'You've definitely got some fight left in you,' Marius says, in a softer tone than before. I imagine him with a hand on Lucy's face. 'We no longer have time for surgery and so I'm going to lay him in the bath and encase him in the expanding foam. It will hopefully hide the smell of his wound until they pass by. You will feed him, keep him quiet and care for him while I figure out what is going on out there. You will obviously try to escape so I think it's best that I chain you to the bath of your lover and then gag you. If he lives then he can decide what to do with you, and if he dies then I will encase you both together in the same bath. But you will be entombed alive, the foam hardening and covering your entire body and face, until you draw your last breath. Is that something that appeals to you?'

I hear her spit, probably in his face. I wonder what these last seven days have turned the beautiful and tender Lucy into.

This time I don't hear any slap, only a brief struggle, then footsteps along the kitchen tiles. 'I need to seal the basement. I'll take that time to consider your response.'

Terry pulls me backwards as the footsteps come towards us. They reach the hallway and stop, only a thin wall separating us from Marius. I begin to think that he knows something is wrong, that maybe he thinks we are in here. My hand is shaking, the gun almost rattling as I think about stepping out and facing him head on, hopeful that the element of surprise would catch him off guard.

353

Finally, he starts walking again, and I see the back of him disappear down the steps to the basement. I turn around to see Terry. 'It's now or never,' I whisper.

She nods and we both creep into the kitchen. As soon as we burst in I see Carlos trying to shout, his voice slow and confused, no full words coming out. He means nothing to me; my attention, regret and my endless love are all directed at Lucy alone. I look at her pale body, tied to a chair, her hair matted and her face bruised all over. I can't move, shocked by the sight of the shell of a woman in front of me. She tries to mouth something through the dirty rag, repeatedly indicating Carlos with her head.

I take my eyes off her for a moment, seeing Carlos trying to get up, his body obviously weak but his mind still with it.

Terry runs past me, her hands quickly pinned over his mouth, and I realise she is trying to stop his screams from carrying their way down the stairs and into the basement. 'Untie her, quickly!' she says, looking over at Lucy.

I nod, suddenly realising where we are. Reality seems scrambled to me, but I do realise that I have finally found her. I lurch forwards, ripping the gag off her and then quickly finding the knots behind her back. As soon as they are loose she stands up, her body next to mine, her red eyes full of tears, as they have probably been all week.

She holds her hands out but it takes me a moment to realise that it's me standing in front of her, as she takes a step back.

My eyes fill up and tears are soon streaming down my face. I shake my head, aware that she is here but still doubting somehow that it has really happened. 'I found you!' I finally say, both of my arms wrapping their way around her as I pull her close. I realise that I have finally succeeded and my grip on her tightens with every grateful second that now passes by. 'I finally found you and I will never let you go again.'

As I drift away from her, my thoughts turning to how we can get out of here and build a new life, I feel her push me away. I look at her and I realise she is looking at Terry.

I turn to see her struggling to keep Carlos down. Both of his hands are on Terry he tries to push her away. His white T-shirt is covered in blood and it's clear even from a distance that the wound is deep, but that doesn't seem to stop him from finding the energy to fight against his rebelling prisoners.

I see Lucy pick up a knife from the table and it's enough for me to know what I need to do. 'Take care of him,' I say to both of them, heading towards the door. I need to kill Marius before he comes back up. We were clever enough to close the doors and put the locks back on, trying our best to hide the fact we had been there, but he must know something is wrong. My only hope is that he has been too busy moving things to hear what has happened here.

I reach the stairs, the lighting in the basement still dim from only a couple of bulbs. I lift my arm and point my gun forward as I listen for where in the room Marius is. My only two choices are to wait or hide; hoping the element of surprise will help me, or I advance and attack. I think of the two of them upstairs, their fight with the wounded bear, and I know that I cannot wait. When I don't hear anything I take the first step downwards, my eyes flicking around, checking for any sign of movement. I only need to hurt him, just enough to put him down on the floor, and then I can take proper aim for my next shot.

But even when I'm three steps further down, I still can't see him, although I notice that a metal box has been placed over the trapdoor. This means he can't be in the tunnel and our escape isn't going to be that easy. I still don't see him and I start to think about moving back up and closing the door, which would at least let us know if he is coming.

I'm about to take that first step back when I see his arms come out from the side of the stairs. He quickly sweeps me off my feet, pulling me into the basement. My head hits the cold floor as I land, the gun dropping onto the floor. I try to reach for it but a kick to my stomach stops me from moving. I grapple with the pain as I see him standing over me, his gaze turning to the gun which he kicks further away.

'You really are one persistent little fucker, aren't you?'

I don't answer, but I look around the room, desperately trying to find something I can use to fight back. With nothing in reach and no chance to knock him down, I'm forced to stare down the barrel of his gun. I look at it, the weapon that will serve a simple purpose in the hands of its trained master, and I think that this cannot be the end. I have come so far, fought so much, only to lose my love in the same minute I found her.

He doesn't say anything else as he points it at my head; his task is simple and his time short. As I see his finger start to squeeze against the trigger I close my eyes, my body exhausted and my mind only wanting to see Lucy. I hear shots ring out around me and the deafening sounds echo around the walls of the basement.

When I don't feel any pain or sense any passing, I open my eyes to see Marius lying on the floor. A pool of blood has already formed around him but he is still wriggling; his body is damaged but not destroyed.

I look up to see Terry standing at the top of the stairs, a gun in her hand. 'Come on, get up!' she shouts, keeping her attention on only Marius.

I run up the stairs, my eyes only on her, as I try to make sure I'm not blocking her line of sight. When I reach the top I turn to see him still on the floor, his right hand gripping two separate wounds around his left arm and shoulder. He looks up at us and then around the floor as he obviously tries to find a weapon. 'You will never get out of here and even if you do then you will be shot or eaten, depending on who and what gets to you first.'

Terry points her gun towards him. 'Not your problem now, is it?'

She's doesn't fire, as we all become distracted by the sounds coming from the trapdoor. It's a kind of growling sound, long and deep, as the heavy box moves.

'That's not possible,' Terry says. 'It has to weigh at least 500 pounds.'

Despite Terry's assessment it moves again; something below is clearly testing that weight. The solid metal box jumps up a good inch from the ground, followed by a second jump that's even higher.

'It's completely your problem now,' Marius says, as he still scrambles around the floor.

Terry lifts the gun higher, ready to take a shot, but I grab it off her. 'I think it's better that he is alive for now,' I say, as I push us backwards. I quickly shut the door and close the bolt, even though I know it will do no good.

I turn to the kitchen, my mind preparing me for seeing the mutilated corpse of Carlos pinned to a chair as blood still drips from his mouth onto the floor. I'm shocked to see he is still alive, his eyes freely following my movements. His hands are tied to the chair and the gag around his mouth still intact.

'How do we get out?' Lucy asks. She is standing next to him, looking down at him with that knife still in her hand. She's shaking, the silver blade resting on his good shoulder, seeming to be fighting against the temptation to drive it into him. She looks up at me, her eyes burning. 'Get me out now before I do it, before I become as evil as he is.'

I move closer to her, holding out a hand, motioning her to come to me. 'Lucy, sweetie, you will never be like him. We are going to get out and we are going to rebuild our lives. You're free now, I promise you.'

She doesn't move as tears flow down her cheeks. She looks at me and then at Terry, as the knife leaves Carlos and settles on her stomach. 'You think we will be free? You have no idea what he has done, what he has given to me.'

I look closely at her as I absorb these words, taking in everything she says, and then I cry. I knew this was inevitable: the thought of what would happen to her whilst held captive had lingered in the back of my mind but had not seemed as important as finding her alive. When

I'm close enough I reach over Carlos and take hold of her wrist, slowly pulling the knife away and letting it drop to the floor. I pull her into my arms and hold her tight. 'All that matters is that we are together. Everything else we will fix, I promise you that.'

She doesn't say anything, but I can feel her frantic heartbeat and hear her muffled crying. I look down at Carlos, who is watching me. His body is still chained and his mouth still gagged, but despite all of this I know that he is still smiling. I think of those things I dare not ask and will never know; things between him and Lucy that should never have happened. Despite how much she hates him, they have secrets now – things that will never be shared, not with me, anyway.

'Aren't we forgetting that there's something in the basement?' Terry asks. 'And I don't think we should wait around to meet it.'

We all fall silent for a moment as we try different doors and windows, all of which are sealed, and it becomes obvious that the only way into this house is through the tunnel.

Lucy grabs hold of Carlos, as she pulls the gag off. 'How do we get out?'

'Marius!' he shouts.

She stuffs the gag back into his mouth, and he shouts and struggles.

Terry moves closer, the gun pinned to Carlos's forehead as she nods for Lucy to remove it one more time. 'There is something trying to get in, so we need to get out. Tell us how and we will take you with us.'

Lucy pulls it out of his mouth but Carlos only laughs, and then coughs up some blood. 'I'm already dead. I just hope I get to watch them eat you bitches first.' He turns to Lucy, his head shaking and his creased face full of what looks like disgust. 'I looked after you, gave you everything, and look what you've done.'

She picks up a knife from the floor, her resolve all but gone; she has been pushed to a place I have never seen her in before.

'Lucy, leave him,' I shout, but don't bother to see what she does, have no interest in watching the already dead when I want us to live. I head towards the back door and wedge the stick of dynamite between the door handle and the metallic, reinforced frame. I have no idea if it will work and no certainty that the hole it needs to make will ever be big enough.

I turn to see both Lucy and Terry running into the dining room. They hide, and I cannot resist looking at Carlos; I need to know if he is finally dead. He is still looking at me, the knife is on the kitchen table and my Lucy is still intact. I smile and flick the lighter and once I hear the hiss of the flame moving down the small rope I run towards her.

As I slam the door shut and put my arms around the huddled mass of bruised and bloody skin I feel the house shake. I move quickly, desperate to know if it has worked. I had expected the noise, but the flames and smoke were not things I remember from the movies. I try to look through the grey plumes of smoke that are filling the house, trying to see if they offer any path to freedom. It doesn't take long for me to realise that the smoke is being pulled out of the house, as I see a glimmer of the outside world.

My body jolts as I hear the sound of gunfire in the basement – four shots from a gun, followed by a long scream from Marius. It's enough for me to grab them both and push them towards our burning freedom. The smoke has cleared enough to see the way out and Terry leads us forward. Lucy takes hold of my hand as we stumble ahead, until we're distracted by Carlos, who is still tied to the chair and looking at us. 'Shoot me,' he shouts.

We both ignore him and I pull Lucy closer. The only thing I want is a safe escape for both of us, for us to get away from whatever is coming to attack us next. If I could have one other wish granted it would be to be equipped with all manner of torture equipment and have ten minutes alone with him. I don't know where I would start but I know where it would end, but since there is no time and the one I love is still in danger, I ask only to be able to escape.

'Please shoot me!' he shouts again.

'Not so secret now, is it?' Lucy says, as she pushes us forward.

I don't ask what she means; I don't want to know. We run through the flaming archway into the chill of the night. Against a background of darkness I see a chaotic light show rage all around us, as we stumble into a desperate battle that has descended on this sleepy neighbourhood. Helicopters circle overhead as spotlights flicker between the gardens and houses. I see flashes of light coming from them, bullets roaring as they fire at things both close to us and then further away. There doesn't seem to be any method to their attack: they all circle in random patterns, then fire quick rounds at anything and everything.

'We have to get to the road,' I shout over the deafening roar.

We all run, as I realise neither Lucy or Terry have any shoes. I look around for the other women, for anything that can help us, but all I see is Lucy's silhouette against the flashes of light and thundering explosions as houses, homes with now meaningless histories of their own, seem to implode and crumble around us. Each eruption of those makes us bow down, still running, still determined. I look at her withered frame, her torn skin, and I wonder how she has anything left to give.

I slow them down as we make it to the road and I take hold of Lucy. We all look up, each of us jumping with whatever energy we have left as we try to attract the attention of the military. I grab my flashlight, trying to point the small light towards the cockpit, but they are moving too quickly and are still high in the sky. It doesn't take much to realise that they aren't here to rescue us – we are in the middle of a battleground.

Lucy grips my hand tighter and then lets out a scream. I look at her and see that she is staring down the road, her body trembling. I follow her gaze, trying to see what she can see, and that's when it comes into view. All I can see at first is a shadow but it's obvious that it's something tall, even though it seems to be crawling along the floor. It remains in the middle of the road, stalking towards us. It roars and we all scream in a combined chorus of horror as we realise the horror that followed us down the tunnel has found us in the street.

A light suddenly lands next to it, showing a muscular form and razor-like talons. Bullets strike the road all around it and I'm convinced many of them hit their target, but it doesn't seem bothered. It suddenly jumps off the road and the helicopter pursues it, still firing in its direction as bullets shatter glass and tear through houses.

The helicopter moves lower, low enough for me to see the soldiers inside it. I see that it's some sort of gunship. The soldiers manning the two large weapons mounted either side pay us no attention. There are two more men in the middle, both looking at large screens while pointing and shouting to the others inside.

Terry suddenly breaks rank and runs towards it, her arms flapping. No one inside notices her but they see something, and the helicopter quickly pulls backwards, the shell casings hitting the floor nearby as they seem to fire everything they have.

It doesn't look to be enough: their enemy comes out of the shadows, leaps onto the side of the helicopter and rips the door clean off its hinges. I'm not sure if it's the same beast or a new one but it's soon inside the cockpit, causing blood to splatter across every window.

Terry is the closest and is first to turn around, as she runs the couple of steps back to us. I know she won't stop and I quickly grab Lucy and pull her around. She screams in pain and I realise she is wounded. I try to carry her but I'm exhausted and so I'm forced to push her along, even though I know how much I know I'm hurting her. 'Please keep going,' I shout to both of them, as another helicopter spirals downwards and I hear the sound of scraping metal on concrete, and I feel the heat of the explosion chasing after us.

As we run I think I can see a shadow in the bushes of the house next door to Carlos's place, but I keep pushing forward, focused only on the many lights up ahead.

Two army vehicles speed past us, their gun turrets firing shots into the dark night, the soldiers on view wearing night-vision goggles and clearly able to see the threat that I don't dare think about. We nearly collide with one of them as it screeches to a halt. The doors open and men in dark green uniforms start shouting at us. I don't know what they're saying, can't hear anything in the haze of this battle, but I feel relief when I see hands reaching out and pulling us in, one by one.

I wait until last and only when Lucy is on board do I take hold of the metal railing. I feel the vehicle moving backwards, the engine roaring as the tyres screech, then I look up to see continuous white flashes spraying out from the roof. I feel one of the soldiers take hold of me, his hand grabbing my wrist as he tries to pull me in headfirst, and I start to lose my grip.

I land on the metal floor and I turn and twist, trying to balance myself. I look around and see men packed into whatever space they can fit into, all of them loading weapons and firing out of different holes – still trying to fight an enemy which seems so different, so powerful to anything they have faced before.

Someone looks at me, and then looks at the women. I think he expected the monsters but not us. 'What are you lot still doing here and where the hell are their clothes?' he shouts at me and only me, as if the burden of an answer is mine alone. I look at his uniform and see sergeant strips on his arms, as I wish he had come along a few hours earlier.

'They were trapped,' I say, looking over at Lucy. 'I was rescuing them.'

Lucy moves forward, snaking her way through the chaos until she has hold of me, her eyes digging deep into mine. Her body might be battered and bruised but those blue eyes still hold every ounce of the women I love. 'You found me,' she says, and then kisses me.

I cry and she cries; we both hold each other so tight, not sure whether we are celebrating or saying goodbye. I want to say that I'm sorry, to make her know how I have battled to find her, but I don't know where to start; don't want to waste a precious second on the past.

The sergeant coughs and then nods, a smile forming across his face as he takes hold of a handrail. The entire vehicle suddenly shakes as it turns around and we both fall back onto the cold metal floor, Lucy's body pressing against mine.

I suddenly hear a scream from above and the boots of the soldier above us disappear as he is pulled from his post. The sergeant starts shouting orders and then shoots at the now vacant hole. He takes one last look at us. 'And now we're rescuing you, and let me tell you that success on that front is very unlikely, so you best say your goodbyes now.'

I look at Lucy and she looks at me, and right now I don't care. I have nothing to say, but I hold her tight, knowing that I will never let her go again.

Friday 26th August – Washington DC

Welcome to the Apocalypse

'I need to call David,' he says to the men in the suits. He turns his head, carefully examining each of them. One of them nods back at him. It's clear evidence that this overdressed man – certainly for these times – is real, that he can actually see him through those dark shades. Larry is used to being the invisible one, and when no phone materialises and no one else makes any effort to help him, he resigns himself to the fact that all he can do is keep asking.

They keep pushing him forward. There is a suit on each of his arms and a further three ahead, plus who knows how many behind him. 'You can make your calls when we get to the bunker,' one of the men ahead of him shouts back. Larry figures he must be the one in charge because he is the one giving orders into his radio, talking in codes that sound incredibly exciting. He's also clearly able to hear all of Larry's cries, pleas and moans. Larry wonders why this man didn't listen in the first place, when he told them he would come peacefully.

David must have made it home by now. He will be pacing around, not knowing who to call or what to do. Larry doesn't know where David will look for him first; it's literally anybody's guess, but with the car so low on gas he knows it won't be far enough.

He thinks of David now, of how much he misses him already, and how he thought they would see the end in together. They had both given up on any plans to fight or to flee and found comfort in accepting an inevitable end. They realised that when they had stopped trying to survive what was coming, and to focus on living instead, they had stopped arguing and started loving each other again. They had it all planned: with all they had stockpiled, they could stay alive for several weeks. From what Larry had managed to find out from his contacts that were still alive, he knew they wouldn't need half this time.

That was until these men burst through the door in the dark of the night. Larry looks at the one to his left. He's a big guy but not bigger than his David. He studies him for a moment and although he finds it hard to focus while being dragged along, his feet barely touching the floor, he thinks he can just about spot a bruise forming under his black glasses. He has never had to hit anyone before and he knows David would be impressed that he managed to do some actual damage to such a burly man.

He smiles but doesn't get long to enjoy the moment before everything changes again. As this small group turn yet another corner he sees two big doors opening ahead of him and realises this is where they are heading. The group speed up, as if they are in a race, all of them desperate to get across the finish line before it's too late. Larry wants to ask what the rush is but since he already knows who they are, and where they are taking him, he sees little point in asking anything else.

'Rear flank collapse back and prepare to defend,' the man in charge shouts.

Larry senses the men who were just behind him now disappear, and soon he hears gun fire echoing through the tunnel behind him.

He looks ahead again, at the doors and what lies beyond them. He suddenly sees soldiers spilling out of the widening metal crack, some of them running and others kneeling down behind makeshift barricades and large machine guns. It looks like something from a war film, and not what you would expect to find beneath a nondescript warehouse on the outskirts of Washington DC.

The leader of his small group is shouting more orders to his fellow agents. His instructions are still precise and sparing with details, but now there is an urgency which Larry cannot understand the reason for. 'Protocol red: we have an immediate breach,' he shouts into his mouthpiece. He then stops and turns around, the machine gun that was previously draped around his neck now held up high. Larry immediately thinks he's going to shoot him, although he does wonder what the point of bringing him here just to kill him would have been – he could have done that at home. And besides, who would want to kill Larry? Although, for that matter, who would want to save him at the collapse of the modern world?

'Get him inside and seal those doors!' the agent shouts, as the men who have hold of Larry keep pushing forward, their fast steps turning into bold strides. They are now practically carrying him towards the entrance, which must lead to this bunker he heard about.

He tries to turn, desperate to see what's happening, but he has to be careful not to lose his glasses. He feels them slipping, a thick layer of sweat almost lubricating their path off his nose and onto the floor. He doubts that any of these busy men would be kind enough to pick them up, not with everything else that appears to be going on. He watches as half of this party of suits collapse their formation backwards and focus on whatever is behind them. They are quickly joined by some of the soldiers, and together they form some sort of defensive line that he can only just make out by stretching his neck until it hurts.

'Get him inside now!' the lead agent shouts. Until this moment Larry saw him as an enemy, a brutal kidnapper who just happened to look good in a tight-fitting black suit, but now he feels guilty for whatever is happening, and whatever they are going to face. He hears a scream, which doesn't sound like something that could have come from the mouth of a man. It's a primal sound and he doesn't need to think about it too much because he knows what it is; he has heard it before and sat through enough briefings to know what is coming.

Then he hears it again, just after the sound of tearing metal. He thinks he can still hear it but against the deafening sound of gunfire he can't be sure. The bullets don't stop as more men are thrown against the beast. The soldiers in front of him are firing at whatever is behind him, and he wonders if those brave, and probably very nice, young men in suits are still alive. The doors are closing now, even though Larry still isn't inside, which forces the two who have hold of him to make one final push.

'It's going to jump!' someone shouts.

They reach the doors and the invisible barrier of air that hopefully signals some sort of safety. The two men who have hold of Larry throw him through the threshold, then turn and point their guns upwards. Larry falls to the floor, but the men on the other side get to him within moments and pick him up, pulling him backwards. He manages to turn and adjust his glasses, catching a glimpse back out there moments before the doors join together. He sees the creature land; its eyes are on him as blood drips from its long fangs. He also makes out what is happening in the distance, sees the ripped suits and mangled bodies spread across the floor. It's a battleground now, and those final few still standing are trying their best to fend this thing off. He sees black-eye take his turn first, and where he defeated Larry with only an unlucky bruise, he fails to win against this thing three times his size, as it tears through him like a knife through butter.

As the two doors finally meet and the screams of those remaining men are drowned out, he listens to the mechanical noises surging through the middle of its thick metal. He realises he is breathing very fast as he bends down and puts his hands on his knees. He thinks of those men who have just lost their lives for nothing; have just left this world in the most brutal way possible. He knows they are far from the first to die like this, but their deaths are still senseless, and he figures they probably knew that too. He lets out a cry of his own when he realises what a sacrifice they have made; he knows that they died for him.

'Electrify it!' someone shouts.

He hears a buzz behind him, realising that something is happening inside the big door, and then he turns to see about 50 men, mostly soldiers, standing there. Some are checking their weapons, while others are keeping them pointed firmly at the door. When he hears banging on the other side he steps backwards, into the arms of a young man in combat gear. The soldier pushes him away, gently, but hard enough to show that he's not as nice as these previous men were. Larry looks around and suddenly feels alone, seeing all of these hardened soldiers staring at him, and only him.

Someone finally steps out of the crowd. It's another man in a black suit, with two others following him. Their once perfectly tailored, iconic outfits now look dusty and worn, their shirts stained, but still they come to work, still they do their duty. When this man eventually makes it to Larry he gestures to him to move away from the doors, which are somehow keeping out the raging monster. He looks Larry up and down, like he's sizing him up for something, and then lets out a long sigh. 'Mr President, welcome to the final bunker.'

*****

'Come this way, Mr President,' this new agent says, leading him towards a smaller door at the end of the large room.

Larry follows obediently. The other two men have taken up positions either side of him, each of them just half a step away. He looks around and realises that this place is big enough to be an aircraft hangar. He sees a separate door open at the other side of the structure and notices three large tanks coming through it. They comfort him, giving him some sort of hope that the American military machine can still be victorious against such a relentless foe.

'I'm Agent Flinch, and the men behind you are Agent Reynolds and Agent Dash,' the man in front says, still charging forward, utterly purposeful.

He looks at both of them and then forwards again, his eyes settling on the back of the agent. He wants to ask who is who again but he doubts he will remember, and besides, he has slightly bigger things on his mind. 'Agent, ummm…'

'Agent Flinch, Mr President.'

'Yes, Agent Flinch. I have a couple of questions, if I may?'

Agent Flinch nods as he walks through the small door, then disappears around the corner for just a moment. Larry also turns, and at exactly the same moment, so do the other two. It's as if they are gliding along, responding to his every movement. He notices they are now in a long, white corridor which stretches quite some way into the distance and which also seems to be angled slightly downwards. He follows, determined to keep up with him and not let these rather dedicated men down in any way. He wonders if they knew the people who have just been ripped apart and if there are actually many secret service agents left. The first 50 or so got carved up and eaten while trying to protect the first president, and he wonders how many more have died since that day.

'What are your questions, Mr. President?'

Larry nods, trying to keep up and trying even harder to focus on the moment, the moment he never thought would come. 'Why are you addressing me as "the president" and when can I call David?'

Agent Flinch seems to think for a moment as he keeps the small group moving forward, his neck repeatedly turning to the left and to the right as they pass doors with numbers but no names. He eventually lets out a small cough. 'You will need to ask your first question to someone in a position of higher authority, and as for your second question, I don't know any David, sir.'

Larry sighs, then nods again, trying to figure things out for himself. He never expected to find himself be here – wherever here is. He has a fairly good idea of what it is, but not its location. When he was expelled from his cabinet duties and told to go home and prepare for the likely end, in whatever way he thought appropriate, that's exactly what he did. That was three days ago and as far as he could tell there was still a working government, one that was still putting up a good fight, and still had no need of his services. After all, at times like this you don't really need to hear the views of the Secretary of Housing and Urban Development.

They reach a door at the end of the long corridor and Agent Flinch stops, standing very still and clearly waiting for something. After a minute or so he nods, happy with whatever is happening, and then turns around. Larry has waited for this moment, wanting to get a proper look at him, and now that he can he sees how young the agent is. He can't be any more than 25, with broad shoulders that comfortably push against all that dark fabric of his suit. He also has the brightest blue eyes that he has ever seen, except perhaps for his David's. Larry takes a deep breath, taking him all in, already forming a fondness for this young man who resembles a David of many decades ago, already praying he doesn't get torn to pieces in the name of protecting him.

Agent Flinch nods back, perhaps as an acknowledgement that their fates are now inevitably sealed together, and that whatever happens to one will happen to the other, meaning that Larry's safety will depend entirely upon him. Or perhaps he's just filling in time, Larry can't be sure. He suddenly turns around, just as some sort of mechanical clicking noise starts. 'Stand still please, Mr. President,' Agent Flinch says.

He does as he is told; remaining perfectly still and only twitching his neck so that he can see what is going on. He senses something closing behind him before he feels a jolt on the floor beneath them. He soon realises that they are moving downwards: the ceiling above him is moving further away and the white walls are turning into grey concrete slabs. He looks up to see something is closing across the gap above them, and as it shuts completely, it plunges them into darkness. He gasps as he feels the men either side of him taking hold of his shoulders, keeping him steady as this sort of lift starts to speed them downwards.

'Nothing to worry about, Mr President,' Agent Flinch says, his young voice still as calm as ever, even if Larry can't see him. 'We are travelling down several hundred metres to the most secure part of this facility. There is only one way in and out and that is via this lift. The creatures apparently hate the colour white, which we only learnt recently. They might be able to tear through metal and smash through concrete but they lose all sense of smell and direction when surrounded by white, hence the colour of the walls and no obvious sign of this lift from within the corridor.'

'So even if they break through that barricade they won't be able to get down here?'

'That's the idea, Mr. President.'

The lift eventually stops and light floods into the small space. Larry has to squint at first, his eyes struggling to make sense of anything. He can see figures in the distance and as soon as the door is fully open Agent Flinch leads the party forward, until they reach a small line of people, dressed in a mixture of suits and army uniforms. When they reach them Flinch steps aside, pushing Larry forward to greet all those who have been waiting.

A general steps forward first; he's probably a little younger than Larry but still in his late fifties at least. He recognises this guy as one of the generals who was advising the third president in what he thinks was the fourth bunker, but most definitely not the one that led off from the White House or any of those top secret and heavily fortified military bases. 'I'm General William Phillips and welcome to the final bunker, Mr. President,' he says as he holds out a hand.

Larry shakes it, feeling the extra padding around this man's hand, the added girth poking out of his uniform. It makes him wonder when Phillips last saw active duty; although right now it's not worth pondering over, and it's not worth mentioning that they have met before.

The introductions continue as he meets a couple of surviving junior officials, the sort who wouldn't normally meet a president in any normal situation. He shakes hands with a few more army personnel, all of whom seem less senior than General Phillips. He also greets a few secret intelligence people, from the CIA and a couple of government branches he has never heard of. He moves on quickly from these particular gentlemen, remembering that before all of this he had spent many hours campaigning for their budgets to be reduced, so that he could spend their money on affordable housing projects across the country. At the end of the line he meets an admiral, an older man who still manages a smile, although he immediately feels sorry for him as there really isn't much of a navy left to command.

General Phillips starts to lead them towards another door at the end of the corridor. Larry is flanked again by his agents, and when he looks around he sees that all of the walls in the corridor are being painted white. Everyone is chipping in, from men in proper overalls to the odd soldier with a brush.

Phillips looks over at him. 'I see that you've been introduced to your secret service detail. They are now the last three left in active duty but I'm sure you will be just fine.' He smiles and winks at him, as if this were just a normal day in the presidential bunker. 'Now, let's get you sworn in and locked in the battle room and ready to do business.'

Larry doesn't like the sound of any of this, especially because they keep going deeper and further away from the world above ground and the person he wants to be with most. 'Look, I don't know why you keep calling me president, and I really do need to phone David.'

The general doesn't turn around as they keep walking towards a white door surrounded by white walls, presumably painted like this to confuse the beast, should it make it this far. He suddenly stops and looks at Larry, a big grin spread across his face. 'I don't know any David but I do know the president when I see him, and that person is you.'

'I can't be the president. Where is Evans? When I left a few days ago he was in charge and doing a good job under the circumstances.'

They continue walking through the door and stop in a small enclosure with a large metal door at one end – the sort you get in a bank vault. He really doesn't want to go in there, mainly because he worries that he will never come out or even worse, that they will be trapped in a very big corner, waiting for the enemy to find its way in. If it does get in, then all it will need to do is get past a line of three secret service agents and one old sea dog before eating up poor old Larry.

General Phillips comes closer to him, his arms held as he politely pushes Agent Flinch out of the way. 'You mean Evans, the Secretary for Agriculture?'

He nods, finding it surprising that this man cannot easily recall every member of the cabinet, even after all he's been through in the last few weeks. Maybe previous titles don't matter anymore, and the only thing that does is what you do with the badge you're given.

The general nods back, almost immediately. 'Yes, he was a nice guy, far better than I expected when we swore him in. After they got passed all the barricades at Fort Hood and ate up President Wilson, and then managed to sneak on-board Air Force One and threw President Harris out the window, we really thought we had got President Evans secured.' He looks around, staring at the secret service guys and then over at the big, complicated bunker door. 'It turns out that they're cleverer than they look and we think they're targeting world leaders deliberately.'

'You mean President Evans is actually dead?' he asks, struggling to keep up. 'But he's still on TV, still broadcasting speeches on the emergency channel. How can he be dead if he's doing that? I mean, I saw him just this morning.'

General Phillips smiles and nods to some people in suits next to him, who pat each other on the back whilst smiling wildly. 'I'm glad the pre-recordings are working. I mean, if you are falling for them and you know who he is, then the average Joe hauled up at home will definitely think it's him.'

Larry suddenly falls down, his head dripping with sweat and his body going numb. 'Evans is really dead? He was a great guy. I knew his wife and kids.'

His three protectors are soon around him, picking him up. Agent Flinch manoeuvres around them until he is in front of Larry, offering the calming gaze of David's blue eyes, as if he knew that's exactly what Larry needed. 'You're the president now, sir, and these people need to see you as a strong leader.'

General Phillips slaps him on the back. 'He's right, you know. Although for now it's probably best the people think that Evans is still in charge. I think the people liked him, and besides we can't keep telling the nation that the president is dead and another guy has been set up in his place.' Phillips walks forward, leading them towards the door as it starts to open. 'But don't take it personally,' he shouts back.

Larry has no choice but to move forward and follow the crowd. As they reach the door he sees a woman standing at the entrance. The background is full of large screens and world maps with red dots and other flashing images all over them. He thinks that he is probably going to end up looking at all of this in a lot of detail.

This woman looks at him but doesn't offer any sign that she notices him. He admits that in any other situation he would barely have noticed her, but in this new world he knows exactly who she is. He's seen her before, in various cabinet meetings and war room situations. Larry thinks he was lucky that he wasn't with any of the presidents when they got attacked, which was more due to his insignificance and total lack of military usefulness than anything else. But with her he thinks it's a different story, because many times he has seen her whispering in the ear of different presidents and yet she was never around when the worst happened.

She doesn't move, doesn't offer a hand as they reach the door; she simply looks him up and down. 'So this is the great Larry Brown, Secretary for Housing and Urban Development, and now the President of the United States of America.'

General Phillips stands next to him, a grin across his face. 'Twelve times lucky.'

She shakes her head and turns around, walking into the room as everyone else follows. 'This isn't a war that's going well. I don't expect you to understand anything that is happening, so as far as I am concerned you are here as a figurehead. Let us make the decisions and you focus on planning for what is likely to be a bleak future for mankind, to which your cabinet role would perhaps be most suitable for.'

He continues to follow as she carries on walking to the centre of the room. When he reaches a chair in the middle he stands still, wondering if this is where he should sit. His secret service trio suddenly leave his side, taking up flanking positions around the room, in places that they likely deem to be the most effective, but he thinks really are the only places not blocking some sort of flashing screen. The large, metal door starts to swing shut slowly but powerfully, just as doors in banks do, except those ones are sealing money in and not keeping monsters out. He hears a large hissing noise which he figures is the air getting sucked out, making the seal even tighter, and the room even more like a tomb.

He looks around as he tries to make sense of this place, seeing monitors lit up everywhere with satellite images and progress updates. It's the world map that catches his attention the most and he stares at it with complete disregard for whatever this attractive, yet utterly miserable woman is saying. The map is really big and Larry can pick out many places he and David have travelled to. He wants to point, to make others feel envious of his globe-trotting – to ask David to get the albums out whilst he puts the coffee pot on. Of course they have them on the iPad, but there's nothing better than the feel of the genuine photo and the smell of a dusty album. He believes it's those memories we mustn't forget; have no time to make more.

He turns to her now and sees that she is finally giving him some attention, as is everyone else in the room. He suddenly feels all these eyes on him, the unlikely president. She doesn't say anything, just brushes back her dark fringe, her head tilted as she examines what has been brought before her.

'What do you think you're doing?' she asks.

Larry looks at her and then back to the map. 'Japan,' he says, his right arm outstretched as he points to the map. 'We never got to go there.' He looks around at everyone else, taking time to find as many eyes as he can, hoping to get some understanding from somewhere in this room. He finally settles on Agent Flinch, who smiles back and nods, the only glimmer of approval anyone in this cavern of contempt has offered him. He eventually lowers his arms and stands still. 'We planned to go there this year but I guess that won't be happening now.'

She suddenly lets out a scream, aimed at the general, as she throws some sort of electronic device across the floor and points at him. 'You believe this man will have the guts to do what must be done? Do you really think we can just keep appointing morons as our commander-in-chief?'

The general has his arms out as he walks towards her, telling her to be quiet in the same way Larry used to tell their neighbours' dog to give him the newspaper back. 'Look, Lopez, we didn't make the rules, did we? He is the twelfth in line to the presidency and we have reached that number. The remaining American people will want to know that we are holding true to the constitution.' He looks at Larry then back to her. 'So that means this guy is now the boss.'

She looks at Larry and then screams again, as he wonders if this is an appropriate moment when his secret service guys should be stepping in, before this hysterical woman yells the place down, alerting whatever is above to their presence.

The General moves closer to her, as does the Admiral and some other guy in a suit. They huddle together, trying to calm her down while whispering in code. He can't hear everything they are saying but he can see that almost everyone else is watching him, apart from the ten or so people who are managing the information feeds and constant updates. He feels just a little bit alone now, standing near the map, away from everyone else. As the huddled group begin to talk louder, crazy Lopez gives him the odd sinister stare, and he thinks about asking his new protectors to come over and talk to him, just so he doesn't feel so lonely.

Larry has never really had a secret service detail of his own before. Once he did need to go to a run-down part of Chicago – some back-of-beyond suburb that even the mayor wouldn't visit – so that he could listen to the residents' complaints that their neighbourhood was being destroyed to make way for a new shopping mall, residential village and luxury hotel. On the day he landed at the airport he got picked up in an SUV by two men in suits – mean-looking sort of guys – but then someone from the White House Press Office made him stop downtown so he could change into a taxi, because they thought it would make him look more down-to-earth and less like a government tool.

That did upset him but at least he still had his two agents to protect him from the mob. They looked quite manly and tough in the front of their land cruiser but squashed into the back of a taxi with him, their ample girths poking through their off-white shirts, he asked the question if either of them had ever served with the current president, or perhaps a previous one. When he found out they were private security and hadn't been to Washington in years, let alone met the top guy, he resigned himself to the reality that he was a nobody, someone who was lucky to get any sort of escort at all. David had volunteered to go with him that day – and, in truth, he would have protected him just as well, and been far better company.

He snaps back to life, remembering that he still needs to call David. He looks around the mass of people, wondering who he could possibly ask for a telephone. He settles on the only person he thinks he can trust, the only one remotely likely to help him. 'Agent Flinch,' he says, walking towards him, never one to demand someone should come to him. 'Would it be possible for you to kindly find me a telephone?' he says, but doesn't give a reason why this time, figuring someone of his importance would never justify a simple instruction.

Agent Flinch smiles and nods, before making his way towards one of the many people nearby, who Larry assumes to be communications operatives.

He smiles back, feeling almost like he has accomplished something. He looks at the many different people, wanting to tell them to get back to work, his one victory giving him the smallest bit of confidence. Inconspicuously, he gazes over at the huddled mass of important people and that woman who is still waving her hands in the air, hitting some invisible target. She says something that he can't quite understand, something about the next few hours being critical and the toughest decision not always being the right one.

He sees General Phillips hush her, his energy seeming to keep the group together. He glances over at Larry for just a moment, before looking back at her. 'We all know that an officially appointed president gives plausible authority to any decision his office makes, and that is what matters right now.'

He doesn't make any comment and in fact pretends that he hasn't heard anything, although he wonders about this official appointment business, considering that Evans is still technically leading the country, even if he is doing it from his grave. All the work and none of the credit – that's what this sounds like to Larry, and that's exactly what his mum said when he told her he was going into government. He started local and worked his way up but it was never about the politics, always about serving someone else and making the system work for the little guy. When Larry was sworn into the latest government he realised that he had probably become just a little politically minded, but by this time his mother had passed away, and he and David were clear on why he was doing it.

He knows that on the day he joined the newly formed government it was still about protecting the little guy, but he never once considered that he would ever become president. He thinks that this is a dark day – 11 other people have died in the attempt and now he's the only one left. There were so many things in place to stop this from ever happening: those next in line not travelling with the president wherever possible, immense security whenever the most important people were together. When they ticked off five from the list in one attack it was probably the beginning of the end. Maybe it was planned and they had waited for the exact moment when they could cause the most damage.

Agent Flinch appears with a phone in his hand and Larry smiles: he is about to complete his first small task, one that means so much. He quickly dials the number from memory. He has always been good at remembering numbers, both cellphones and landlines. He wonders how many people bother to memorise their partner's cell numbers when they can just be programmed and forgotten. He's never been one to think of an emergency, something where he will have no choice but to dial the number; it's just that he grew up without these gadgets and their long, identifying digits. He remembers his parents getting their first phone, his first trip to a payphone, and the day he unboxed his first cell. He still has his filodex on the desk in his office, despite his personal assistant having shown him how to use the online phone list a hundred times. He finds something reassuring in doing things the old way; he finds a kind of healthiness and balance in clinging to bits and pieces of the past.

As the phone starts ringing he feels his victories starting to form into a small pattern, hopefully building into many successes that will lead him out of this place and back to David, which is exactly what he plans to tell him.

Someone picks up and Larry is about to scream with excitement but then the line goes dead. He looks down at the phone and then holds it up to his ear, before holding it at a slight angle so he can properly see through his glasses as he tries to find the redial button.

He doesn't get a chance; instead, he realises Lopez is next to him. She grabs the phone from his hand and throws it across the room; it smashes into one of the large screens. 'What do you think you're doing?' she shouts.

He doesn't look at her or offer an answer as he looks at the flickering screen, seeing that most of Australia is now just a series of cracked lines. He thinks that if she keeps throwing electrical objects across the room at her current rate, then they will be back to pen, paper and maps within hours.

She smacks him across the chest and then lets out a long scream, clearly frustrated at his lack of fight. It's enough to bring Flinch back towards him, as the agent holds out his arms, politely fending her off. She pushes him away and it's enough to make him back off, as he still tries to indicate a truce. Larry wonders if he is genuinely afraid of this woman. He has watched enough encounters between secret service agents and senior government officials to know that they are good at defusing tensions without actually shooting anyone, which might turn out to be a real shame in this particular situation.

'No outgoing phone calls without my express approval,' she says, as she straightens her blouse and stares at him, clearly expecting an apology from him.

General Phillips appears from nowhere, as he walks towards her and coughs.

She looks at him and then back to Larry. 'No outgoing calls, *Mr. President.*'

Larry nods back at her as she turns and walks away, telling everyone else to get back to work, which is all that is required to make everyone else focus back on their monitors and other various duties that he doesn't yet understand. He thinks that maybe he should be the one who is issuing these orders, but since he hasn't got himself up to speed he thinks it best to let her carry on.

Phillips soon takes her place, standing next to him but looking a lot more pleasant. Larry thinks he is a genuinely happy fellow, the sort of person who would be ruthless at work but then go home and entertain the grandkids with the best of them. He taps Larry on the arm and guides him towards one of the large screens. Against a background of America and Canada are many flashing lights, which seem to change between red crosses, green dots and black skulls. He notices that the black skulls are the most numerous, and since they don't look very positive he wonders if it's even worth asking the question as to what they signify.

Phillips points to the very top of the map, drawing an invisible circle. 'Alaska think they can go it alone,' he says. 'They always think they know better, always want to play by their own rules. What do you think about that, Mr President?'

Larry thinks about this for a moment, wondering how any of what he sees here is even possible, not understanding how any form of order and organisation can still remain.

Phillips celebrates his absence from the moment by slapping him on the back again, which he has to admit is starting to annoy him. 'Nothing to say yet? Well, I'm sure you'll get the hang of this commander-in-chief business pretty quickly. Best you just listen to the advice you're offered and let us worry about the finer details.'

Larry quickly shakes his head, entirely disagreeing with that abdication nonsense. He doesn't really want to sit in the chair but he also knows that if he is given a task to do he will always follow it through as best as he can. He remembers an online personality profile he once did: according to his results, he was someone who always wanted to be perfect. To him, if a job was worth doing then it is worth doing right. He looks at the General and then touches him on the shoulder, focusing on the map. 'Alaska wants to go it alone? Is it doing them any good?'

Phillips pauses for a moment, frowning and then smiling, seeming to take time to genuinely think about this. 'Actually, they seem to be repelling the beasts to the point where they are withdrawing and moving back into Canada. But this is probably because of how much white stuff there is in Alaska, which is giving them a slight tactical advantage.'

Larry smiles. 'Well it looks to me like we need some snow across the entire land.'

Phillips laughs, sending a deep and booming echo across the room. 'In the middle of summer, I hardly think so.' He looks at the screen and then back to Larry, before grabbing him and pulling him towards another screen. 'Let me show you some more and see if our new president can make any other useful observations.'

Larry tags along, having no choice but to move with the general. He catches a quick glance at Flinch who gives him a purposeful nod in return. He smiles back at him and, for now, he completely forgets about home and David, and how they so meticulously planned to meet their end together.

*****

Larry really needs to go to the restroom. There have been many times in his career where he has been in such vital meetings with the cabinet, the president and other very important people and he has desperately needed to go, but has had to hold it. Otherwise, he would risk missing out on crucial decisions, or looking like a weak, old man who can't keep it together. But it's getting really painful and since he's the president now he wonders if anyone would be able to stop him, or if anyone would dare to make a bold decision in his absence. He looks around at the different doors, but he can't see a restroom sign anywhere, which is perhaps because this place was built so hastily that they didn't have time to put the signs up.

He's thankful to be sitting down and even though he's in the main chair, still the guy in charge, it is helping relieve some of the pressure on his ageing bladder. He looks around at all the coffee cups spread across the desks that surround his chair. He didn't drink all of them – they're his predecessors', still stained around the rims with the marks of sipping lips, some with cold liquid still floating at the bottom. Where there isn't a cup there is a folder, full of desperately important information for the commander-in-chief. Right now, Larry doesn't think any of this 'Highly Confidential' information could be more desperate than his need to release bodily fluids, but people still keep coming up to him with yet more information. He wonders when they are going to run out of paper or ink and what they will do then.

He looks down at these folders that he has arranged like a hand of cards. He used to love playing poker, and every time a new folder is handed to him he reads the title that's printed on the brown cover, before he sorts it into what he believes is the correct place in this rather complex hand. The problem is that they all seem so awfully important, all containing details of yet more terrifying events that are unfolding, which means that he doesn't seem to have any that you would call a crap card. He has also noticed that he's getting far more folders than he is giving back, yet no one seems to be bothered about this, either.

That's it, Larry decides. He thinks enough is enough and he resolves to go to the restroom and then ask for everyone to come together to give the president an update. He's especially intrigued by the increasing number of black skulls stretching up the west coast, which was the only untouched place until this morning. The east coast fell early, except for Washington DC, which one of the presidents, Blackmore, he believes, decided would be held at all costs as a strong symbol for the people – the city that houses the power of our country remaining intact. He doesn't know whether he should be thankful to Blackmore or not, since on the one hand it is the reason why he and David have survived so long, with their house in a suburb on the outskirts of the city. However, had Washington fallen already then none of this would be a problem for them. He eventually decides that this is a moot point because what is done is done, and besides Blackmore isn't around to hear his thoughts anyway: having chosen to ensure Washington remained heavily defended, he was then stupid enough to fly out to an aircraft carrier to rally the troops.

Larry and David had both sat at home in stunned silence when the press showed the carrier sinking off the coast. The president and the remaining members of his secret service detail had tried to escape to the shore before being pulled under. Thankfully, there were only a few images of the actual assault and the press were quickly silenced, as per the NATO agreement that the general public, as much as humanly possible, should not see what it was that was attacking humanity.

Of course most people knew about the lurkers, as they were eventually named. These attackers quickly became humanity's newest and biggest threat. At first people thought it was some sort of virus but that turned out to be a distraction to keep the authorities busy, which worked rather well. What followed was an endless series of poor decisions by government agencies, and when the real attacks happened the planet simply wasn't prepared enough.

But all that has happened has actually made Larry even more determined that he will make the right decisions when they matter, although it would have been helpful if David was here so he could bounce some ideas off him. He looks back around the room, trying to spot some allies in the desperate muddle of white shirts and jumbled information. He looks back over to Agent Flinch and gets the same nod as always, reminding him that he is still here, has still got his back.

After a final sweep of the room Larry concludes that he really is alone. He decides to call Flinch over and to ask him to make a journey into the unknown to get David. He stands up, stepping down from his throne, now very clear in his mind that two heads are better than one. He heads towards the young man, resolving to find the restrooms, and also ensure his partner is brought to this safest of places, although he's not sure how easy that will be if the enemy is still outside. That's the art of delegation, he tells himself, remembering that it is other people who will need to worry about the details of his commands.

He hasn't yet made it to Flinch when the USA screen starts bleeping and the West Coast suddenly turns into a sea of red, as skulls replace every one of the major cities from San Francisco to San Diego. He starts to hobble his way over, knowing he will have to wait a little longer to relieve himself. 'What's going on?' he asks.

'Ah, damn it, we've just lost L.A., which means we've lost the whole goddamn West Coast,' General Phillips says, walking up to him, shaking his head. He taps a few buttons on a device in his hand and the big screen suddenly changes to show a map of Los Angeles, all divided into the newly formed districts. A prolonged battle had been going on in Los Angeles for days and the districts were supposed to make defence easier. They were based on key geographical barriers and all lined with various explosive traps, so if one district was lost the enemy couldn't just walk into the next one without meeting a new line of defence. Larry doesn't know much about war but when he first heard about this he thought it made sense, and for a while it had seemed to work, meaning that survivors could easily be moved to a numbered zone that was deemed safer and not just wherever they wanted to go. Admittedly, at the start of the attacks the United Kingdom and Japan had done a good job of that, but since they had much smaller geographical areas and far fewer people to organise, it had probably been easier for them and that's why they lasted longer.

He knows something about how people behave from his years in urban planning, so he thought President Wilson was onto a winner. It was a shame he never made it past day four because Larry thought he might just vote for him, if things ever returned to some sort of normality. At that point, just over a week ago, most people were convinced that humanity would prevail. You only had to look at all the years of Armageddon-related movies, dealing with threats from alien invasions to zombie hordes, to be reminded that there is always some resemblance of the human race left to rebuild, and they always need a government to lead the planet's recovery. He looks up at the screen; he knows that things are different in this real life version. This isn't like some movie but rather a documentary from hell, meaning nothing is likely to work out with any resemblance of a happy ending.

'Attention everyone,' General Phillips shouts out from somewhere above. Larry looks up to see he is standing on a table and surveying every corner of the room, clearly waiting for everyone to fall silent. 'We just lost the West Coast.'

He hears a lot of gasps around the room. A few people fall to the floor, while others stand firm, clearly determined to continue. The people down here have probably been at this for days, having little sleep, with not a lot to motivate them, which is something Larry hadn't given much thought about until now. He had freely accepted his disposal-from-office order from the last president. He and David had both accepted defeat and run away to let fate do whatever it felt appropriate. He simply hadn't realised just how many people were still putting up a fight; putting on a brave show for the American people and the rest of the world.

Phillips holds up his hands, calming everyone down. 'It's night-time there and as we know, that's the best time for them to attack. By the looks of it our troops have put up a brave fight. We got a lot of survivors out, but Fort Hope and Fort Valliant were both destroyed.'

People keep shaking their heads and Larry knows why. Both forts were newly built strategic defence points. They were built on the same concept that is still holding Washington together, with several layers of high walls and many self-contained defence turrets, each of them fully equipped and self-sustained units that the soldiers can defend from. The military learned quite early on that these lurkers don't stay in any sort of formation for long and although they turn up in packs they go off and do their own thing whenever there is a confrontation, much like the one that has followed Larry to the bunker. The majority of the defences in Washington DC are still holding but the odd beast gets through. Whether as part of a greater plan or not, no one is really sure, but this city is fast being named as the place that humanity will make its last stand. Sometimes others follow and join in the attack, and other times there is just a single lurker. When they are alone they tend to fail, because eventually a bullet or two manages to get through their thick, armour-like skin. The problem is that bullets don't get through often enough – even though there are only an estimated hundred-or-so of the enemy across the world, that's still too many.

'I know you all feel that this world is just getting scarier by the minute but we have to remain strong. The enemy has now defeated 80% of our armed forces,' Phillips says, looking around the room, trying to meet the eyes of as many people as possible. 'But they haven't won yet, and they haven't found many of our secret weapons either.'

Lopez seems to look bored and eventually steps forward and stands in front of Phillips. She comes up shorter but no less formidable than him. He looks down at her but doesn't say anything else; it's as if he's some sort of puppet on a string.

Larry really doesn't like Lopez, so he's surprised to find himself moving forward and approaching the centre of the room. He has never been someone who wants to stand out in a crowd, preferring to work quietly and efficiently in the background, letting someone else take all the glory. But this time he can't be that person; he must stand up for what he believes in. He coughs, attracting all attention to him. 'The human race needs not just to survive, but to win, and I think we need to start thinking about how we can help as many people as possible to do just that. Our military is virtually defeated, but if I'm reading this map correctly, there are still people spread across the United States, and all over the rest of the world. So, our real challenge is how can we help these people to get to places of safety, and set up effective communications, as well as gathering resources in order to survive for as long as possible.'

The room stays quiet as she seeks him out in the crowd, clearly having given no thought to where the president was actually standing when everyone was called together. When she finds him she takes slow and pronounced steps towards him, as a few people move out of the way, clearing a path for her. As she approaches he wants to remind her that he's the president but he doesn't think it will actually help. When she finally makes it to him she looks him up and down, her eyes probing his every move. 'What?'

Larry looks back at her and wonders what she is asking him. He wants to answer her question with a question; he wants to ask why they aren't already working on this. After only an hour down here he can see that they have been focusing only on the fight and not enough on the flight. If they cannot win then they need to survive, and since only 20% of the military is left he doesn't see anything wrong with changing the strategy. A surge of confidence flows through him as he wonders if perhaps this is fate – perhaps he was meant to become president at this exact time. He would have made a rubbish military leader but remaining invisible and working hard are what he's best at, and that's exactly what humanity needs to do right now. He points to the map, picking out places he thinks would fit the bill. 'Have we considered setting up a series of safe havens? Places with natural defences, such as Alaska, which is already proving that it can win the fight?'

She looks around the room and then back to Larry. 'I'm sorry, but are you unhappy with our performance? Do you think we've been doing nothing down here, and don't you think we haven't already looked at every possible option available to the United States of America?'

He ignores her and walks closer to the large map, weaving through the various people and politely asking them to move. When he gets close enough he points to Iceland – that insignificant, little island that everyone wants to visit but where few chose to live. 'Have they fared any better than us?'

He doesn't get the response he was hoping for, as several gasps come from the crowd. People shake their heads and walk back to their stations, as a few of them look over at Larry, at the president, but none of them seem to want to give him an answer. That is everyone except Lopez: she glares at him as if she wants to burn her pure hatred into his brain so it stays there forever.

Larry isn't sure how, but Phillips suddenly pushes him forward, forcing him in front of Lopez sooner than he would have liked. He sees the general raise a hand in the direction of Flinch, who nods in return, presumably that it's okay to lead Larry the lamb to the slaughter.

When he is finally facing her, he wonders if perhaps he has hit a nerve and that perhaps they could have done more. At the start of the attacks they focused solely on understanding and defeating the enemy, but Larry does remember a short time where they spent more time trying to ensure the human race survived, until another change of president brought with it a different set of orders to follow.

Lopez shakes her head. 'Here you stand, the president of the world's most powerful country. You're such a small man to be responsible for so much, don't you think?'

He doesn't answer her but it's not because he wants to disagree. He looks at the map and then back to both of them, knowing it doesn't take a genius to realise that the end of the world has arrived. He doesn't want to know any more than that but he has no choice. It's a simple fact; the hardest to accept yet the easiest to see. He really wants to be at home, with David, as they prepare for this end together but he knows that's not going to happen.

'Every president wants something different,' she says, still looking him up and down. 'First we had the big fight, followed by an even bigger fight, and then we had to try to reason with them. Then we got a president who wanted revenge, which you can't blame him for, especially when they killed so many of us in one night. Somewhere in the midst of all this we had a quiet voice, a lone president, who wanted to think about the people, about how we ensured the continuing survival of our species.' She steps closer to him and leans in to his ear. 'Let me tell you that there is no survival. You will be the president who reigns over the biggest cloud of dust and debris ever created, as the human race is pulled into a chasm of judgement that is has created. The only solace you can take from any of this is that there will be no one left alive to remember what you do, or don't do, on this very pathetic night.'

Larry thinks for a moment as he shakes his head, trying to deny the things he doesn't yet know he is capable of.

She walks past him, towards the general, clearly having nothing else to add. 'Get him ready, because you and I both know the time is fast approaching,' she says, as she continue to walk away, the taps of her shoes echoing throughout the bunker and signalling an end to any further debate, or any of the endless questions Larry has on this particular subject.

When she is gone Phillips looks at the president, and Larry looks at the general.

'What happened to Iceland?' Larry asks.

'Iceland?' Phillips says and shakes his head. 'Well, it's not really there anymore.'

He looks up at the map and then back to the general. 'What do you mean it's not there anymore?'

The general only seems able to mumble something as he looks to the floor. It's too quiet, too vague for Larry to understand. Whatever Phillips means by this is not enough of an answer, and he decides that he will keep asking the question. 'Iceland?'

'You don't give in do you?' Phillips says, smiling again. 'We will need this attitude over the next few hours, I can promise you that.'

'Iceland?'

'Okay, I hear you!' he says, as he leads Larry away from the group and towards his presidential chair. 'So, Iceland's not there anymore because we nuked 'em.'

'We did what?' Larry says, as he absently follows the general.

'It sounds bad, doesn't it?'

'If you're telling me that we used nuclear weapons on an entire country then it is bad.'

Phillips sways on the spot, his arms moving up and down, as he tries to mentally balance just a couple of the many controversial decisions made in the last few days. 'Well, we weren't looking at it as a country, more of an island.'

He shakes his head. 'That doesn't make it any better.'

The General shakes his head in return, playing a game of ping-pong in his head with what is wrong and perhaps not quite as wrong. 'We needed to see what happens to the beasts when we deploy a tactical nuclear deterrent. We thought that if they saw what we were capable of they might withdraw their attack, so when we found they were attacking Reykjavik, President Harris made the only real decision available at the time.'

'What about the snow and the people? Some of them might have made it to the mountains and survived.'

The general shakes his head. 'We didn't know about the white back then and besides, no one survived it, and we wanted to show what kind of damage we could do.' He keeps pushing him forwards, leading him to the chair where he is likely to be chained to all the future decisions he is yet to make. 'Anyway, it was technically the British who fired the missiles, although we would have done it if they hadn't.' He looks at Larry now as he straightens his tie and stands up straight, his right foot hitting the floor as he makes a bold salute to the map. 'God rest those bastards, they put up one hell of a fight. Talk about that British stiff upper lip – they held the line for days without the public knowing just how close the enemy was to London. Rumour even has it that when the lurkers got to Calais the Royal Marines went down the tunnel to greet them. I bet that was one welcome party they weren't expecting.'

Larry examines the General's face; the greasy folds in his skin bring him to life as he talks about the good fight. It makes him feel proud and utterly humbled that there are people all over the world doing all that they can. Not like the coward, Larry Brown, who was happy to be discharged from his office so he could cower at home and wait for someone else to win the war – or, more likely, for the beasts to turn up at their door and rip them to pieces. He wonders if David could really have done what he promised, to break Larry's neck as they forced their way into their home – and if he did have the guts to do it, would he still have had the time to finish himself off before those same horrors made it upstairs?

Phillips lets out a long sigh. 'The weapons worked but it didn't stop them from continuing their attacks, and we know they won't stop until we're all dead, so now we have to decide if we die alone or if we take those bastards down to hell with us.'

Larry sits down, thinking about what Phillips is saying, about the reality of the situation they now face. He has completely forgotten how badly he needs to relieve himself: it's too much to think about right now, and there is only one thing on his mind, only one decision he thinks he will not be able to make alone. He looks up to the general. 'I really need to call David.'

****

'Congratulations, Mr. President,' Phillips says, standing up straight and making another salute, this time at Larry, with several other key military personnel doing the same.

The bunker has fallen silent again, just for a moment, so that they can acknowledge that Larry has been formally sworn in as the 56th president of the United States and, perhaps more appropriately, the 12th president since this whole thing began.

He looks around the room as he thanks everyone, although he's not sure if that's the appropriate response. He doesn't feel he's earned this position and it's not one he ever wanted. Even so, he gets a lot of nods back. Perhaps his couple of sharp observations so far have earned him some respect, and maybe some people think they stand a chance with him around. Larry wonders about that for a moment and soon admits to himself that it's much more likely that those in this bunker are worn out and know the end is coming, and perhaps they just want to get on with it. This thought makes him sit down in his chair, signalling for everyone else to go about their business and that he will do the same.

As everyone silently obeys, he looks over at the one person who has paid no attention to these short proceedings, and seems to have no interest in him or his new title. Lopez has spent her time wisely: she kept two men back from the ceremony and has been commanding them to tap things into their computer screens. It doesn't take long for Larry to work out what she is doing, as every time she barks an order another line is drawn across the large map until it becomes a tapestry of doom covering the entire planet.

He doesn't have time to ask the most obvious question he feels he must ask, and quickly finds himself surrounded by people, all wanting to speak to him. It seems as if he was invisible before and now this short, but symbolic meeting has given him a status he never wanted. Phillips steps forward first, probably assuming he is the logical starting point, holding a clipboard in his hand with many scribbled notes, clearly desperate to speak.

Larry quickly holds out a hand, politely asking him to wait. 'Could I hear from Agent Flinch first, please?'

Phillips thinks for a moment, then nods and starts to shuffle on his feet, like a desperate child wanting to be noticed by their busy parents.

Flinch takes one look at the general and then calmly steps forward. 'Mr. President, I'm afraid to report that we have been unable to get hold of your partner, David, on the phone and have been unable to deploy any local resource to find him. Although, even if we did, I'm not sure we would be able to get him into here, as the one beast has been joined by several more, making entry to this bunker now impossible.'

Larry nods back, all too quickly, all too accepting. He thinks that if he is going to do a good job as the President he will need to toughen up and be more demanding. He wants to be like this with Agent Flinch but one look into those eyes stops him making any further demands, or asking him to leave this place of safety and fight the many monsters outside. 'Thank you, Agent Flinch. Please keep trying.'

Flinch nods back. 'Of course, Mr President.'

'And the security of this bunker?' Larry asks, suddenly thinking that David might be safer outside this place than he could ever be inside, where the beasts will continue to hunt him and his newfound title.

Phillips steps forward again, unable to keep quiet any longer. 'Our brave men and women are doing their best to hold them back, but I fear the main doors will not hold much longer. Once they are breached I give our defensive perimeter about ten minutes before they are defeated, and that's only based on how many lurkers there are now. If more show up to the party then for every two extra that arrive you can knock a minute off that time.'

'And then what will happen?' Larry asks, feeling braver by the minute, finally brave enough to ask a question that – from the fate of his eleven predecessors as president – he already knows the answer to.

Phillips gives a solemn nod in return, almost knowing this question was coming, the answer seeming to live on the tip of his tongue. 'Well, once they carve up our boys and turn over our tanks, then we only really have the white maze to protect us. They might not come near us and they certainly can't dig this far down. There is a high chance that if they cannot come near the whiteness then they won't be able to search for the lift shaft.'

'And you're sure it's the colour white that they don't like?'

Phillips looks around at the small crowd, his head tilted, like he wants to nod but he's not quite sure he wants to do it alone. 'They have withdrawn from any snow-covered, mountainous region where people have been hiding, and since they can easily climb and jump, we have to assume it's not the height that's the issue – it's either the snow or the colour.'

The admiral raises his hand, realising he finally has the chance to speak. 'And since we know how well they can swim in any ocean, regardless of the temperature, then it's safe to assume that it's not the cold that repels them.'

Phillips nods to his counterpart. 'Since we believe they come from the deepest part of the ocean, where there is nothing but darkness, then it's logical to assume they are confused by the light colours, of which white is obviously the brightest.'

Larry nods back to both of them; it certainly makes sense. 'So, if we believe that they will not be able to come down here, then why don't we move those men and women from the perimeter into this bunker?'

The General stares back at him, not able to answer such a simple question.

Lopez suddenly appears, having crept up in the silence. She leans down and takes hold of Larry's neck, her claw-like grip digging into his flesh like she's trying to connect with him at the most primal level. 'It is because they really are inconsequential to the bigger picture.'

'No one is inconsequential, especially if I am to believe the calculations of how many human beings are left alive.'

She growls at him, her frustration at their contrasting views growing by the minute. She grabs his chair and turns it towards the main screens before grabbing his head, her sharp nails digging into his skin, as she forces him to look at all the skulls spread across the flattened view of planet Earth. 'Don't you see that we are nearly defeated, nearly destroyed? Everything we built, every human achievement, is slowly being torn down. Those people out there will die in a glorious but very short battle, as are many others around the world. They will die out there because we don't have enough space down here, because they need to protect our lines of communication for as long as possible, and because you need to be focused on the bigger picture and not your precious David, or those dear little boys up above who are giving their lives to protect you.'

Larry tries to block her out, to refuse to listen to the obvious ending that she has already painted for them all, one that he freely accepted just hours before. He thinks back to his science lessons, to what he learnt about the human race and its climb to the top of the food chain, making it the reigning species on this planet. 'We can rebuild. It might take hundreds of years, but we can do it, if we just preserve enough of our people to start again.'

'Leave us,' she says to everyone, as she releases her grip on him but still keeps her narrowed eyes on him, as if she's ready for this debate on the fate of the world that no one can really win.

Everyone quickly obeys her and walks away, even the general, who gives Larry one small nod that silently tells him this simply isn't his fight.

She steps in front of Larry and kneels down, her movements slow and pronounced, like she needs to know he is giving her his all. 'Do you think this is the first time we have met these beings? And do you think we called them lurkers last time they attacked us?'

He shakes his head. 'You're saying they have attacked us before?'

She nods back. 'These creatures have been keeping us in check for centuries. The Mayans, the Egyptians, the Greeks and the Romans. Do you really think all of these great civilisations would just have fallen to pieces of their own accord? Do you really think they could all just suddenly turn to dust, and not one of them would endure?'

Larry looks into her blazing eyes. 'No one alive truly knows what happened to them.'

'But you know something happened, don't you? You know that they existed and that some of their secrets still survive today, like the depths of the pyramids, the predictions of the Mayans and the wisdom of the Greeks. These creatures who attack us are our greatest conscience, our biggest enemy and the strongest opponent to our collective progress. They come out every 10,000 years or so to keep us in check, pushing humanity back into the darkness for more generations than we could ever count, burying our precious past with the dust of our ancestors from countless millennia.'

'You're saying all this was planned?'

She nods. 'Knowledge is power, Mr. President, and so much of the past has been kept from the public. People only ever believe what they are told and trust me when I say that planet earth is coated with more millennia of dust than you could ever conceive. Sure, you are allowed to know that Stonehenge exists, allowed to walk the Great Wall of China. But why do you think they built that wall in the first place, and how did they ever get those stones in place if they weren't half as capable as we are? The clues are everywhere but most people don't see them as anything more than curiosities. There are many dead civilisations buried on top of even older ones, all were powerful and all were destroyed as easily by the lurkers.'

'But why would they do this?' Larry asks, desperate to know their purpose, unable to accept the simple storylines from the many movies that never really prepared anyone for this darkest milestone to face humanity.

'Why not? And why should they bother to tell us? Do you tell a pig why it must die? Do you ever sit it down and explain that its death will serve a bigger purpose – that it will be chopped into something that will never again look like what is was when it lived, breathed and walked this planet?'

He shakes his head, seeing these as very different things. 'Humans have superior intelligence, whereas pigs don't understand what is happening to them.'

'How do you know that these things don't see us as primitive as we see cattle? And do you really believe we are that intelligent, especially as individuals? I am part of a bigger group and we have been preparing for this while everyone goes about their daily business. Why else do you think we invented nuclear weapons, or travelled to the moon? On this next judgement of our entire planet, we will still lose but we are getting closer to defeating them.'

'I have one question,' Larry says, staring back at her. 'So why aren't we winning?'

She nods back and stands up, looking down at him with what Larry almost thinks is a glimmer of respect. 'The survival of our race will always be a very long game. One day we will reach distant stars and spread far beyond this one small planet. Maybe they are here because they don't believe we are ready, or perhaps they have always been here since the day that mankind lit its first fire, their only task being to keep us at bay, keep us small in such an endless and unknown universe.'

'You think they hate us that much?'

'Perhaps it's their job to hate us, sent down here by whatever we believe to be our God, or maybe they fear us. Perhaps it's easier for them to dominate the galaxy if they stop us from growing into what we could become. Maybe it's their role to crush our progress every time we get close to a certain population size. Ten billion people ready to leave this planet and spread themselves across the universe could be a scary thought to other civilisations.'

Larry isn't shaking his head anymore, isn't interested in giving an opinion or an answer. He only wants to hear what Lopez clearly believes is right in every version of this world that she knows. 'But what gives them the right?'

'What gives you the right to crush a termite's nest before it gets too big, too close to your home? They build such amazing things, working together to create underground labyrinths and stunning surface architecture; it's especially incredible when you consider their size. But you still don't want them to find your foundations and let these little creatures destroy all that you have built, and so you pour boiling water into the mound, put chemicals down there until they are no more, and then you think nothing of it until the next year.'

'You're not seriously comparing the human race to cattle and insects?'

She leans closer, her face nothing but serious. 'You think that we're better just because we evolved first? Do you really think that every other species on this planet was put here just to service our needs? We are being exterminated now, just as we exterminate pests and anything else that gets in the way of our stability or progress.'

He slumps downwards, his whole body aching, his mind exhausted by all he is being forced to endure. He is getting so many answers to a question he never wanted to ask in the first place. 'And you're saying we will be defeated again, just like before?'

'I told you, it's a long game. Some of us will survive: they don't seem to want to enslave us, or even eat us, but they do seem to want us to forget. And so we will forget for now, as our billions of bodies fertilise and re-energise the soil around the world. Although, I know that this time will be different. This time we have the power to damage them as much as they hurt us. We will leave even better clues and we will make sure that in our next life we will grow back before they do. We will help those who forget to somehow remember, not just what happened but to look to the stars for escape. You have a role to play, because you are our leader now and everything hangs in the balance of your limited wisdom. The Egyptians marched an army of millions to attack them, the Chinese built the biggest wall ever imagined, and now it is our turn to strike a blow at our mortal enemy.'

Larry looks away from her and down to it, to the new addition to his commanding chair. He saw it when he came back from the restrooms, after he was distracted by the update from the world map that showed how less than 20% of the planet remains untouched. That red button sits under a small layer of glass but it is no less imposing.

'Those soldiers will fight upstairs for you to survive long enough to make the right decision; to do what must be done. Whilst men and women went about living, collecting the badges of holidays and houses, writing about love – despite most of us knowing little more than lust – some of us were doing more. Fate has now made you one of those people who will do more, whether you like it or not.'

He looks back at the button and wonders whether it will even work. Not just if it will actually do the job she claims it will, but if it will actually fire the many missiles needed.

She doesn't answer, doesn't think to offer him any comfort. She leaves him now, going back to her calculations, quickly bringing more people into the fold as she demands that they prepare. There is no emotion left, no sad faces. He wonders if others around the world are doing the same, if there are even any world leaders left. He picks up a folder that sits next to the button. He finds it ironic that it's titled 'The Best Chances of Survival.' He has already looked through, having participated in putting it together a few days ago. He shuffles through the paperwork at random, only stopping at the ideas that interest him the most. He sees a satellite image of Japan, the fortified walls they built around two of their main islands, which, as it turned out, wasn't enough to help them survive.

He smiles at the British decision to sail their remaining fleet out to sea and create a sort of island in the Atlantic Ocean. Sure, it had some major drawbacks, because as the saying goes: 'water, water everywhere, but not a drop to drink.' It was projected that they would be able to survive at sea for less than three months before extreme lack of supplies forced them back to land and to the waiting enemy. It turned out to be a lot less when they found the lurkers were very good swimmers and didn't have any intention of waiting that long.

He turns to the last page, to an intelligence report from the Caribbean islands, about an ingenious plan to launch a large platform thousands of feet into the air. The intelligence officer gave it a 50% chance of working which, when compared to the other options, was actually quite high. He looks at the name of the officer and thinks about trying to find him, but since they will have been based at Langley, which was destroyed days ago, he doesn't see the point. He does wonder if it ever got off the ground, ever managed to save just a few.

Phillips reappears and disturbs his thoughts, the clipboard still in his hand. Larry notices it's full of scribbled notes with percentages next to them. 'Is now a good time for a progress update, Mr. President?'

Larry gets up, making himself stand shoulder to shoulder with the General. 'I'm not sure there will ever be a good time, but I guess I need to hear it.'

Phillips nods back, looking at his notes as if he's trying to find the best place to start. He taps the pen on the plastic as he makes a ticking sound with his mouth, until he seems to find what he was looking for. 'Let's start furthest away from home and work our way backwards,' he says, as he ushers them over to the large, interactive map of the world.

They soon reach the workstation of a young soldier and Phillips taps him on the shoulder, making him jump as they distract him from whatever important work he was doing. The screen zooms in until it is only showing a red Europe, as Larry realises he is going to get a continent-by-continent summary of how screwed the world really is. He sees the many skulls covering the landmass and he wants to laugh. He is seriously impressed by how much data the American war machine can collect from around the world, but he also knows that this cannot stop the beasts from winning.

Phillips coughs and then looks down at his notes. 'So, Europe has taken the biggest hit with only 30% of the population is left there. This is probably because, as we know, they seem to attack world leaders and centres of power, and that's where there is the largest concentration. They crept through Africa days before anyone knew and didn't bother themselves with anything but the biggest cities. After that Spain got hit next, as they simply walked out of the ocean and onto the beaches. It took them a while to work their way through the Spanish countryside, and then through France, and at that point the majority of world powers still didn't know what was happening. When they eventually reached the rest of the European countries they realised it might not be a virus or plague.'

'And we still don't know why they are attacking world leaders?'

Phillips doesn't answer, but he holds out his hand, keeping his focus on the pad. 'Don't stop me now, Mr. President, I'm on a roll.' He taps the shoulder of his helper who in turn starts tapping commands onto the computer.

'The Nordic regions are almost gone, probably because the population is concentrated in a few major cities. Russia put up a good fight and we think there are several thousand in the mountains, but since we have limited intelligence over there it's hard to say. Asia, India and the Middle East have taken 70% losses so far and the battles are still continuing, so we should definitely nuke them. Australia is very big and a few thousand of the population remain but with the main cities across the coast destroyed, the majority of the surviving population will die of starvation.' He taps his pen again, as he looks down his list and then up to Larry. 'South America isn't worth writing home about and Canada has gone the same way as Russia. So, all in all, I would say about 40% of the world's population from before this started is now left, and further war casualties are projected to take us down to around 20%.'

Larry leans down and takes hold of the desk. 'So, less than two billion will survive?'

Phillips quickly shakes his head. 'Oh no, Mr. President, it's nowhere near that high. Even if we assume the creatures are all destroyed, the direct assault of the nuclear tactical deterrents will kill off another billion or so, then add on the fall out and radiation, which will finish off at least another 500 million, if not more.'

He looks at Phillips but doesn't say anything, somehow knowing he's not finished yet.

'And so we're left with about 500 million. Now, this is where it gets interesting. You then need to assume that we have only killed off 60% of the lurkers, so they will easily manage to kill another couple hundred million of us. We will then probably manage to halve our numbers, when you think about everything that Mad Max has taught us. Then add in famine, disease, lack of modern medicine and the fact that we're going to be dropping down a few rungs on the food chain, which will finish off another 60% of whatever remains.'

'So we are left with less than ten million survivors?'

Phillips shakes his head again, as he flicks through more pages on his clipboard. 'Our best scientists predict less than a million of us will be alive this time next year. When you then consider that people aren't going to be having babies any time soon, the on-going fight for survival means that in a hundred years' time we will be down to less than 50,000.'

Phillips nods, finally giving Larry and the human race the break they deserve. 'Assuming the beasts don't hunt us down to the last man, we will then steadily grow. Other than our current enemy there is no other creature on earth that has the capacity to grow as fast as we can. And since we're several hundred-million years ahead of any other species we should reach our current numbers by the year 10,000.'

Larry shakes his head, looking down. 'That sounds so unbelievably distant,' he says, as he looks over at Lopez. 'And so we have to trust her theory that some of the population will survive and grow, and that we will get back to where we are now?'

Phillips nods and smiles. 'The population of our planet in 1800 was about a billion, so that gives you an idea of how it took us to recover last time. If you think that in the last 200 years we have grown by eight times from that original billion people, so it shows just what we're capable of. It's getting back to the first billion that's the real hurdle.'

'You believe her, don't you?'

Phillips stops and remains completely unmoving for the first time since Larry has met him. 'Mr. President, I don't know what to believe but right now we have very little time left, so both of us need to pick something and grab hold on tight, before it's too late.'

Larry looks at him and wonders if he should say anything, offer any words of wisdom from his own perspective. He looks at Phillips, who looks back, looking almost as if he needs something from his commander and chief.

'What do you think, Mr. President?' Phillips asks, clearly unable to bear the silence.

'I think humans are living for no reason and so they can die for no reason just as easily.'

Phillips lets out a long, bellowing laugh and slaps Larry on the back. 'Oh, come on, Mr. President. Think about all that we achieved in the last thousand years: it's clearly incredible, but the saddest fact of all is that it hasn't been enough. We just took too long to find the clues, spent too long fighting with each other and not enough time preparing to find their hiding place or getting enough of our people off this planet and onto another one.'

Larry nods, sort of agreeing with him, especially in the absence of any better theory. 'If we had just been given another ten years then the Mars missions would have at least got a few people off, perhaps given us a small chance.'

Phillips leans forward, close to his ear. 'You're the president now, so I'll let you into a little secret. There were two spacecraft launches that the general public was never aware of. The first one only had robots onboard and we managed to get another one off the ground last week with human astronauts as well. The whole public recruitment drive for the Mars 2025 mission was just to keep the press off our backs, so that we could pretend to launch test craft and the like.'

'You mean people made it off our planet?' he says and pulls away. 'But how many?'

'Well, only five humans plus the two robots. The chances of them surviving the journey are pretty slim but at least it's another possible option for the human race.'

'And if they don't survive?'

'We have left clues everywhere, hoping that our distant descendants will find them and realise sooner than we did that the inhabitants of this planet have a bigger purpose than simply existing. We want them to know that we don't have all the time in the world, and the lurkers are the most brutal of timekeepers, waiting to strike whenever we grow. Hopefully the next batch of humans can save our race from destruction again, in another few millennia.'

'I'm assuming our distant ancestors left clues, otherwise how would we know all this?'

Right on cue, Lopez, who has a habit of creeping up on people, appears next to them. 'Look at how much the human race has moved forward in the past hundred years. Before 1900 we bumbled through a few new advances, invented the wheel and agriculture, discovered electricity and learnt to use it for ourselves, but imagine what we have achieved in the last fifty, twenty and even the last ten years. Do you really think that it's possible for so many technologies to just be invented in such a short space of time?'

Phillips is nodding away now, smiling at everything Lopez says. 'We found out properly about the creatures a hundred years ago and ever since then we have done all we can to prepare. Think about the space missions, nuclear fusion, miniaturisation, the internet and many more – all these came from our ancestors. The day we found out about them was the same day we found all the knowledge that has shaped the last century, and the last two decades have seen the most significant advances. Why do you think we have been such a hurry to get to the moon, or create weapons of mass destruction without this knowledge?'

'The lurkers seem to hibernate until something awakens them. We are lucky they didn't attack dead on the turn of the millennium, because we would never have been prepared.'

Larry sits back down in his chair. 'We aren't really prepared now, are we? Perhaps if we had told the population of the entire world and got everyone working together on this purpose we could have done much more.'

She stands next to him and then gently rubs behind his ear. 'You are a nice man, too nice for this task that has fallen upon you. You fail to understand that the human race can never work together and will always rely on the few to do the work of the many. And while humanity has kept itself busy putting dogs on leads and plants in pots, there have been a few who have looked ahead, who have prepared us for the next millennium and the wars that haven't even been written yet.'

Larry looks up to her, wanting to argue, but not knowing where to start.

'Humans are wired to be individuals, thinking their own life is the centre of their world and therefore that the universe revolves around them. Before the turn of this millennium we consciously leaked the many predictions of our doom to the many inhabitants of the so-called developed world, believing that this would be the dawn of the attack. It never came and that's a good thing, but look at how few even took heed of the warning. Telling people of the specifics would have made no difference but it might have forced an attack earlier, and we needed time to prepare.'

'And what did the extra 15 years give us?'

'It gave us the time we needed to prepare for what we believe to be the tenth destruction of the human race. We have left our clues, passing down the knowledge from our ancestors, having made our own additions.' She looks down at his chair, her gaze finding the red button that sits next to him. 'They didn't have this on the dawn of the last attack. It was only an idea, formed shortly before the fall of what we call the Roman Empire. It's something we have taken and shaped into a devastating weapon, sacrificing many of our own kind to ensure that it is as deadly as it can be.'

General Phillips is still with them, seeming mesmerised by all that Lopez has said, and when she mentions the nuclear weapons he nods and looks down at the button like it is the juiciest snack imaginable, like an oasis in the desert of despair. 'Our time has come to destroy more of them than we ever did before. When they go back into hibernation our numbers will start increasing again, so that in another thousand years we will be ready for a fight that they cannot win. Perhaps they will not even turn up for it and maybe we will have left for the stars by then.'

Larry shakes his head, doubtful that this could ever be possible. 'What if they don't go back and hibernate? What if we anger them so much that they hunt us down to the last human and wipe us off the planet for good?'

Both of them shake their heads in unison; after the months and years of preparation they refuse to believe this could even be possible. 'You don't understand. You haven't seen all the evidence.'

'Then show me,' Larry says. 'Help me to understand that pressing this button is the correct thing to do, because right now it sounds like I will be killing more humans than lurkers.'

Lopez turns to Phillips. 'I knew he wouldn't have the backbone to do this. Why appoint another President when we have everyone we need down here?'

'You know why,' the General says.

She shakes her head, looking at Larry. 'Judgement is upon us and you must do what is right for the future, not what is right for you or for the present. Do not look to the past and do not think of love, friends or any other selfish notions. We have no time for them down here.'

He wonders how anyone could not think of love at a time like this. As Lopez starts shouting commands and General Phillips moves towards the bunker doors Larry shouts out to anyone who will listen. 'I need to call David.'

*****

Larry sits in his big chair, looking down at that red button. It haunts him more than the evil outside that is threatening to get into this place and tear the remains of the American government to pieces. People rush around him, shouting things to each other about which countries are now in range, and which allies are synced and able to fire in unison, all this planning leading to the ultimate firework display that will signal the final performance for planet earth. Lopez is standing in front of several screens, emotionlessly shouting orders.

Larry is distracted by the flash of something black in the corner of his eye, as he watches Agent Flinch walk past with a machine gun dangling from his shoulder and another one in his hand. 'It's been an honour, Mr. President,' he says, as he offers Larry one solitary nod before he joins his fellow agents and a scattering of marines at the vault door.

He knows what's coming; he's preparing for the end. Larry wishes more than anything that he wasn't here, that he wasn't the one with this enormous burden. He wonders that if he was still at home with David would they already be dead by now. That would be a blessing, he thinks.

'Mr. President, I have David on Line One for you,' a voice says from somewhere; it's hard to hear through all the frantic shouting.

He looks around, wondering where the voice came from but he can't see anyone looking at him. He clambers around his desk, pushing folders out the way to find a phone that works, but he still can't see it.

General Phillips suddenly appears with an arm outstretched and a phone in his hand. He still manages a smile as he hands it over. 'Suggest you make it snappy, Mr. President.'

He grabs the phone, nodding back to Phillips, liking him more by the minute. 'David?' he says. 'Where are you and are you okay?'

'Larry, is that you?'

'Oh David, it's me. I can't believe I finally got you. Where are you?'

'I thought you were dead. I've been looking everywhere for you. They attacked the neighbourhood so I fled and found some other survivors. We are holed up in an empty police station, but I'm not sure how long we can last.'

Larry laughs as he wipes tears from his eyes. 'I knew you were alive, I just knew it.'

'It was touch and go but I'm okay and I'm coming to get you,' David says, his tone so smooth and calming, despite all he has clearly been through while hunting for his husband and rescuing anyone he found still alive on the way.

'David, that's not going to be possible, however much I want you to rescue me.'

'Don't be stupid, just tell me where you are and I'll be there,' he says, fulfilling every possible aspect of the hero Larry knows him to be.

Larry doesn't say anything, mainly because, selfishly, he wants to tell David exactly where he is, and demand that he fights every possible monster until he is in his arms again, however impossible that may sound.

'Larry, something is happening, isn't it? When I got this phone call it said to hold for the president. No offence but I didn't expect it to be you. I thought it was the president calling to tell me that you were dead, although I wondered if he would really have the time for that sort of thing.'

'Well, it's a funny thing, but I might just have gone and got myself the presidency.'

'You're in that Washington bunker aren't you? I'm coming to get you.'

'Ninety seconds until we lose total world satellite coverage,' Lopez shouts.

'It's now or never, Mr. President,' Phillips shouts, having taken up position with his boys at the vault door. 'It turns out the lurkers aren't that bothered about white things, but people survived better in Alaska because there are far less of them in the snowy mountains. It seems once a group numbers only a handful, then they aren't that interested in us.'

Larry nods to Phillips, trying to take it all in. David is still asking him a lot of questions. 'No, David, it doesn't matter where I am. What matters is that you listen to me very carefully because the end of the world is almost upon us, and although I want nothing more than to spend it with you, that isn't going to happen.'

'What do you mean?' David asks.

Larry takes a deep breath as he wipes his glasses. They are so dirty and he wants to be able to see properly, to think clearly. 'Although this will probably be my end, it doesn't have to be yours. I'm faced with such a difficult decision and I don't know what to do.'

'Don't do anything until I get there,' David says. Larry hears nothing but calm determination in his voice, despite all the obstacles he would face.

Larry doesn't answer when he is distracted by banging on the vault door, as the judder against the metal announces the reality of what approaches. He looks at the general and then at Agent Flinch, into those very special eyes he shares with David. As the brave few prepare for the end Larry can only smile, feeling thankful that he was at least able to speak to David at this final moment, and that he's far enough away to perhaps survive and create a new life.

Hearing the first gunshot, he suddenly jolts forward. He looks at the main door but it's still holding strong. He hears Lopez shouting and looks over to see a body lying on the floor near her, a pool of blood forming around its head. She is shouting at the others, all of whom have guns to their heads, telling them not to give up so soon, to wait at least until the beast gets in.

Larry puts the phone close to his face, like he wants to whisper what he never thought he would say. 'David, do I plunge the planet into a nuclear winter in the hope of a recovery in a few thousand years, or do I do nothing and hope for our survival tomorrow?'

He doesn't answer at first and in the absence of a reply from the person Larry trusts most, all he can hear is Lopez shouting. She throws a tablet across the room as she moves towards him. 'Do your duty and do it now. It's your destiny!'

'Larry, are you still there?' David says.

'Yes, I'm still here but probably not for much longer.'

'Well, could you please ask whoever that squawking woman is in the background to be quiet for just a moment? I'm really trying to think.'

He laughs, wiping tears from his cheeks. 'That isn't going to happen, because she wants me to do something very important. It's now or never, and if I make the wrong choice, the repercussions will be felt for literally thousands of years.'

'Nuclear weapons?' David asks, seeing no need to ask any more.

Larry nods but doesn't answer him. He looks down to the button. It seems so small and insignificant and he wonders if it's what they wanted all along. Maybe they do surface every few thousand years and attack humanity, or maybe this is the first time. But what if mankind using its deadliest weapon on itself is exactly what happens every time? Larry wonders if this is perhaps a cycle that has continued for many millennia. Maybe, just maybe, he is here to break that cycle?

'My dearest Larry, only you can make that decision, because you are there and you are a good man. Why shouldn't it be the best of us who are burdened with this decision?'

She is getting closer to him now, her dark eyes blazing into his as he hears the soothing tones of the one he has always loved. 'The fate of the world will be in your hands for less than 60 seconds!'

'I give the vault door half that time,' Phillips shouts.

Larry looks at the general and all the people standing next to him. He holds the phone close to his ear, as close as he can get to David. 'I don't want you to come find me, David. I want you to fight until you get to the place where I think you will be safest. It's your turn now, and the human race will endure because I'm passing this responsibility over to you. Take as many people as you can find and head deep in the Alaskan mountains, cold and covered in snow. Look for places that are white and cold, because that might just help. You will gather and hunt, build and grow, because I know you are capable of all this.'

'But you're not in Alaska.'

'Go there, or anywhere that's out of the main cities and as remote as possible. Don't come to the bunker because we are about to bury many of those bastards in a thousand tonnes of concrete. They're attacking now, coming to take me and everything that we know, but the more we spread the word, the more we tell people that we are a race which should be aiming for the stars, the more we stand a chance of doing just that.'

'Stop this nonsense and tell me what's happening.'

Larry watches as the door is ripped away from the white walls and the lurkers enter. The general, Agent Flinch and the bravest of men fire everything they have, but it does very little to stop this newest and perhaps final onslaught. Larry turns to Lopez, who continues running towards him, no doubt determined to do what he might fail to do. Everyone else is screaming at the beasts as she is screaming at him, but he doesn't hear what she is saying. He lifts up the glass cover, his hand shaking, as the red button flashes and presents itself to him.

'David, I love you with all my heart and I always will. That love has guided me this far and I won't let it change what I know is right. Knowledge is our greatest asset and our collective determination our biggest power, so please spread the word.'

David answers back – of course he does. He tells Larry he loves him and that the decision he makes will be the right one. He tells him that Larry's ethos that a job should be done properly, or not at all, will help him lead the humanity down the right path.

But David cannot see what is happening, cannot understand just how little time Larry actually has to make this big decision. Doing something or doing nothing are equally important, and as Larry hears David's voice, he sees his own reflection in Lopez's eyes, as she leaps over chairs to get to him. He already knows that she will never make it in time, never be able step in and do what she believes is right, because although she's near to him, one of the lurkers is just as close, yet it's far more deadly than she could ever be.

He sees it now, the face of his judgement – its body is covered in scales and fur that lines its back. Its eyes are as red as the blood that flows through his veins, and this creation from the depths of hell is charging at him like he's the most important man left alive. Larry has always wondered about his end, about what would happen afterwards; he just never expected that everyone would meet the same fate at the same time as him. His life has always been his own, his decisions so small and limited to such a tiny part of a bigger realm he never bothered to ask about. He knows he's not alone in having these thoughts, but he also knows he could have done much more, and now it's too late because this world of so many individuals has come to an end, and everyone is fighting just to exist.

He can still hear David talking, as he looks at the woman and then the beast, both of who seem to see the best and worst in him. And so with one shaking hand above the button he closes his eyes and says out loud, for all to hear, 'welcome to the apocalypse.'

The end… Hope not!

If you look on Wikipedia there are 153 detailed accounts of what would happen at the end of the world (as of May 2015), ranging from 66 CE through to 2013 AD. There are a further 15 future predictions, with the next one being September 2015 (if this book got published and you're reading it from a cave, or a zombie shelter, then best of luck to you) And then 2020 seems the next most exciting end for those of us who are still hanging around. If you're interested then take a look on Wikipedia for yourself (just search end of world future predictions). I was especially intrigued to see that the Doomsday Argument says that we have about 9120 years left as a human race (that's not too bad, is it?), whilst another prediction says the earth will run out of carbon dioxide in about 500,000,000 years, give or take a millennium or so.

So, hopefully we have a little bit of time left before we all get wiped out, but we may never really know when our end is coming. And what should we do with this remaining time, however long it is? Should we reach for the stars and spread mankind across the galaxy, ensuring our future survival as we suck dry a few more planets? Maybe we'll discover spiritual enlightenment and all transcend to a higher astral plain, or maybe we'll download all our brains into a very big computer and become some sort of crazy collective, all talking at the same time, hoping to somehow be heard through all that noise?

Maybe someone knows the answer and maybe no one does but more importantly, what will you do with the unknown time that you have left?

THANKS :-)

I start as always by thanking Laura O'Toole and Rose Hicks for reading my work, offering their thoughts and above all just believing in me. Without both of you I don't know where I would start each time I embark on the crazy idea of writing another book.

Thanks to all my friends who gave me encouragement, support or even the odd distraction. All of these things mean so much. And finally, thanks to anyone and everyone who has supported me so far, either through buying my books or simply passing on a good word. It's all appreciated!

ABOUT LEE KERR

This is Lee's third book and one of his ten bright ideas to be published by 2020.

He lives in London and works full time. You might spot him one day tapping away on his next big story in a coffee shop somewhere. If you see him you should say hello as he doesn't have many fans. You can see what he looks like and learn more about his work at **www.leekerr.net**. He's a bit of a dreamer, sometimes funny, but not when he laughs at his own jokes. He's got this crazy idea that we're all chasing something – a dream, a career, money, love, or just a better tomorrow. Do you think he's right?

If you enjoyed this book then you can find his others in all the usual places, or you can…

Follow him on twitter @leekerrwrites

Like him on facebook.com/leekerr.writes

Check out www.leekerr.net for some random reading group questions.

Or simply tell a friend.

Whatever you're chasing, do it with a smile ;-)

ALSO BY LEE KERR

'QUEUES LIKELY'

Meet Ryan, the guy who has it all – the body, the girls, and the perfect pad in Canary Wharf. His career at Global United Eradication is flawless, as he helps them in their quest to sanitise the entire planet.

He's climbing his way up that golden ladder and doesn't care about the lives or the past stories of those around him. He's playing to win; competing against a shadow set by his father, and trying to please his ever-demanding boss. Even when he struggles through his daily routine, fighting against endless traffic and tube delays, he thinks only about his future. And with the help of his crazy friend, Ken, they plan to break as many of the company rules as needed to beat that long corporate queue to the top.

But as his boss's demands become more sinister, Ryan finds out that the past he had no interest in is very much alive. As he uncovers a darker part of Global United Eradication, those who gave him his lifestyle ask for too much in return, and he realises that he must put things right and help the people he previously climbed all over. With no one around him that he can trust and time running out, he learns that having it all can still mean you have nothing.

ALSO BY LEE KERR

'CHASING 30'

Of all the things you could chase, what would it be?

As Josh celebrates his twenty-ninth birthday, his closest friend gives him a ring with a simple inscription: *Chasing 30*. It's supposed to be a message to tell Josh to chase something more than his talented career, to stop running from his past, and to embrace the world he has hidden on the edge of for so long. It's a plea that asks Josh to accept his sexuality and to recognise their friendship for what it could be.

But Josh refuses to admit any feelings, as he slowly pushes everyone away in favour of quietly struggling with the ideas of being a good gay, an honest son, and a real friend. He soon finds his world shattered by bizarre encounters, small adventures and interfering people, as he wakes up to see his friends have silently fought against life's complications, addictions, depression and unspoken love.

When he finally makes a stand against his grinding existence, he enters into a race against time to help his friends, and to find the courage to admit an unspoken true love for the best friend he never wanted to lose.

Printed in Great Britain
by Amazon